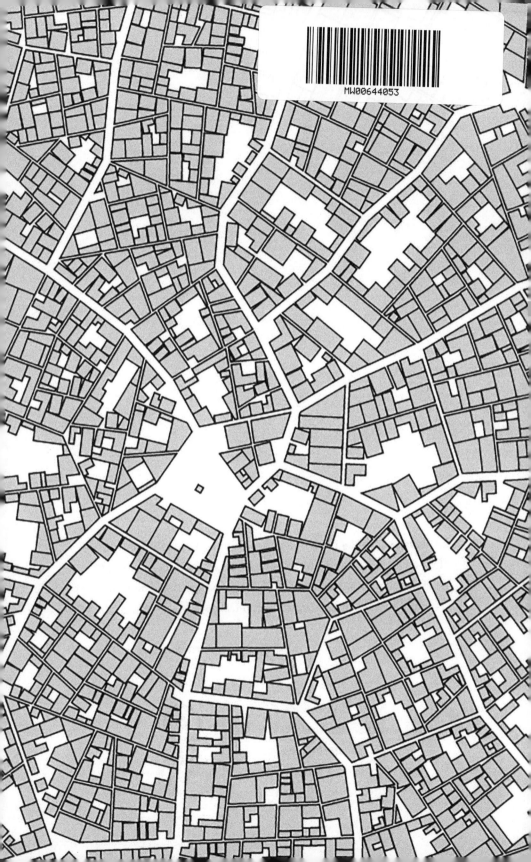

Broken Eye Books is an independent press, here to bring you the odd, strange, and offbeat side of speculative fiction. Our stories tend to blend genres, highlighting the weird and blurring its boundaries with horror, sci-fi, and fantasy.

Support weird. Support indie.

brokeneyebooks.com
twitter.com/brokeneyebooks
facebook.com/brokeneyebooks
instagram.com/brokeneyebooks
patreon.com/brokeneyebooks

nowHereville

weird is other people

NOWHEREVILLE: WEIRD IS OTHER PEOPLE

Published by Broken Eye Books
www.brokeneyebooks.com

Cover illustration by Meredith McClaren
Interior cartography by Oleg Dolya's
Medieval Fantasy City Generator
Cover design by Scott Gable
Interior design by Scott Gable
Editing by Scott Gable and C. Dombrowski

Published in advance at *Eyedolon* (patreon.com/brokeneyebooks):
"Y" by Maura McHugh © 2017
"Patio Wing Monsters" by S.P. Miskowski © 2017
"Underglaze" by Craig Laurance Gidney © 2017
"A Name for Every Home" by Ramsey Campbell © 2018
"Urb Civ" by Kathe Koja © 2018
"Like Fleas on a Tired Dog's Back" by Erica L. Satifka © 2018
"Walk Softly, Softly" by Nuzo Onoh © 2018
"The Vestige" by Lynda E. Rucker © 2018
"Night Doctors" by P. Djèlí Clark © 2018
"The Sister City" by Cody Goodfellow © 2018
"Tends to Zero" by Wole Talabi © 2019
"My Lying-Down Smiley Face" by Stephen Graham Jones © 2019
"Nolens Volens" by Mike Allen © 2019
"Vertices" by Jeffrey Thomas © 2019
"Luriberg-That-Was" by R.B. Lemberg © 2019
"The Chemical Bride" by Evan J. Peterson © 2019
"The Cure" by Tariro Ndoro © 2019
"Over/Under" by Leah Bobet © 2019
"Kleinsche Fläche of Four-Dimensional Redolence"
by D.A. Xiaolin Spires © 2019

978-1-940372-47-1 (ebook)
978-1-940372-48-8 (trade paperback)
978-1-940372-49-5 (hardcover)

Nowhereville

weird is other people

tales of the urban weird
edited by Scott Gable & C. Dombrowski

TABLE OF CONTENTS

Introduction: Toward a Weirder Tomorrow

SCOTT GABLE

ETWEEN THE *IMPOSSIBLE* OF FANTASY AND the *Inevitable* (or at least *Very Plausible Given Our Current Understanding*) of science fiction exists the *Maybe* state of the weird. Simply put, weird fiction is the unknown. It lies between the real and the unreal, bringing our fear and ecstasy to life as we're confronted by what we don't understand.

If one could map all the stories ever told and yet to be told on a vast theoretical, multidimensional architecture, how might that look? Imagine each dimension, ticked off by different measures and serving as axes for plotting stories on this vast landscape. For the purposes at hand, we're only interested in the portion relating to speculative fiction, so let's spin the dials and shift our gaze through the appropriate porthole—

There! That particular spectacular and shifting lobe contains all of speculative fiction.

Charting the Weird

If one were to attempt to map **speculation**, at one end might lie **fantasy** while at the other **science fiction**. And caught in between is the **weird**.

❖ **Fantasy** represents the *impossible*, at its core. These are the stories presenting pasts that have already happened (but differently) and the stories relying on elements that the consensus has deemed impossible (see also magic and dragons, such that while perhaps there is indeed more to understand about Universe, there is nothing substantive pointing toward it ever actually happening). These are the tales, whether heroic or dark, that don't try to replicate our reality in every detail but that create worlds beholden only to their own internal logic, either from whole cloth or by reweaving the existing fabric of history (whether baldly or subtly).

❖ **Science fiction**, on the other end, represents that which is *inevitable*, that which is *perfectly likely*, and even that which *might very well happen to us as a species at some point in the future maybe*—at least based on how we understand ourselves and Universe here and now. At its core, it is an extrapolation of our current reality, building social and technological advances or curtailments as befits the time of the writing. It is all of our possible futures based on our current understanding.

❖ The **weird** (now that we've set a foundation) falls in between those prior two giants' extremes. It is more proximal to our current state of being. It is our *unknown*, us trying to give name and shape to the darkness and to the ecstatic—to that which we don't understand. It is often labeled as "supernatural" or "weird science," depending on which side of the scale it tips, toward fantasy or toward science fiction.

Compared to fantasy, it is anchored more firmly in the *known*: rather than rewriting all that exists, it instead merely pokes holes and pulls strings, tearing down or building up, layering upon the *known*. (Supernatural horror and folk horror and fabulism are some weird subgenres that often tilt toward fantasy.) Compared to science fiction, weird fiction is less certain. It relies on established principles, on a "science" and "nature," that while perhaps imagined they have no accepted model. (Slipstream and "soft" science fiction are often the more science fiction–leaning of weird tales, exploring themes of death, dreams, psychic abilities (even time travel and artificial life can be weird adjacent)—the very nature of reality—and similar realms where science's final word quite possibly hasn't yet been said.)

Now, back to our massive map! It is comprised of axes, each a continuum of some quality, each further expandable into its own multidimensional spectrum as needed. But the three such measures of a story that might be most helpful now are **proximity** (or time), **realism**, and **emotion**.

❖ **Proximity** is simply the past-present-future of the story, and this measures how close the reader is to the narrative in spacetime. Does it take place in a projected future or a derived past, or is it relaxing into a present-day approximation?

❖ **Realism** is how far the fiction deviates from consensus reality. (The zero point here is our consensus world—this is realistic fiction and not speculative at all—and the opposite extreme is absurdism, or bizarro fiction.) So to what extent does a story speculate? Is there only a touch of the unreal painted on an otherwise "healthy" reality (as in magical realism), does it enter the surreal, or maybe sail on clear to the absurd?

❖ Proximity and realism generally represent the setting of a story, the time and place and culture. But you still need to add in the plot and tension and mood, so there's a third axis: **emotion**. This now makes such modes as horror, comedy, slice of life, and romance possible (all of which only intersect with speculative fiction some of the time, though they are free to intermingle with all speculative genres).

To counter the idea that weird fiction and horror are interchangeable, key takeaways here are that 1) weird is not solely horror (just as horror is not solely weird) and 2) horror need not be considered separate from science fiction and fantasy; science fiction horror and fantasy horror and weird horror are all perfectly valid.

I suggest here that all of speculative fiction could be measured on the space defined by **proximity, realism,** and **emotion**. We could certainly refine this by unpacking the axes further and even adding more dimensions, but at the core, this feels a good approximation of **speculation**. And it is independent of style (existing anywhere from literary to pop).

Weird fiction encompasses the stories that take place in the realms between science fiction and fantasy, between non-speculative fiction and bizarro—between its borders with other genres. And these frontiers are evershifting. The weird sits in an "uncanny valley," or rather an "uncanny sea," of speculation, snug between *impossibility* and *certitude*, *realism* and *absurdity*.

In Weird Times

Perhaps more than other genres, weird fiction is very much a function of the era in which it is written. A given fantasy's probably never going to stop being fantasy. Science fiction, of course, changes as we shuffle inexorably forward in spacetime, relying on our current *knowns*, occasionally becoming dated subgenres of itself (such as steampunk and cyberpunk) and celebrated on their own merits (and perhaps becoming more fantastical in their continuation). Weird fiction, however, relies on our current *unknown*, on the fears and desires of a people, probing the accumulated questions and assumptions of an age. It is a speculative lens of its time.

By way of illustration, I'll invoke religion and folklore. Religion exalts the divine, building on the visions of its believers. It is real to the faithful, even if untouchable to scientific inquiry and unassailable to otherwise-believers. Likewise, folklore guards against the tribulations of an everyday life under constant scrutiny of ever-present supernatural malice and whimsy, circumstance proving causality in the face of need. My point for bringing this up is that these tales tend to slip into fantasy from our modern vantage: Gilgamesh no longer holds the same deific significance, the fair folk no longer curdle our milk in real time. But myth and folklore were all too real to people at one time, or rather all too weird.

❖ We revel in the ecstasy! Religion never dies, so there will always be a weird space for the ecstatic. Tales of the Greek pantheon may never again reach outside the bounds of fantasy, but there are more than enough religious experiences, whether modern or fictional, to feed the emerging weird.

❖ We brave the unknown! Eventually our fears get turned over, mulch for a new generation, but the bogeymen just change, again and again. They always change: demons and devils and faeries, witches and werewolves, vampires and ghosts, aliens and their gods. There's always a new monster of the era.

What we now view as fantastical may have once been just the other side of the darkness, just the other side of the known world. Those earliest tales would have fit right at home with our current estimation of the weird. The mythic and the fey are to the weird as steampunk is to science fiction—they are the "old weird," the weird of a different era. As time moves on, our weird drifts with it. The words may not change, but how they reflect our relationship with the world certainly does.

But then we also, since those early days, started questioning reality itself. The previous examples illustrated the more supernatural side of the weird, but in later narrative, there emerged a more scientific bent. If not earlier, then at least with *Frankenstein*, we saw scientific inquiry rise to high weirdness. And though we've come far, there's still much we don't know about Universe, so there's more than enough fanciful conjecture and uncertain outcomes to fuel all the weird science of our dreams and keep us always twirling into the future weird.

All this is to say that weird fiction is very much reliant on our perspective. What was once weird is no longer. What is now weird may not always be. And who can tell what tomorrow's weird holds. But let's find out!

Nowhereville: Weird Is Other People

And that brings us to the book at hand. *Nowhereville: Weird Is Other People* contains nineteen original tales of urban weird fiction. These are the tales of the high weirdness inherent in clusters of people, in people interacting with others.

We cut right to the quick with the targeted, citywide body horror of Nuzo Onoh's "Walk Softly, Softly." From there, we zoom the microscope in on some very personal apocalypses with Maura McHugh's "Y" and P. Djèlí Clark's "Night Doctors," dripping with agency and even popping back to 1937 America in the latter. Following that is a string of quiet personal horror and slice-of-life tales, focusing more on interpersonal weirdness, the weirdness that we impose upon ourselves and others, before we bounce into some tales of future weird landscapes. The last third of the book tends to intermix the personal with the sprawl of urban life until we send you back to your home reality with the final course of R.B. Lemberg's "Luriberg-That-Was" and Cody Goodfellow's "The Sister City"—both spiraling the reader through potent fabulist-surreal landscapes.

So that you can think on what you've done.

Many of these tales are dark, but as I've suggested above, it's not my intent to provide you with just a horror fiction anthology. There are horror stories in here, absolutely, of varying degrees. This is, though, an exercise in weird fiction, intentionally drawing from the various shores of weirdness, from the Uncanny Sea, to explore all that might entail.

(The stories herein were first published to our Patreon website, *Eyedolon*, over the previous couple of years. Going forward, similar such anthologies will be collected in the same year as the stories' online publication.)

Stay weird. Read books. Repeat.

September 18, 2019
(published in part to *Eyedolon* in 2018)
Scott Gable

Walk Softly, Softly

NUZO ONOH

O BI'S SLEEP WAS INTERRUPTED BY A BURNING URGE TO piss. The pressure in his groin was so great that he feared an embarrassing accident before he made it to the toilet across the corridor. His hand reached up to the light switch as he rushed toward the shut door of the toilet. The dusty bulb overhead flooded the dark corridor with a sickly yellow glow as he pushed open the rickety wooden door of the communal bathroom.

Earlier that evening, he'd gone overboard at the popular establishment Karma, Madam Joy's secret brothel, bingeing on the icy palm wine offered by the fat woman till his stomach could hold no more. The result had been the usual violence that accompanied the poison in his bloodstream. By the time he was done with his prostitute, her own mother would have struggled to recognize the battered features of the screaming girl. Madam Joy had thrown him out, threatening to ban him for good from her house of pleasure.

Obi had stumbled out of the bar, cursing, punching, and spitting at some of the waitresses within his vicinity. Their angry screams followed him out to the street where he'd boarded the three-wheeled keke napep to his bedsit in the decrepit building located in the notorious slum Nike, a drug-infested area of the city, boasting robbers, kidnappers, murderers, and witch doctors as residents. Karma was just a mile away. On a good night, he would walk his way home, just as any other twenty-something, healthy, young man would. But on binge nights, he rode the bright yellow keke napep.

As he got out of the keke napep, he'd felt a sudden chill descend over him. It attacked him in waves, layering his skin with goose pimples and bringing an inexplicable dread to his heart. He shook his head vigorously, shouting out a loud greeting to some familiar figures, loitering neighbours hugging the railings of the balcony above his second-floor place. Their mocking laughter followed him into the building, together with someone else who walked silently behind him. Obi didn't know who it was that had followed him into the building, didn't really care to know either. Save for the person's massive black shadow that waved before him, obliterating his own like a total eclipse, he wouldn't even have known that someone else followed him up the stairs. The shadow seemed to grow, swell, spread across the uneven concrete like a solid black river.

That was when an uncomfortable sensation pierced through the drunken fog clouding his mind. The chill was back, this time with a vengeance. Obi felt the chattering of his teeth as his body trembled with a mixture of cold and terror. It was a terror that hit him without warning, a fear that came from the sudden awareness that he heard no footsteps behind him, felt no human presence with him despite the evidence of the dense shadow. His heart began to beat, pound with the thunder of a hundred war drums. He stopped midway up the staircase and turned.

He was alone. No one followed him. He swerved and stared at the solid black shadow that flowed upward like a blanket of tar, hugging the uneven angles of the stairs. He raised his arms and waved them frantically. The black shadow remained still, masking his own into invisibility. Obi began to run, race up the stairs in an attempt to overtake his dark companion. The black shadow raced with him, toyed with him, flowing first to his right and then to his left, before rushing ahead of him along the long narrow corridor that led to his bedsit. Obi saw it flow underneath the gap of his locked door as he fumbled for the room key in his pocket. His mind, cleared of its alcohol poison, pondered over the phenomenon. *Was he hallucinating from his binge? Had the bitch at the brothel spiked his drinks with some ganja to knock him out before robbing him? Was it his own shadow after all rather than some terrifying entity his muddled mind had conjured?* There was only one way to find out.

Obi turned the key and opened his door. He reached for the switch and flooded the room with light. He heaved a silent prayer of thanks. Power supply was so erratic in the city that it was a miracle to have light on any given night. His red-hued eyes did a rapid scan of the room, seeking the black shadow. *Was it hiding under the thin blanket on his single mattress? Or perhaps lurking underneath the metal bed?* His frenzied search revealed nothing except his own familiar shadow, following his manic movements across the untidy bedsit littered with unwashed laundry and dirty plates. The chill freezing his veins vanished, together with the black shadow. In fact, Obi felt beads of sweat across his forehead as he slumped on his bed, overtaken by a sudden bone-weakening weariness.

Sleep had been an instantaneous and deep affair, filled with distorted dreams of sinister, cackling women and a faceless, fearsome entity that bore an eerie resemblance to fat Madam Joy of the dubious house of pleasure, Karma. Obi had tossed and lashed out in his sleep till the need to piss dragged him out of his sweat-drenched mattress. He didn't bother shutting the toilet door behind him as he reached inside his shorts, groaning softly in desperation.

His hand grasped nothing.

Obi froze. A sudden chill seeped into his marrow, chasing away the last of his sleep fuzz. His fingers began a frantic search, trailing the flat skin of his lower abdomen, his inner thighs, the terrifying emptiness of his groin, reaching almost to his rectum.

Nothing; no familiar turgid length and soft eggs nestled between his thighs. His palm was bereft of the expected warm hardness it had cupped from the day he abandoned his pee-deluged baby terry napkins for hand-directed aims. His heart skipped a beat, leapt into his throat, almost choking him. The movements of his hand underneath his shorts became more agitated, manic, almost violent. A low moan escaped his lips, a groan of agony. The pressure in his groin was now a scorching pain, drenching his face with hot sweat. *He had to piss; he must piss immediately or die.* He pushed down his shorts with frantic hands, kicking them off violently as if they were infested with squirming cockroaches. He leaned forward, bending low from the waist. Then his eyes widened, his mouth forming a silent O. His heart started to race, pound, tighten in a killing grip that stole his breath.

Obi began to scream.

By the time his housemates rushed to his aid, Obi had passed out on the cold, cement floor of the toilet. They found him unconscious, clasping the empty space between his thighs that had once housed the glory of his manhood. And by the time the sun began its journey to the west that fateful day, four more men would experience the inexplicable, sudden disappearance of their prized rods, and the entire city would be thrown into dark terror.

II

Sanusi bristled as he listened to the raspy voice of his boss, the state commissioner of police. His brow furrowed as he strove to contain his irritation. From his seated position across the commissioner's desk, he watched his boss light up yet another cigarette, leaving two half-smoked sticks smouldering in his ashtray.

"I expect you to round up this thing by the end of the week," the commissioner said, taking a puff of his cigarette before stubbing out the end in the ash-filled bowl on his massive desk. With reluctant fascination, Sanusi watched the commissioner pick up one of the half-smoked cigarettes and stick it back in his mouth, his actions distracted yet executed with expert precision. In the background, the humming air conditioner dispersed the smoke generously around the room. Numerous files littered the desk, awaiting the commissioner's attention. He pushed a thick file across to Sanusi, who eyed it with ill-concealed distaste.

"So far, there's been seven reports of men losing their genitals, all within a four-week span," the commissioner continued. "One of the victims claims his penis disappeared after shaking hands with a woman he suspects to be a witch. Another states he was offered cocaine-laced palm wine and a prostitute at some street brothel operated by a fat woman who later came into his dreams and stole his penis. However, two other victims of the 'vanished cocks' epidemic claim to have miraculously recovered their penises after intervention by their church pastors." The commissioner's fingers curved an inverted comma as he barked out a harsh laugh that ended with a hacking cough. He took a deep gulp from his Heineken can before drawing another long puff of his cigarette. "So that leaves us so far with five remaining victims, supposedly with vanished penises. Everything's in that file," the commissioner shook his head, amusement and exasperation dancing in his dark pupils. "These Igbo people! They fill their cities with churches and universities and yet allow themselves to be ruled by crazy superstitions."

"So why are we even bothering to investigate these stupid claims, sir?" Sanusi could no longer contain his anger. "Why can't we send out a local officer who speaks their language to investigate this stupidity?" The cultured tone of his voice was icily polite. Underneath the immaculate cut of his grey pinstripe suit, his wiry body quivered with rage. *He would be a laughingstock amongst his colleagues when they discovered he'd been assigned the case of the fucking vanished penises. He hadn't spent three years at a top British university to come back to this farce.*

"Sanusi, you know you're my boy. We come from the same tribe," the commissioner smiled at his favourite detective. "Normally, I would send a police constable who speaks the Igbo language to investigate a ridiculous complaint like this one. But this time, we need someone who isn't biased. I need someone who has a different culture from these people and is professional enough to deliver an accurate and objective report. I need someone with some brains. In fact, my brother, I need you. You're the only detective here with a British degree, and like me, you're not from the Igbo tribe. It seems one of the victims is somehow related to the governor, and he has requested my assistance as a personal favour. We both know there's nothing to these claims. You should be done with it in a few days. Write up your report over the weekend and bring it to me first thing on Monday. You'll be travelling with me to the UK for a seminar next week. So ensure you apply for travel leave without delay so that your allowances can be paid in British pound sterling."

Sanusi's heart leapt. He could not suppress the wide smile that wreathed the sharp features of his face. *He would face a million teases from his colleagues for the chance to get out of the country to his beloved England with its great pubs and available white women.* Sanusi still recalled his student years at Coventry University with nostalgia. But for visa restrictions, he would have stayed on for much longer after his degree. Nonetheless, he was grateful for the doors his British degree had opened for him in Nigeria. He knew he would never have earned a quarter of his present salary in England. But then, he wouldn't have been expected to deal with ridiculous claims like this one he was now lumbered with, sweetheart deal and all. Still, as the commissioner said, there was no rationality to the claims, and he should wrap things up nicely within a couple of days and start packing for his trip to the UK. Sanusi smiled. *Who knows, he might even squeeze in a nice train journey back to Coventry, maybe look up that white whore, Sue-something or maybe Chloe-whateverherlastnameis, and enjoy a few days in those passionate arms. There would be no need to tell his white women that he was now a married man with two children; no need to tell his wife that she couldn't do for his libido what those white whores could do. Women! Always the cause of every trouble in a man's life . . .*

III

The street was unlike any other street Sanusi had visited at nighttime in the city. Due to the incessant power cuts, most streets were cloaked in darkness and silence, save for Sunday nights when Pentecostal churches blazed with generator-powered brilliance and Jehovah-powered shrills of the faithful. But this particular street was different, alive with a seedy brightness that reeked of corruption and desperation. Sanusi walked from shop to kiosk, restaurant to pharmacy, inspecting the displayed wares, the greedy sellers and hungry buyers. He'd heard that the Nike area of the city came alive at night, and it wasn't an exaggeration. The deafening roars of whizzing automobiles with their blasting horns competed with the loud music from a nearby record store and louder singing from a church. Generators spewed smoke and noise as they powered the street into dazzling brilliance. Hawkers shrieked out their wares—oranges, peanuts, batteries, handkerchiefs, bottled water, fried fish. Beggars harassed passersby, though Sanusi noticed that the male beggars avoided the women, no doubt afraid of losing their genitals. *Idiots!*

Sanusi fought to suppress his mounting irritation. The whole thing was a waste of his time as he'd known it would be from when he spoke to his last victim, some chap going by the name of Obi. Stupid man claimed that he'd been given spiked palm wine by a fat woman who ran a brothel and that he'd woken up to discover his penis had vanished. Yet when Sanusi asked to carry out a private inspection, Obi claimed his penis had miraculously returned to him the next day, just like all the other four victims he had interviewed . . . *fucking idiots.* By his own admission, the wretched man was so sozzled, it was a miracle he'd managed to find his drunken way back to his doorstep, much less locate his bloody penis. Sanusi was still to interview two of the seven complainants, one of them the governor's brother-in-law, the blasted man responsible for dragging him into this mess. Their families claimed the men had disappeared, vanished without trace into the big metropolis, Enugu, the Coal City. Sanusi thought the fools were too embarrassed to face him after coming to their senses. Left to him, he would arrest the entire bunch and chuck them into prison for wasting police time . . . *his fucking time.*

Obi had refused Sanusi's request to go with him to identify his attacker at Karma. The look of pure terror on the man's face at the suggestion had left Sanusi no option but to carry out his investigation by himself. All he had was a description of the accused woman, Madam Joy, and the location of her brothel. The other victims had claimed not to know the identities of the various women they blamed for their sinister attacks. The only thing they all had in common was that their woes had been caused by women, evil witches wandering the congested streets of the city day and night, seeking unwary men to rob of their most prized possession, their genitals. Obi was the only victim who could pinpoint his attacker and her location.

One thing was clear to Sanusi: the entire male population in Enugu was living under a dark cloud of terror and suspicion. In the four weeks since the rumour first surfaced, there'd been an unprecedented spike in violence against women. The famed courtesy for which the Igbos were known had been thrown to the garbage dump. No one shook hands anymore or clasped arms in friendship. Men avoided all forms of body contact with women, even their wives . . . *especially their wives* . . . in homes where domestic violence had been the norm before the rumours circulated.

In the workplace, the situation was no better with bullying and harassment of women on the rise. Taxi drivers refused to carry women in their keke napep cabs, leaving women stranded in the streets at all hours. In the hospitals, men refused to be attended by female nurses, resulting in an alarming rise in male fatalities in emergency rooms. Religious institutions, previously the main stronghold of the womenfolk, now overflowed with male congregations. Churches were operating seven days a week, day and night, as spirit-possessed pastors spoke in mysterious tongues, casting out witches and returning lost penises to a multitude of traumatized men. Witch doctors, determined not to be outdone by the pastors, set up their mats and relics by the roadside, offering protection against witches and powerful charms to safeguard penises. Sanusi had been accosted by a couple of witch doctors in the few minutes he'd been in the Nike area. It was becoming clear to him that the entire Coal City was close to meltdown. *He was close to a meltdown with the fucking heat.* Sanusi dabbed his face delicately with a clean white cotton handkerchief. Left to him, he would arrest anyone caught spreading the lies and dump them in the mosquito-infested jail at force headquarters. *That'll give them something to talk about, the fucking rice-brains.*

Sanusi made his way toward Madam Joy's brothel. It didn't take him long to locate the nefarious house where the crime against Obi had supposedly been perpetrated. It was a several-storey building painted a bright red and yellow, just as Obi had described. The massive signboard at the top twinkled from the multi-coloured neon bulbs used to write the name of the brothel, Karma. At the front of the house, there were several plastic chairs and tables overflowing with male diners under wide canopies, noisily enjoying an abundance of palm wine and local dishes. Loud music blasted from huge speakers mounted by the steps, leading up to the front door. Bright, alternating coloured light turned the place into a rainbow wonderland, hiding the vice and corruption in its radiance.

Sanusi paused at the entrance, surveying the clientele, mostly men. A fat woman in a dirty kaftan emerged from the building and greeted him with a cheerful smile, inviting him to one of the tables. *Madam Joy!* Sanusi recognized her instantly from the description given him by her erstwhile victim Obi. He forced himself to sit on the offered chair, resisting the urge to flee from the suffocating squalor of the place. Flies and ants fought for right of space with the humans who simply waved them away or squashed them underfoot before carrying on with their meal. Scantily clad girls served the men, allowing themselves to be pawed as they exchanged vulgar jokes with their favourites. Sanusi noticed that the pretty prostitutes received generous tips while the ugly ones were shouted at by the men and bullied by Madam Joy. He noticed two sour-faced prostitutes in particular who were on the receiving end of the worst of the abuse. He eyed them with contempt, revolted by their ugliness. One thing he couldn't abide was fat, dark-skinned women. He was ruthless in his interrogation when they fell into his trap. It would have been easier to simply pull fat Madam Joy aside, question her, slap her around her pig-face, and leave the filthy place. But he preferred to observe his quarry first before striking, disarm them, take them unawares, and beat the truth out of them.

"Oga, what you want drink?" Madam Joy spoke to him in pidgin English, automatically identifying him as a stranger in their midst. Sanusi still couldn't fathom how these blasted Igbo people could distinguish him from themselves, considering he was a Fulani man and as light skinned as most of them. But in the short time he'd spent in their city, Sanusi had come to realise that the Igbos were a very cliquey tribe. They could spot their kind blindfolded. When they spoke to a person in English instead of their local lingo, they automatically consigned the person to the "stranger" realm. He gave an inward shrug, put his mobile phone into his pocket, and turned his attention to Madam Joy.

The fat madam bustled around him, crowding his meagre space with her sweaty bulk. A rank odor wafted from her body, a pungent stench of rottenness, sour yet sweet. Sanusi gave his nostril a discreet squeeze, leaning away from her. *Little wonder that idiot Obi had been convinced the woman was a witch. With a stench like this, she could easily kill the staunchest penis in the world. Wonder was why anyone would want to eat anything she offered in her filthy brothel.*

"Just a bottle of Coca-Cola will do." Sanusi pulled out a naira note. The woman looked at him, a peculiar look in her small, dark eyes that were almost smothered within the sweaty folds of flesh on her face. Something pricked his neck, an uneasy dark cloak on his shoulders. He felt like the criminal and not the police, like a prisoner instead of the judge, a trapped insect under a microscope.

"Hurry woman, and don't waste my time," Sanusi's voice was harsh, angry furrows on his brow. He felt the sudden thudding of his heart and hot sweat on his face. The woman looked at him for several seconds after his outburst, a considering gaze like one studying an unusual specimen.

Then she smiled, a wide obsequious smile that made his skin crawl. He wanted to get up and walk out of the filthy joint, put as much distance between himself and the woman. He wasn't a superstitious man, not by a long mile. But he was a trained officer, and every instinct in him screamed that something was wrong with the woman. He could not pinpoint what the something was, but he knew evil when he came across it. In his job, he had encountered enough evil to bring the "No Vacancy" label to hell.

"Bottle of Coca-Cola sharp-sharp, sir," the woman waddled away from him, taking her reek with her, bringing temporary relief to his fuzzy brain. Sanusi shook his head. He cursed himself for his fanciful thoughts. *Hell! This bloody case was fast turning him into an ignorant and superstitious fool like the rest of the wretched residents of the city. Damn it all! The sooner he questioned the bloody woman and wrapped up his investigation, the quicker he'd get home and prepare for his trip to England, back to civilization.*

The woman returned with his drink, a can opener in her hand. She made to uncork the lid, but Sanusi stayed her hand. He didn't trust her. The last thing he wanted was to leave with food poisoning and whatever else the vile woman had on offer. He felt a sudden kinship with the fool Obi. Having met the woman, he didn't blame the man for his suspicions despite knowing there was no truth to them. And yet a niggling feeling remained with him, something that couldn't be tidied away into a rational box, a wrongness about the five men he had interviewed, an unnatural defect in their makeup: their voices for one thing . . . *their identical high-pitched feminine voices.*

Each of the five men Sanusi had interviewed spoke in the same unnerving female shrill. All of them, together with their friends and families, swore they'd each owned a different voice, a deeper masculine tone that vanished the same day they lost their genitals. More unsettling was the black shadow they all claimed to have seen, coupled with the identical dreams they also shared, nightmares about a faceless, terrifying entity that bore an uncanny resemblance to Madam Joy. Now he'd met her, Sanusi could understand why she could haunt men's dreams. She was the stuff nightmares were made of.

Except she was a total stranger to the men whose dreams she haunted. With the exception of Obi, none of the victims had been to Madam Joy's filthy brothel. None of them had laid eyes on the fat woman. Yet each of the men he'd interviewed had described the madam with an accuracy that turned the hot sweat trickling down his spine into chilly, skeletal fingers.

IV

That night, Sanusi returned home and thrashed his wife to within an inch of her life. He had caught her without her veil, the second time in the week. The first time it happened, he'd put it down to an accidental oversight. This time it was different. Zainab had spent her day with more of her liberal Igbo friends, brash Kardashian-wanna-be women, drowning in thick makeup and expensive perfumes. They were fast leading his hitherto chaste Muslim wife into their liberal lives of Christian immorality. Sanusi was determined to nip things in the bud before they got any further. He derived extra pleasure in kicking his wife's bottom. *The stupid bitch needed the fat kicked out of her wobbly arse.* But for his need to keep on the right side of his commissioner, who was a right moralistic prick, he would have sent Zainab home as soon as she began piling on weight after their last son was born.

The next day, he woke up with a cold. It felt like the flu, and he could barely speak. His throat hurt when he tried to swallow, and his body was a mass of shivers and aches. For a brief second, Sanusi wondered if he had picked up a virus from Madam Joy's brothel. But he'd been very careful and had even restrained himself from smacking the fat pig on her sweaty face when he interrogated her about Obi's missing penis. *He had restrained himself . . . he had definitely restrained himself. He was sure of that.*

Madam Joy had laughed at him when he posed his question, looked him squarely in the eyes without fear and laughed at him as if he were no more than one of her ugly servant girls. He'd raised his hand to knock out her front teeth, bring the swelling to her dark, piggy eyes. But his fist had refused to obey him. His right arm stayed stiff against his body; his left arm equally resisted him, bringing unfamiliar thuds of panic to his heart. And all the while, Madam Joy cackled, her laughter raucous and evil, glee glittering in her dark icy eyes. She walked away from him, waddled her way back to her business still laughing. Her laughter had rung in his ears for hours. Even as he thrashed Zainab, he'd still heard that maniacal screech underneath his wife's agonized screams.

He could swear he'd also heard that evil cackle in his dreams, though he couldn't recall the dream. Sanusi pushed away his morbid thoughts, swallowing a couple of paracetamol capsules. *He was probably coming down with malaria. Everyone knew malaria came with weird dreams.* For good measure, he took some malaria tablets and prepared for his final round of interviews. He planned to make a last attempt to contact the two missing complainants, get their statements, tie up some loose ends with Obi, and write his report for the commissioner before calling it a day with the stupid case.

Sanusi arrived at Obi's house a little after midday, having found the other two men still missing. All he could get from their terrified and confused families was that the men had disappeared with the same inexplicable suddenness as their vanished penises. Everyone had seen them retire for the night, but no one ever saw them awaken to the new dawn. They had both taken nothing with them, neither their clothes nor their car keys. In the case of the governor's in-law, the man's international passport was still intact with wads of dollar notes from his previous trip to the United States. Sanusi had initially suspected foul play as each of the men had several wives and mistresses who seemed to harbour little affection for them.

That was until he saw the dollars. No Nigerian felon, certainly no Igbo wife or mistress with murderous intentions, would abandon dollar notes, not for God or country. But in the absence of any credible evidence, he could not pursue the case any further. He crossed out their files and walked away from their compounds. He was done chasing after the two men, especially the governor's wretched brother-in-law whose disappearance had sparked the investigation. *Bloody governor could stick it in his pipe and smoke it. The commissioner too.* The whole thing was simply some stupid urban hysteria that strong-arm police tactics should soon nip in the bud. He intended to recommend robust policing in his report, starting with that vile Madam Joy's brothel, Karma. He would give her karma, alright, and personally supervise the closure of the place and the vigorous whipping of the filthy woman in his police cell afterward. *That should cure her insolence, the dirty, fat bitch.*

V

Obi was nowhere to be found when Sanusi arrived at his building. His neighbours said he had vanished the previous night. His mobile phone lay on his unmade bed, and his bedroom door remained wide open. Sanusi searched the room, looking for signs of a struggle, anything that would suggest foul play. But there was nothing out of place. The room had an air of normalcy as if the owner had just popped out for a shower or a chat with a neighbor. Except he never returned. Sanusi questioned the neighbours, searched their rooms vigorously. No one demanded a search warrant. Only a fool would risk his freedom and safety by making such a ridiculous demand.

He returned home that evening, fighting frustration and some unknown ailment. His malaria symptoms had disappeared only to be replaced by a feeling of anxiety and a nervous twitch that had him constantly glancing over his shoulder. He felt a dark claustrophobia shrouding his being as if the very air he breathed was littered with a million black eyes, following his every move. A sense of urgency drove him, rushing back to his house and up his staircase, ignoring his wife and kids in the living room. Halfway up his stairs, something halted his steps.

Sanusi stared at the black shadow spreading across his stairs. A sudden chill shook his body, swelling his head. A sense of déjà vu engulfed him, a bad recollection. He stared at the shadow, his brows knitted. He strove to bring some calm back to his stunned mind. *He was a detective, a British-trained detective, versed in dealing with hard facts. There was no place for superstition in his world. He wasn't a fucking Igbo, ruled by fantastical beliefs and crazy conjecture.*

Sanusi stooped low to touch the carpeted flooring of the stairs. His fingers made contact with something old and cold, a slimy iciness that was as real as the burning pain it inflicted on his fingers. Sanusi shouted, leaping back, almost stumbling down the stairs. The black shadow jumped with him, seeming to fly over his head, engulfing him briefly in its icy molasses before streaming out of his house. Sanusi rushed up the remaining stairs, stumbling into his bedroom and slamming the door behind him. His breath came fast and hard, loud and harsh. Sweat poured from his forehead as if he'd been caught in a sudden tropical storm. His body shivered, his limbs trembled. He stumbled toward his bed feeling his head swell, expanding and contracting, bringing sudden darkness to his pupils. Sanusi crashed on his bed just as oblivion stole his mind.

VI

He is in a dark place, a place filled with women. It looks like a market, a night market run by women, fat black-skinned women who all bear an uncanny resemblance to Madam Joy. They all look at him and laugh at him, calling him names, vile names: Mr Little-Cock, Mr Wife-Basher, Mr Sexual-Disease-Giver, Mr Rapist-of-Beautiful-Female-Prisoners, Mr Love-Rat, Mr Adulterer, Mr No-Respect-for-His-Mother, Mr Big-Useless-Nothing . . .

By the time he hears the last "Mr," Sanusi finds himself drowning underneath the weight of countless, vengeful, fat women. They hit him with their plumb fists and slap his face with their saggy breasts. Their hot hands reach into his trousers, pulling his penis, squeezing and yanking till he can scream no more, and he gives in to the dark call of unconsciousness.

He awakens in another place, a different place from the night market of angry fat women. This time, he finds himself in a bright place, a place of light and colour, a place of beautiful light-skinned women and greedy men. The women look at him and smile. Their smiles are leers of corruption. They beckon him over, call him "Sister." He wants to tell them they're either blind or rude. He's no sister. He is a man. He starts to speak and instead ends up screaming. His voice mirrors their female tones, high, shrill, all woman. The women begin to giggle, cackle as evilly as the fat market women. The greedy men turn to look at him, rise to pull him into their passion-crazed arms. Sanusi starts to run, seeking escape from the mad room of light and vice.

He doesn't run far. They catch him and hold him down. The men mount him and violate him. They hit him as he struggles, slap him as they take their pleasure on his body. And all the time, the women hoot at his ravishment, cackle in the identical voices of their fat market sisters. When they're done, the greedy men leave him where he's sprawled on the red carpet of the house of sin, covered in blood and snot, semen and tears.

He crawls toward the red door, feeling himself swooning, fighting the darkness that threatens to steal his mind and sanity. Just as he gets to the door, he feels a hand, a powerful hand, pull his arm, yank him forward . . .

Into a familiar place, a place he'd visited just the previous night. Karma! Madam Joy stands before him, tall, mammoth, powerful . . . and darkly deadly. Gone is the cheerful smile, the air of affable congeniality. She towers over twenty feet tall, her girth spanning several yards like the gigantic statue of an ancient, forgotten god. Except she's not a lifeless statue. She is all power and fury, a coal-black pitiless entity of malice and vengeance. Her black shadow flows down her body like a living river, flooding the floor in dark iciness. Sanusi feels his skin burn as Madam Joy's black shadow swirls around him.

"Foolish man!" her voice booms like the roar of thunder, bringing the shivers of terror to his jellied limbs. "Useless little man!" She stoops and lifts him till he dangles in front of her face, her terrible, dark face that brings the hot piss to his groins. "You men go through life abusing my daughters, stealing their pride, killing their hope. You believe your powers are from above, that you can stride the earth with your bold walk, your loud voices and hard fists, wreaking pain and misery on my daughters. My earth is flooded with the tears and blood of my daughters; their pains fertilise my soil. Yet I hold my rage because it is only by your seed that we can keep ourselves in existence. The seed of a good man is the perfection of unity I weaved for my daughters, a tree and its fruit: one, faithfully hard, the other, sweetly soft. But men like you, perverts, psychopaths, abusers, and manipulators, have soured that tree of paradise. Your brutality and wickedness have tainted the purity of my work. You would have been better off staying above with your creator than coming down to my earth.

Madam Joy pauses, piercing him with her terrible black stare. Sanusi shuts his eyes, trying to shut out the terror that quakes his heart, steals the final vestige of his male pride. Madam Joy's voice drowns out the pounding of his heart. "Listen *well, pathetic creature. I have made some cities female cities, cities that house my soul and my powers. All over your human world, there are male and female cities: cities that house the soul of my brother, Sky, and cities that house my soul, Earth—cities like this one, Enugu, the Coal City. Just as my daughters never fare well in my brother's cities, you men will never flourish in my cities. The wise ones amongst you know to walk softly in my cities, to speak softly and live quietly. But others like you, foolish men who insist on strutting my lands with brutal arrogance, get their comeuppance. Prepare for my judgment, foolish man. You'll soon feel what it is to be one of my daughters, the ones you abuse with impunity."*

The mammoth terror lets out another loud cackle, her towering mass trembling like a river of black molasses. Fear steals his breath and sanity. He shuts his eyes but cannot shut out her voice, her chilling cackle. He gags from the terrible stench of decay oozing from her skin, the stench of death and putrid corpses. "Like all the others before you who have used the symbol of your manhood to suppress my daughters, you shall be turned into a woman and experience the same pain and humiliation you've dished out to my daughters throughout the dawn of the deities." Madam Joy's voice rings with his doom. "Look around you, pathetic little man, and see with a clear vision. The ugly servant girls you so despise were once swaggering men like you, each boasting high connections and great wealth. Yet like you, each of them are soured trees, killing their fruits before they ripened and shedding them like worthless junk. Soon you'll join them in eternal servitude to me. Perhaps in your next incarnation, you will choose your city wisely and steer clear of female cities, my cities, cities that house my soul and my powers."

Madam Joy lets him go. The evil cackle returns to her lips as her black shadow swirls up, rising to engulf him. Sanusi begins to fall from the great height. He tumbles and screams . . . falling . . . drowning . . . falling . . .

VII

He awoke from his nightmare with a low moan. His head pounded, and his heart raced. He jumped off his bed as if it was infested with razor-toothed bugs. Images flashed in his head, memories of a terrifying dark entity, something about women, angry women, cackling women. He struggled to recall his nightmare, searched his mind for recollection. There was a wild urgency in him, a desperate need to remember. All he received were disjointed pictures and a disquieting sense of doom. He felt the sudden pressure in his groin, a burning need to piss. He stumbled to the door toward the family bathroom by the landing. His hands trembled as he pressed the switch, flooding the white-tiled room with blinding light. His fingers pulled the buckle on his belt, zipped down his trousers, reached inside his underwear to yank out his penis.

Downstairs, Zainab heard the bone-curdling screams of her husband as she stooped to lift her son from the couch. She froze. Her limbs went weak. She let her son drop back onto the sofa. Heart pounding, she raced up the stairs toward the toilet from where the screams came, high-pitched female shrieks, screams that sounded uncannily like her own pain-filled cries when Sanusi subjected her to one of his brutal beatings. And from the open door of the empty bathroom, along the carpeted flooring of the landing, across the glossy painted walls, a thick black shadow flowed its steady black stream out of the house, taking with it an invisible passenger whose shrill screams followed the undulating course of the black shadow to a dark realm of eternal misery.

ℬ

Nuzo Onoh is a British writer of African-Igbo heritage. Popularly known as "The Queen of African Horror," Nuzo was born in Enugu, in the Eastern part of Nigeria (formerly, the Republic of Biafra). She experienced the Nigerian-Biafran war as a child refugee, an experience that has influenced some of her works. She first came to England as a teenager and attended the Mount School, York (a Quaker boarding school), and St Andrew's Tutorial College, Cambridge, from where she obtained her A Levels. She holds a law degree and a master's degree in writing, both from the University of Warwick, Warwickshire, England.

A keen musician, Nuzo plays both the piano and guitar and enjoys writing songs when not haunting church graveyards and the beautiful Coventry War Memorial Park. Her book, *The Reluctant Dead* (2014), introduced modern African horror into the mainstream horror genre. Her other books include *Unhallowed Graves* (2015), *The Sleepless* (2016), and *Dead Corpse* (2017). Nuzo has two daughters and her cat, Tinkerbell. She lives in Coventry and is an active member of the Coventry Writers Group.

MAURA MCHUGH

"WHY IS THE WORLD WRONG?" FIVE-YEAR-OLD Ygraine asked her mother for the first time.

Nerthus didn't respond for a moment. She was perched on the edge of the couch in the darkened den, an intent crease in her forehead as she watched a lurching black and white film on the telly. Old chiaroscuro dreams sculpted her features.

She blinked, picked up the remote, and froze the image.

"What did you say?"

Ygraine flapped a free hand to indicate the entire shadowy space (her stuffed rabbit Zepher was clamped in the crook of her other arm). "Why is everything . . . *wrong?*"

Nerthus sat back and regarded the serious expression on her daughter's face. She drummed a slow beat with the pen in her hand across the notepad balanced on her knees. It seemed to Ygraine that this was the first time she had ever captured her mother's complete attention.

"What's wrong with everything?" Nerthus asked.

Frustration spiked Ygraine's belly like one of Mikael's ugly cacti in the conservatory. She didn't have words for the wrongness. It was a bone-deep knowledge that she was misplaced. Every morning she woke up expecting to be *someone else* and *somewhere else*. All Ygraine knew was that she and the world were out of sorts, and the pain from this mismatch had become a constant numbness in her heart.

"It's not *right!*" she cried. She twisted her bunny's head, and a black desire to rip it off rose in her. *That* would demonstrate her feelings.

Nerthus patted the cushion to her left, and with sullen, reluctant steps, Ygraine moved to her side and plopped down. Nerthus placed her arm around Ygraine's shoulders, but Ygraine did not relax into it like another child would, seeking comfort. She suffered the touch.

Nerthus did not act offended. "The world is a difficult place to live in, Y."

It was the first time Nerthus abbreviated Ygraine's name, and she pronounced it *ee*.

(A click registered in Y's mind. This name felt *almost-right*. An approximate of what *should be*. She instantly claimed it as her own.)

"It doesn't make sense half the time," she said. "It's a confusing place even for adults." She bent her head and looked directly into Y's eyes. "You have to unlock the puzzle of life on your own terms. Don't believe what other people tell you. Most of them make up their solutions and pass them off as truths. Find your own logic to the nonsense."

The one thing Y liked about her mother is that Nerthus spoke to her as an equal, but that meant she didn't always grasp everything she was told. She frowned.

Nerthus broke her gaze and sat upright. She gestured at the books, papers, and photographs spilled on the coffee table and the DVDs stacked around the TV in the corner. "This is how I decode the messages of the world. I break them down and reforge them in a way that approximates my inner landscapes."

She straightened her spine a little. "Just don't expect people to like it if you show them unsafe territories."

She tapped Y on the head, and Y knew she was dismissed. She returned to her bedroom, sat on her bed, and stroked Zepher's head roughly. She thought about her mother's words until Mikael's deep voice called her for dinner.

It took two decades for Y to realise that it was the best conversation she would ever have with her mother.

The landscape outside the bus window rolled past desolately. Y considered how it mirrored her experience of the world: an observer separated from people and places by an invisible barrier. Rarely connecting with anyone truly, never feeling at home in any place. "Distant" is what most people called her. "Aloof" if they were being passive aggressive. "A fucking psychopath" was Levi's summary at their last meeting. The fatal shot in their breakup duel.

What a mistake, Y thought and adjusted the seal of her headphone ear buds, so the music of Sigur Ros pushed out the thrum of the bus engine and the chatter of the two schoolgirls in front of her.

The stench of warm egg sandwiches left half-eaten on the seat across from her was harder to ignore. She wanted the view and the swell of the music to overwhelm all her senses. The bleak landscape and the slate skies soothed her in a way that was unusual. She sensed she was coming close to the next place she needed to live—somewhere isolated and surrounded by rock and sea. She'd felt this urge coming upon her for a year and had finally given away most of her possessions to travel in Europe and find the location that drew her.

Things meant very little to Y, apart from her laptop and smartphone. They were tools for her work, creativity, and social interaction: the online articles she wrote for income, her social media personae, and the obscure discussion boards she moderated. All her photographs, articles, and notes were stored on encrypted cloud servers, so even if she lost her devices, the data would remain. Those intangible files were her tether to her ongoing attempt to decipher the signs she had relentlessly followed since she spotted her first clue at age sixteen.

That initial marker had been an unassuming concrete wall in an underground car park at a supermarket. Nerthus and Gawain were loading up the car with groceries, and Y noticed a strange pattern out of the corner of her eye. Plain square pillars lined up like a colonnade before the wall splotched with abstract grey patterns. A pool of black water slicked the floor before it, reflecting the cold white strip of the overhead light.

All those elements, seen in a moment, clicked in her mind. The same way her name, Y, had fitted some unconscious lock. It was the first time a piece of the puzzle presented itself.

She drifted toward the space, feeling as if she was floating. The screech of car wheels and the clash of shopping carts receded. As she moved, her hand scrabbled in her satchel for her camera. It had been a birthday gift from Mikael the previous week—her first digital camera. Nerthus had huffed about it. She was a purist and preferred film, so she assumed Mikael had done it on purpose to annoy her. Instead, Mikael had just listened when Y said that's what she wanted. Y had no ambition to be a photographer or a director like her mother. She just needed something to document the signs.

A week earlier, she'd had a dream.

The signs, a voice thundered at her from darkness, *follow them!*

She'd woken up shaking from both excitement and fear. The emotions were so raw and unaccustomed she felt woozy, like the time Mikael had given her too much cough medicine.

Y swung the camera up, flicked off the flash, and was snapping images before she thought about it consciously. At the same time, there was a pressure on her skull like a giant hand slowly squeezing. The *certainty* that she needed to photograph this arbitrary array of clean lines intersecting with grey stains was so strong she ignored the weirdness and kept clicking the button.

"What'cha doing, Y?"

Gawain had slouched up behind her.

She hated her brother for making her speak. It disrupted the connection. "What's it look like, jerkface?"

"You're photographing a wall, dumbass. Mum wants you to get in the car."

She could feel the moment slipping away.

"Come on!"

It was gone.

She whipped around, a fury boiling up her body in an instant.

Gawain stepped back from her anger. She took a photograph of him for spite. It neatly captured the surprise—and fear—on his amiable features.

She shouldered past him, yanking on her headphones, and climbed into the back seat of the car. She slammed the door, hard, and switched on her music, loud.

Y turned her face to the window and blanked her brother and mother in the front seats. She vaguely heard a mumble of conversation but steadfastly ignored it. Instead, Y stared at the wall, which no longer seemed possessed of secrets.

Yet that night, when she repeatedly scrolled through the odd assemblage of shapes on her laptop, it unsealed a conduit, and something *whispered* to her.

Bring Her back, it seemed to say. *Find Her.*

Who was Her?

Y still didn't know. Not after years of eclectic study at college, followed by a nomadic existence in three different countries and ten different houses and apartments.

At the arrival of each sign, Y could feel herself closing in on this mysterious person. It also signalled a change or a move. A week after she photographed the wall, Mikael died of a massive heart attack. Y did and said all the necessary things, but she found it difficult to care in the deep way everyone else seemed to feel about the death of her father. When they lowered Mikael's coffin into the grave, upon which lay the three white roses they'd thrown in, she only experienced the typical dullness in her chest.

Then Gawain grabbed and squeezed her hand, and she glanced up at him: his tousled hair limned by the sun, tears shining on his agonised face, and a throb swelled up. He had always been her lone, tenuous human connection.

She hugged him, and he cinched her so tight she gasped—it felt *real*, and a few tears escaped, followed by a scald of sobs because she'd always thought herself incapable of such sentiment.

The bus braked suddenly, and Y was thrown against the seat in front of her. Dust burst out of the cheap material. She coughed and pulled back in disgust. She was re-evaluating her decision to take this tour of the Clare coastline in Ireland. The vehicle rumbled slowly up a steep corkscrew road to a cliff overlooking the vast Atlantic Ocean.

They would have had a good view of the fields of grass and folds of limestone rock separated by rough stone walls except for the silver mist that hung in the air. The higher they climbed, the more it closed in. Beads of water rolled down the outside of the glass pane, and a film of condensation built up on the inside until only smears of green and grey were visible through the window. A chill pressed in and enveloped Y.

Close now, some innate knowledge told her. She trembled a little, not sure if it was the cold or the coffee she'd been sipping throughout the trip.

The bus heaved up the final ascent and levelled out with a strained gasp of relief from the engine. A few minutes later, shapes of houses and shop signs emerged from the gloom. The bus pulled in at a dingy petrol station, and its door wheezed open.

"Half an hour stop," the driver announced. The passengers disembarked and streamed through the mist toward the dim light of a neon café sign that advertised CHIPS.

The driver stretched and strained the buttons on his navy rayon shirt as Y paused, ready to alight.

"Where are we?" she asked.

"Kilcailligh. It's a hole of a town. I don't normally stop here, but the weather's shite, and I need a piss."

"Kilcailligh," she said, enjoying the way it rolled on her tongue. She stepped into the damp, turned away from the café, and followed the narrow winding street.

Pale two-story houses hunched against each other on either side, but after a minute, they thinned out leaving only a country road that merged with the haze. Unseen seagulls shrieked in the murk. She tasted salt on her lips.

She noticed a stile cut into the stone wall and climbed over it. Her boots crunched on a gravel path as the mist pushed in. A dark, hooked shape began to materialize: a hawthorn bush, no doubt hammered into its crooked contour by constant storms. Y drew abreast to it and considered how the branches appeared like a woman's hair rippling in a perpetual breeze. She reached out and touched its slippery, black-brown surface. Its gnarled roots clamped into the rocky ground in an obstinate fashion. *It could be eternal,* she thought idly.

An owl hooted to her right, and she swung around. The outline of a derelict building hung like a watermark in the moist veil. She moved toward it, and the curtain pulled back to reveal the roofless shell of an early stone church.

Weathered, listing gravestones littered the area around the bare walls. Humps of grass hinted where nubs of stone had been overgrown. Ivy choked tomb slabs dotted the area—some of which were broken as if those interred had smashed free of their confines. Only a pair of yew trees seemed to thrive there. Twin green guardians of the ruin of people's faith.

The owl perched at the apex of the church walls and stared at her. She nodded at it, and the woozy feeling slipped over her.

This place was significant.

She almost tripped over a mossy lump and staggered into a semi-circular wall built of smooth stones. It protected a massive granite boulder, the top of which was sheared off to form a flat surface. Five depressions were carved into it. Water pooled in them, so they looked like black mirrors.

She'd read about this in the guide book for the area. They were bullaun. In the past, people used to place polished pebbles in the indentations and turn them—for good luck or to curse. It was a strange practice thought to pre-date Christianity.

Y bent to examine the base of the boulder and spotted piles of stone lying about. She didn't consider her actions, merely moved on instinct. Over the years, she'd learned to trust the wisdom of the moment.

She dropped a stone into the middle pool and, for a fleeting instant, hesitated at putting her hand into the icy water. The notion that something might grab her fingers or cut the tips off flashed into her mind. She glanced over at the owl, but it had disappeared—there was no instruction except her intuition's urging.

She inhaled, bracing herself, and dipped her hand into the little pocket of water. Her finger tips numbed instantly, but she discerned the shape of the pebble below. She turned it five times counterclockwise and left the stone inside its well. She picked another stone at random and repeated the process until she had turned a stone in each of the pools.

"It took you long enough."

The woman's voice behind her was so unexpected Y yelped.

She turned and froze at the sight.

The woman perched on a low headstone that had been worn down with age. She was naked, sitting on her heels with her arms wrapped around her knees. Her skin was red, like brick. The first thing Y noticed were her bird-like feet: her toes were impossibly long and weirdly jointed. There was a ring of white bone around each one just before the curved talon. A ridge of feathers grew out along her forearms, and her hands were similar to her feet, except they looked more agile.

Her face was the most arresting: heart-shaped with a chin that came to a fine point, framed by a beard of feathers. Her eyes were large, upswept with yellow pupils and a black, reptile irises. They glowed. Her mouth curved into a cynical smile. A mane of scalloped white feathers edged in black flowed in a wide strip down her skull and back, between her glorious wings.

The woman's strange beauty dazzled Y, rendering her speechless. The void in her chest vanished as a warm familiarity flooded her. Y felt she knew this being better than her own family.

A soft breeze stirred the mist in eddies around them.

The woman jumped down from her roost. Her breasts were small, and the nipples pierced with the same bone rings. Her pubis was bare. She was shorter than Y, but Y did not believe she had a single advantage over her.

"You called, and I came," the woman said, her accent odd but melodious.

"I followed the signs," Y said. She wondered if this was a dream and if she was still jaunting along in the bus. "Who . . . ?" she couldn't continue.

The woman cocked her head. "You don't remember, sister?"

Y shook her head slowly.

The woman shrugged. "You never remember. I thought it might be different this time."

Y pondered this. "What should I call you?"

She laughed, an almost whistling sound. "There are so many names. I don't think I trust you with the important ones yet. How do you identify yourself?

"Y," she said.

"Then call me Aan," she drawled the vowels. "Who needs complicated names when you know who you are?" She laughed, and Y knew she was being mocked.

"What now?" Y asked, her tone sharp.

Aan darted forward, and it took all of Y's control not to flinch. She stood close and gazed up at Y. Y could smell her—a mixture of incense and sweat that was oddly arousing.

"Are you ready?" she said intently. Her bright eyes wide and mesmerizing. "To bring Her back."

"Who?" Y asked, but in her mind, a shape had begun to form. A column of fire and black smoke and, roaring inside it, a heart forged for destruction.

Aan placed her hand upon Y's arm, and it electrified her.

Y dipped her head and kissed Aan, deeply, passionately. The pillar of fire in her mind erupted. Lust gripped her. It had never been like this before: not with Levi or with Alice or any of the partners she had sampled over the years.

"Nothing is forbidden, all will be made anew!" a voice cried joyously, and Y realised it was her voice.

Y pulled off her coat as Aan ripped open Y's blouse. Buttons pinged. Aan's fingers were remarkably agile, and sliced through Y's bra and were massaging her breasts in moments. Y groaned from deep in her belly. Her knees gave slightly from the intensity.

She wanted to rut in the grass with this woman-creature. To roll in the soil among the graves of the deceased. She wanted the dust-mouthed dead in the underworld to be stirred from their leaden existence by Y's and Aan's cries of pleasure, to envy the flickering glory of life.

So she did.

Afterward she lay naked and panting beside Aan. Small cuts and bruises throbbed on her arms and legs, but she had never felt more alive. Over the years, she had sometimes wondered if she were merely a flesh golem, magicked up by her parents.

Yet the warmth subsided, the connection eroded, and dissatisfaction needled its way into her mind again. She sat up.

Aan stretched and preened and, in a flash, was perched on a headstone again.

"It won't last," Aan commented. "Not while you're in that body. Not while the world remains this way."

Y glared at Aan, suspicion slipping into her thoughts.

"Why?" she shouted, and the hatred at being *wrong* flooded through her again. "Why was I made like this?"

"You have a choice," Aan said. "To call Her forth and bring about a new world or to remain as you are, eternally unhappy in this one."

"What?"

"It was an ancient curse. We were separated, Her avatars. You, to be reborn, again and again, each time with the choice to bring Her back. Me, to wait and to offer you the choice."

"I've never chosen Her?" That seemed impossible, already the pillar of fire held Y's devotion.

Aan's expression darkened. "Nothing will survive Her return. Not even us."

"That's not . . ." she was going to say possible, but already she knew it was. The vision of the planet burned to smouldering pitch and prepped for another race's emergence resolved in her mind.

Gawain would be roasted. Her mother melted to slag. Her past acquaintances and lovers would be incinerated. She and Aan would be the last witnesses to the razing of the world before they too writhed in the final flames.

All for a promise that what would come after would be more marvellous— and even as she contemplated the notion, Y sensed the beauty beating at the edges of this world. It wanted to come into being so desperately. All that stood in its way was Y's decision.

The responsibility crushed her. It was too much to ask of any person. She pulled on her trousers, grabbed her coat, and buttoned it up. The mist chilled her again now the heat of passion had died.

"This always happens!" Aan screamed and sprang into the air. Great wings extended outward and beat, so she hovered above Y, her expression livid. Y's coat flapped in the gusts.

"By living with them, you become attached. You swallow their teachings about self-sacrifice and 'the greater good' and choose martyrdom rather than renewal." She spat. "And what do I have? Centuries of loneliness, interspersed by moments of hope. Always dashed. And sometimes you never come. Generations pass without any contact."

Aan darted high into the air, keening.

The thunderclaps of her wings buffeted Y. She grabbed onto an old stone cross and wished this had never come to pass. Hatred scored her heart. She craved death rather than to endure such pain and to cause it in others.

Aan dove down instantly and grabbed her arms.

"If you wish for the end, at least bring on transformation! Don't leave me behind, waiting again upon another choice and another rejection."

Y closed her eyes against the pleading. "Nothing will remain," she whispered.

Aan's talons tore into Y's coat sleeves and gouged Y's arms. She cried out.

"Choose!" Aan bellowed and threw Y away from her.

"I can't." Tears streamed down Y's face.

"You have," Aan replied, and her words were ice.

She leaped into the air and vanished.

Y lay crouched on the grass, sobbing. The emptiness inside her returned, worse than before. She welcomed it. The void would swallow confusion and pain. She had lived like this before: a meat shell containing a vacuum.

Calm settled upon her again.

Y stood, dragged fingers through her hair, and brushed grass off her coat. She was prepping the mannequin for display.

She returned through the mist, over the stile, and down the road to the bus station.

Stranger than everything else, the bus waited for her.

Y stood at the open door expecting the driver to be aghast at her appearance or chastise her for tardiness.

He sat with a newspaper draped over the steering wheel. He glanced up and gave her a nod. "You're early. No one else is back." Then he returned to his perusal of headlines and scandal.

Y climbed into the empty vehicle with leaden feet and plodded down the aisle. She dropped onto her seat and clutched her bag to her chest.

Outside the dewed glass, a line of ghostly figures approached the bus. Unreal forms moving through an unreal life.

The driver turned the key in the engine, and it growled and vibrated, awaiting the impetus to depart.

The smell of spoiled food filled her mouth.

She jumped up.

"I have to go!" she cried.

Y raced past the rows of seats and shoved through the protesting bodies.

The pillar of fire in her mind roared and exploded until she could feel the flames bursting through her bones.

She scorched a path through the mist, and behind her, there remained only ash.

§

Maura McHugh lives in the Irish countryside in a house watched over by rooks and visited by hares. Her short fiction, poetry, and essays have appeared in publications in America and Europe. She's published two collections—*Twisted Fairy Tales* and *Twisted Myths*—in the USA. She's written several comic book series and is also a screenwriter, playwright, and critic and has served on the juries of international literary, comic book, and film awards. Her latest book is a monograph on David Lynch's iconic film *Twin Peaks: Fire Walk With Me*, published by Electric Dreamhouse Press/PS Publishing. Her website is splinister.com, and she tweets as @splinister.

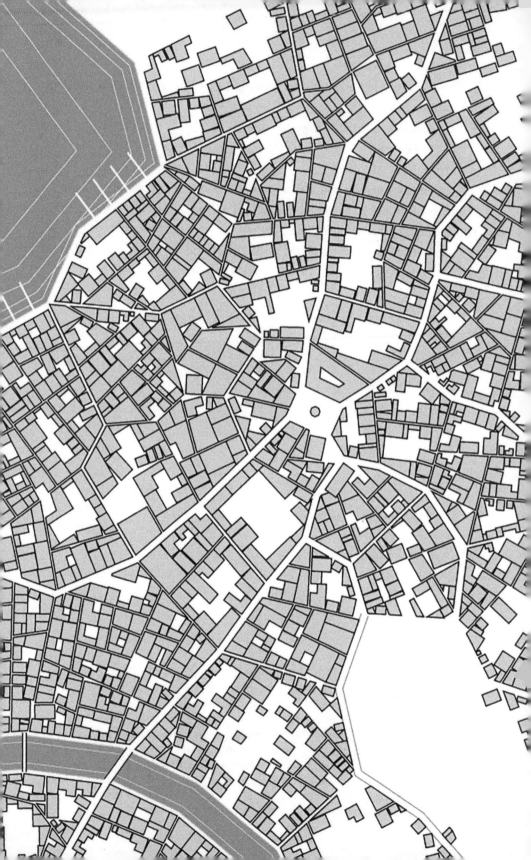

Night Doctors

P. DJÈLÍ CLARK

"De only Ku Klux I ever bumped into was a passel o' young Baltimore Doctors tryin' to ketch me one night an' take me to de medicine college to 'periment on me. I seed dem a laying' fer me an' I run back into de house. Dey had a plaster all ready for to slap on my mouf. Yessuh."

—Cornelius Garner (ex-slave, Virginia),
interview by Emmy Wilson and Claude W. Anderson,
May 18, 1937 (*Weevils in the Wheat*, 1976:102)

Y ARRIVAL IN DURHAM COMES ON A sweltering August afternoon in 1937. I am here on work with the Federal Writers' Project, tasked to conduct interviews of former slaves, to collect their stories, memories, and folkways, as that generation is daily dying out and will soon reach its end.

Securing lodgings comes with its usual difficulties as Jim Crowism is as rampant in this city as any other in the South. From experience, I can assure that if there is anything a Southerner dislikes more than a colored man it is one who shows education and learning.

The proprietor of the local Chanford Motel informs me that he does not "rent rooms to niggers" with further invectives followed by a hail of saliva and pungent chewing tobacco. I wipe the detritus from my spectacles and leave the establishment, not altogether surprised.

After some investigation, I am able to secure lodgings in the city at the place of a colored butcher, a squat anvil of a man with arms suited to his profession. He tends to his work while we haggle, hacking at a knuckle of meat with a wide hog splitter and cleanly slicing flesh from bone with a thin knife.

"Well, I'll take you on. Mr. Bisset, is it? Gonna have to get yer food someplace else tho'. Mama Elsa's just round the corner. One of the finest meals you'll ever have in town. 'Less you like yer meat rare."

He chuckles, wiping his apron with ham-fisted, bloody smears before showing me up some side stairs. The room is clean but Spartan: a small bed, a closet, and a window that opens to an alley.

"You can comes and goes as you please. Gonna have to put up with the smell tho', when I'm butchering." I surreptitiously sniff the air where a coppery scent seeps into every pore and crevice.

"You say you a writer?" His eyes move to appraise my supple hands. "And you here to ask old folk 'bout slavery times? Government pay colored men for that?"

I explain that many of the old Negroes prove reluctant with white interviewers. The Works Progress Administration hopes that colored men and women such as myself can alleviate their recalcitrance.

He laughs. "President Roosevelt makin' a job for everybody. And what you thinkin' to find out 'bout slavery times? That white folk had as much of the devil in 'em then as now?"

We share a knowing smile before he departs—the one that unites the colored race across region and caste in our sacred knowledge and unwritten scriptures on the ways of white folk.

When he's gone, I open my suitcases, laying out my clothes and removing a leather book that I place beneath the mattress. Then I set out for dinner.

True to the butcher's words, Mama Elsa (a matronly woman who is a wonder in the kitchen) provides me with a fine meal of the Southern Negro variety. Learning I am from the North, she sits to talk with me over jars of iced tea and raisin cake, suggesting where I might find older Negroes who remember slavery. When I return to my room, I plot out my plans for the next day, turn down the lights, and retire.

I wake up sometime after 2 a.m.

I pick out a white suit from my belongings: a full jacket, vest, and pants with white socks and white shoes. Fully dressed, I grab up a matching cloth bag and make my way down the side passage of the butchery until I step outside. Pulling a white bowler down to keep it firm, I enter into Durham's still night, keeping from the main roads and remaining hidden behind buildings and shadows until reaching my destination. When I rap on the door with a white-gloved hand, the face of the man that greets me looks confused. Perhaps from being roused from sleep. Or at the sight of a tall Negro man dressed in white, wearing a surgeon's mask.

The blur of silver cuts a clean line across the man's throat, spraying bits of crimson onto the white apron I assiduously placed over my wears. He clutches the open wound, shock and pain marring his sharp features. He does not try to scream, not that he can with the severed trachea. Instead he tries to hold in the fluid that leaks over his hands, staggering back and knocking over a small stool as he falls. I follow and close the door behind me.

The proprietor of the Chanford Motel lies on a disheveled rug, his bare legs kicking from beneath a blue robe. Righting the stool, I seat myself and watch. The condescension that had once filled those gray eyes, when he'd earlier hurled slurs in my face, is gone. There is only fear now in a gaze that is fixed singly on me as if I have become his whole world. It is an animal's terror—unable to look away from the predator that has captured it. He watches as I remove a cloth bundle from my bag, spreading it upon the floor. The silver instruments within are sharp, made for cutting and slicing. I run a finger over them and am reminded how similar a surgeon's tools are to a butcher's.

A wet gurgling comes from the specimen laid out before me—a failed attempt to speak through ruined cartilage. I imagine it is asking why, so I answer.

"You may think this is vengeance for our earlier uncivil encounter. But I can assure it is nothing so base." I draw out my leather book, opening it to show notations and sketches. "I'm a curious man, you see, looking for something. And you, I believe, offer a fine sampling."

Those panic-stricken animal eyes remain on me as I cut open the specimen's abdomen. They stay open long after I begin my search within the reek of bile and organs.

In my book, I jot down my findings.

My first three interviews the next day yield little result. Two of the Negroes were children at the end of slavery and remember little of it. A third is so addle-minded he does little more than glare.

It is late afternoon when I arrive at the home of Miss Maddie Shaw, who lives with her granddaughter in a humble shack at the city's edge, near woods untouched by electricity, plumbing, or paved roads.

Miss Shaw claims to be 97 years of age. She is an ideal illustration of the old Negro type: black skin, white teeth, and woolly hair. Her face, with its wide forehead and prognathous jaw, bears a regal countenance that looks descended from the Amazons of Dahomey. She is bound to this place by infirmity and lords over it like a Kentake of old Meroe. When I tell her why I've come, she is guarded.

"Can I tell yer 'bout slavery days? Sho', but I ain't going to. Most of it I can't remember. And the rest's too awful to tell. Don't need to know all that old talk no how. You got sweeties? I lak sweet things and don't get dem too often."

At learning I have no sweets, she turns away from me with disinterest. Her granddaughter, younger than myself (though aged unnaturally by a life under Jim Crowism), is my savior. She prods the elder, telling her I've come to put her story into a book. Miss Maddie Shaw shifts in her rickety throne and eyes me contemplatively.

"Well, I'll tell yer some to put down in yer book. But not the worse. Where I'm from? Was born and raised right here. Same as my mammy and pappy, back when dis was all Payne land. My ol' missus? Dat be Miss Emma Payne. How she treat me? Lak a missus treat all her slaves. She'd slap and beat you wit' her hands and every now and den take to you wit' a switch till you raw. But her husband was the tough one, hang you up by the thumbs in the barn and den whup you till the blood run. Did he beat women? Why sure he beat dem, jes' lak men. Beat us naked and washed us down in brine on Sundays, right fore he gon' to church."

She makes a bitter face.

"I ain't gon' tell yer much more. No, I ain't. No sense for yer to know 'bout all dose mean white folk. Dey all daid now. Is dey in heaven? Lord no! Dey don't deserve heaven nor hell. Wish the Night Doctors had took 'em!"

Those last words jolt my spine. Setting aside my writing pad, I reach into my bag for my leather book and bid her to continue, trying to hold back my eagerness.

"Night Doctors? Oh, dey was a fright round here back'n when dis was Payne land. Night Doctors was men, you see, only dey was not men. Used to come round at night and snatch away slaves to 'speriment on. Best you up and die 'fore the Night Doctors git you. Dey take you to where dey stay, a great white dissectin' hall, big as a whole city, and cut you open right dere and show you all yer insides!"

Old Miss Shaw reads my face as if it were etched with runes and grins at deciphering them.

"Oh, I sees what you lak. Ain't stories 'bout slaves and white folk you want to hear. It's stories 'bout haints and witches, raw head and bloody bones. Old Maddie knows dem stories and better. You come back wit' sumtin sweet, might jes' tell you more."

With that, her face closes. I shut my book in turn and bid her farewell, thoughts of Night Doctors whispering in my head.

"Night Doctors?"

Mama Elsa squints at me over the frosted rim of a mason jar. "Now what you want with them ol' stories?"

I explain that the Federal Writer's Project is interested in the folkways of ex-slaves, and I share a particular interest. In fact, I tell her, I am collecting such stories for a book.

She raises a sculpted eyebrow and removes a flat tin flask from somewhere in her voluminous saffron dress to top off our iced tea.

"You writer folk sho' got queer ideas. I just know what the ol' people say. Night Doctors was supposed to be men what snatched away slaves. They'd leave traps to get you. Some of em' had black bottles full of ether or needles to prick you with. Other times, they put plaster round yo' face. They'd experiment on you. Slice you up while you was still alive even!"

I ask if she believes such stories.

"Did when I was little. My auntie used to tell us. Said she heard them from our grandmammy. Used to give me a fright. But I knows better now. Night Doctors was made up by white folks. Was the masters theyselves, you see, dressing up and scarin' the slaves to keep them from running off the plantations."

I nod thoughtfully. Night Doctors, Night Witches, Night Riders, Bottle Men, and Needle Men. My first hearing of the tale was back in Washington DC in medical school, conveyed to us as a curious superstition of Negro migrants so plentiful in the city. Much as Mama Elsa relates, it's commonly held that the folklore arose with slave masters. Others claim it began with the all too common practice of selling deceased slaves to medical colleges as cadavers. Night Doctors lingered on with freedom, with some mistaking the Klan for "Ku Klux" Doctors. The stories are common among Negroes throughout the cities of the South: Charleston, New Orleans, Birmingham. And though told with slight variations, they share a remarkable continuity.

"Suppose you asking 'bout these Night Doctors because of what's been happening here in Durham," Mama Elsa says.

I work my face into befuddlement, and she leans forward to whisper.

"It's all folk can talk 'bout! Four white people found dead in the past week. They was cut open and then sowed up—like somebody took they insides out and put it all back in again!"

I round my eyes to match her alarm, asking if they've caught anyone. She shakes her head.

"They ain't know who done it. But they saying it got to be some kind of doctor. They checkin' all the white folk work up at the hospital."

I sip from my jar. Of course, in Durham, the culprit would be expected to be white. Negroes were suspected well enough of delinquencies—stealing, robbery, rape, even casual murder. But nothing like this. Nothing that required such skill.

Had anyone cared to look, they would find a pattern to the specimens. The storeowner who viciously beat a colored boy of 12 for the offense of not removing his hat in a white man's presence. The public defender that conspired to shuffle his clients into chain gangs. The old carpenter who bragged openly of the Negro he once helped burn alive. The thread that connected them was gleaned from the whispered chatter picked up in spaces like Mama Elsa's, of the many sins of this city—like the others. It should have been easy to see but was rendered as invisible as the crimes each had committed.

"Them killings done started up talk 'bout Night Doctors," Mama Elsa went on. "Some saying they even seen a man in white skulkin' round the back streets at night."

I remind her that she doesn't believe in such things anymore. She returns a wry grin. "There's what you don't believe in Mr. Bisset, and then there's what you 'fraid of." She pauses. "We used to sing this song 'bout Night Doctors when we was small." She puts on the wide eyes and hoary voice of an ancient storyteller, mesmerizing her clansmen about the fire:

Yuh see that house? That great white house?
Way yonder down de street?
They used to take dead folks in there
Wrapped in a long white sheet!

An' sometimes when a nigger did stop,
A-wondering who was dead,
Them Night Doctors would come along
An' bat him on the head!

An' drag that poor dead nigger chile
Right in they dissectin' hall
To investigate his liver, lights—
His gizzard and his gall.

Take off dat nigger's hands an' feet—
His eyes, his head, an' all,
An' when them doctors finish up
They wasn't nothin' left at all!

She finishes with a whoop of laughter.
"Maybe you can write a book bout that!"
"Perhaps I will," I answer. And I sip my tea.

It is a week before I return to see Miss Maddie Shaw. I find her alone, her granddaughter having gone into Durham to do domestic work. I ask if she remembers me.

"Well sho' I do. See you come back to ask more questions for yer book. Colored folk sho' come up high in the world. You git to learn from books in all dem big schools wit the white folk? No? A school jes' for colored folk? Well, ain't dat sumthin'. What dey learn you dar?"

Medicine, I tell her, discarding my earlier pretenses. I learned how to be a surgeon. But I was a curious man, and I now search for something beyond what my learning could teach me. I tell her I think she might be able to help. She listens and shrugs.

"If so you say. You brung sumthin' sweet?"

I offer up a bag of caramels, and her old eyes light up. She takes one between thumb and forefinger, plopping it in her mouth and sucking joyfully. I wait for her to finish and ask about the Night Doctors.

"Lak I say, dey was men that was not men who snatched away the slaves. Dey come mostly for the sick and old ones. Did Marser Payne know? Pfshaw! White folk ain't pay no mind what slaves say. Dey lose a healthy nigger and dey thinkin' he ran off. Dey lose a sick or old nigger, jes' one less mouth at the trow'. Did dey like to scare us? Sho'. Nothin' made dem happier than scaring niggers, exceptin' whipping 'em. When I was small, Marster Payne used to put out a trow' and have us little ones eatin' from it lak hogs. Remember, he'd say whoeva finish last he gonna cut and hang up like a piglet and have us for Easter dinner. We eat fast den, and he jes' laugh and laugh. Used to scare me powerful, thinkin' of hanging up in dat smokehouse, all salted and ready fer marster 'n' missus to eat."

I tell her that I've heard about Night Doctors too. I tap the leather book in my lap. I explain that I've collected stories about them from old slaves like her, from all around the country. I ask if Night Doctors weren't just white men like her master, trying to scare the slaves. She hoots at this.

"Men in sheets? Night Doctors not no men in sheets! You figurin' some ol' white man in a sheet gonna scare a big field hand lak Jeremiah? Who was he? Only the biggest buck you eva seen! Strong too. One time, the overseer tie him to a tree stump. Jeremiah pull dat stump right out the ground and walk round wit' it draggin' behind! He wasn't scared of nothin' or nobody neither. Exceptin' the Night Doctors."

Did this Jeremiah see one, I press? A Night Doctor? She takes another caramel, sucking for a while before answering.

"Jeremiah's wife, Adeline, she take sick. Marster send out his nigger doctor, same one who look after horses and mules. But he say she burning up wit' the fever and gon' be dead. Was late dat same night the Night Doctors come. Jeremiah hear a knocking outside. And he knows nobody come calling 'round dat time. He shout for dem to leave. But Night Doctors don't heed what you say. Dey come right in under the door! Yes, under the door is what I say! Dey can squeeze dey bodies like a rat do, right up under yer door and appear big as day! When Jeremiah see dem, he try to hold on to his wife.

"But dem doctors just start talking dey whisper talk. Dat's how dey get on, whisperin' right inside yer head. Adeline hear dat whisperin' and jump out dat bed lak she not sick! She start walkin' to dem. When Jeremiah try and stop her, she turn back to him. But not her whole body, jes' her neck, all twisted 'bout like an owl! And when she open her mouth, only dat whisper talk come out. Dat just 'bout make Jeremiah crazy. He starts to hollerin' and the other slaves come running! But the Night Doctors wus gone. Take Adeline wit dem."

My hands are shaking as I write. I've recorded many stories about Night Doctors. But Miss Shaw tells them with a clarity I've never before encountered. Overcome, I lean forward and spill out my own truths.

I too believe these Night Doctors are more than folktales, I tell her. And whoever or whatever they are, I believe they can help me in my work. Help me in my great search.

"And what you lookin' for, Mistuh Bisset? What you thinkin' some Night Doctors can help you find?"

Hate, I tell her. I'm looking for hate.

Most people would greet my words with bewilderment. They might even think I was mad. But Maddie Shaw only reaches for another caramel and speaks again without prodding.

"When Adeline was took, Jeremiah swear he gon' git her back. He sneak off to see a conjurin' woman what live on a near plantation. She tell him to go into the woods a ways at night and look for the daid Angel Oak. Dat's the way to where dem Night Doctors stay. He gon' on do it, traveling to the big white dissectin' hall and get to fussin' wit' dem Night Doctors 'bout Adeline. Dey don't give her, but dey let him come back. When we find him, he 'bout half-daid and wit no eyes in his head. Yes, I say! No eyes! Wasn't nothing dere but bloody holes starin' out at you! And he tell us what he learn, why it is dem Night Doctors come."

She reaches out to grab my arm. The hand that holds me is old, but the grip is tight—marked with scars and callouses, made strong by enduring hardship.

"It's our sufferin' dey want! See, dey ain't got no feelins where dey comes from. Dey empty and dried out inside. Don't know nothin' 'bout pain or misery. And ain't nobody seen more pain and sufferin' in these parts than us poor

slaves. Dat's why dey take jes' us. Why dey leave the white folk be. Dat's why
dey take Jeremiah's eyes, 'cause he done looked out on so much misery in his
life. That was the bargain what won him free."

She releases me then and settles back, but her eyes are as firm as her grip.

"If you go to see dem Night Doctors, dey gonna set a price 'fore you can leave.
Or you don't come back. Wat you ready to give, Mistuh Bisset?"

That night, I walk the woods just on Durham's edges, a ghost in white. Old
Maddie Shaw's instructions play in my head. Find the dead Angel Oak. I'd
know it when I see it. But I had to *want* to see it, she'd said. And how I wanted
that so badly.

In medical school, we learned of the discarded notion of humorism, begun by
those wise Hamites of Egypt and passed down to the Greeks, Romans, and onto
the Hindoos in their Ayurveda medicine. It believed in the existence of bodily
fluids that made up each man: blood was the first and foremost humor of life;
yellow bile was the cause of aggression; black bile was the source of melancholy;
and phlegm, apathy.

In our hubris, we've disparaged this wisdom for modernity. And it is our
loss, for we are kept ignorant of the human condition. I believe there is another
humor yet unaccounted for: hate. I have seen enough of its workings in this
world to know that it exists. If it can be found at its source, perhaps its essence
can be counteracted or drained away, to ease the senseless and injurious emotion
that has caused humanity such incalculable harm. I looked for it in dissecting
halls and in the cold cavities of cadavers. But it remained elusive. So I took my
search to living specimens. My travels have offered me unique opportunities
to continue my pursuit. And these Night Doctors, who understand the hidden
inner workings of the body, have been my inspiration.

I cannot say if it is I who find the dead tree or if it finds me, but it stands out
suddenly in the shadowed forest. Where the hickories that surround it are tall
and dark, the dead Angel Oak is squat and bone white. Generous branches grow
out from its trunk, splitting into further limbs that spill out upon the ground
and reach up into the air. The skeletal remains of dead things cover the tree in
a decaying moss, and as I draw near, I can see that some are fused to the pale
wood: rib cages and the vertebrae of spinal columns, even teeth, all taken from

more beasts than I can count. I place my hand to a hefty bough and find it solid, but not hard, and warm to the touch. Opening my razor, I draw a gash across the colorless bark. It splits open and oozes blood thick as sap.

The dead tree, I decide, is oddly named.

I walk to the trunk, wondering fancily if the tree's many appendages might snatch me up like some horrid kraken of the deep. From my bundle of tools, I select the bone saw and set about cutting. The jagged iron teeth tear into red pulp that gives way like tough meat. By the time the hole is made wide enough, I am spattered in arboreal gore. I reach into the fleshy interior, pulling apart hardy muscle and gristle. There is soft, sucking warmth when I push myself into the gaping wound. I take a breath and thrust deeper. For a terrifying moment, there is only suffocating darkness, and I imagine my body becoming trapped within, digested by this monstrous tree, my bones fusing to its pallid branches and left to knock together like chimes in any errant wind. Breaking through, I tumble out onto hard stone, covered in the sweet metallic pungency of my birth blood.

I am in a hall.

To call it cavernous is to do an injustice. It is gargantuan, and I am but a Lilliputian in turn. Its high walls and ceilings are made of white stone that look continuous, with no bricks or seams—as if carved from one block of massive ivory. The opening I entered through is now a blistering wound, knitting back together like skin before vanishing altogether. I reach a blood-soaked palm to touch where it had been, leaving an imprint on the now unblemished stone.

I turn about to look down the hall and can now make out corridors as well. They are endless and flow on and on, like a small city of stone. There is nothing to do now, I surmise, but continue my journey to seek out the masters of this nether realm. As I walk, my shoes reverberate in the silence. It strikes me that there is no sound here. But for the trail of blood left by my footsteps, all is pristine, sterile.

I reach the first corridor and peer down its length. It is as swallowing and seemingly infinite as the one I now follow. Another on the opposite side is much the same. There are no windows or doors. And I am left to wonder if this hall is all there is to be found here? I am deciding my next course of action when I hear the first noise other than my own. It is a dull shuffling, like many bare feet running upon stone. And it is growing. Base instinct sends me darting into one of the corridors, wary of being seen. Back flat against the wall, I peek around the edge to find a monstrosity emerging from another passageway.

I bite a clenched fist not to cry out. The thing before me is a horror from a fevered nightmare. It resembles a great colorless centipede, easily the width of an automobile and longer still, with a segmented body of armor topped with a fused spinal ridge. It is so uniformly white it blends with the stone as it pours out from the corridor, winding along the ceiling on a multitude of legs, each of which ends in a long-fingered hand. Clinging to the wall, it snakes down to the closed opening where I entered. Two protracted antennae twitch as mandibles upon its eyeless head open to lap up my bloodied handprint. It stretches to the ground: half of its elongated bulk still clutching the wall while a torso of wriggling legs, fingers, and feelers scours the floor clean of the first of my bloody footprints.

I turn and run, knowing now that I am being hunted.

Panic grips me in my flight. I imagine this monstrosity is the guard dog of this place. Or perhaps a scavenger, set to maintain its purity. And I am terrified of my fate were it to find me. I think to remove my bloodstained shoes, cursing at not having the wits to do so earlier. It is as I pause to look over my shoulder to see if I am being pursued that something seizes me.

I am pulled off my feet, landing hard on my back. My head strikes the stone floor, and my world threatens to go dark in a blossom of pain. But I chase it away, forcing my mind back to coherency. I am being dragged by my legs, my body limp and arms splayed at my sides. I cry out, thinking the monstrous scavenger has captured me! But when I crane my neck to look up, I find I am held by giants.

They appear to my eyes at first as impossibly tall men. Their bodies are draped in long white robes over frames that seem almost skeletal. The hands that hold me are pale with desiccated skin stretched tight over long slender fingers. I shout, demanding to be released. But when one turns back to me, I am stricken silent.

There are no features on that colorless face: no eyes, nose, or even a mouth. There are just folds of wrinkled skin on an elongated head. As I stare into that blank visage, I know then that I have found the beings that I have so long sought. The Bottle Men and Needle Men of old Negro folklore who stalk the darkness and shadows. The Night Doctors.

We stop, and I am lifted, deposited unceremoniously atop a raised block of stone. I attempt to rise, but a whisper fills my head: a cacophony of voices that shatter my will. My body obeys this eldritch power, and I lay immobile as six-fingered hands reach to tear away my clothing, discarding my soiled suit and stripping me bare. I am unable even to blink, leaving me to stare as another block of stone descends from above. This one is lined with silver implements, the first hint of color I've seen. One looks like scissors with four serrated blades. Another is cruelly hooked like a scythe. Others are pointed, barbed, or covered in thin needles. The otherworldly lords of this realm arrange themselves about me, each taking one of the silver devices in hand. I know what they are then: the tools of a surgeon.

Grasping their intent, I am fast overcome with that animal terror: the very one I have seen in the eyes of my specimens. It threatens to envelop me, drown me in its depths. But I have come too far to end things here. I grapple with the terror-stricken animal within, caging it and wresting back control as a blade descends to part my flesh.

"Wait!" I shout. "I want to talk! Wait!"

I watch the blade move closer and wonder if my words will reach them. Were the amoeba on my petri dish to voice its lament, would I hear? Were the frog in my dissecting tray to cry out to stay my hand, would I listen?

I remember then Old Maddie Shaw's words. They would set a price. "I can pay the price!" I scream.

The blade mercifully stops and hovers.

The Night Doctors turn to regard each other, and the whispering begins again, filling the silence in the spaces of my mind. I do not understand, but when it stops, one of those terrible faces leans down to loom over me. The voice that comes is a whisper, alien and cold, that hammers my skull.

Price. What do you know of the price?

My words spill out in a rush. "I know what you seek! The pain! The misery! I know it! You didn't take me like the others! I sought you out. I came here willingly! Because I know about the price!"

Fools come here willingly.

I'm not certain if it is the same voice or another, but I give answer. "I'm like you, an explorer. I search for something. Something more than the misery and pain you've come to savor. Help me find it, and I will offer it to you!"

One of the cyclopean heads tilt, appearing curious. *Name this thing you would offer. Name this new price.*

"Hate," I whisper. "I will give you hate."

The Night Doctors share looks and new whispers. I don't need to understand to know their meaning. It is confusion. They turn back to look down at me.

You will explain. Hate.

I am struck silent. How am I to describe hate to beings such as these? How do I put meaning to the insensible?

I am still in my thoughts when the blade descends, cutting deep into my abdomen with a searing fire. A primal scream pours from my depths, and the caged animal howls in unison, throwing itself at its bars. I watch as the glistening ropes of my intestines are pulled free. The Night Doctors probe its fleshy contours, heedless of my cries. A hand reaches back inside me to retrieve a pink mass I know is my stomach. It is passed around among my hosts, one of whom slits it open to spill out the putrid contents. My liver is pored over by slender fingers, investigated as one would a book.

And it is only then that I understand: *you will explain, Hate.*

They are reading me, seeking to comprehend what could not be put into words. It must have been them, I muse, who long ago visited the Babylonians, delivering the lesson of hepatoscopy—the reading of entrails, passed on to the Hittites, Etruscans, and priestesses of old Rome. With this final knowing, I surrender to the pain, my shrieks coming in a holy litany. I sing to these lords of viscera, I tell them of hate, of Negro bodies hung from trees like fruit. In the cooked hearts and severed fingers distributed as souvenirs. In the postcards to celebrate the bonfires made of men and women for no other crime but Negritude. In the daily rituals of humiliations and oppressions that engulfs the whole land. I sing to them of the hate that consumes men's souls like a ravaging cancer. When my eyes are plucked free, leaving only tears of blood to streak my cheeks, I am still singing.

It is not yet morning when I stand again before Miss Maddie Shaw. I am dressed once more in my white suit, my white shoes, my white bowler hat, and holding my white doctor's bag. She awakens at my presence, blinking up at me.

"You come back," she says plainly.

I give a slow nod. "I have been to the place where the Night Doctors live."

Her eyes meet my empty bleeding sockets.

"Look like it so."

Her granddaughter murmurs from a pile of blankets on the floor. I whisper a command, and she eases back into sleep. My attention returns to Miss Maddie Shaw.

"They have shared with me their secrets and returned me to do my work." In truth, they had done more than that. They had initiated me, chosen me as their conduit to this world to seek out this promised feast of hate.

"I thank you," I say, "for showing me the way."

The old woman grunts. "Seem like you knows the way long 'fore I tell you."

I grin at this, and she flinches. When I turn to leave, she calls out a question.

"What you give them to learn dey secrets? To let you come back?"

I look down, beneath the white suit, to a body now emptied of organs and entrails and blood, of all that it once held.

"All of me," I answer. "I gave everything."

With those parting words, I collapse, flattening like a rat as I squeeze beneath the door of her cabin and out into the night.

§

Phenderson Djèlí Clark is the author of the novellas *The Black God's Drums* (Summer 2018) and *The Haunting of Tram Car 015* (Winter 2019) from Tor.com Publishing. His Tor.com novelette *A Dead Djinn in Cairo* (2016) made the Locus Recommended Reading List and was listed as one of the Notable Stories in *The Best American Science Fiction and Fantasy 2017* as well as republished in *The Long List Anthology Vol. 3* (2017), featuring stories from the Hugo Award Nomination List. His stories have appeared in online venues such as *Daily Science Fiction*, *Heroic Fantasy Quarterly*, *Apex*, *Lightspeed*, *Fireside Quarterly*, *Beneath Ceaseless Skies*, and in print anthologies including *Griots*, *Hidden Youth*, and *Clockwork Cairo*. He is loosely associated with the quarterly *FIYAH: Magazine of Black Speculative Fiction* and an infrequent reviewer at *Strange Horizons*.

The author resides in a small Edwardian castle in New England with his wife and pet dragon, where he writes speculative fiction when he is not playing the part of a mild-mannered academic historian. He rambles on issues of speculative fiction, politics, and diversity at his blog The Disgruntled Haradrim.

The Chemical Bride

EVAN J. PETERSON

SCENE 1

(Lights up on two women. They huddle around a glass-and-iron tank. The masses floating therein suggest human limbs. One woman is dressed in filthy rags, the other in a blood-stained blouse and pants. Both wear leather aprons. The set is dressed to suggest a rudimentary alchemist's laboratory.)

CREATURE

You delay. When will she be finished?

VICTORIA FRANKENSTEIN

Easy, easy. This is delicate work. The branches of nerves and vessels must find one another, like streams merging into a great river. Should we remove her before those loose threads join, she will be a pitiful thing, constantly in pain and bleeding inside. Do you want a bride in never-ending seizure?

CREATURE

Make her better than you made me. But not too.

VICTORIA FRANKENSTEIN

She will be. You, I assembled from the damps of the grave, unhallowed and piecemeal. A life of death. She has never truly lived. She will decide when her healing and coagulation are complete. She's too precious now, like a map sewn from chrysanthemums—

HLOE BROKE CHARACTER. "DO YOU REALLY WANT ME to say that?" she asked, only half-rhetorically. "That the bride is a precious flower?" Chloe gazed into the nearly empty seats of the darkened theater and tried to distinguish the silhouette of her director.

No response.

Chloe continued, "I mean, I thought this was a *feminist* horror story. That's what I signed on for."

She looked to Natasha, but Natasha avoided her eyes and stared silently at the murky tank of viscera. Even without the prosthetic makeup, her costume of bloodied rags disquieted Chloe.

The voice came reverberating through the cavernous building, a sound like frosted clay, making Chloe and Natasha both jump. "Did it occur to you that Victoria Frankenstein herself is not a feminist?"

Chloe scanned the house. Maria's voice continued to haunt, hidden from view like the orchestra to a silent motion picture.

"There have been no changes to the script since your first read-through. We are decontextualizing the female body, exploding it to give birth to a new sex. Victoria Frankenstein is a pioneer, like Wollstonecraft and her daughter. And like them, Frankenstein herself has a far way to go yet. Did you read the books I gave you?"

Dust motes danced in the stage lights. Chloe looked to Natasha, the young costar who never missed an opportunity to play sycophant to the avant-garde director. Natasha found an opportunity to please both women now, telling Chloe, "I think chapters five and six of *Speak the Skin* might help you understand what Maria is after."

Natasha had in fact played a supporting character in every one of Maria's productions for years until finally given the part of Macbeth in the much-lauded production that made Maria Dorn a hip name to know.

Chloe wiped her forehead on her loose, surgery-stained sleeve. "I'll check those out again."

Maria wasn't done. "Didn't we discuss this accent you keep lapsing into? Victoria Frankenstein is Swiss, not some American approximation of British. Learn a Swiss French accent or drop it entirely."

Chloe sighed. "I know, Maria. I'm working on it."

"Lights up." At Maria's command, the house lights erased the black glamour obscuring her. "Lunch for an hour."

Chloe found that Maria had indeed changed seats since the lights had gone down, moving in that unnervingly silent way. Chloe turned to leave the stage, but Maria's words caught her again. "The two of you will take lunch together every day for the next two weeks. Your chemistry reeks. Your characters should be inseparable, practically indistinguishable by the end of the script."

Chloe sighed again for stage. Directors were directors, male or female, stage or screen.

The whole production was a gamble for Chloe Clinkscales. An eighties teen idol, her best-known work consisted of a suite of saccharine films that climaxed in inevitable house parties. Back then, she'd been Chloe Kay, a name easier to sign and pronounce. Softer.

Besides playing an abused trans woman (with of course a heart of gold) on four episodes of the police procedural *Sensitive Cases*, she'd done nothing of critical note since the nineties. It was also the closest she'd ever been to going public with her bisexuality. Not the same thing, she knew, but it was a small victory. Now, Chloe was lucky to have her kitchen safety show for children, *Cooking with Chloe*.

The all-female production of *Frankenstein* held so much promise and so much risk. Was L.A. ready for it? Maria's all-female *Macbeth* smashed theater records in London, but it had a mixed response in New York. Would L.A. go for a sapphic *Frankenstein*?

Either they'll love me or I'll go down in flames, Chloe thought. *Either way, they'll talk about me. I could host a game show . . .*

She lunched with Natasha in a café two blocks from the theater, a little organic place frequented by aspiring models and other L.A. women on never-ending diets. It was a dead place, tiles too white, ferns too yellow.

Natasha led the awkward dance of conversation. "How are your children?"

Chloe reached for her phone. She showed Natasha a pic of two awkward, ginger-haired teens. "Aaron's getting ready to graduate. Madison's almost caught up with him. Maybe she'll lap him if they both move on to grad school."

"He's handsome. Does he take after his father?"

"He does. Their dad's away at college too." Chloe put her phone away and stared at her brown rice penne, the pesto unnaturally bright green.

"That's . . . cryptic." Natasha stabbed her salad. Chloe wondered how anyone could eat salad with such a mix of brutality and elegance. Maybe it was a British thing.

"We separated last year. He went to go find himself. Being a stay-at-home dad left him existentially lost. Or something." Chloe caught herself giving a stage sigh and reminded herself of her New Year's resolution to be more authentic off stage. "But the kids are awesome. So bright. Aaron is studying medicine. Madison wants to be a computer programmer."

Natasha's brows perked up. "Not following you to the screen?"

Chloe tried to mimic Natasha's sophisticated way of stabbing the food. "They're way too smart for that. My career has been dormant for two decades. They want more reliable work." The penne she put into her mouth was too chewy. *Why the hell make pasta out of rice?*

Natasha changed the subject. "What do you think's at play with our missing castmate? There's always a plan where Maria's involved. I think it's why she wants us to get closer."

Chloe sipped her fizzy water. "She wants you to teach me to sound Swiss."

Natasha laughed more enthusiastically than necessary. Chloe went on. "I doubt she's even cast the bride yet."

Natasha squinted and shook her head. "Oh no, no. I think she cast her *first*. Or him. She loves to surprise. When I was in *God Hates Women*, she had us rehearse the entire thing for weeks, and then two weeks before the show, she told us we'd all be wearing masks for most of the production," she said between bites of chicken and kale. "And she'd *hammered* us on our facial expressions. She does that."

Chloe's eyes narrowed beneath her ginger brows. *I've stood up to bigger prima donnas,* she thought.

"Maria never tells me what's up. She wants me to be just as put off as the rest of the cast and crew. Didn't you know that about her before you signed on?"

Women at a nearby table chatted about reiki for cats. Chloe pushed her food around the plate and said, "I knew she was an extraordinary perfectionist. She's supposed to be like Kubrick for the stage."

"No, not Kubrick. He was too . . . quantifying if you get my meaning. Like his films were some kind of equation. No, Maria is like no one else I've ever worked with."

Chloe knew the intensity of her own look as she met Natasha's gaze. "Natasha, how many other directors *have* you worked with?"

She looked somewhat hurt by the question, but Chloe suspected that behind Natasha's unassuming persona, a calculating survivor played the game. Chloe saw herself there: spunky, underestimated ingenue, working with the same director again and again, typecast only as long as she needed to milk the paycheck. Ready to awe critics and audiences alike when she showed what she was truly made of. She hoped that Natasha could make a better transition than she had.

Natasha answered, "I've worked with several others. Mostly men. Maria is my steak and potatoes, I'll admit."

Chloe took in the image of Natasha's curly brown hair. "Did you and Maria ever . . . you know?" Chloe blushed at her own question.

Natasha laughed lightly. "Oh no! Almost once or twice, but we're better as friends. And there's something untouchable about her. I'm not sure she has sex, to be quite honest."

That was curious information. They finished their meals. Returning to the theater, they found Maria directing the crew in a manic burst.

Natasha straightened. "Shit. Here we are then. Are you ready?"

Chloe clutched her purse closely. "For what?"

"You two!" Maria marched toward them, her boots clomping along the stage. "I hope you're ready to work overtime. You're each going to play both roles."

Chloe looked to Natasha, her own mouth open with shock. Natasha just shook her head, resigned to Maria's inconvenient strokes of genius.

"I want you two to switch roles every other performance. This will help you finally get inside one another's skins." The director turned, just like that, and trotted over to the costumers.

"Now wait!" Chloe shouted, expecting to bring the entire crew to a halt. No one even hesitated. "Wait!"

Maria did an about-face, her straight black hair winging out with the momentum and settling just as quickly. She crossed her arms around her brown pinstripe vest.

Natasha grabbed Chloe's elbow. "Please, Chloe, don't. Just go with it."

Chloe swatted Natasha's hand away, clucking her tongue against her teeth. "I signed a contract, Maria. You can't just pull this shit on me. I have an agent!"

Maria approached her new star with precise steps. "Chloe," she began in her unnervingly calm tone, "why did you join my cast?"

The one question Chloe was unprepared to answer aloud, though she knew the answer well. "I—"

Maria sat down on the apron of the stage and dangled one boot over the edge. She remained silent.

Chloe didn't care if the crew could hear and blab to the gossip sites. "I want to be taken seriously. I want to prove to the world that I'm not Becky Walsh from *Sweet Sixteen*."

Maria cocked an eyebrow. "And?"

"And I want to stop hosting a goddamn children's cooking show. I want to feel like I've done something with my life other than . . . that."

Maria stood, gazing down from the stage like a soft-butch Medusa. "And that, my dear, is why you're going to do everything I tell you. This show is going to make or break the both of us. So buck yourself up and get made."

Maria turned her back, calling over her shoulder, "I want to see both of you on stage in ten." She disappeared into the wings.

Collecting herself in the bathroom, Chloe examined her forty-six-year-old face, its lines, the places it slackened. *Maybe I'll get a lift if I go back to film.* For stage, she believed no one would scrutinize her face that closely. One perk of the medium.

Voices came from outside the ladies' room, rising and falling as Natasha and Maria walked past. Chloe thought she heard Maria say something about "tension" and to "Do it for me."

Natasha's words came through more clearly: ". . . always a game with you. I'll do it because *I* want to, not because—" and the last part drifted out of earshot.

Chloe looked back at her image in the mirror. *Lesbian Frankenstein. I'd better get a game show out of this.*

She bowled through an intense week of memorization and rehearsals. Restaurant delivery every night. Natasha arrived Sunday afternoon with pizza and wine. "I know you host a cooking show. I thought you might like a break from cooking."

Chloe smiled at her warmly, holding the door open for her. "You don't know me very well. It's been takeout all week."

"Maybe I know you better than you think," Natasha said, sassy for the first time Chloe had ever seen.

They ran lines for an hour and a half. Natasha's phone buzzed a few times with texts. She peered at some and unlocked the phone but didn't reply. She left it facedown beside her.

Chloe grew silent and said, "I'm worried I can't pull this off. I mean, I get it—they're both monsters. Every horror fan knows that. But playing both roles?"

Natasha moved closer on the white leather couch in the pseudo-art-deco living room with its glass brick shoring up despair. She gently massaged Chloe's shoulders, and Chloe jumped at the touch before relaxing into it.

She couldn't remember the last time she'd been touched like that.

Natasha cooed over her. "You're going to smash this role. And so am I dammit. This isn't something you let defeat you, Chloe. If you fail, you had better fail luxuriously. You don't just give it a dodgy little effort."

Chloe made a loose fist and tapped it awkwardly twice on Natasha's denim-armored knee. "Thanks, kiddo."

"Where's the WC?"

"The what? Oh, the bathroom? Past the stairs on the right."

The younger woman stretched and disappeared around a corner. Her phone, left on the couch cushion, buzzed again. Chloe snuck a look.

It was Maria. It said only, *Counting on you.*

Maria reserved the next day at the theater for Chloe and Natasha. The crew worked in a nearby studio. In their last hour together, Maria called for an improvisational exercise.

The stage was empty except for three chairs. Chloe and Natasha sat, their chairs arranged about two feet apart, squared parallel and facing the same direction. The third chair faced them, close enough to kick. Maria stood behind it.

"Put on the blindfolds," Maria commanded. Both of her actors tied burgundy satin scarves around their heads. Chloe pulled hers tight, loosened it, tightened it again. Whatever fresh humiliation Maria had concocted, Chloe would use it to drive her own performance.

In the ruddy darkness, Chloe waited, listened to the boots stepping around her. The director's voice came through the dark. "Concentrate on your breath. Clear your thoughts. If you begin thinking, come back to your breath."

Yoga? thought Chloe. She came back to her breath.

Maria continued. "Concentrate on what I describe. You're in a laboratory. It smells acrid. Looking around, you see limbs and organs isolated in tanks and on dissecting tables. You see an arm, a foot, a breast. You see a beating heart on the slab, attached to lungs that draw breath and exhale."

Chloe heard Natasha's breathing grow louder. She felt lust stir along the floor of her pelvis.

The guided meditation, or whatever it was, continued. "There is a person with you in this laboratory, female, but what makes this person *female*? Is it the body? The mind? What part is woman? Is the liver female? The vertebrae?"

Chloe envisioned a faceless entity at first, one that had only one breast. Natasha's face then, and her body stripped of clothes, of rags, both breasts intact, clean and plump and fertile.

The exercise lasted a few more minutes as Maria told them to imagine the woman experimenting with herself, exploring her body as unlimited potential. Chloe pictured Natasha running hands all over herself, finding the wells and wilds of her skin.

"Now. Remove your blindfolds."

Chloe held her eyelids closed for a moment to adjust to the lights. Opening them, she shrieked.

In the previously unoccupied chair that faced her, a wretched girl sat. Forehead protruding and lower jaw oversized with an underbite, the features combined to further dwarf the birdlike eyes staring into Chloe's own.

The skull bore no ears, merely smooth-rimmed holes at the sides. A few thin clumps of hair draped unevenly around the equator of the head, their presence somehow worse than being simply bald. The lips grimaced, opening and closing by a centimeter.

What the fuck? Chloe almost said aloud.

The girl's head rested on a twisted body. On her neck were striations— scars?—that looked like gills. Her trunk arched forward and slightly to the left, presenting a small bust. One arm hung shorter than the other, the longer ending in a claw-like hand of fewer than five fingers. A pale and breezy dress, perhaps cotton chiffon, draped her torso, ending just above the knee. Chloe noticed that the girl's legs were quite beautifully shaped. The toenails had been painted gold.

After a breathless span, Maria finally spoke. "Here at last is your castmate, the bride. You needn't know her name. You won't take lunch with her." She walked over to the girl and stroked the stringy hair. The girl groaned.

"Shhhh. I'm proud of you. You're doing beautifully," Maria said.

Natasha, sideswiped but not shocked, gave a low chuckle. "Brava, Maria. Brava."

Chloe's disquiet shattered any compassion she had for the disfigured person staring at her. "Who's doing beautifully? Who *is* this?"

"My finest discovery," Maria announced. "The most compelling actress the world has ever seen. I've already brought her into her character, and in character, she'll stay until the show closes. You will never see her in the dressing room or anywhere offstage. Do not in any way suggest your ideas for her character. I've created the perfect territory for her to make the role entirely her own. I ask you both to uphold the sanctity of that."

Chloe looked desperately to Natasha who contemplated their new castmate with malicious curiosity, like a child watching something die under a magnifying glass. Chloe looked back to the girl.

"I'm Chloe. It's nice . . . to meet you. I'm Chloe."

The girl looked up at Maria and groaned something that sounded like, "Herrrr."

Maria answered, "Oh no, they're just surprised. You did well," and she gave her little friend a tea biscuit. "Elsa Lanchester would be proud. Okay, that's enough excitement for today. Go home, and get a good night's rest. Tomorrow we begin the next phase."

With that, she gently guided the new girl away. Chloe fled for the ladies' room.

Natasha followed, closing the door gently behind her. "Are you all right?"

Chloe sobbed out her newest frustration. "She's some kind of sideshow freak! I know that's a shitty thing to say, but fucking look at her! Can she even talk? Is this even legal? What the hell kind of production is this?"

Natasha merely shrugged. "Maria's a genius. They do some foul things. She's been obsessed with Francis Bacon lately. Both of them. And Tod Browning."

"I don't know who the hell Francis Bacon is. Some kind of Arctic explorer? Like in the novel?" She opened the tap at the sink and washed her face with the cool splash. She thought about her children, how she'd wash their faces when they were little and they'd throw tantrums.

Natasha didn't correct her. "Do you spend a lot of time in bathrooms, pulling yourself together?"

Chloe laughed just for a second, sniffed, and grabbed a handful of paper towels. "It's the only place around here I get close to privacy." She ran the towels over her face.

Natasha hesitated and walked closer. She put her hand on Chloe's elbow and said quietly, "Would you rather be alone?"

Her words still resonated across the ceramic tiles of the bathroom as Chloe grabbed her and slipped her tongue into Natasha's mouth. They did not get the good night's rest their director had prescribed.

Chloe had them all in stitches. In her heyday, critics lauded her comic timing. She felt that power again, real admiration.

"I mean, have all of you read the novel?" she said and took a swig of wine. "Victor Frankenstein is a textbook narcissist with a *boner* for corpses."

Natasha put her arm around Chloe and said, "I love the way you say *boner* in that American accent." Chloe leaned in and touched her forehead to Natasha's.

Maria sat at the head of the table, presiding like a papess over the dinner party. To her left sat Chloe and then Natasha and Annie, the assistant director. Kent, head of costuming, sat at the foot of the table. Opposite Chloe sat Keisha, stage manager, and then Amy, a curiously butch casting choice for Elizabeth. One of Maria's L.A. investors, Clementine, sat nearest Kent.

Clementine, for Christ's sake. Chloe examined the woman's fuchsia hair.

Maria smiled at her two stars but didn't laugh. She'd prepared a Swiss-themed dinner, inspired by the locales of *Frankenstein*. Her verbal invitations emphasized, "Tell me beforehand what your food allergies may be, and I'll tell you if you should simply stay home."

Keisha twirled her fork and asked, "Have you thought about what's next, Maria? If *Frankenstein* is a success—"

"It will be a success," Maria cut off.

Amy brightened. "Ooh, would you do an all-female *Little Shop of Horrors*? I would kill to be in that! Can I be the S&M dentist?"

"Would you?" Maria replied, completely deadpan. "If I asked you too?"

Amy froze. The other guests looked at their plates or laughed uncomfortably.

Kent asked, "Maria, did you invite what's-her-name? The bride? I had a hell of a time dressing her. I wish you would've warned me you were getting a . . . a special-needs actress."

Maria narrowed her eyes and said, "She's allergic to this sort of food."

Natasha quipped, "I think all actors have special needs."

"Could you imagine that, Kent?!" Chloe nearly shouted. "Staying in character the whole time at the table!" She laughed so hard she could barely choke the words out.

"Why is that funny?" Maria asked. "You see? This is why none of you are allowed to see her offstage. You'd ruin everything."

Chloe took a sip of wine but giggled, and a trickle of it came down her chin and onto her shirt. "Oh, God! I'm sorry. Dammit. Where's the—oh, what did you call it the other day?" She ran a fingertip down Natasha's bicep. "The WC?"

Maria said, "It's in a redundant little alcove. Follow that hall, and it will be on your left."

Chloe left the table and entered the hall. *Damn, kiddo, you do spend a lot of time pulling yourself together in bathrooms.* She pulled the stained section of shirt to her mouth and sucked on it, a trick her mother taught her to prevent stains from setting.

Several doors lined the passage but nothing recognizable as an alcove. She reached the end of the hallway and hadn't seen the bathroom. She turned around, a bit drunker than she'd realized before standing up from the table.

She heard something, something like dripping water behind a door. Walking slowly up the hallway, she listened for it, traced it to a doorway that indeed nestled a bit recessed from the frame around it. *I guess this passes for an alcove.* She turned the knob and entering without knocking.

Stairs led down to a dim floor. It didn't smell like a basement. Instead of musty odors, Chloe detected a more acidic scent, mellow and vinegary, like the kombucha Aaron and Madison learned to brew at home. As she descended, her eyes adjusted to the faint glow of several lighted tanks. Each seemed to contain some curious organic thing in torpor, aquatic and godforsaken. Here, a ribbony mass that may have been some sort of jellyfish. And here, a tank occupied by something with two slim, dark legs but no detectable arms or head.

The array of tubes and tanks and apparatuses felt like a set, but Chloe hadn't seen these yet, and the show would open in a week. Would Maria pull these out so late in the game?

Then she saw the last tank. In it, what at first appeared to be a clustered tumor was actually four fetuses, all conjoined along their backs, their four skulls merged into a single bulb of many faces. It was too lifelike, too disgustingly perfect.

"Jesus Christ," Chloe said aloud. "Maria . . . what the hell are you up to?"

To Chloe's shock, Maria answered. "I call her the Blastocyst."

Chloe whirled to face the director and let out a quick animal rasp.

"I almost got it that time."

"Maria! What the fuck have you been doing in here?"

Maria looked around, the glow of the tanks bathing her in murky light. "Research."

Chloe raised her arms as if to argue but dropped them.

A tear crossed Chloe's cheek. "I'm sorry, I just . . . I don't understand."

"Oh no, I think you do," Maria said. From the shadows emerged the misshapen girl, the nameless actress playing the nameless bride. She loped over to Maria and clung to the woman's hip. Maria stroked the bulbous skull of the homunculus and said, "Shall we play out the scene in which you launch your futile arguments against what's already been done?"

"This is sick." Chloe pointed to the Blastocyst. "Sick, Maria. I don't know if I can be part of this." Her face burned.

"No," Maria said, looking back to Chloe and cradling the bride's chin in her fingers. "This isn't sick. The *world* is sick. This is art. This is healthy and beautiful."

"So what? You're like a mad scientist now? The feminist alchemist?"

Maria lowered her eyes dramatically to her creation. "And this is my beautiful daughter. It's all quite cliché really. But I've reinvented it. Skinned it for a new century."

"Beautiful?" Chloe barked.

Maria snapped her gaze back to Chloe. "Will you lower your voice? The others needn't know. This is just backstage business."

Chloe looked back at the tank with the Blastocyst, the little faces. Tiny eyelashes.

"Chloe, I'm asking you to help me usher in a new age. Stop teaching children to fry eggs, and do something extravagant. This is alchemy—femme alchemy. We'll turn ourselves into gold. We're going to start an artistic revolution—the art of making people."

At least the manipulation was blatant. "Nice, Maria. Why not just rub your palms together while you reveal your master plan. So was Natasha part of it, or does she actually care about me?"

Maria's face softened. "Why not both? She's been my biggest star, but imagine what a company we'd create. You and I and Natasha. And all the coming children."

The bride dug snot from her nose and ate it.

Chloe knew the view from a corner. Any woman, Hollywood or not, knew it. "If I quit? Are you going to kill me? Threaten my children?"

Maria scoffed. "How insulting. No. If you quit, your hungry little understudy steps up, and I do what I can to talk the executive producers out of suing you blind. Natasha will be fine. She always is. As for all this, it's just a set. Like every room you walk into. And I wanted you to see it. I think you're ready."

Chloe squatted, careful not to touch the laboratory floor, moist with God knew what, and put her head into her hands. After a moment, she stood up again. "No one gets hurt?"

Maria dipped a finger into the Blastocyst's tank and rubbed the liquid against her thumb. "I haven't killed anyone, you realize. The opposite if anything." Maria reached out a clean hand. So did the created girl.

Chloe joined hands with each of them. What else was there to do?

Maria admired her work. "I'm counting on you."

DRAMATIS PERSONAE

VICTORIA FRANKENSTEIN   Foolhardy scientist & chirurgeon

Chloe Clinkscales / Natasha Burton

———

THE CREATURE   First woman created through science

Natasha Burton / Chloe Clinkscales

———

ELIZABETH   Victoria's fiancée and adopted cousin

Amy Treadway

———

THE BRIDE   Frankenstein's second creation

???

Natasha sat in the makeup chair, the prosthetics team applying her burns and scars and stitches. They stayed well away from her mouth. Maria insisted that her Creature speak with eloquence, not clumsiness. *Her mouth is the only part of her that's lovely.*

Chloe, stage-ready in her shirtsleeves and blood-dewed leather apron, crossed to the chair and laid her hands on Natasha's shoulders. "Looking good, kiddo."

Natasha kept her eyes closed as the makeup man and woman continued to corrupt her skin but said, "May I have a moment with Chloe?"

The prosthetics team applied a few more daubs of gore and left her to set. Natasha opened her left eye, the right partially eclipsed by latex. "You're interrupting me getting into character, you minx. Should I come bother you when you're in this chair tomorrow night?"

Chloe leaned in and kissed the elegant mouth, careful not to smear the freshly faked wounds. "Yes. You should."

The misshapen trinity of Francis Bacon's *Three Studies for Figures at the Base of a Crucifixion* presided over the public debut of the bride. The homunculus girl floated in the cloudy liquid of the tank, amphibious and atavistic, breathing through gills.

Madison and Aaron sat second row center. Chloe tried not to make eye contact with them as she delivered her lines.

"She will decide when her healing and coagulation are complete. She's too precious now, like a map sewn from chrysanthemums."

The bride twitched and began to pound on the lid.

Natasha, as the Creature, shouted, "No! She is already perfect!" She tore Chloe away from the tank, flipped the lid, and brought the howling bride into the air.

The audience gasped. Hundreds of eyes took in the marvelous naked body, its three breasts, its flaring gill slits.

"She is *magnificent*!" exclaimed Victoria Frankenstein.

It took no effort at all to believe it now.

§

Evan J. Peterson is the author of *Drag Star!* (Choice of Games), the world's first drag RPG, as well as *The PrEP Diaries: A Safe(r) Sex Memoir* (Lethe Press). He is a Clarion West alum and author of the horror poetry chapbooks *Skin Job* and *The Midnight Channel* as well as editor of the Lambda Literary finalist *Ghosts in Gaslight, Monsters in Steam: Gay City 5*. His writing has also appeared on Boing Boing and in *Weird Tales, Unspeakable Horror 2, Queers Destroy Horror,* and *Best Gay Stories 2015*. Evanjpeterson.com can tell you more.

Patio Wing Monsters

S.P. MISKOWSKI

THE PHYSICIAN TOLD HER THE TINGLING—A GRADUALLY receding numbness followed by random pinpricks of nerves coming back to life—might continue for a long time. If she stuck with her regimen and if she committed to the counseling, group sessions, yoga, recreational therapy, and PT, she could be back home in a couple of months. But the prickly sensation in her arms might go on for years.

1

Patio Wing was designed to imitate home life. Six casually decorated rooms were arranged in a semicircle around a palm tree court. Next to the exit gate, a nurse's station faced the center of the court, its sliding glass windows and fluorescent lighting a stark contrast and a reminder of reality behind the suburban veneer.

The ranch house atmosphere was intended to soothe and reassure. All of it was created according to a long forgotten theory. Nothing about it fooled the teenagers assigned to Patio Wing. Beyond the open-air setting, beyond the wrought iron gates and the kidney-shaped swimming pool, the cinder-block fences stood ten feet tall. On the other side, the desert ran for miles in all directions. Not an inescapable hellhole but enough to give the residents pause.

Gillian shared a room with a captured runaway named Sid whose regimen included emotional reprogramming instead of yoga. Sid's mom had hired a private detective to track her down. After she was located in a compound in Wyoming, her mom brought her home and had the family doctor perform an abortion. As a safety measure, Sid got six months on Patio Ward in the company of eleven other teens with similar problems, all part of a process to "reestablish her baseline identity."

"As what?" Gillian asked. "A prisoner of boredom?" She was paired with her roommate because both were fourteen and their actions were deemed self-destructive rather than antisocial.

"If my mother took a good look at herself for even one minute, she would *die*," Sid told Gillian when they had been sharing the room for a week. "She's a size twelve at least. Unbelievable! She's been taking fertility drugs ever since she married her fourth husband. The hormones are making her crazy. One time, I found her in the backyard, staring over the barbecue pit at the desert. Not moving or anything. Frozen like a fucking statue or like she was waiting for something to come slithering out of the rocks and call her name."

"Why did she make you come back from Wyoming?" Gillian asked. "If all she wants is a new baby, why doesn't she leave you alone?"

"Jealousy, of course. She hates the fact that I can have a baby and she can't. You wait and see. Rory's coming for me, and when he finds out where I am and what that bitch did to me, he's going to split her head open with an axe. Then you know what I'll do when she screams and wets herself and begs me to save her life? I'm going to laugh! I'm going to put my head back, like this, and laugh all fucking day!"

Gillian was pretty sure Sid had plucked this idea from a movie. It sounded like one of the gruesome horror flicks the teens gathered to watch and make fun of on Friday nights in the rec room. The angle of Sid's head, her valentine-shaped face surrounded by blond dreadlocks, made Gillian wonder if the girl's middle-aged boyfriend would risk everything to rescue her.

"So what's *your* mom like?" Sid exhaled a stream of smoke with a sputtering sound.

This was the question everyone asked. Everyone had to answer it.

. . . *my name is Danny. I'm a kleptomaniac Mormon, homeschooled. What's YOUR mom like?*

The one point on which all twelve Patio Wing residents agreed was that their mothers ought to be here in their place. Their mothers were monsters who couldn't make children the right way. Somehow they left out crucial parts or managed to break the engine. Most of the teens hated their dads too, but it was a lot more satisfying to hate their moms. It was more fucked up. Someone said it was Freudian. Anyway, comparing mother notes made them laugh while they waited out their time on Patio Wing.

"Mine is classic," said Gillian. "Middle-class, well groomed, obedient."

"She sounds like a poodle," Sid told her.

"Pretty much. Poodle monster."

They were sitting on the concrete walkway outside their room with their backs against the outer wall. Adjacent to Patio Wing, two more buildings offered adult patients either "minimal supervision" (Sunrise Wing) or "higher security care" (Cactus Wing). Higher security patients were not supposed to interact with the residents of Patio Wing. Because it was forbidden, the two groups were understandably curious about one another. Every sighting of an adult from the "rubber room" in Cactus Wing caused the teens to whisper behind their hands and snicker while a glimpse of young people taking their turn in the swimming pool was enough to trigger a Cactus Wing rash of undressing, ranting, and escape attempts. None of these actions were directed at the teens. They didn't seem to be an object of desire but merely a reminder of something lost, forgotten, or never attained.

Interactions between Patio Wing residents and the minimal supervision adults of Sunrise Wing occurred only during an optional workshop in drama therapy. Sid refused to sign up because she said she had enough drama coping with her mother. So Gillian and two other teens accompanied a nurse through the gate every Tuesday and Thursday morning, navigated the sparkling clean halls of the central building, and joined ten sheepish grown-ups in a series of exercises intended to excavate and relieve trapped emotions. They did this through roleplaying games and stretching, and they ended each session with a "trust reassurance." The person whose life had been played out in tearful, excruciating scenes was cradled by the entire group, touched gently and non-threateningly, and lifted into the air to be rocked for a few minutes in a safe and loving environment.

Gillian found these exercises easy yet ridiculous. They were unlike anything the patients would ever encounter in real life. The center of attention was always some drab, lonely person who was never hugged or listened to outside of a hospital setting. He or she would mumble a tale of disappointment, sob in the therapist's arms, and then light up with joy when the cradling began.

The hard part of the session was the roleplaying. Watching the therapist pretend to be a parent or grandparent, while the patient adopted a vocal pitch to portray himself as a child, was the absolute worst. Gillian dug her nails into her jeans to keep from laughing. Later, during the cradling, she could let loose a cough, a strangled guffaw that passed for emotional release. Invariably several of the adults cried during the cradling. When the group separated, there were smiles all around and a smattering of applause. Then the three teens headed back to Patio Wing where Gillian would reenact the session for Sid's amusement. Best of all, guaranteed to elicit shrieks of derision from Sid, was Gillian's imitation of the Emoting Woman.

Horsey and tall with large eyes, her hair sculpted into a fancy bouffant from a much older generation, the woman seemed unable to control her expressions. She was never neutral, never blank or at rest. Her face was in perpetual motion, frowning with sympathy and then smiling encouragement, forming an O of surprise with her mouth and raising both eyebrows until she resembled a cartoon version of amazement. Gillian practiced switching from one expression to another until she and her roommate were sick with laughter.

On the fifth Friday night of Sid's stay in the hospital, her forty-two-year-old boyfriend, Rory, parked a van next to the outer wall. While residents and staff were distracted by the week's hoary old horror movie in the rec room, three of Rory's friends scaled the wall, and a teen resident helped hoist Sid up and over to freedom. She was never seen again.

Tom, the boy who assisted in the escape, was given a day of solitary confinement in Cactus Wing. Afterward he returned with a smirk, an implausible tale of old men loudly masturbating in private cells, and one more thing.

2

"The lost nurse," Tom said, handing a cigarette to Gillian. "Everybody over there's heard of her."

They were sitting on the concrete walk the way she used to hang out with Sid. Several other teens gathered near them, sharing a smoke and quizzing the recent delinquent hero on his twenty-four-hour exposure to grown-up madness.

"You can't get lost in a place that small," said Jack, a thirteen-year-old who had attempted suicide twice and spent seven months in the county asylum before balancing out on prescription drugs and being downgraded to Patio Wing. "County's about ten times bigger than that building."

Gillian observed the custom of never asking Jack about his time in the asylum. There were whispers—that he'd been raped by a male nurse and received electroshock treatments at his mother's insistence—but no one knew for sure. They accepted as truth any detail Jack offered and left it at that.

"This nurse," said Tom. "She ain't real. She don't walk on legs. She kinda drifts in the air. Only in the morning just before the sun comes up, and only in solitary where I was."

"Does she make a noise, like 'wooooo' or something?" Jack asked.

"Naw," said Tom. "It's like she's pushin' a metal cart, and the wheels squeak. You know the worst part? It's when the squeak stops—because she's right outside your door!"

The night after Tom told this story, Gillian dreamed about Cactus Wing. She was walking down the hall toward the only light, shining in a dull arc next to a door with a barred window. She was aware of doors on either side of her as she walked along. These had no windows, but she could hear living creatures behind them—some human sized and some as large as the rooms they occupied— groaning and murmuring.

She forced herself to face directly ahead and ignore the sounds. Only gradually did she begin to feel the handles in her grip. Then she could see the cart she pushed was covered in trays and paper cups full of pills.

When she reached the arc of light, she stopped and faced the door. She had to rise up on tiptoe to gaze through the barred window. From there, she could just make out a curving surface in the far corner of the room. Shivering, a bright sheen of sweat glistening even in the shadows, an enormous swath of pale skin vanished as quickly as she could recognize it.

3

When she woke up, Gillian lay in the pre-dawn gray of fading moonlight and listened for the squeak of wheels in a corridor. There was nothing. Even the doves nesting in the eaves beneath the roof were silent.

She glanced at the vacant single bed on the other side of the room. In a few days, she would undoubtedly be paired with another girl her age, another cast-off or runaway recovering from an overdose or failed self-annihilation.

No one ever inquired about the railroad tracks skittering down the inside of Gillian's arms, just as they never asked Jack what the asylum was like. One look told them what they needed to know, and this was followed by a slight, swift nod as if to say, "Got it." They were members of a special club, not merely fed up with the world but ready to fall invisibly into silence and darkness to be rid of it.

On Tuesday, she was more reluctant than usual to attend drama therapy. There would be no one to entertain with an account when she returned to her room. But she knew the length of her stay depended on cooperation. Sid had known too. Gillian assumed that was why her ex-roommate had enlisted Tom, who had already received a couple of detention notices for smoking in his room and for putting his hand through a window, to help her abscond with her boyfriend.

It wasn't that Gillian wanted to go home to her frantic, color-coordinated mother and her engineer dad who refused to attend the monthly family nights. She wasn't anxious for the silent meals, the mandatory music concerts, the lectures on grooming, or her mother's obsession with SAT scores and "life skills" and extracurricular lessons in everything from modern dance to baking. She just wanted to know how it would feel to be on her own again. Would the darkness come rushing in again? Would she collapse into it, the slow sensation of tumbling downward to nothing? Or would the weeks of counseling and "healing" make a difference? Was she different now? She didn't feel different. She still hated her parents' life, their sour misery and devotion to routine. She still didn't care about school, the endless parade of tiny achievements and worn-out advice from middle-aged teachers who had given up. But she wanted to know. She wanted to walk out the front door and know.

The drama therapist was quiet while the patients gathered in a circle and sat cross-legged on the floor. As usual, the overhead lights were dimmed, and the room was full of soft cushions. The therapist held her silence for another minute and then asked everyone to hold hands.

Another teen, Marisa, clasped Gillian's left hand. They were fellow sufferers, not interested in the group yet acknowledging with a rueful grin that this was a necessary part of their rehabilitation.

To Gillian's alarm, the Emoting Woman took hold of her right hand. It was the worst thing that could happen. The woman had been praised numerous times by the drama therapist, singled out for her empathy and her ability to "connect" with others. There was no one in the group Gillian disliked more, and she was baffled by the therapist's insistence that a continuous stream of vicarious emotion was better than simply standing still, being quiet.

By contrast, Gillian had been called out more than once for going blank and not appearing to care about her surroundings. In the group, she pledged to try harder and care more. In private, and for Sid's benefit, she had referred to the therapist as a bitch, a fraud with an acting degree, and worse—a "helper." This was the term all of the teens used to describe the guidance counselors, pastors, priests, homeroom teachers, and relatives who had played a role in having them incarcerated. Helpers were adults who helped to find out what was wrong with you and then helped to have you locked up for it.

Gillian could feel the Emoting Woman staring a hole in the side of her face, searching for a feeling she could latch onto. On her left side, Marisa let out a little chuckle and tried to disguise it with a cough. She wasn't a close ally, just a girl Gillian knew from movie nights and meals in the cafeteria. Marisa's only accomplishment in drama therapy was learning to stop rolling her eyes while other people were talking about personal tragedies.

With a kind of peripheral sixth sense, Gillian was aware of the Emoting Woman shifting into general sympathy mode, a pursing of the lips and a determination to "be there" whenever Gillian decided to blurt out all of her thoughts. Which would be never. She grimaced when the woman clenched her hand tighter and gave it a little pump of solidarity and understanding.

"I'm sure all of you have noticed Dave isn't joining us today," said the therapist.

Gillian and Marisa exchanged a look. Marisa lifted her shoulders slightly. Neither of them had any idea who Dave was.

"This is deep work," said the therapist. "Painful, mining the very core of who and what we are. No one tried harder than Dave, no one was a greater inspiration to me as a caring individual, and out of respect for Dave's effort, I'd like to let you go today, to reflect and to meditate on the timeless struggle we all face."

Around the circle, the patients let go of one another's hands. The adults murmured goodbyes. Some of them stood and embraced, and some wandered off. Only the Emoting Woman remained until Gillian pulled her hand free and turned her back, shutting the woman out.

Marisa shrugged. "Guess this Dave guy must be dead, huh? What do we do now?" she asked.

"Go back to our rooms," said Gillian. "I guess."

She dropped her shoulders with relief when the Emoting Woman left the room. Nearby, the third teenager—a boy with long hair and a scar on the side of his neck—gave them a wink and headed out the door. He had figured out what they were only beginning to realize. The therapist had failed to inform their nurse chaperone that they would be released early. Adults in minimum supervision were allowed to wander throughout the building, back to their rooms or the sun deck or the rec room. Only the outside doors were locked. Teens from Patio Wing were supposed to be accompanied at all times, but in her grief, the therapist had forgotten all about them.

Marisa stuck her hands in her pockets and made for the door. In a second, she was gone, traipsing down the hall, looking for entertainment.

Gillian considered joining her but decided instead to give in to her bladder. She had neglected to stop off at the women's bathroom on her way to drama therapy. A quick look revealed no orderlies or nurses in the hall.

Letting the door ease shut behind her, she scanned the cool tile and pristine porcelain sinks. There were three stalls. The farthest, against the wall, was large, and the door was closed. Gillian chose the stall next to it. She was ashamed at the sense of relief she felt every time she peed. She wondered if it was the one time she felt real emotions. She would have asked the drama therapist if her "peeing face" conveyed enough feeling, but she knew this would only lengthen her stay in Patio Wing.

When she finished, she pulled up her underwear and adjusted her jeans and T-shirt. She reached to flush and heard a noise from the larger stall next door.

It might have been crying if animals cried. Or it might have been snuffling in search of food if humans behaved that way. The underlying note was one of grief, a stifled keening from deep in the chest. The person inside the stall had to be an adult, yet the noise had the broken sound of an inconsolable child. Its despair seemed muffled beneath an unimaginably thick blanket, the blanket itself a useless attempt at comfort.

Gillian's flesh felt as cold as the tiles beneath her feet. She stood there, afraid to make a sound by flushing or by opening the door to her stall. She wondered how silently she could slide the metal bar on the lock, fling open the flimsy door, and run away. She was reaching out her hand in slow motion, to make the attempt, when the entire stall next to her gave a shiver as if the person inside had expanded until the stall itself became an outer shell threatening to break.

This should have been enough to send Gillian dashing through the halls back to Patio Wing. And yet she couldn't move. She was paralyzed by the sudden, vivid memory of another dream, one she'd experienced many times. She had seen the grass under her feet racing by and heard a buzz. Her arms had stretched and stretched on either side of her body, making larger and larger whipping circles in the air until the grass below sank away and dropped off, and her body climbed high into the air over a field, a marching band, a street with no traffic, a lake littered with boats, a park, and the tiny figures on the ground grew more distant until they disappeared.

Gillian crossed her arms. She ran her fingers over the railroad tracks of her skin, the scar tissue that would never go away.

In the next stall, something quivered, drew breath, and stood up. Gillian glanced down at the floor and saw no feet, no shadow, nothing at all.

When the noises resolved into a minute squeak of porcelain grinding against metal, Gillian tilted her head to take in the shadow rising on the ceiling overhead and beginning to spill onto the wall where she stood waiting. Whatever it was, it was climbing over. With all her heart, Gillian began to hope for a real monster, something huge and indescribably hideous, something she had never seen before—anything but the sad, stupid face of the Emoting Woman crying alone in a bathroom stall. Anything would be better than that.

§

S.P. Miskowski is a three-time Shirley Jackson Award nominee. Her short stories have been published in *Supernatural Tales, Black Static, Identity Theory*, and *Strange Aeons* as well as in the anthologies *Haunted Nights, The Madness of Dr. Caligari, October Dreams II, Autumn Cthulhu, Cassilda's Song, The Hyde Hotel, Darker Companions: Celebrating 50 Years of Ramsey Campbell, Tales from a Talking Board*, and *Looming Low*. She's received two National Endowment for the Arts Fellowships. Her novel, *Knock Knock*, and three related novellas (*Delphine Dodd, Astoria*, and *In the Light*) are available from Omnium Gatherum. Her SJA-nominated novella, *Muscadines*, is available from Dunhams Manor Press. Her second novel, *I Wish I Was Like You*, is published by JournalStone. Her story collection, *Strange is the Night*, is published by Trepidatio, an imprint of JournalStone.

Underglaze

CRAIG LAURANCE GIDNEY

HE HOUSE WAS PROBABLY GRAND IN ITS HEYDAY, Maureen thought as she parked. It had a large front lawn of topiary that was so overgrown you couldn't tell what shapes they'd originally been. She could detect, just barely, the bulbous forms, like chess piece pawns and bishops, their silhouettes imprecise and sloppy. The house itself sprawled over a hill in a single level. It was painted yellow, though the paint was peeling, revealing the red brick skin beneath. Maureen passed a bird bath, streaked with old droppings and filled with black water. Only the printed sign that said Estate Sale taped on the door let her know that she was in the right place.

The door was unlocked. Stepping inside, Maureen felt like she had entered an alternate timeline, one in which the decor of the 1970s was still popular. The vinyl floor tile was bright orange and patterned with sunflowers. The light fixtures were molded plastic in organic yet mathematical shapes. And the furniture in the sunken living room had modular furniture in tones of avocado-green and harvest gold.

The house appeared to be empty.

She resisted the urge to announce herself. There probably wasn't anything she wanted here anyway. Her husband accused her of being addicted to estate sales. He might have been right. She couldn't resist them. There was an adrenaline spike that moved through her body every time she saw a sign for one. The thrill, though, was not in buying things. That was where Cyril was wrong (in spite of the many purchases she'd brought home). Maureen was addicted (if indeed it *was* an addiction) to exploring other people's houses. It was like walking into a person's memories. And the things she actually bought were messages from the dead to her. A vase or chair or painting wasn't just an object. It was a piece of the person's soul.

In the absence of any official, Maureen began to wander the house. The deceased woman collected odd things, that much was for sure. In one room, possibly a study, there was an antique rolltop desk. The price, at $350, was pretty good, considering the excellent condition of the stained cherry wood. Maureen rolled up the ruffled desk covering.

She almost dropped her purse. A collection of yellowed skulls was concealed within. Bird skulls, mouse skulls, and the skull of some slightly larger creature, perhaps a cat or a ferret. The skulls themselves didn't bother her. She'd been in several boutique shops where animal bones and pinned butterflies were sold along with other tchotchkes like pocket watches or Limoges Boxes. She personally found such things macabre, but to each their own. What Maureen found disturbing was that someone had painstakingly placed objects in the eye sockets. The "eyes" were baubles of all colors. Little diamanté eyes of green, blue, pink, and yellow all gazed up at Maureen as if she had disturbed them. Maureen closed the desk, leaving the bone beasts to glitter on in darkness.

The next room she stepped into was filled with lamps that were also sculptures of African boys in turbans and balloon pants. The boys were all in servile poses and their painted "skin" was a shiny black that stood out against the bright white of their flowing outfits. Each of the black boy sculptures (there might have been twenty of them) grinned widely, their lips as red as blood. The lamps sat on the floor, on side and end tables, on an ottoman and a wall-length buffet. All of the bulbs in the lamps were on, and each bulb was a different color. "Party Lights," they were called at the home improvement store. Maureen saw pink, green, and blue light illuminating the blacker-than-black bric-a-brac. She even saw a couple of black-light bulbs. Black-light always nauseated her, and the purple glow on the fake black skin intensified that feeling. Maureen backed out of the room and closed the door for good measure.

The final room she entered was occupied by a thin, beaky looking woman in a fluorescent-green polyester blouse from the seventies, gray high-water pants, and penny loafers. Her brown and gray hair was styled like a mushroom cap. This woman flashed Maureen a toothy grin.

Maureen smiled back even though she was uncomfortable. The woman's bespectacled gaze was intense. As she glanced away, something caught her eye.

There was an ugly curio cabinet in which three plates were vertically displayed. The plates looked like standard blue-and-white Willow-ware china, but the pattern was slightly blurred, and the blue was much, much richer. It was a beautiful blue that seemed to glow. It even bled onto the bone-white porcelain, staining it. The rims of the dishes were loops of blue that looked as if they could have been an elegant script she couldn't make out. The center of the plate had the portrait of a woman in an old-fashioned hoop skirt. She looked like a Southern belle in crinolines. Then the face changed.

Metamorphosed.

It became the face of a long-haired Persian cat with fur of spun cotton in the antebellum dress, like a feline Scarlett O'Hara. The blurry pattern changed again, right before her eyes. The figure in the dress had the face of an owl. Even in dark blue glaze, the eyes were wild and piercing.

Not unlike the owlish face of the woman with the mushroom cap hairdo.

"How much for the plates?" Maureen asked her.

The woman peered at her through her face-shielding bifocals. "The azure porcelain is quite lovely. They are quite rare," she said. Her voice was high and fluty. "The chemical compound for the transfer glaze is unknown. Legend has it that the glaze would stain the potter's hands. *Permanently.* How awful that would be: to have azure hands for the rest of your life. My word!"

"That sounds terrible," Maureen replied. "But how much?"

"Let me check the price list." The woman picked up a printout of old style computer paper, the kind with perforations and striped green and white. Maureen noticed that the print was dot matrix. The whole house was trapped in a time warp.

Maureen waited for what seemed like an awkwardly long time as the woman peered at the printout. Behind the large spectacles, her eyes narrowed and widened as if they couldn't focus on the text in front of her. She gave an exasperated sigh and flung the printout down on a side table.

But when she looked at Maureen in the eye, her face settled into a semblance of calm, and she smiled. Her teeth were tombstone white.

"Mrs. Ingrid LeFevre was my mother," said Mushroom Cap. "Momma was, to be frank, quite eccentric."

Maureen nodded, even though she had no idea of where this conversation was going.

Mushroom Cap continued. "It could be very exasperating."

Maureen made a noncommittal sound in response.

"She had certain, how shall we say, queer notions about some of her objects."

"I see," Maureen said. "If you'll excuse me . . ."

"No, I fear you don't understand."

"Pardon?"

"Momma believed that certain possessions should, upon the occasion of her death, be bequeathed to deserving persons."

"I don't know what that means? Three hundred is my limit."

"Oh dear," said the woman, who was quickly getting on her nerves. "What I mean to say is this: Momma wants—or wanted me to ask you a question about the plates before the estate should part with them."

"What's the question?" Maureen knew she sounded short, but her patience was wearing thin.

"The question is simple. What faces did you see in the Azure Porcelain plates—the three that are displayed?"

"That's it?" Maureen glanced at the plates in the cabinet. And found that she was somewhat speechless. What she saw was amazingly nonsensical, but to speak it aloud would be madness.

She spoke nevertheless. "The plate on the right has the face of a goat. There are hooves sticking out of the sleeves. The face in the middle is some kind of anthropomorphic root vegetable. I think it's a turnip—isn't it clever how the stalks are arranged like hair? And the last plate, I see a squid. It has a friendly face as far as squids go. I guess."

"How splendid," said Mushroom Cap. "You may take the plates."

Maureen fumbled in her purse for her wallet.

"My dear woman," LeFevre's daughter said. For some reason, Maureen thought she looked like a Hortense or a Mildred. She had the look of someone who would have an ugly, old-timey name redolent of floral perfume, tart lemonade, and licorice. "There is no reason whatsoever to pay. Ingrid wished this sui generis set of azure porcelain find a home with 'a kindred spirit.'"

"Did she now?"

"Indeed. I shall wrap them up for you. Momma would be happy knowing that they have found a new home."

Maureen didn't respond to that as she hefted the box up. What was there to say?

Cyril was singing in the kitchen when she got home. Singing and cooking. Maureen saw raw flank steak, a colander full of fresh spinach and a bowl of quartered red bliss potatoes. Cyril didn't hear her coming because he was listening to music on his headphones and pulsing the food processor. The counter was full of tiny messes, including discarded basil stems and papery garlic skins. She also noticed a pink bakery box on the table. She placed the box with the plates next to it.

"You got the job," Maureen said after Cyril had taken off his earphones and kissed her hello.

"I start next Monday," he said, beaming. "I even get a corner office. With a good view!"

"So you thought you'd celebrate," she said. She smiled at her husband. "Let me guess: steak with chimichurri sauce, garlic mashed potatoes, and red velvet cake."

"Close but no cigar," Cyril said and swatted her on her butt. "That's not a red velvet cake in that box. It's—" He stopped, noticing her own box. "What's that?"

"Something I picked up from an estate sale," she said.

"Lord," he said. "You and your garage sales."

"It was an *estate* sale," she said, "and you won't believe what I found. And you really won't believe the price." She opened the box and began removing the plates, which were all swaddled in newspaper and bubble wrap. She removed the wrapping from three plates, setting them down. The hue was intense against the white kitchen table. "Aren't they gorgeous?"

Cyril silently hovered over the three dishes. The woman in the dress in these plates had the head of a lioness, an antelope, and a heron. The faces slowly changed. The optical illusion was amazing. "They sure are *something*," he finally said.

"You don't like them?"

"Well," he said.

"Well, what?"

"Well, they are odd. Are they supposed to be antique or something? The faces look like those inkblots that shrinks use. Someone must have screwed up at the China factory."

Maureen looked at the three plates that lay on the white table.

"You don't see her?" Maureen said.

"See who, honey? All I see are a bunch of Jackson Pollack paint splatters where a head ought to be. The color's nice though. How much did they cost?"

"They were free," Maureen said. The big reveal was anticlimactic. To her at least. She was disturbed by the fact that her husband, and apparently Mildred/Hortense, couldn't see the ever-changing faces in the ceramics.

Cyril said, "That's good news. I can't imagine that they were worth much."

"You hate them."

"Oh, now, honey. They're not to my taste. But what do I know? I would be happy filling the house with pictures of dogs playing poker."

She unwrapped another dish of the set. This time, the azure lady had the face of a weasel. The weasel's eyes were soft, the whiskers so expertly rendered Maureen could imagine the whisper-tickle against her skin.

"I've got to finish up dinner. Maureen, would you mind setting the table?"

She pulled out another dish. This time, the azure lady had the head of a bear. A great grizzly with massive paws poking through the dress sleeves. The bear seemed to be smiling at her beneath the glaze.

"Maureen? Honey? Did you hear me?"

She put the plate down gently. "I heard you. Should we have a Cabernet or a Malbec?"

Every now and then, Maureen suffered bouts of insomnia. It wasn't often enough to warrant a prescription. She could make do with over-the-counter sleep aids. The problem was, she usually diagnosed her insomnia in the small hours of the morning. Any medication she took now would keep her groggy well into the next day.

Oh well. She'd drink lots of coffee at work and maybe leave early. Right now, she was wide awake. There wasn't a hint of exhaustion anywhere. She was wired, just as if she'd had several espressos. She heard Cyril lightly snoring next to her. In the half-light, she could see his relaxed face, his mouth slightly open.

When she got bored of looking at his child-like slumber and the cracks on the ceiling, she sat up and got out of bed. After gathering her robe and her tablet, she left the bedroom and headed downstairs. She planned to read in the living room.

But Maureen found she couldn't really concentrate on the words on the small screen. She couldn't absorb them. The book club had picked this novel, titled *Caw*, because it was short and had won a major literary award. But it was densely written and confusing. Every labyrinthine sentence had multiple meanings. Even the character names were symbolic. Or maybe they weren't; it just seemed awfully on-the-nose to name a clashing married couple Cyan (the male) and Ruby. The author was fond of repeating images, or motifs. Seagulls showed up with alarming regularity, and at one point, both Ruby and Cyan believed it was the same seagull who may or may not have been the ghost of their dead drowned child. Dreary sea imagery popped up. Green waves, gold waves, white foam, spume, clumps of algae. The grey sea, the azure sea. It was the sort of novel that Mildred or Ingrid might enjoy, Maureen decided. *Caw* was grotesque and impenetrable.

Maureen turned off her tablet. She found herself drifting toward the kitchen. She was through the double doors and at the table and began unpacking the dishes. She saw a vixen, a wolf, and a raven. The twelfth and final plate had the head of a seagull. It was a very Beatrix Potter like seagull. She even wore a dainty hat. Each of the creatures had warm, soulful eyes. In fact, they had the same eyes. Whereas the ornate gown and the fur and vegetable matter had all been rendered in exquisite detail, the eyes were all simple. They were just pure circles. Blue orbs, like marbles. A child could have drawn them. And yet, they seemed to be alive.

Maureen shuddered. She remembered the diamanté eyes of the skulls in Ingrid LeFevre's house. And how the eyes of those turbaned black boy lamps stared at her. She shrugged the queer feeling off and stacked the plates. She lifted the box, intending to break it down for recycling. It was heavy; more than just discarded bubble wrap was in that box. Maureen dug through the trash until she reached the bottom and unearthed the thirteenth plate.

Like the others, it was the same rich azure color and featured the ornate, ruffled, and lace-adorned gown. But it was missing a face. Where a face should have been, Maureen saw a storm cloud of chaos. It was an azure inkblot, just like her husband had said all of the dishes were. A wild and careless mistake that stood out in stark relief against the delicately etched dress. The "hands" were also explosions of blue, a child's drawing of a bomb going off.

This plate, like all of the others in the set, had a filigree decoration around the rim, a series of fine swirls that mimicked elegant script but was essentially nonsense. But on *this* plate, it seemed to spell out something. She couldn't make it out, but she was sure that there was a message in those azure letters.

Maureen decided that this plate with the faceless woman was her favorite. She couldn't say why. She turned the kitchen light on to examine the plate more.

The formless mass where the face should have been was, somehow, an even more intense color. If it were a pool, she would swim in its depths. Even the clearest cloudless sky couldn't compete with this blue. She could have stared at it for hours. It was so beautiful.

Maureen found herself in the fridge, taking out the bourbon pecan tart. She cut a slice of the pie and put it on the azure plate.

The change was immediate and inexorable. The slice turned blue. Crust, the gelled syrup filling, the pecans. It was bright, glowingly so. Maureen paused. She should really wake her husband, if only to share this miraculous, supernatural moment with him. But Cyril slept like the dead and woke up evil. Besides, didn't he say he couldn't see the designs in the dish sets? Maybe he couldn't see this slice of sea and sky.

She took up her fork. Paused, thinking of paint-based poisons. But only for a moment. She devoured the pie. It tasted of a hidden grotto where the shrine to a forgotten sea goddess sat with offerings of flowers—candles flickering and water lambent. It tasted of a sky where no cloud ever floated or bird ever flew, just a flawless expanse of blue. It also tasted of bourbon, butter, and pecan.

The slice of azure was gone, wolfed down. She lifted the thirteenth plate, intending to wash it. She saw crumbs of blue pastry on the surface. Before she could get to the sink, they were absorbed by the faceless blue face. She saw the specks go under the glaze and into the blue void. Then they disintegrated.

Cyril was up and out of the house before she woke up. There was a hastily scrawled note about a 6 a.m. conference call with clients in Shanghai.

"You must of had some kinda dream," he wrote. Maureen twitched; Cyril was always saying (and writing) "must of" instead of "must have." It was a pet peeve of hers.

Maureen had gotten to back to bed after her midnight snack. She fell asleep shortly after that. The dreams, which she remembered in scraps, were vivid and quite wonderful. Maureen was on a boat made of porcelain, on a turbulent sea. At various points, she was visited by the jewel-encrusted bones of sea creatures. She recalled a giant squid made of opals with chocolate diamonds for its eyes and beak.

She felt well rested and clearheaded. But apparently, she'd done something in her sleep to disturb Cyril, which was odd. Cyril had slept though thunderstorms with hailstones that sounded like castanets on the roof. He'd even slept through a mild earthquake that had managed to destroy a fair amount of the glass figurines she'd been collecting.

Maureen shrugged it off, making a note to text him about it later that day.

"I really like that scarf," said the barista as she foamed the milk for Maureen's morning latte. She had a pixie cut that was dyed bright pink, and her ears had hoops marching up and down her lobes.

"Oh, thanks," Maureen replied absently. She was slightly embarrassed that she'd been caught staring at the girl, whose arms were also heavily tattooed sleeves. The tattoos were a busy swirl of color, but Maureen saw shapes in them. On the right arm, there was a cat's face, an owl's head, a goat, a bear, and a lioness. On the right, she saw a fox, a wolf, and a seagull.

"Where did you get it?" the barista asked. Her name tag identified her as Jinwen.

"This? It was a gift from my mother-in-law." Maureen reflexively touched the cheaply made scarf, looped around her neck at the last minute before leaving the house.

And gasped.

The scarf that Aimee, Cyril's mother, had given her years ago had been a washed out pale powder blue, prosaic and ordinary. It had probably been bought on sale at a dollar store. The scarf Maureen now wore was azure, heading into sapphire. It was a piece of the sea wrapped around her throat. It almost hurt to look at.

It was the same color as the plates.

"Ma'am? Your drink is ready." Some impatient douchebag in a Panama hat looked up from his iPhone, gave her the "hurry up" gesture. Maureen looked from the blindingly blue scarf to see that her latte was perched on the counter. She took her drink.

Jinwen's foam-art was one of the many reasons this coffee shop had a loyal clientele. She crafted steamed milk into hearts, tulips, and Hello Kitty. The white cloud of foam was sculpted into the shape of a woman's profile, her hair up in a fancy chignon. But there was no face. There was a void with a trail of bubbles trailing out from the empty gaze.

It was through sheer force of will that Maureen did not drop the cup. She carefully walked over to the sugar and cream station and set her cup down. She took her phone out, snapped a picture before dropping in sugar packets, which destroyed the image.

"I am not going insane," she said aloud on the walk to her parked car. There was no one else there, and she wouldn't have cared even if there were. She vocalized her thoughts all the time. It helped her focus.

She got in her car and sat down. Took a few sips of her latte.

She took out her phone and opened her browser.

"Azure Porcelain" was the first thing she typed. She clicked the first link and read.

'Azure Porcelain' was a brand of novelty ceramics made by LeFevre & Co from 1900–1920. It was a parody of the popular Flo-Blue (or Flown Blue) style of dinnerware. The scenes on the dishes were often whimsical with references to (then) contemporary doggerel and drinking songs. They were discontinued due to poor sales and not, as rumor had it, due to the toxicity of the chemical glaze. The story, that the glaze was derived from a strong cyanotoxic algae, however, encouraged the collectability of intact sets.

"Okay," Maureen said aloud. At least this wiki was convinced that the idea that the azure dishes somehow *stained* their owners as ridiculous. Because of course that was ridiculous. Mildred/Hortense with the mushroom cap hairstyle was crazy. But there was still the fact of the luminous azure scarf. And the faceless woman in her foam art.

Maureen asked her phone, "Search for Ingrid LeFevre."

The first and second hits directed to LeFevre & Co. The third link was productive, being a history of the LeFevre family. She scrolled past the bios of company founder Arvid LeFevre and his brother Osvald until she found what she was looking for.

Ingrid LeFevre was pictured, an old-timey photographic portrait that had a slight plum-colored hue to it. She was a white woman with wide eyes, a heart-shaped face with her ringleted hair fashioned into a bun on top of her head.

"You've got to be kidding me," Maureen muttered.

The dress Ingrid wore was an exact replica of the ornate gown that the many-faced lady wore on those plates.

"Where did you get that lipstick, girl?" asked Diane, one of the secretaries, when she walked into the office.

"I love those shoes," said Justin, one of her fellow instructors.

She passed an obstacle course of admiration before she made it into the ladies' room. She stood in front of the mirror, shocked and unsurprised at the same time.

Maureen was covered in azure. Everything was beautifully and terrifyingly blue. Bright, electric blue. The simple black tunic dress she'd thrown on was blue. As blue as the scarf around her neck. And her shoes. And her makeup, both lipstick and eyeshadow.

"I look like a damn smurf," she said to her reflection. Or that little girl in the Willie Wonka movie who turned into a blueberry.

Even so, Maureen had to admit, she looked good. Azure *was* her color. It played nicely against her dark skin.

She reached up to flake off some of the eyeshadow. It was a little too thickly applied; she'd been running late. A piece of it chipped off. It had an oddly *solid* texture. The chip hit the bathroom counter. And shattered, like a piece of pottery. Maureen felt a tickle at the spot where the flake of eyeshadow had been. It was a pinprick, small but insistent. She ignored it, and focused on the piece of eyeshadow on the counter. It was jagged and crystalline in structure. She touched it.

"Ouch!"

It stabbed her finger before turning into powder. She put her finger into her mouth and slowly backed away from the mirror.

Maureen didn't have to teach any classes that day. She just had office hours, during which no student visited save during finals. She closed the door to the room and continued searching on the internet for Ingrid LeFevre.

She found a death notice from a month ago.

INGRID LEFEVRE (March 30, 1926–April 9, 2017). Heiress to the LeFevre company. Socialite, trailblazer, patron of the arts, collector of oddities. Survived by her daughter Harriet Ohm. In lieu of flowers, please donate to the LeFevre Foundation.

"*Collector of oddities.*" The phrase caused her spine to tingle with disgust. She saw the silent stares of black lamp boys and the glittering eyes of the skulls. She no longer liked the plates. They were no longer whimsical.

"Harriet Ohm?"

"Speaking." Maureen immediately recognized the fluty voice.

"Hello. This is Maureen Sexton. We met yesterday. At the estate sale on Sunday?"

"Are you scheduling a delivery? Let me get the number of the moving company—"

"No. I'm not having anything delivered. You gave me the dinnerware? The Azure Porcelain?"

"Oh, yes! I remember you. Quite the lucky girl, you are! You know, they are collector's items . . ."

Maureen bristled at being called *girl*. She let it slide though. There were more important things to contend with at the moment. More of her eyeshadow had crumbled off. Chips of azure pottery littered her work desk. "Was your mother the model for the lady in the dress?"

"Why, yes. She was quite the belle de jour! Her father thought it would be a scream to have her immortalized in ceramic."

"I . . . thank you. Thank you very much," said Maureen. She hung up the phone; she knew what she had to do.

Immortalized in ceramic.

Even now, her bones made a hollow scraping sound like the tines of a fork against fine china.

By the time she got home, the lines in Maureen's hand were blue, like veins of lapis lazuli. The glazed fingernails on her left hand were fissured like the surface of an antique vase.

Maureen stumbled into the kitchen where the plates were. The color was no longer intense. The design was washed out, the color of faded blue jeans. All the plates were ghosts of what they had been. All save one.

The faceless woman was no longer sitting in her circle. She stood, facing Maureen. The void where her face should have been was an undulating, turbulent oval of lovely blue. It was both an eye and a mouth. The nonsense script encircling the rim of the plate burned azure.

Without a moment's hesitation, Maureen picked up the plate and smashed it on the floor.

It shattered in large pieces, the large blue void still intact. Did the fragment look like a heart-shaped face? Maureen looked at the other plates. She had a hunch. She watched as the ceramic animal faces—eyes, whiskers, and noses—blurred inexorably into pools of azure underglaze.

ß

Craig Laurance Gidney is the author of the collections *Sea, Swallow Me & Other Stories* (Lethe Press, 2008), *Skin Deep Magic* (Rebel Satori Press, 2014), the young adult novel *Bereft* (Tiny Satchel Press, 2013), and *The Nectar of Nightmares* (Dim Shores, 2015). He lives in his native Washington, DC, in a library hoard full of weird books. Website: craiglaurancegidney.com. Instagram, Tumblr & Twitter: ethereallad.

The Vestige

LYNDA E. RUCKER

AVID WOKE AS HE WAS ROUGHLY JARRED IN HIS BUNK. Halfway between sleep and wakefulness, he cried out—and was surprised when a soothing female voice, heavily accented, replied in English. "They are just moving us to a different rail gauge," she said. "They are going to pick us up with the crane now."

Gauge. The rail. He was slowly coming back to himself. He was on a night train out of Bucharest to Moldova, and he must be at the border because he'd read about this, that car by car, they would actually be picked up and deposited on a separate track.

The voice said, "It is for defense, you know? From Soviet times." He said, "How did you know I speak English?"

"You woke up once and you said, 'What's happening?' That—what is it you say? That let the cat out of the bag, right?"

He smiled at her, even though the light in the sleeping compartment was too dim for her to see him, and rolled onto his stomach to gaze at the sullen debris of the rail yard and the grey lightening sky raked by bare winter branches. Through the night, he had imagined that he wasn't sleeping at all as the heater blasted stifling hot air, leaving his lips and skin and eyes parched. But now he remembered stirring out of fitful dreams once, when someone came in and claimed the opposite bunk. He'd felt briefly disappointed before falling asleep again; he'd been lucky to get a compartment to himself, and he hated the idea of sleeping with a stranger so close and the inevitable awkwardness that would ensue in the morning when they couldn't communicate. It hadn't occurred to him for some reason that it would be a girl, which changed everything. Although he didn't actually know what she looked like, she *sounded* attractive.

"I'm Anna," she said and stuck an arm out across the gap between them. He reached out as well. Her grip was surprisingly firm. "You're American, right?"

"Anna," he said. "That's my cousin's middle name. The one I'm visiting. She used to call herself that sometimes when we were teenagers."

She said, "I don't care what your cousin is named. What is *your* name?"

"David," he said. "How'd you know I'm American? The air of general cluelessness, right?" She laughed. He had made her laugh. That was good. He wasn't used to being the kind of guy who made attractive girls laugh. He could tell she was rummaging around for something and then her face bloomed pale and ghostly above a flashlight. "This is me," she said. He'd already made a picture of her in his mind, and the face before him didn't match it—and why would it? She was less conventionally pretty than the Anna he'd conjured up. On the other hand, her features were more interesting, and the imagined-Anna couldn't quite hold her own before her flesh-and-blood counterpart and disintegrated with less than a whimper. The girl across from him had dark hair and wide eyes, a strong nose and chin, and an interesting scar above her left eyebrow that, like its right twin, was decisively unplucked. As she grew older, he thought, she would be what people used to call a "handsome woman."

He said, "Let's turn the lights on."

"No, it's more fun like this. Like secrets. Here. Now you." She passed the flashlight across to him. He had the absurd sensation that he was auditioning for something.

"Ooh," she said. "You are very handsome. This is good news for me, I think."

He was a little taken aback, even though he'd heard somewhere that European girls could be more forward than American ones.

"Oh!" she said. "Listen!" He did, but he couldn't hear anything. "Now we must turn the light on. They are coming to check our passports." She was rummaging in her bag again, and he reached over by the door and fumbled for the light. They blinked at each other in its dull incandescence, at the drab fake wood paneling of the train car, the worn and not-quite-clean look of things.

He said, "You were right about not turning the light on," and rummaged for his own passport.

But it wasn't in the pocket of his backpack where he knew he'd stashed it; it didn't seem to be anywhere else either, he quickly established, checking his bunk, the floor around him, digging into the bag itself and pulling out fistfuls of socks and T-shirts and underwear.

"It's gone," he said, "someone's taken it." Someone had come in while he, or they, were sleeping and taken his passport. But who would do that? Who would know he had a passport worth taking? Had someone overheard him buying his ticket and followed him to see which compartment he took? Not Anna; what kind of thief stole from somebody and then bunked with them? He could hear something now in the corridor, voices as they neared.

Anna tossed her covers back. "Get in my bunk!" He was too astonished to protest, even when she reached over and killed the light and demanded, "Give me your blankets and pillow!"

"What?"

"You cannot travel without a passport and visa! Are you crazy or something?" She was acting as though he'd be thrown into prison, put up before a firing squad. He said, "I'll just explain—" but her panic was contagious. "Get down under my covers!" she said. "They will think I am the only one in the compartment. A messy sleeper, maybe, but alone." She snatched at his arm across the gap between them.

Later he would wonder why he obeyed her so unquestioningly. It must have been the disorientation of being woken, of the strange surroundings, of the lost passport. He burrowed down in her bunk. If it hadn't been so unbearably hot, it might have been intoxicating; he was tangled up in her bare legs, which were hard and muscled. She snarled at him, "Don't say a *word*," moments before someone rapped at the door of the compartment. He had a final moment of wondering if it might not be a better idea to come clean with the passport officials, surely they'd seen it before, but the door slid open, and it was too late. He couldn't understand what anyone was saying; they were speaking either Romanian or Moldovan, but there were two of them, a man and a woman. Anna made her voice sound sleepy and reproachful, and he could tell she was saying *no, no, no* as they reached for the light switch. She must have convinced them, for they stepped into the lighted corridor to examine her documents. They all sounded awfully chummy, he thought. Maybe it was some kind of trick played by all three of them. Maybe it was an elaborate scheme to get him into some kind of trouble, plant drugs on him, disappear him to some unknown cell block in the former Soviet Union. Maybe it was like that one movie he saw about the rich people who paid lots of money to torture tourists. Maybe they were terrorists. Maybe he was really, really paranoid.

Anna was laughing now, and a twinge of jealousy surprised him—hadn't he made her laugh the same way just a few minutes ago? She hadn't thought he was funny at all. She was making fun of him. Briefly, dangerously, he thought he ought to jump out and surprise them all.

"Okay," she said. "Okay, they are gone." She flicked back the covers. "You can go now."

He said, daring, "I was hoping that was what passed for a courtship ritual in your country," but she didn't laugh again, and maybe the vocabulary was too difficult, but he felt himself flush as he settled himself back on his own bunk. She tossed over his blanket and pillow and reached into her own bag.

"Hungry?" she said. "Thirsty?" She passed him something wrapped in a napkin and a tall, plastic water bottle. The thing in the napkin proved to be a bit of sweet, crumbly cake.

"This isn't water," he said, and she laughed. "Of course it is not water," she said. "It's wine. My family made it. All Moldovans make wine." He took an experimental sip—he didn't know anything about wine, but it seemed okay. She laughed again. "In Moldova, we drink it like shots, like this," and she mimed doing it.

"But I don't have a shot glass," he said.

"Never mind," she said still laughing. "Noroc! You have to say it. It means good luck. Drink some more, and then give it here to me. You need some good luck."

He did as she said and passed it back. She took a swig as well and returned his "Noroc!" Now she was looking at him intently as he finished the slice of cake. "Do you have any money?" she said. "Or have you lost that too?"

He checked. This time at greater leisure, if indeed it could be called that, with the frantic taking and shaking out of everything in his pack to discover that no, he had nothing: no passport, no money, no credit cards, not even his phone, which he'd dutifully used to photograph all of his important documents in case of just such an incident.

"We will need money to bribe the officials when we get off the train in

Chisinau," she said. "I have some."

"A bribe, really?" he said. That sounded dangerous. And unnecessary. And dramatic.

"Of course," she said sharply.

If this was a scam that she was a part of, it had to be one of the weirdest ones ever. Maybe it was some kind of mail-order bride thing. David tried to figure out how that might work. He said experimentally, "I'm engaged, you know. To someone back in America."

She was counting out her own bills, and she looked at him. "What has that got to do with anything?"

He was embarrassed, self-conscious, suddenly all too aware of his helplessness in a foreign place. "I don't know," he said. He thought about Claudia back at home, prickly and impatient, to whom he was sort of engaged. In a manner of speaking.

"Right," she said. "I will pay the officials. You can pay me back when you get back to America, whatever, okay? Once we are off this train, just follow me and don't talk. And do what I say."

He said, "My cousin's meeting me at the station actually. That's what I'm doing here, visiting Natalie. She works here. With the Peace Corps."

"Good, then your cousin can fix things for you I am sure, but"—Anna's tone darkened—"let me get you off the train first. Trust me on this."

Did he have any choice?

The sun was reluctantly burning its way through the clouds when they arrived at the station in Chisinau. In their tiny cabin prior to deboarding, Anna had dressed with skilled modesty and made herself up, transforming into something formidable in a miniskirt and spiked heels and (David thought) too much makeup. She ushered him past officials as she said she would, shoving small wads of cash into their hands and chattering away, and then they were safe and outside the train station, yet there was no Natalie.

"Perhaps you can phone your cousin," Anna suggested, and he'd had her number but stored in the phone that was missing along with everything else that mattered.

"I have her address!" he remembered, and he dropped his bag and went pawing through it again, and this time, thank goodness, finally something going right, he found the little memo book where he'd scribbled it down in case his phone battery died along with a folded-up map he'd printed off Google.

Anna took the memo book from him and looked at the address with an expression he couldn't read. When she lowered the paper, she said, "Is this some kind of joke?"

He didn't know what to say, so he didn't say anything.

Anna said, "This is *my* address. How did you get my address?"

This was too much. This was too far. This was definitely an elaborate scam although he couldn't make head or tails of it.

He said, "You must think I'm an idiot," and he heard Claudia saying it to him as well. *Lost your passport? And your money? Went off with some woman . . . honestly, David, do you expect me to believe this?*

I don't really believe this, he thought. "It must be some kind of mistake," he said. "I must have written the address down wrong," although he knew he hadn't, knew he'd been painstaking because he'd been so worried about getting lost in a foreign country.

Anna looked both angry and hurt. Of course she was pretending, he told himself. "What is wrong with you?" she said. "I helped you when I didn't have to. Go on then. Go to your embassy, or go try to find your cousin *at my flat*. I have had enough of your problems."

He watched her walk away, so decisively that he thought she was not bluffing, and he must have been wrong. But that he would write down the wrong address and that it would be hers was a coincidence that simply beggared belief. She got into a taxi and was gone. Off to find an easier mark, he told himself.

He debated trying to find the embassy or consulate first, but he only had the paper map to Natalie's, and anyway, he was exhausted and confused and desperately wanted a familiar face. He found himself wanting to talk to Claudia as well, but of course he had no way of phoning her, and anyway, she would only be disapproving. *This call is costing too much money, David.* And, *you always screw up the details.* He just wouldn't mention any of it to her, even though he had the feeling she'd get it out of him one way or another. It was something he'd admired about her even as it frightened him, her scathing intuition and dogged determination to get to the bottom of him. It was, he supposed, what love was all about, someone knowing you better than you knew yourself.

He estimated that the walk to Natalie's would take about two hours. That wasn't so far really, and she would be able to help. She'd take him to the embassy and help him get to the bottom of it all. He wouldn't be the first traveler the embassy staff had seen who'd been robbed. And as soon as he got to Natalie's, he could print out all the documents he'd sent to himself as well. David set off, glad for the sunny day and—despite the growling in his stomach and a passing wish for coffee—feeling hopeful. It had been a weird night. It would be a weird story to tell later (to everyone but Claudia). At least he still had most of his belongings. He hitched his pack on his shoulders and set off toward Natalie's apartment.

The parts of Chisinau he walked through weren't much to look at. The train station itself had been colorful on the outside, but soon enough, he found himself walking through a section of the city that grew increasingly shabby. He wondered how long he had been walking, but the phone had been his only way of telling time.

He was looking forward to seeing Natalie again. They'd been close as children but drifted apart as time and growing up got in the way. He spent his adolescence in his room playing video games. Natalie ran away from home three times. But she was the kind of rebel who always landed on her feet. She'd joined a punk band, married and divorced, finally got it together and gone to college where she studied education, and taught inner-city school kids before joining the Peace Corps and moving to Moldova. After he got engaged to Claudia, he'd found himself overcome with a desire to see Natalie again, even though they hadn't spoken in years and had lived such different lives. He'd gone to a community college, gotten a business degree, and worked as support staff in offices since graduating, still living in the same town he grew up in. A timid life or at least it felt like one to him. When they were children, Natalie had always been his defender, the fierce one of the two of them. He knew instinctively that she and Claudia would not like one another. Maybe that was why he needed to see her one last time.

He'd never traveled outside of the United States before in his life, though at Claudia's insistence they were planning a honeymoon at some resort in Mexico. The night train had been cheaper than a direct flight into Moldova, but more importantly, it had also sounded exciting. The flight into Bucharest, the journey to the train station, and the process of purchasing the ticket and boarding the train had all been new and almost impossibly adventurous. Now, he was frightened and alone and was sweating in his dress clothes—button-down shirt, nice trousers—he'd unwisely donned, thinking you had to look respectable when you traveled. The sun was quite warm, and as he made his way past streets of concrete apartment buildings, he felt certain he would never be able to figure out which one was Natalie's. He cursed himself again for his carelessness. But why had Natalie not been there to meet him in the first place? She had promised.

The buildings had the grim look of American high-rise housing projects from the seventies. When he'd followed the map for as long as he could and still found himself unable to choose between them, he approached a group of young people with Natalie's address held out before him. They watched him warily, and he found himself gesticulating as though he were mute. He was embarrassed to speak English in front of them. Finally, one of them, a blonde girl with a big grin who looked about fourteen, took him by the arm and led him away. She chattered away the entire time without seeming to mind that he clearly couldn't understand a word she was saying.

He was glad it was a girl and not the boys because he'd have been wary of following them into the bloc she led him into. Inside, it was in even worse repair than he'd imagined. Graffiti scarred the walls, and the cold cement stairwell they climbed was unlit and crumbling and smelled of mold.

The girl moved just ahead of him, still chattering away, casting the occasional charming smile over her shoulder at him. He was a little concerned she'd misunderstood what he wanted, but she said "Natalie" a few times, so she must know her—or maybe he'd said Natalie's name first before he lost the ability to speak at all? He couldn't remember.

At last, they were out of the terrible stairwell and round a corner, and the girl skipped ahead of him and rapped hard on the first door on the left. When she did so, it swung open of its own accord. For a moment, he expected Anna to step out and berate him. Instinct pushed him across the threshold, a sense of emptiness before he confronted it. He took the place in quickly; it felt like a museum. Natalie had said she was renting an apartment from a family that had gone to the UK to work. He was surprised by the care and delicacy that had gone into its decoration: the touches of lace, the cabinet of what must surely be heirloom bric-a-brac, the heavy curtains that disguised the outside world, and the fabrics and overstuffed furniture that gave the modest room a palatial feel. It was, or should have been, as cozy as the rest of the building was grim.

It should have been and was not because no one had been inside this apartment for a very long time. A gentle coating of dust lay across everything; the temperature, the atmosphere, the smell inside was the same as on the landing outside. He knew if he crossed to the stack of books on a small side table, they would be swollen with moisture and stuck together with mold.

David turned back to the girl. "I was looking for Natalie," he said, but the girl was gone.

He realized then that he was exhausted: the heat, the hunger, the wine, the stress, all of it combined, and at the same moment, he realized he had nowhere to go. He reeled over to the sofa. He tasted dust as he fell back onto its cushions and fell into darkness.

David woke without opening his eyes and without confusion. He knew exactly where he was—on Natalie's couch in Natalie's apartment—and he thought he would lie there for a little bit longer with his eyes closed while he worked through the possibilities of what might have happened. One was that the woman who called herself Anna (for surely that was not her real name) had drugged him, so his own perceptions could not be trusted. He could not think of any other possibilities, and he lay there a little bit longer with his eyes closed.

He suddenly missed Claudia so much he found her absence difficult to bear. He missed her calm, her dogged expectation of incompetence from everyone else that nevertheless ensured that things almost always ran smoothly because she was prepared for every contingency. She was so capable. None of these things would have happened to him with Claudia along. He felt that a part of him might have been passing an unfair judgment on her earlier, mentally constructing a Claudia out of her worst qualities and none of her good ones. He opened his eyes.

Doing so proved to be anticlimactic, for there was only the ceiling overhead and silence. He turned his head and saw the apartment as it had been on his arrival: the lace, the bric-a-brac, the heavy furniture. He said, "Natalie?" experimentally, and there was no reply. Of course there was not. He admitted to himself for the first time that he was afraid. He said it out loud, trying it out. "I'm afraid." *Don't be silly, what are you afraid of, David?* That was Claudia's voice. *I don't know,* he told it. But that was a lie. *I'm afraid to say the things I'm afraid of.*

Just in case, he tried again. "Anna?" She had written him letters when they were kids that she signed that way. *I'm Anna when I get tired of being Natalie.* Of course there was no reply to that either.

He thought of Natalie as she'd looked in her most recent photos on Facebook. Last time he'd seen her, years ago, her honey-colored hair had been dyed black and styled like Betty Page. But now she looked like the stereotypical California girl she was again, all healthy glow and wholesome toothy smile. He thought of her harder then, as though thinking of her could conjure her, her voice that was just a little lower than you'd expect, the way she smelled of roses and cigarettes and beer. She'd quit the last two, she'd told him, and the roses, well, she probably hadn't really smelled like roses. It was just the cheap body spray she'd worn as a teenager, but when he stood close enough to her to smell her, it had enraptured him.

Natalie. Where was she in this city? Where was he for that matter?

There was nothing else for it. He had to go to the embassy himself. He'd head back toward the center of town and surely there had to be a tourist office, something, someone somewhere who spoke enough English to direct him there, and they would fix him up with a new passport, and Claudia could wire him some money or whatever it was you did.

Or was it the consulate he needed? Were they even the same thing? His knowledge of such matters came from stitched-together pop culture references in action movies and spy thrillers. He hadn't really done any research prior to his trip because he'd expected Natalie to shepherd him around. If he wandered around asking people where the American embassy was, surely they could direct him. But then he imagined a foreigner coming to ask him how to get to their own embassy in a large American city. He'd have no idea.

He thought about wandering the streets, listening for an American accent that might indicate someone who could help him. The idea exhausted him. How many tourists even came here anyway? He was still very thirsty, so he got up and went over to the kitchen area and found a dusty glass in a cabinet. The water came out brown at first but then looked okay, and he rinsed the glass and drank some of the water. It tasted gritty and strange, but he supposed it wouldn't poison him. He found himself wondering if there was anything to eat in the apartment and began looking through more cabinets before remembering an apple he hadn't eaten on the flight. He found it in his bag and sat on the edge of the sofa eating the rest of it. He half-expected it to have turned to maggots, all in a tenor with this strangest of strange days, but in fact, it was sweet and bright and crunchy, the only thing that seemed alive in this awful dead room.

He wondered why it had occurred to him to think of the apartment as dead. He got up again and walked around and into the second room that completed it, looking for some sign of Natalie. He opened a closet and saw some clothes hanging there that might be hers, but how would he know? He opened drawers, looking for something personal, looking for one of the letters he had written to her, but found nothing.

The young blonde girl had either played a trick on him or misunderstood who or what he was looking for. It was the only explanation. Nevertheless, he did not want to leave; he found some sense of respite here in this gloomy and forgotten place, and he knew it would be gone again the moment he stepped back out into the street. He heaved the backpack onto his shoulders again and trudged back down the stairs and outside again, back toward the train station.

In the end, he stopped people on the street until he found a couple who spoke English, and they looked up the embassy on their phones and mapped its location for him. After that, everything had seemed easy because he had imagined he would get to the embassy and would be unable to prove that he existed, would in fact not exist, would find his email account gone and a collect call to Claudia rejected because he had stepped into a parallel world where he did not exist in Claudia's life. There was some hassle—he had to make a police report for one, no small task—but both they and the embassy staff had dealt with foreigners with emergencies before, and his was relatively easy to solve with all of his documents saved in his email and a girlfriend who could wire him the money he needed. Claudia herself wasn't angry at all when he reached her by phone, only concerned. By the close of day, he had cash in hand, a temporary passport on the way, and a story to tell, though he wasn't sure who he could tell it to.

In some ways, he found himself disappointed that it had all been as easy as it was. Natalie's absence would make more sense if he were missing from the world as well.

But there would be a logical explanation; there had to be. Mixed up dates, mixed up addresses, all the mix-ups in the world converged at once, and when he contacted Natalie the following day it would all make sense again. No more mix-ups.

Instead, he spent the next few nights in a youth hostel. He'd found an internet cafe and looked up Natalie's address and phone number again in his email. The address matched the one he had on paper, and all their messages back and forth still existed, sitting on a server somewhere and appearing one after another on his screen as he clicked to open them. The phone number appeared to be out of service. He wrote her an email and sent it off without hope. He went to the train station the next morning and waited for the arrival of the night train from Bucharest, and he watched people deboard, expecting Anna to be among them or Natalie to be wandering about, waiting for him on the wrong day, but he saw neither of them.

He hailed a taxi outside the station and handed Natalie's address to the driver. He had the sense that if he tried it again on a different day he could get it right. The driver took him back to a familiar set of buildings. David tapped on the address and held out cash to the driver, pointing to the building and hoping he was indicating he wanted the driver's help in finding the place. The driver took him back up the stairs to the same apartment. David tried to pay him extra, but the driver refused, seeming anxious to be away.

He went back again, three times in total. The door was never locked, and each time, he waited and listened in the solitude for someone who never came.

Each time, he dozed off. The third time, he woke and found a slice of cake wrapped in paper and a water bottle full of wine, sitting in the middle of the dining room table, and a sense of someone having just left. No—someone was still in the apartment. He bolted upright and raced into the other room. Again the sense of a presence. Someone was here and not here. He could almost smell the person, almost hear the person in a silence that he could almost but not quite put a name to.

He ate the cake and drank some of the wine and left the rest of it. He knew as he did that he would not return again. He said, "Noroc!" when he drank the wine as Anna had told him to.

In the evenings, he went out for shish kebabs or Turkish pizza, both of which seemed to be popular menu items in Chisinau restaurants. He ate, and he drank wine and listened to the chatter around him, which he could not understand. There was a great comfort in it, like being invisible.

On the last day, he stopped by the Peace Corps office to ask after Natalie. It was anticlimactic as he'd known it would be, and that was why he had not bothered to do so earlier. It was more a matter of tying off a loose end than expecting any progress. They had not heard of her or said they had not anyway. And what reason would they have to lie about it?

He shared a compartment with a boisterous family on the train back to Bucharest where his flight was delayed. He sat in a bar at the airport and had three quick shots of whiskey, one after another, until a woman came and sat two stools down from him. He felt her looking at him and shifted his body in the opposite direction, so he could not see her. He could smell her: like roses. He left his fourth shot untouched, glancing her way when he left and caught an impression of wide eyes with an interesting scar above one unplucked brow.

He waited in a departure lounge, looking out at the night sky. That was something he and Natalie had enjoyed doing when they were kids. Imagine, they would say to one another. Imagine we sent people up there once. Imagine if aliens came down from there. What would they do or say? Maybe we were the aliens, he'd said. Maybe we came here from another planet. Natalie said, that's silly. Haven't you ever heard of the fossil record? Everything and everybody leaves traces behind. Nothing just disappears.

Of course, here at the airport, there was too much light pollution, and the stars themselves might have gone out for all he could see of them. They left no traces of themselves at all and still appeared to be missing as his plane lifted off and sheared the oblivious sky.

§

Lynda E. Rucker grew up in a house in the woods full of books, cats, and typewriters in southeastern United States, so naturally she had little choice but to become a writer. She has sold dozens of short stories to various magazines and anthologies including *Best New Horror, The Best Horror of the Year, The Year's Best Dark Fantasy and Horror, Black Static, Nightmare, F&SF, Postscripts*, and *Shadows and Tall Trees* among others. She has had a short play produced as part of an anthology of horror plays on London's West End, has collaborated on a short horror comic, and is a regular columnist for the UK horror magazine *Black Static*. In 2015, she won the Shirley Jackson Award for Best Short Story. Her first collection, *The Moon Will Look Strange*, was released in 2013 from Karōshi Books and her second, *You'll Know When You Get There*, was published by Swan River Press in 2016. In 2018, she edited the anthology *Uncertainties III* for Swan River Press. She currently lives in Berlin, Germany.

The Cure

TARIRO NDORO

F THE TELLING OF TALL MARIETTA'S TALE WERE TO BE LEFT TO the old wives of Eldorado Park, it would begin with Marietta appearing on East Avenue from absolutely nowhere, wearing a faded pink dress and the sort of flat shoes that nurses wear, her brown hair tied back in a simple bun.

"Jinne! I just saw her with a brown suitcase in hand. It was a Thursday . . . I remember now because Elaine and I were baking scones for the church benefit there by the verandah, drinking Horlicks whilst we waited for the last batch of scones when we heard a rumble. So I said, 'Elaine, what's happening in the street today?' We both went over to the fence, and that's where we saw it—I mean her. Twelve feet tall, I tell you. Twelve feet. I crossed myself, I promise you. I've never seen a woman so big."
—Marjorie Price, an Eldorado Park Housewife

The old wives of Eldorado Park tell this story to every young wife or visiting relative. They say that after her mysterious appearance on East Avenue, Tall Marietta walked all the way down to Lucas Street where she used a combination of muti and juju to make "poor" Mr. Engelbrecht rent her his dilapidated old house.

Of course, in this version, they won't tell you that no one had ever felt sorry for "poor" Mr. Engelbrecht before this happening and that no one else would ever feel sorry for him in the future either. He was a cheat, to be sure, and the house he offered was a dump.

That had been Marietta's first day in Joburg, but it wouldn't be her last. Any sadness she felt because she hadn't found a good place to rent was intensified by the unsuccessful job hunt that followed. They wouldn't take her as a nurse or a nurse aide—she scared the patients. They wouldn't take her in the library for the blind, for although her appearance wouldn't scare those who couldn't see her, she could scare them with her great crashing feet.

They never told her this to her face. No. The year was '95 and South Africa was new, so they told her what they said to everyone else who didn't fit the part: "We've filled the vacancy, but leave your CV under that pile, ne, and we'll call you if we have space for you." They never called her.

This fuelled the second part of the old wives' tale—that Marietta was positively involved in some kind of juju. It's true, the only job Tall Marietta found was as a cleaning lady in a funeral parlour because no one else wanted the job. Marietta's new boss, a small miserly man named Athol Smith, figured with a tall body like hers she could help with the heavy lifting.

She spent most of her free time at the Joburg Zoo, watching the caged animals because she felt as much of a spectacle as they did, but that didn't stop the old wives of Eldorado Park from calling her Juju Queen behind her back.

They told their children not to misbehave or Tall Marietta would get them. She became a legend, and local children threw rocks at her to see if she really breathed fire, and newcomers took pictures of her when they thought she couldn't see.

Seasons came and went, and years later, they posted the pictures on Twitter and Instagram, tagging them #JoburgGiantSpotted and other such nonsense.

It is true Marietta came from a dusty little dorp in the middle of the Free State where the roads are dusty and everything is brown when it doesn't rain, including the sheep. Where there's a church called Nederduitse Gereformeerde Kerk that everyone attended except Marietta and her mother (God rest her soul). This little town is right in the middle of nowhere, but that isn't quite the same as *nowhere*, so the housewives of Eldorado Park are wrong when they say that Marietta came from nowhere.

How did she get to Joburg then? Oom Kobus Viljoen gave her a lift to

Bloemfontein, and although he refused to take the R100 note she offered him, he *did* force her to sit in the back with the sheep. Marietta wasn't sure if it was because she was too large to sit in the front of the truck with him or if it was the colour of her skin that scared him, but now she'll never know because she didn't ask at the time, and Oom Kobus Viljoen's gone to his maker.

From Bloemfontein, she took the Greyhound to Joburg and landed in Roodepoort where she jumped into a cab because she was lost and couldn't ask for directions. *The tsotsis will rob you blind if they ever smell your fear,* her mother had always said. It was the cabbie and not the wrath of God that had deposited her at the top of Lucas Street.

Why did she leave the little town in the first place? Certainly not to terrorise the little boys of Eldorado Park who listened to their elders for fear of being devoured by Tall Marietta. But because her mother was dead—she couldn't bear to live in a one-street town where everyone looked at her slyly as the one whose mother had carnal relations with a giant from the circus.

It is true, Marietta's father was eleven feet tall, and he'd been a part of a travelling troupe. People paid to see him the way they paid to see the dancing elephant and the juggling monkeys, but Marietta had no such luck. They stared, pointed, and took photos, but if anyone had ever paid R10 to see her face, then she must have been sleeping when it happened because her money never stretched as elastically as the month.

It is also true, the other girls in the dorp where she grew up got married straight after they finished matric, and some even before that, but when Marietta left the Free State, she was a twenty-year-old spinster, and by the time she fell in love for the first time, she was twenty four.

It happened on a train on her way to the morgue, though it can never be referred to as love at first sight—she smelt him before she saw him. It was the fine smell of hay, hard work, and honesty that caught her brain before she noticed the awkward man huddling on two seats of the train because he couldn't fit on one. He looked up for a second after she saw him and stared and stared, obviously happy he'd seen one of his own. They continued this way for a while as they were on the same commute, and it took no less than three weeks for him to get the courage to say hello.

As things go, he joined her in her home in Eldorado Park, the ramshackle house where the roof leaked and the walls groaned if you shut the door too roughly. They got on very well at first, sharing stories about the wide open air and country life and future dreams and perhaps children who would be as tall as their gap-toothed giant father, but after a few years of arguments, Vince realised that the gold mines on the outskirts of the city were more lucrative than the construction firm he worked for. After all, hadn't the wealth of Johannesburg, the great Egoli, been built on the foundations of gold mining?

He also realised that the wondrous city girls were more welcoming of giant men than of giant women, though one would never have caught him saying that his Marietta was ugly; he just never said the opposite, so Vince left Marietta for the fast lane. Suffice to say, he no longer smelt of hay, hard work, or honesty.

Marietta didn't mind the golden age of Instagram with all its #JoburgGiant sightings. The great Internet boom had brought her the distinct knowledge that she wasn't alone in the world; there were other giants, and they united the same way other outcasts did—online. From MySpace fora to Facebook groups and Twitter threads, they existed on every patch of God's green earth, and not all of them were poor morgue janitors whose fathers had been circus attractions.

Take Hank Jones, a giant from Texas, and Janek Slovisch, a Chechen ogre, for instance, who were what kids these days would refer to as ARGs (or alt-right giants). These two believed in creating a homeland for giants where no one would throw bricks at them or try to exorcise them with garlic water. Hank and Janek had decided to crowdfund an island as a sort of mecca for all Tall People, and a rich Swiss giant named Jan Sommers had pledged the necessary billions to buy it, but Hank and Janek had never been able to decide whether they preferred to buy a Caribbean island or something off the coast of Mozambique.

A veteran giant woman who went by the moniker of GGBigs believed in integration. She was there for the earliest struggles for giants' rights and had started the Integrated Civil Rights Movement for Giants, Trolls, Fairies, and Elves, but the civil rights movement and the women's movement had stolen her thunder, and she was still trying to find a way to revive interest.

Our Marietta had no great political aspirations. She was just there to enjoy the camaraderie and the cat videos that a giant from Nelspruit kept posting every Friday.

One day, a rare thing happened. During a lull in the lobbying for an island and the cat videos and the strange flirtations between Sunday Thompson (a Lagosian giant) and Anais L (a Madagascan troll), a giant from Australia posted a link that screamed—

Click HERE!! ARE YOU TIRED OF BEING A FREAK OF NATURE ? CLICK HERE!!

—in bright red, fourteen-point Helvetica.

Marietta was indeed tired of being treated like a freak of nature. She was tired of people calling her a witch, she was tired of vicariously living through the Internet, and most of all she was tired of overhearing mothers whisper, "Cheryl, I swear to God if you don't clean your room this instant I'll feed you to Tall Marietta!" She felt as much a freak show as her father was said to have been.

GGBigs promptly typed a comment, reminding the other giants that the forum was for solidarity not for spamming and scamming. Hank and Janek agreed with GGBigs and, more importantly, each other. They rightly predicted that their dreams of the giant utopia would go kaput if there were no longer any giants to unite. In fact, there was even chatter that the Swiss giant was considering making the transition to becoming an HASB (or historically advantaged short being). A gaming giant commented that the link probably led to some virus-infected den of trouble that would corrupt all their hard drives. Marietta was afraid of computer viruses. She didn't know much about computers except how to use social media and look at videos on YouTube.

Yet something pulled at her insides; she was tired of being oversized. She was tired of having no friends. She thought she could win Vince back if she was smaller and dressed like Lisa, the receptionist at the morgue. Her ovaries were aging, and she wanted children. Marietta clicked on the link and held her breath.

"Hi, I'm Martha, and I used to be a giant," a chirpy voice said from the other end of her secondhand smartphone. The body attached to this voice was an attractive woman with long black hair and striking blue eyes. Marietta had a hard time believing the woman had ever been an inch above seven feet.

"Humans and their children used to tease me. I lived up in the mountains where no one could get to me. My father was hunted down during a witch hunt, and my mother raised me on her own. People set fire to our house during the night sometimes, and life became very difficult."

At this point, slow sad music began to play, and pictures of Martha and her mother were displayed. Marietta was reminded of the Verimark infomercials that SABC 2 aired on Saturday mornings.

"Luckily for me, Dr. Havershnak Fitzgerald created a revolutionary cure-all for our condition. Nowadays I live a normal life. I'm getting married in June, and I have a regular job. If you would like the revolutionary formula to change your life like it changed mine, click on the link below, and for just $15.99, the life-changing formula will be sent to your home."

Marietta's heart rate sped and slowed and sped again. Could it be? She dared not hope. Back on the forum, Hank and Janek castigated the advert vehemently.

How dare they call our beautiful heritage a condition? typed Janek.

I say we boycott this and write them a strongly worded letter, responded Hank.

I would like to try it out, one giant typed a minute later.

You do that and we'll kick you off our forum, traitor. Janek could be a bit passionate.

GGBigs intervened, *Her body her choice.*

Marietta closed the tab and put her phone on the charger. She made all the motions of going to bed, but she hardly slept a wink, *What if . . . what if her life were vastly different from what it is now?* That night, she dreamt of herself being a successful society lady with young men trailing after her and young women asking her for fashion advice. She would throw tea parties that real people would actually attend.

At the funeral parlour, she was distracted all day. Mr. Smith almost yelled at her, but he remembered that she had half a metre on him and could easily beat him to a pulp, so he let her be. She burnt her dinner that night and hardly noticed. She was so preoccupied and ultimately read through everyone's comments once again. At last, she clicked on the bright red link and watched the entire presentation again. Before she could chicken out, she clicked on Buy and entered her credit card details and postal address. Marietta was finally going to experience what it was like to be a *real* woman.

It arrived on a Saturday in a brown box with Amazon markings, and it was all Marietta could do to stop herself from tearing it open the way a six-year-old attacks a Christmas present. Carefully she removed the tape that ran along the middle of the box and opened the two yawning flaps. Marietta expected the potion to be sitting right there in front of her, but instead there were acres and acres of bubble wrap and styrofoam.

Before she gave up, Marietta spotted another box within—like a Matryoshka doll. She opened the white box, and right there were two vials, one red and one blue, and a leafy instruction manual.

She lay her human-sized dress from Woolworths (why not splurge?) on the bed and brought the blue vial to her lips.

"Three, two, one," she counted down before downing the whole thing. She waited a few seconds and peeked shyly at the mirror. No change. After another ten seconds, she was in a full tizzy. She grabbed the instruction manual and read it from cover to cover. She'd done everything correctly.

She felt itchy. Her skin tightened like it had been stretched thin, and her eyes started to go in and out of focus. It was as though she was being pulled into a great vortex, and her stomach garbled in protest. Down, down, down her stomach went, ticklish like when she was a little girl and played on swings.

As suddenly as the pulling and stretching began, it stopped. Marietta's hands were smaller. Funny, the mattress was closer to her than it was before. She rushed to the mirror, which wasn't shorter than her any longer, and looked seriously at her features for the first time since Pieter Labuschagne from her hometown had told her she was uglier than a hippo with German measles.

She pinched her cheeks and looked herself over, this way and that. Her dress had pooled at her ankles, and now she put on the frock from Woolworths.

"Beautiful," she announced. "Jy is pragtig." She giggled and blushed for the first time since Vince had walked out on her.

The city of Joburg was not ready for Marietta. Marietta herself was not ready for Marietta. She hit the elevators first. She had never been allowed aboard elevators before. Whenever she'd tried to climb in, others had looked at the crinkled sign that said, "Maximum weight 950 kg," and they'd looked at Marietta and shaken their heads. Now that she was five foot six and weighed sixty-five kilos, the possibilities were endless. Men blew her kisses in the streets, there was a new spring to her step, and women wanted to be friends. For the first time, they saw her face before they saw her size. She didn't scare babies anymore.

In under a week of her molecular makeover, Marietta found a new job waitressing at an upmarket restaurant. The hours were awful, but the men gave her tips upward of 20 percent, and some of them smiled at her and scribbled their names and numbers on the bills. These were not farmhands and morgue attendants but men who wore suits from Saville Row and smelt like Old Spice.

After a month, she was able to move to an apartment in Newtown, and she stopped reading the giant forum because she was no longer sad nor lonely. She forgot about the previous life she led. The photograph of her mother got buried under a pile of new clothes from Woolworths and Identity. Marietta felt that she was *really living*.

Marietta shared her flat with another waitress, originally from Bloem. Her name was Veronique, and she'd moved to Joburg to be an actor, but this and that had happened, and well, twelve years later, she was still a waitress at Mario's, working the six to ten with Marietta. Most nights, they closed at eleven. By that time, it was so dark that they had decided to live together, so they needn't travel alone, Joburg being Joburg.

Every two months, Marietta received her next brown box from Amazon with one blue vial and one red vial. (Jan Sommers had made sure there would be a constant supply by buying shares in the company and donating a production plant.) Marietta locked herself in her room each time and drank the entire contents of the blue vial, bottoms up. Her roommate suspected her of drug abuse but didn't say anything; she herself had gone through a bad stage just a few years ago. She shuddered just thinking of it.

One night, Mario's closed late. Some hotshot lawyer had rented the place for his birthday. His guests had so much fun that they stayed for hours and hours. Mario hinted about closing time, so one guy slipped him a wad of cash. That had been that. The lawyers had left at midnight, and by the time the wait staff had cleaned the dishes and righted the chairs, it was two in the morning. Mario locked up and rushed into his waiting sports car—the winter wind biting that night.

Veronique and Marietta shrugged deeper into their coats, watched Mario's car recede into the inky tar, and checked on their Uber guy for the eighth time. The guy was running late. Should they have stayed and waited? Maybe. Should they have called a regular cab? No one will ever know.

"It's not safe here," Veronique said. "Maybe we should walk to the Music

Factory. There'll be people there."

Marietta frowned at the wind and looked up to the sky. She couldn't see the stars the way she had back in the Free State. She didn't feel like music, but at least, there'd be people there.

"Besides, it will be warmer in there," said Veronique. Marietta began to walk toward Nxumalo Street. Veronique kept pace with her. With every step, the electro house music from the club seemed louder and louder. Marietta relaxed a little. A speeding car full of drunk youngsters drove past them.

"Jinne! These kids will kill themselves one—" Marietta was saying and then something cold and sharp was at her neck. The smell of cheap wine before her.

"If you scream, you die," a voice said. It must have been connected to the hand holding the blade at her neck or the hand clamping her mouth shut. She tried to struggle, but like a freshly shorn Samson, she had no power. She twisted her eyes as far as they could go, and she saw Veronique was in the same predicament as her, tears streaming down her face. They had come face to face with the city of Joburg, and they hadn't won.

She stumbled into the apartment at four in the morning, clothing torn, no purse, no house keys; she had to ask the caretaker to let her in. He asked her where her roommate was, and she shook her head. Gunshot wound to the abdomen, not usually fatal but it had taken her a while to revive after the blow to her head. Vero was still breathing, but there'd been no phone to call an ambulance. So she'd staggered to the nightclub, the pavement biting into her feet since they'd taken her shoes.

If you ask the residents of Newtown, they'll say Marietta fainted after telling the club bouncer what had happened, that he had called the cops and offered her his jacket.

Some say this never happened, that she never changed to a human and was always tall. But in this version of the tale, Marietta took a shower when she got home; it was okay now that they'd taken evidence from her body. She slept till nightfall and went to Mario's.

"Look, Marietta, we're all upset about what happened last night. Take the week off like I said. You'll be paid as normal."

Mario's eyes were sincere, but Marietta still changed into her black slacks and white shirt. She painted her lips a demure colour and carried menus to the customers' tables. That night, Marietta served more tables than she had in her life, and when the other servers threw questioning stares at Mario, he shrugged and said, "Can't get her to leave."

She wouldn't take a lift at closing time. Not from Mario, not from Thabo, and not from Kelly. She told them there was closure in walking, and they all nodded like they understood. Except Kelly sat in her Prius and watched—she'd been robbed before and promised herself she'd sit there till Marietta got a cab or got to her apartment. But Marietta simply wandered around the back alleys until she heard a scream. Kelly called the cops from inside her Prius, and Marietta walked toward the sounds.

This time, it was one woman. She wore ripped jeans, and her eyes looked as though they would pop out of her face.

"Let her go!" Marietta said.

"Hey, Nico, it's the woman from last night. She has more money to donate, ne?"

"Let her go, or I'll make you."

"You and what army?" the one named Thinus asked.

Marietta slipped her hand into her purse.

"Ha-ha, you think she's packing?" Nico asked.

Marietta's hand emerged from her purse, and there were six red vials in her hand. She drank from them all in one go.

"This one thinks she's Popeye the Sailor"

Kelly in the Prius grabbed for her mace and hoped for safety in numbers. She'd called a while ago, but the sirens of the cavalry hadn't sounded yet. She thought of all her wasted taxpayer money. Kelly stepped out of the car and ran toward the fracas, but before she got there, a miracle occurred before her eyes. Marietta transformed.

She grew bigger and bigger, bursting out of her clothing, and she didn't stop until her eyes were level with a five-story building. She bent down and picked the girl between her index finger and thumb. She flicked Nico and Thinus away with her middle finger and turned sideways, nodding at Kelly. Kelly peed herself.

"What's your name, girl?"

"Nonhle."

"Where do you live?"

Nonhle pointed in the direction of Four Ways. It seemed speech was too much just then. Marietta carried her in the palm of one hand and negotiated her way to Four Ways.

There are those who thought it was an earthquake. Fanatics decided the world was ending. They say Nico aged several years in one night and Thinus died of fright, but these rumours have not been confirmed. Veronique was buried in the Free State on her parents' farm. Her parents offered Marietta shelter, but she was having none of it. The streets of Joburg were full of menace, and who better to scare the rascals if not a woman as tall as a building?

The women of Eldorado Park say many trolls and ogres and giants appeared after Marietta saved the girl. The tall ones no longer hid near the Drakensburg Mountains but walked freely in the cities and in the towns. The ARG finally secured funds to buy a giant utopia, but on the day of leaving, no other giants showed up. GGBigs must have been proud. Yet who knows if any of this is true? After all, housewives have been known to tell tall tales.

§

Tariro Ndoro is a Zimbabwean writer, poet, and typical millennial. Her short stories have appeared in various literary venues, including *Afreada, Moving On and Other Zimbabwean Stories, Hotel Africa: New Short Fiction from Africa, La Shamba, New Contrast, Fireside Fiction Redux Literary Journal,* and *Omenana.* Her debut poetry collection, *Agringada: Like a gringa, like a foreigner* (Modjaji Books) was published early in 2019. Tariro's work has been longlisted for the Writivism Short Story Award (2017) and NOMMO Short Story Award for African Speculative Fiction (2018) and shortlisted for the DALRO Poetry Award (2017) and the BN Poetry Award (2018). When Tariro is not reading experimental fiction and contemplating the meaning of life, she can be found working on a collection of short stories or at least trying to. Links to her stories, poems, and essays can be found at tarirondoro.wordpress.com.

Kleinsche Fläche of Four-Dimensional Redolence

D.A. XIAOLIN SPIRES

PEERED INTO THE MANY TRANSLUCENT FLASKS AND VINTAGE atomizer bottles, the contours of my face perverted by the curves and flexures of the glass. My cheeks warped, my eyes bloated, jaundiced, and then chromed—alternating from fuchsia to jade— as I passed the line of merchandise.

I picked up one specimen, an aqueous cocktail of sea green. I pushed the metal knob with a finger, spritzed it onto a scentless swatch I grabbed from a tight stack. The spray left behind no color on the sheet but trailed a salty scent of deep oceans. I placed the swatch onto the discard pile.

I reached the end of the table and turned around, looking at the rest of the group of mostly women before I eased into my seat. Sunlight diffused through the window and highlighted the empty chairs, washed in white. I didn't know how I got talked into this. I think it had to do with a free lunch and the imploring, expectant eyes of a gregarious former clerk in the office.

"Let's wait a few more minutes before we get started. I'm still waiting for Vedhika and her husband. And Becky. She's bringing her two kids," said Mie.

We socialized until the stragglers arrived and took their seats. After greetings and exchanged apologies, Mie began.

"Thank you for giving me the opportunity to introduce my new and fabulous line of perfumes, Redolence. Many of you know me as the talkative one in cubicle 12-B on the third floor. At least, that used to be my headquarters before

I was handpicked for the pink slip during the big March layoff half a year ago. But it was a blessing in disguise.

"Some might know my health was suffering. The stress of the job was wearing on me. But that was secondary. The main thing was the terrible allergy I developed using commercial cosmetics. I had been buying them since a teen, not knowing they were grating on my body day after day. Just the kinds you find at the pharmacy. Nothing fancy. I had no idea they were loaded with toxins and especially harmful for sensitive people like me.

"So I'd like to thank you for giving me a second chance to show you how wonderful these perfumes I designed are. How different they are from the mainstream commercial stuff. I spent months with scent specialists, dermatologists, and allergists. I visited spice farms and talked to local purveyors. I spent my own capital, funneled R&D into this enterprise until I felt good about my products. I felt like I could use them on myself, but not only that, they smell glorious. They are attractive, splendid perfumes. So I present to you this limited line of fragrances—Redolence."

Once she took out the bags with the logos, I knew. Everyone knew. Josephine's. The magenta bag. With the curling *J* and the loopy signature. We breathed a collective sigh of recognition. It was no wonder she had the bags hidden under the table, nestled between the sheets of tablecloth, biding its time until the proper moment to be unearthed.

What Mie failed to explain during her spiel was that Redolence was a small line of products appended onto a bigger venture—Josephine's. Josephine's sold everything from perfumes to lipstick to underwear. The kinds of build-your-own-business catalog products that sustained an ever-trickling clientele of want-to-be entrepreneurs, waiting to swindle others as they themselves were swindled. In short, a teetering Ponzi scheme.

Most of the products Josephine's sold were second-grade stuff, tolerable for home use but hardly exceptional. Things that look nice 2-D and shiny in a brochure but just don't cut it in person. Items you couldn't pass on as gifts even if you were arm-twisted to make a purchase.

I wasn't going to say anything, but the loudmouth from cubicle 15-C, who somehow managed to hold onto his job, got up and said, "You said you designed these. I thought Josephine's sold premade stuff?" as his husband kept trying to shush him.

Mie nodded. She was nonplussed. Probably had done this a hundred times.

Even hoping the question would come up, so she could give her curated answer. "I think a lot of you are familiar with Josephine's. Their standard lot is in their brochures. But Josephine's now offers a place where new designers can pitch ideas that can be appended to their brand. It goes through a rigorous screening process, and my line of perfumes passed the test. Josephine's called it 'edgy and adventurous' while still safe and with only natural ingredients. They said that the sillage, that is the wake of the scent of the perfume, is 'dreamy and evocative,' warranting the proposed name Redolence.

"The good news for you is that sponsorship and support through the Josephine brand mean less risk on my end and more savings on your end for meticulously crafted high-end products."

Her reedy voice, carrying through this pasty white living room with too much sunflower-print upholstering, reminded me of the gatherings my mom often went to when I was a child. Their houses must have looked exactly like this, pale but lived in, decorated but unthreatening. Bland with a touch of kitsch. I must have gone, but the exact memories escape me. But I did remember opening our cabinet doors to Tupperware tumbling. I'd had to dive to catch the falling treasures. My mom would justify her purchases with a smile, saying she was proud to support her financially venturesome girlfriends.

We milled about. It was only noon on a weekend, but I wished Mie had the foresight to prepare some wine. Something that would ease our preconceptions and lubricate our pockets. Really it would be a win-win situation. I made note of her wallpaper, choice of rugs, and the company she kept. Some of the other couples gave in and signed up for perfume delivery on a regular basis. Heck, maybe they really liked the perfumes.

I hovered over the snack table and munched on some cucumber strips dipped in generous amounts of ranch dressing, trying to wash down my distaste with the dill-flavored oil emulsion.

Figuring I should have the decency to appear at least remotely interested, I finished off a few more cut vegetables and walked over to the table where a crowd had gathered. Mie was demonstrating yet another scent. The aromas now mingled in the air, fused into the very molecules around us, circulating about this room that was in desperate need of more ventilation.

Holding my nose for some respite from the olfactory onslaught, I pressed my fingernails against the glass of one of the vials, a clear hourglass form beside a blocky pink one. I pretended to think about which one to order.

I could feel the room brimming with pretense, not just from me but emanating from all the bodies, all the artful articulations around me. "Well, this one smells like a summer tangerine. That's a very bright scent. I bet Florine would like this." And "How did you come up with these, Mie? They're ingenious." I kept my mouth shut but at least played the part of an interested buyer, fumbling with bottles, letting the scents invade my nostrils. Mie had helped me find my job after all, so I owed her that at least. Maybe I'd make a purchase and give it away. I tried to think of who I could unload the merchandise on.

I was still coming up with a name, perhaps a distant cousin I might see during the holidays, months away, when I saw something under the table glint in the sun. The brightness was emanating from another carafe-like object resting upon a half-open suitcase.

I was determined not to show curiosity toward any particular product unless I was committed to buying it, but curiosity overtook me.

"Hey, Mie," I said, extracting her from another conversation. "What's that perfume over there?" I pointed toward a spot below the table, behind where she was standing.

"Where?" she said, looking around. "You mean this Cucumber Lush?" She held up a long thin bottle that looked slightly like a leaping dolphin.

"No, the one down there," I said, my finger now more urgently spearing toward the vicinity below the table where she was now shifting her legs as if to cover it.

"Oh, that's . . . that's not for sale," she said.

"Is that one you made?" I asked.

"It's still a prototype. I haven't gotten it approved under the Josephine's label. It hasn't gone through the marketing circuit. We haven't even settled on a name for it yet."

"Can I see it?" I asked.

"Yeah, you know, after we're done here. I'll let you be the first to test it out," she said. "But I think Vedhika is looking for a receipt over there, and Becky's eyeing a whole set for her nieces. This is great. My best sales so far. Take a look at some of the ones displayed. I know you haven't tested them all out yet. I'll be back."

Now it would be hard to make my grand escape as my curiosity kept me ensnared in another round of discounts and prizes. Magenta bags inscribed with the logo disappeared into cars, and soon Mie was down to just a few bottles left. I waited until it mostly cleared out and committed myself to the smallest vial possible: a 135-ounce pill-shaped travel spray of the least offensive scent, one of cloves and cinnamon, reminding more of baked cookies and spiced nuts than something you'd want to wear on a first date. I figure I could palm it off as a Secret Santa if I couldn't figure another way to dispose of it before then.

I was finishing off the rest of the tortillas, looking out the window to her backyard, thinking of the pool later today and wondering what I needed to buy for the beach outing next week, when Mie tapped my shoulder.

"They're all gone," she said with a conspiratorial smile. In her hands was a large, vintage suitcase, almost a shipping box, angular in mahogany-dyed leather and with shiny metal clasps. "Come on, let's take a look."

She hefted the suitcase onto the table that once held her pet line of fragrances, now empty except for a few doilies.

"Watch this," she said. She pressed down on two metal clasps on either side of the handle. The suitcase cracked in half like a clam, opening up to the most exquisite pearl of a flask I had ever seen.

"What is this?" I asked. I resisted the urge to touch, to approach it and breathe onto it. Taint the glass with my foggy breath.

"It officially doesn't have a name. But I call it Anamnesis," said Mie.

"Anamnesis?" I cocked an eyebrow. "Isn't that a bit pretentious of a—"

"Yes, I know. But look at it. Isn't it a beauty?"

"It is," I breathed, not even a whisper.

Before me stood the flask, quite large, the size of a generous decanter. It boasted a pear-shaped bottom, plump and round, that curved up into a tube. The tube, a dignified mast of iridescence, stuck out from the top like a plume that then looped back around in an arc and intersected with the flask at one of its sides. That side glittered in the sun, the seam of the tube crossing into the flask itself, hidden in a flood of light, continuing from there inside as a negation of space, an inner hole, a hollow pipe within. It emptied out into the bottom. Altogether the tube looked like almost but not quite an S shape, weaving into and out of the flask.

"A Klein bottle," I said.

"Is that what it's called? I always thought it looked like a coiled snake," said Mie, laughing.

"I saw some of these forms for sale online. It's some topological anomaly, isn't it? I thought of getting one for my nephew who's into these kinds of strange science paraphernalia, but they were always so expensive. Is this commercially viable?" I asked. The colors inside were mesmerizing, a neon prism of liquids intersecting and flowing within each other. A dynamic fluid.

"I bought it at a party much like this one. The man running it looked like he had come from an apothecary. The things he was selling! You'd have a hoot if you were there. Concoctions of all kinds. He said that he drew some of his distillations from the Antarctic. The kinds of colors and smells I never would have imagined in my life. Like the insides of locker rooms, pungency of mold, and the piquancy of fruit from distant tropical lands I could kind of perceive but couldn't really pinpoint.

"'Titillating, abhorrent, isn't it?' he'd said, clearly rhetorical. 'Evoking all kinds of visceral reactions.' He had this long white beard that he would stroke as he displayed his products. He only took cash, and he wouldn't say when he would come back for another party. It was at a friend of a friend's house on the outskirts of the city. I don't think I'll be going there again. The traffic was terrible. But oh, he was such a character."

"Sounds like one," I said. I thought I could sniff out something like that piquancy in the air right then. An elusive but tangy quality.

"I wasn't really impressed with his fragrances, to be honest. They seemed like the kinds you could throw together with some rubbing alcohol and a stirring wand, but he jazzed them up with some commercial essences he probably got at bulk discount, which was why they were so strange. Probably had been sitting around too long, fermenting in a dank basement.

"He told me I was a hard sell. He went to his car, an old, rusty baby-blue Volkswagen beetle covered, absolutely slathered, in bumper stickers that contradicted one another. "Save the planet" with a picture of a bear and a recycling sign. "Littering is not a crime when this whole city is garbage." "Baby on board." "Stop being a baby and learn how to drive." "My kid's an honor student." "The only honorable thing you can say about your kid is nothing." Some of us looked out the window and shared a good laugh. The whole car was like this, an eyesore, perhaps some kind of post-modern outburst of irony. I don't know. Seems like it would be eye candy for any policeman trying to make quota. A target saying, 'You know what I need right now? A ticket,'" said Mie.

"Maybe he runs a bumper sticker printing company?" I offered.

"Could be. He sold enough stuff. I could believe it. And well, you might be right. If you only saw what he came back with. You could tell me he sold anything, and I'd nod and say, 'Probably.' So what did he fish out of that craze-mobile? A canvas sack filled with all sorts of strange stuff. He pulled out each one as the other guests were leaving. Some of the guests made purchases, a lot left empty-handed. They didn't seem worried that they'd offend him. I was still there. I mean, I couldn't help myself. I was amused, maybe a bit mesmerized even.

"It was like watching a magician and his enchanted hat. What will come out of there next? 'A dodo beak,' he said, reaching in and pulling out a rather phallic looking yellow object. I'm sure it was just plastic. 'An unbreakable spider web, a Cantor-set processing chip, Koch-snowflake Christmas tree decorations.'

"I must have mentioned I sold perfumes because he looked a little sheepish, probably from his dismal selection. He said he had something for me. 'Totally violating vile vials,' he said, winking. He went back to his car yet again and stacked boxes upon boxes, coming in through the door like he was moving in.

"Well, a lot of it was junk. And I had to admit, some was really gorgeous junk. Vials perhaps not exactly wild but at least a bit wicked. Ones that seemed to have flames inside, probably just some trick of the light. Ones that glowed with some phosphorous compound, or at least, that's what he said it was. Ones that looped in eerie shapes, like a snake eating itself."

"An ouroboros," I said.

"Yeah, something like that," said Mie. "Just all kinds of wild shapes and braids, forms I thought I would only find in challah bread, tangled shoelaces, Escher paintings, museums of the architecturally strange. Like seasoned sea navigators in glassblowers' bodies, heaving out such intricate sailor-knot creations.

"And then he pulled out this suitcase, and the color captivated me. Completely enraptured. Had my eyes locked on it like it was prey. A beautiful warm color, rustic and rich. When he cracked it open, something like reason left me. I just had to have it."

"It was this flask here?" I noticed the intersection where tube met bottle, like a majestic handle, was not really a self-intersection at all. It looked blurry, still drenched in the golden rays of the sun, but I tried to probe through the brightness. The intersection looked like it wasn't even there, as if the tube flowed naturally into the bottle. Was it some trick of the light or a flickering of four-dimensional space? I shook my head, ridding the laughable reverie.

"Yes, it's such a beaut, isn't it? But it's not just the looks. I experimented with it. Everything I put in there took on such a complex fusion of smells. A kind of earthiness we perfumers know comes from galbanum, a resin naturally occurring in Iranian plants, but I didn't put a drop of it in there. Chypre— citrusy mixed with the animalic, usually infused with the secretions of whales and of the anal glands of felines you'd find in tropical rainforests more so than in your local suburban backyard. Really expensive stuff that I can't afford to put in my line. But my nose picked them right up. Balsamic notes, sweet and warm, often associated with an Eastern flair, vanilla, myrrh, and shrub resins. Frankincense essential oils."

While Mie rattled off perfume lingo, all I could think about was Frankenstein. And my mind started wandering to the kinds of animal secretions that might end up on our skin for such lofty goals as allure and seduction.

"Frankincense?" my lips managed to utter, stupefied by her tsunami of fragrance trivia.

"Yes, frankincense, one of those scents used in aromatherapy and stress relief. Well, okay, let's put it this way. You gotta take a whiff yourself," she said.

She lifted the Klein flask. It looked so exquisite, almost fragile. Like it was quivering, waiting for a single, wayward high note to send it into shambles. I could imagine an opera singer tearing that delicate specimen into shards. The fluid in there continued to dance, eddies of a nonexistent river, swirling and passing off hues in haste like itinerant baton racers.

"These fragrant notes, they're not usually all in one mix, but there they were, all in there. Each time I made a fresh batch, they had all those traces."

She reached toward the bottom of the flask, and at the very center was a ring, lying flat and attached to a stuffed cork, plugging up the only opening to the strange form. She pulled the ring up and twisted it and cajoled the cork out.

I smelled nothing.

"I know what you're thinking. It's scentless. You have to get in closer. There's something about the dynamics of the bottle that circulates the scent. Some of it will pass through eventually, right out this hole and onto the surface. But the smell is . . . viscous, I think. Sticks pretty close to the bottle. You have to get close."

My skeptical nature didn't stop me from pulling in next to the bottle. If anything, my scientific mind had a few wayward hypotheses I was eager to dispel. There was only one way to find out.

I bent over, nose breaching the tubular void, and inhaled.

My sensory system overloaded. Scents I had never in my life explored flooded through my nasal cavity. Mushrooms upon mushrooms. Oranges upon oranges. A myriad of them. Tangerines, clementines, grapefruits, ones from the recesses of my mind, trips eastward with tropical drinks and expensive teas, calamansi, yuzu, and shikuwasa, topped with a colorful toothpick umbrella or upon a tinkling porcelain saucer. Earthy fungi that grew in dark woods, that sprang where no sunlight dared to graze. Things I could not name and did not even know had existed as a sensation.

A chemosensory violation. Coffee beans, old leather baseball gloves, honeysuckle, antique cabinets, newspapers, horse dung, fresh laundry, wet dog fur, durian, the humid pause before the rain, rare cheese, animal seepages. I could smell the fragrances branching off into more strands of smells, fractals of derivative and associated odors, some pleasant, some not so much but graphically charged nonetheless.

I recalled an old documentary I came upon while idly flipping channels on a late Saturday evening. It was about the limbic system, the oldest, most primitive area of the human brain. The olfactory bulb—that sounded so much like tulip bulbs to me—with its army of sensory receptors, shoots messages to the limbic system whose jurisdiction includes memories and emotions. The olfactory bulb nestles comfortably next to the hippocampus, part of the limbic system, vital in memory access and processing. The documentary narrator said in his low, pointed voice, "This is the hub where memories are formed and stored, a diary for later retrieval."

Ominous music cued, suggesting a frightful turn, and the narrator, his trendy thick glasses and blazer suggesting a cool, knowing authority, said, "For those who have experienced damage to the hippocampus, they lack the ability to create new memories."

I thought of this now, knowing my hippocampus was healthy and must be lighting up, neurons cavorting in fireworks displays, seizing time that has passed and gone, and drudging them up for me to bear.

I thought I saw the flow of the aroma, the mists of the perfume, flowing onto the outside surface of the flask and siphoning back in through the tube, an endless cycle that violated *outside* and *in*, that destroyed notions of the boundaries of self and the other, of interior and exterior, of foreign and local, all diametrically opposed concepts rendered meaningless.

I breathed in deep, engaged with the wild mists, the surging effluvium, letting them course through my body and flow out from my invisible, topologically wondrous tubes.

I remembered my birth, my mother's womb, and the amniotic fluid that spilled in spawning aggression. I recalled my first birthday at four when I got a new bike and gashed my head on the roadside upon my fall. My mind fast-forwarded; it invoked my teenage years with braces and bottled-up hybrid emotions, crushes that rang with the pang of youthful infatuation, gym rooms and bra straps and cliquish humiliations.

I remembered the sweetest of all sixteens, a party that never happened and that my parents could not afford, but I had run off with my best friend, Sam, and we spent a beautiful evening in the woods, bitten by mosquitoes, lacerated by forest branches and leaves, but jubilant nonetheless. I could see the leaves now, smell the woodsy bark and the stench and ferocity of the little wild mammals.

I remembered the darker years, the one-night stands, the self-doubt, the intensity of partying and alcohol. I could smell it now, the barf, the hanging over the toilet despite the excrement particulates, the hair laced with smoke laced with the stale taste of liquid paralysis stuck on my tongue, spreading across the roof of my mouth.

And the feeling of death that weighed on me, the trauma of one lost embryo and then another, the antiseptic tang, and my crooked smile that could never right itself. The smell of the alley, next to the garbage where I let it all out and decided to forget about it, cross it off in my journal as never happened. The oceans that took me, that grabbed me from an instant of yes, and I was sailing off with a mostly unknown partner on a voyage I could not really write in all its saturated details of corals, beaches, locals, and customs officers I bribed for docking.

And the train wreck that creeped on me until it veered into a blight, the morning coffees and chilled silences, the escalations of strained muscles in ecstatic animosity, bodily discharges and the fetor of undone laundry, used disposable chopsticks strewn on rugs and wedged in sour-cream-and-onion-potato-chip-sprinkled couches. The efflorescent hints of my partnered demise, the drunken lows of pungent morning bloody marys.

My humble, pressing imminence of the story of my life wrapped up into a course of vapor that chased itself round and round my torso, through my mouth, out all my cavities, and again and again, not quite as mathematically perfect as the *Kleinsche Fläche* that stood before me, its Germanic name coming to me like a rush of instinct as if conjured from an encounter long ago, a primitive rush of knowledge.

She capped it.

I straightened my dizzying self up, looked at the offending source of this befouling miasmic gas. I gave Mie a smile that I thought must have looked enigmatic if I were able to see it from her eyes.

She looked at me on tenterhooks, her eyes as sharp as claws as if picking the scavenged meats of my time-traversing flights of fancy.

I realized I must have encountered her years and years ago, perhaps lifetimes ago, a wily sage of chronologies lost, twisted and returned back to sender. Redolence of raw affect continued to flow through my system even as I surfaced to the present.

"So you'll sell it," I hear myself saying across the void from a space of mental peregrination.

"If it's commercially viable," Mie said, her smile turned impish, inward. "Which by the way, I'm guessing from your experience, it would be. No one can escape its purchase on retrospection and emotional revision."

I reached over and with a shaking hand grabbed the cork and pulled. And with a strength I never knew I possessed, I stuck her face into it, letting her nose peep through the void.

She was sucked in, the whole of her stretched out and thin at the cusp of its opening like light attenuated at the event horizon of a black hole.

I capped it and watched her slosh about inside. At first, her stretched self just flowed through in an endless loop, but she eventually became fixed in this non-orientable surface, no longer mixing, no longer circulating through the outside and in.

Still.

I wedged the flask with the lightness of her weight and all into the mauve velour lining of the suitcase. I pushed it in until the flask seemed to hold, molded into the protective foam, and pulled it shut.

With my hands still shaking, I snapped the clasps shut. I didn't know where I would be taking it, but I thought far, far away. Not even in an alley. Perhaps a faraway ocean, farther than the corals and beaches of journeys past, a no man's land where only the vastness of space could find it.

As I walked, my step was lighter, and I thought of the perfume name. *Anamnesis.* A Platonic concept, it referred to the knowledge of lives past that accumulate and exist within, that circulate with every reincarnation. The redolence of life itself, of experience and reawakening, of coursing through the very soul.

I trapped that malignant midwife who dared to awaken this recognition through advertent exposure of closed spaces. She violated the terms of the outside and in, of dormancy and activity, of containment and emptiness, stirring juices, defying the consistency of time.

The smells changed me; I was no longer the same, and the longer I walked with the suitcase in hand, the more this was true. The suitcase dragged so heavy minute by minute; its leather bottom threatened to graze the heat-soaked asphalt. I felt my shoulders shift, my legs contort. Every step betrayed me, revealing a savage bounce that I tried to but could not repress.

§§

D.A. Xiaolin Spires steps into portals and reappears in sites such as Hawai'i, New York, various parts of Asia, and elsewhere with her keyboard appendage attached. Besides *Nowhereville*, her work appears or is forthcoming in publications such as *Clarkesworld*, *Analog*, *Uncanny*, *Nature*, *Terraform*, *Grievous Angel*, *Fireside*, *Galaxy's Edge*, *StarShipSofa*, *Andromeda Spaceways* (Year's Best issue), *Diabolical Plots*, *Factor Four*, *Pantheon*, *Outlook Springs*, *Mithila Review*, *LONTAR*, *Reckoning*, *Issues in Earth Science*, *Liminality*, *Star*Line*, *Polu Texni*, *Argot*, *Eye to the Telescope*, *Liquid Imagination*, *Gathering Storm Magazine*, *Little Blue Marble*, *Story Seed Vault*, and anthologies of the strange and beautiful: *Ride the Star Wind*, *Sharp and Sugar Tooth*, *Future Visions*, *Deep Signal*, *Battling in All Her Finery*, and *Broad Knowledge*.

Nolens Volens

MIKE ALLEN

ONJA COULD NOT ABIDE THE MAN'S BLOODSHOT STARE any longer. "Mr. Reynolds," she said, pointing, "who is that at your window? Do you know him?"

Reynolds stopped his spiel and swiveled his massive head toward his office's luxuriant bay window. "Mrs. Delgado," the attorney said in his deep plantation drawl—stretching out the *MIZZ-zuhzz*—"I don't see a single body out there."

Sonja followed his gaze. No one stood at the window. The lushly seeded lawn gleamed green. Even though she had just watched a man in faded camo, dark brown skin offsetting hair white as fleece, limp from the street to the window across that very same lawn, his cane spearing the soil, fierce eyes fixed on her the entire time. In the instant she had spoken to Reynolds, the man had vanished.

"He must have . . . have ducked below the windowsill," she said, knowing how silly she sounded as soon as the words left her mouth. "He was standing right there, staring at me."

Reynolds glanced over Sonja's head at Ferguson, the PI in his employ: a short, wiry man with a face like leather stretched over a wooden mask. Sonja turned in time to see Ferguson shrug. "I'll go check it out," he said in a voice rough as pitted pavement.

Reynolds offered a non-smile and, as the office door shut, rumbled, "You all right with talking business while we wait?" From a desk drawer, he withdrew a sheaf of papers, dense with small-print paragraphs. Feverish sapphires in his wide pink face, his tiny blue eyes scanned her expression. Every bit of the wealth the man had amassed seemed manifest in his swollen girth, the bulge of his jowls. "I think you'll find it's an extremely generous contract."

"You've not even said what you want me to do. I'm not signing one thing until you tell me."

"Now, obviously, Mrs. Delgado, I'm requesting your services as an interpreter for someone whose spoken English isn't so good. I know what I'm offering you triples your usual compensation."

"Which makes me suspicious."

"Of the job or the person offering it?" His smile bared large teeth between the cotton of mustache and beard.

She ignored the thrown gauntlet. "What case is this connected to?"

"One we're gonna get tossed out tout de suite with your help."

He awaited her next question, but she chose to let the silence stretch. The man at the window had tipped her out of equilibrium. She needed to regain her balance.

She regarded the attorney's face, beady-eyed to the point of cartoonish villainy. ¡Que feo! Behind the moon of his head, the shelves of alphabetized law books spoke to a fussbudget nature at odds with his rumpled suit.

To her knowledge, Reynolds's heart held nothing but loathing for her gender or her race. His crony Mickey Burkhart had won election to council yammering garbage about secret Muslims sneaking across the Mexican border. The fact that Sonja's father was a Cuban refugee would make no difference to his ilk. Yet he wanted to offer her a lot of money based on professional reputation alone, so he claimed. Strings had to be attached.

He finally said, "I've been retained by Jefferson Dalton III."

Dalton was a scion of old money with a huge brick rambler of a house in the city and an even bigger one out in the northern quadrant of the county. Mona Rae Hunsaker—Dalton's flamboyant, bottle-blonde, young-enough-to-be-his-daughter mistress—turned up dead beneath the I-93 overpass two weeks ago. Police had released damn near nothing to the press, but Sonja had overheard just enough courthouse scuttlebutt to know that a throat slit ear-to-ear and a disconcerting absence of blood spatter severely undermined any substance-abuse-fueled-suicide theories.

Of course, Dalton had hired Reynolds. "You were expecting me to gasp in surprise?"

"If you give this a moment's thought, you might instead jump for joy at this windfall I've brought you."

"Judge Golden's assigned me a lot of cases this month. I'll need to check that list, make sure there're no conflicts of interest." If so, Reynolds's offer was DOA, and maybe that was a good thing.

He smirked. "I know there's no conflict. There is *nothing* on the dockets concerning my client, and with your help, there never will be."

Ferguson leaned in to whisper in Reynolds's ear. Sonja jumped, her chair scraping backward, her hands leaping to her heart. "¡Puta madre!" She had not heard the PI reenter the office.

The men ignored her. Reynolds's bushy eyebrows lowered, but whatever the unhappy news was, neither shared with Sonja.

When the PI straightened, he said, "You told her what we want yet?" He turned to Sonja without a pause for breath, speaking over her as she tried to ask about the man in the window. "I bet you think Jeff Dalton the Turd is a douchebag, and I don't blame you, but he didn't kill that girl. I got a lead on a witness who can clear our client, but he doesn't speak the language so good."

Sonja bristled. "The only language you bothered to learn, you mean."

Ferguson shrugged. "I know how to speak money and drugs. That's what matters in my line of work."

Sonja had heard such macho-sounding claptrap before, mainly from police officers justifying the bruise-covered faces of inmates. She gathered up her purse, shouldered the strap, and gripped her attaché with the test of good intention it contained still unsprung. "Sounds like you don't need me."

"Hey, hey, hey, I meant no offense." The PI's tone softened to a surreal degree, this gentle immediacy a complete mismatch coming from his pinched mouth. "This is only about acquiring a reliable affidavit from a Spanish-speaking witness." His gesture included Reynolds. "We lack the skill set for that. You come highly recommended."

Sonja knew better than to buy into obvious performances. Still, she sat back down.

"There's no doubt in my mind that what Jorge Mercado-Guerra has to say will prove our client's innocence. But to be sure, we need you."

"You're a neutral party," Reynolds chimed in. "Beyond reproach. Rare in this town. Exactly what we need."

"What makes you think he'll cooperate?"

"We know he wants to." Ferguson put his hands together in imitation of prayer. "He's made some mistakes in his life, but he has a conscience. He's devout, and it's not just a show."

"Uh huh. And what did you offer him?"

"A trustworthy translator." Reynolds again proffered the sheaf in his meaty hand. "Will you at least review the contract?"

She took it, noted the template it was drawn from, flipped straight to the page that specified payment. More than four times her standard court-appointment fee.

"I want to think about this," she said. "In the meantime, may I talk to you about something else?"

"You mean whatever's inside that sharp-looking briefcase?" His amusement grated between her shoulder blades.

"Yes," she said, keeping her voice free of inflection, a skill she'd honed over four years laboring in this city's hick-run legal system.

Even as she withdrew a pair of pamphlets, he went on, "I think I can save you the trouble of a speech. You're planning on a song and dance about that Erasing Barriers Foundation and what a help it is integrating the folks here who don't speak English."

Sonja stiffened, knowing full well how Reynolds viewed "Mexicans."

He reached out. "Lemme see."

Sonja passed him a pamphlet. He glanced over it and opened another desk drawer, retrieving an old-fashioned, extra-wide checkbook bound with metal rungs. He flipped past a couple dozen carbon stubs to a blank white form and scrawled across it, handing the filled-out check to Sonja with a flourish. "A worthy cause."

Sonja had anticipated the attorney's refusal as the excuse she would need to end this conversation. Instead, she gasped despite herself. She was staring at a $200,000 donation.

"I'd prefer my support stay anonymous," Reynolds said.

Sonja had not completely lost her head. "What are you expecting in exchange for this?"

Reynolds waved a hand at her. "What a cynic you are, Mrs. Delgado. I expect nothing whatsoever. I'd have done this a long time ago if anyone had thought to ask."

Sincere or not, he had just given the EBF enough funds to hire two more instructors.

"And it's yours whether you take the job or not," Reynolds said. "Whatever you're of a mind to do, I need to hear by tomorrow noon."

By the time she left, she'd completely forgotten about the bloodshot-eyed watcher at the window.

The microwave clock changed to 10:11. She stared at her cellphone (which read 10:09), willing Ferguson to call.

She reread (yet again) the text message the PI had sent at 9:15: *off 2 get jorge will txt when en route 2 office stand by*

Nothing about this meshed with normal standards and protocols. It even violated that bedrock axiom: no attorney liked to work after 5 p.m., especially not a plush tomcat like Reynolds. Contrary to television farces, nothing that involved attorneys ever unfolded in a hurry.

For Reynolds to make arrangements to collect an affidavit at midnight, Jefferson Dalton III must have paid exorbitant cash up front. He had to be terrified that the long arm of the law was actually going to touch him.

She waited in silence at her kitchen bar, her phone the only object on its polished, faux marble surface. She could have clicked on the radio to help time pass but didn't. When Eduardo was still alive, before the cancer sprouted in his stomach and tore him apart from the inside, he would have scolded her to relax. *Staying wound up won't make this go faster,* he would say.

In the bleak moments, when she and the bedroom clock lock gazes at 3 a.m., she's wondered if his "que sera, sera" attitude is what sent him to the crematorium, his determination to light the dark corridors of her life so great that he refused to acknowledge the ball of agony growing inside him.

The house she once shared with Eduardo had reflected all his eccentricities: indoor brick facades and gardens of white pebbles, an abstract painting of a spiny red-and-black orb that he insisted was a portrait of Eleggua. The duplex she lived in now was bland beige and showroom neat as if she could abandon it at any moment, even though she had lived there three years. Eduardo would never have stood for it, but he had no mouth and no say.

The phone shook with an insect wing buzz, and the screen lit up. It wasn't Eduardo's voice that came to her just then but her mother's. *Sacude todo el dinero que puedas de ese comemierda, mi Luz. Y no confíes en él.*

Oh, mama, I know, she thought. She put Ferguson on speakerphone. "Yes?"

"He's with me, and we're on the way. See ya at the office."

"My billable hours started with your text at 9:15."

The PI barked a laugh. "That's the fat man's problem, not mine."

When Sonja arrived at Reynolds's law office, Ferguson's scarecrow form awaited her, silhouetted in the open front entrance. Goose pimples rose on her skin as she pushed past him, moving from the muggy night to a mausoleum-cold interior. The PI clanged the doors shut behind her.

Jorge sat across from the moon-sized lawyer in the same yielding leather chair Sonja had sat in for her audience. A small fellow: shorter than Sonja, skin browner, hair gelled in a pompadour, he wore a black T-shirt printed with an image of a nude woman embracing a skeleton with angel wings. His mouth hung open. When his gaze alighted on her, his lips stretched in an almost-smile.

Reynolds nodded his ponderous head in greeting.

Ferguson handed her a sheet of paper smudged with photocopy toner. "Before we record anything, we need you to read this to him."

Sonja glanced at the paper—some sort of poem was printed on it, lines grouped in couplets—and studied Jorge's slack jaw. "Is he stoned?"

"He's doing great," Ferguson said. "He's waiting for you to read him that."

The poem was written in English. "You want me to translate *this* for him? Why? It's gibberish."

Reynolds harrumphed. "It's code. He won't utter a word until he hears it."

"That makes no sense—"

"It's not supposed to," Ferguson said. "Like Mr. Reynolds said, it's a code. It's gang-related. A nonsense rhyme makes a way more complex password than one word alone. I got this from a DEA source who slipped it to me from a sealed court file. But I don't know how to say it in Spanish."

Sonja shook her head. "You can't be serious. I can translate that, but it still might not come out the way he's expecting to hear it. If you're not just shitting me."

"I'm paying you," Reynolds said. "Quite well. That's all that matters."

Ferguson touched her shoulder. "Mrs. Delgado, I know you ain't got nothing in common with Jorge here. You never ran with a gang in your life. Gangs though—hard life, hard knocks—those are things I'm up to speed on. It won't hurt you to do this, and we won't get anywhere until you do. You'll see."

She glanced over the poem. It was strange, but wasn't poetry always strange?

Split my tongue and I become the serpent
Slice my heart and I become the vein
Pith my mind so I become your servant
Pierce my eyes and I'll embrace the pain

She took a stab at the first line. The translation came easily, as if another mind moved her lips and tongue, breathed through her throat. Her voice adopted a sing-song cadence. Reynolds was speaking in the same cadence as if he was reciting it with her except the basso syllables he uttered were neither English nor Spanish. She made out a phrase, unfamiliar syllables: *nolens volens*.

When she finished, she had no memory of the words she'd just recited. Jorge stared at her with glistening eyes, his lips stretched into a four-cornered rictus.

"Ask him if he's ready to talk now," the attorney rumbled.

Sonja intended to do nothing of the sort. She intended to demand an explanation from Reynolds, but instead she obeyed his order.

"Si," Jorge answered in a monotone.

"Please tell him that we're going to start recording."

She relayed the message, hardly registering her own voice. Jorge's head jerked as if he struggled to nod or struggled against the gesture. Ferguson took an eon to place a finger on the tape recorder perched on Reynolds's desk and push the play button down. *¡Qué raro! ¿Quién usa cinta de casete en estos días?* Sonja thought, a junk thought.

"Mrs. Delgado, this is where you earn your keep," Reynolds said. A dark, freezing cloud bloomed from his mouth.

"*Did you drug me?*"

"*Now, Mrs. Delgado, when could we have done that?*"

"*What's 'nolens volens'?*"

"*It's just Latin. Lawyer-speak.*"

"*Something happened . . .*"

"*Something wonderful. You were perfect. I cannot thank you enough.*"

The conversation took place in a dream for all Sonja knew. The nightmare of her husband's return blazed many times more vivid.

Lying atop the covers of her own bed, she had no memory of how she got there. Eduardo crouched naked between her bare legs, his weight distorting the mattress. The beautiful brown of his skin had blanched under the twin assaults of cancer and chemotherapy, but even in death, he'd never drained so pale. His bones strained against his skin. His bloodshot eyes fixed on her crotch.

He raised an arm. The skin of his hand had molted at the wrist, an empty flap like a rubber glove peeled loose from rot-moist, asphalt-black flesh and new fingers twice as long as before.

He touched the inside of her thighs, and each fingertip was a red-hot skewer searing into her fat and muscle. She screamed as he pressed down, her flesh boiling out around his acid palm.

Again she awoke screaming. This time, she resisted the exhaustion that kept dragging her back into sleep, only to frighten her awake with the same dream.

She blinked into curtain-filtered sunlight that banded the room at the wrong angle to signify morning.

She wore the camisole and pajama bottoms she always chose for sleeping. Her purse slouched atop her dresser where she never ever put it, a white envelope tucked into its side pouch that turned out to contain one of Reynolds's elongated checks, an amount scribbled across it that more than satisfied the terms of her contract. Her phone perched on her nightstand, fully charged.

Words glowed across its screen from a number she didn't recognize: *your handiwork is all over the news*

She grabbed up the phone and called the foundation, reached the after-business-hours automated response. Then she noticed the date on the display, which couldn't possibly be correct. She called the court clerk's office, again an automated response. She half-staggered, half-dashed, downstairs to the den. The Spanish newspaper sat in a neat stack atop the coffee table, the way she always positioned it. She grabbed the top copy: *Sábado, el 22 de Marzo,* the same date on her phone display. She had no memory of placing the papers there. She had no memory of anything beyond the interview with Jorge five days ago. And it was after 6 p.m., according to her phone. She never slept that late in her life.

all over the news

She scrolled through her social media feeds on her phone. A tingling like the jabs of hot needles spread from her chest and neck as she found the first relevant headline: "Authorities probe apparent suicide: man charged in Hunsaker slaying found dead in jail." Before she even read his name, she knew the "suspect" would be Jorge Mercado-Guerra.

He had turned himself in to the police Wednesday morning. No mention of Reynolds or even Dalton in any of the articles or video clips.

That pricking sensation descended her spine as she finally thought to check voicemail and found none. Not even missed calls. She had lost five entire days, missed a week's worth of meetings, classes, court appointments, and not one person had checked on her?

She wondered if television news might tell her more. Idly she regarded the screen, shiny and black as Eduardo's hand in her dream. Behind it, beyond the curtains that draped the sliding patio door, a shadow moved, a blurred silhouette of someone framed in sunlight. The figure took another step to the side and jumped.

Sonja recoiled toward the stairs with a shriek, but her eyes had deceived her. Nothing slammed against the glass doors.

¡Dios mío! ¿Qué caramba fue eso? But it could only have been a trick of the eye.

She yanked the curtains aside. The patio furniture gleamed happy colors, the unoccupied deck immaculate.

Head spinning, she rushed to the kitchen, threw open a top cupboard, and seized a bottle of Kahlúa that had sat unopened for more than a year. She downed half its bittersweet contents in a single desperate swig.

The last drops were disappearing down her throat when the doorbell rang.

"¿Quién está ahí?" she croaked.

It rang again. Mind swathed in woozy warmth, she squinted through the peephole. A black man with white hair leaned on a cane, his red-rimmed eyes looking back at her.

A swarm of angry flies buzzed in her brain, driving her to speak before her fear could stop it. "I saw you at Reynolds's office."

"And I saw you," he replied evenly, his voice like moist honeycomb.

"Are you part of what they did to me?"

"I might be your only hope of fixing it." His lips curled in a sad smile. "But first you'll have to help me figure out exactly what it is they did."

She tottered, caught herself against the door. "Why would you help me?"

"That lawyer's people once did me a wrong, but they didn't finish what they started. That's all you need to know." That smile widened, and she mirrored it. She couldn't help herself.

Sitting at her kitchen bar, still wearing his threadbare camo jacket, he introduced himself as John Hairston, "But my name don't matter one damn bit. That asshole Reynolds has a pact with the Boneyard, but I got one of my own. Now tell me what happened 'cause I have a hunch, and I wanna know if I'm right."

He spoke nonsense, but a compulsion to hang on every word kept Sonja rapt. In the back of her mind, her mother's voice repeated with increasing urgency, *¡Corre! ¡Corre!* "Carter Reynolds hired me to interpret for that man who killed himself—"

"I don't care about that. Tell me about the incantation."

Tipsy, bewildered, angry, she wanted to tell him off for talking over her, and at the same time, she needed, for reasons not at all clear, to voice everything he wanted to hear. She resisted both impulses. "What do you mean, incantation?"

"Was there a song? A riddle?"

"Yes!" At once, she felt better. "They made me translate a poem."

Hairston leaned in, his breath reeking of something that wasn't alcohol. "How did the poem go?"

She shook her head, furious with herself. "I can't remember!"

"Did it start with splitting tongues and serpents?"

A shadow memory of her mouth moving while some other force spoke through it. "I . . . think so."

"And the patsy was compelled to confess. And a poor man died in a rich man's stead." She had her hands clasped on the bar, and he placed his atop them, engulfing them to the wrists in furnace warmth. "Was there anything else?"

There was. "He said Latin words. 'Nolens volens.' Said it was legalese."

"It sure is. Means 'willingly or unwillingly.' The right words for this situation."

He squeezed Sonja's wrists. "You live clean, don't you? Like a nun?"

"What? I have a husband . . . had a husband . . ."

"That's just fine," he said. "I think the fat man finally fucked up. I think I can restore your mind. If you want me to. If I do that though, you're gonna understand what got done to you. That might save your life, or it might make its ending even worse."

An ending. An escape. The thought pushed against the compulsions that held her fast.

"You have two ways out of the mess you're in, ma'am. The quickest way is the most painful. Do nothing—what's coming for you will find you, and it'll be over. The other way, your life will never go back to what it was, but you get a chance to live. Not a good one but a chance."

That growing urge to flee finally found a voice. "I don't want to die."

His smile glowed from an abyss. "You accept my help then?"

"Please."

"Then listen." He recited a poem of his own.

She clutched the strings of Hairston's words, permitted herself to act in ways that made no ordinary sense. Throughout, she retained consciousness and clarity.

She drove to a crumbling slum she'd never been to before, parked by an alley too narrow for a car, and followed it into an empty courtyard lined with windows like plucked-out eyes. She whispered, "Nolens volens," three times. When she left, a shadow trailed her.

She went back to her apartment and watched television, the images passing the time without coalescing into meaning. The black thing stood behind her, reflected in the television screen every time the images went dark. Whenever she got up to relieve herself, she was alone in the den.

After midnight, she selected the longest knife from the kitchen and a small screwdriver from near the furnace and went for another drive, a shiver of pleasure tickling her spine as the shadow climbed into the car behind her. More joined it, crawling onto the roof, clinging to the undercarriage, even running beside the car on two legs or four as she led them all out into the country.

She had never driven that stretch of road, never seen that driveway burrowing through the trees, but she killed the headlights as she reached it and navigated every subsequent turn in the dark. She killed the engine before the tree line thinned. She emerged into an immaculate yard, moonlit silver, that encircled a luxurious plantation house, the columns of its full-surround porch proudly gleaming, its gables arched in condescension. No lights shone from the windows.

One of the shadows returned from a foray, projecting a picture into her mind, a guest-room window with the inner sash open, outer screen loose. A voice in her mind, her own, shouted *¡Esto esta chiflado! ¡¡Qué estoy haciendo!?* but she popped the screen out with the screwdriver. The gap beneath the sash was narrow. Lucky that she was such a tiny woman.

As she padded through rooms and halls and up the stairs, a horde moved with her, their presence sending joy through her veins.

She found the bedroom door ajar. Beyond, a huge shape pulsed under floral comforters.

She wanted to run down the stairs, out the door. She pushed into the room. Heavy breathing filled the stuffy space.

Like a would-be parlor magician, she ripped the covers from the bed in one swooping flourish, exposing the monsters beneath.

A pale, quivering mountain covered with hoary down, Reynolds lay stark naked and erect, his tree-trunk-sized thighs spread wide. A woman that Sonja didn't know was squeezed between them, using both arms to push up his belly, so she could suck on the organ it shaded. She was older than Sonja but much younger than the lawyer.

Sonja struck with the knife, drawing a dark, liquid line into the fat above his groin. She spat, "Nolens volens." Adding after a moment, "¡Muera, comebola!"

Reynolds's lover sprang upright as he bellowed, propelling herself straight into the arms of the shadow-thing crawling up behind her. Her skin sizzled and boiled as soon as it contacted the creature's black flesh. Her scream didn't stop when the creature shoved a hand into her mouth. Red ichor gushed out around its wrist. Five more creatures joined it on the plush bed.

Somehow her muffled, gargling scream grew louder until the creature's acid flesh eroded the roof of her mouth, and its fist punched through into the bowl holding her brain.

Reynolds too was repeating the phrase, "Nolens volens," just as she had in the courtyard, but the creatures, already claimed by her incantation, ignored his attempts to conscript them to his will. The strings of Hairston's willpower guiding Sonja imparted this knowledge to her, what Reynolds was trying to do, why it wasn't working.

Tendrils of joy coiled through her belly.

The shadows corralled his mass, their limbs clamping around his and eating into his adipose like hot knives into marzipan. His chant became a howl.

The lead creature discarded the woman's limp body and crawled toward Reynolds's blood-streaked groin. It dipped its glistening head, and Reynolds screamed ten times louder. The creature kept crawling forward, the skin of its scalp dissolving the flesh it contacted, its head disappearing inside the attorney's belly. It continued, relentless, its shoulders burning against his wobbling thighs. Reynolds shrieked, a giant infant experiencing the reverse of birth.

Liquefied innards sloughed onto the mattress. Sonja marveled that the attorney was still awake, still shrieking, the creature hidden to the waist inside him now, and just as before, she just knew, rejoicing in the revelation, that the shadows knew how to inflict hideous damage without triggering death, prolonging the cruelty to sweeten the sacrifice.

Reynolds's voice went silent, but his mouth kept working as if his cries had shifted into frequencies beyond human hearing.

He slumped, and the shadows went still.

The phantom ecstasy faded from Sonja's bloodstream. Her nerves thrummed with terror. She was alone in an unfamiliar bedroom with two corpses and a platoon of shadow-creatures, their slate-blank faces all turning toward her. She had been meant to die as a result of Reynolds's curse, as doomed a lamb as Jorge Mercado-Guerra. With Hairston's intervention, the attorney had died in her stead, but now the spell was at an end, and the shadows had no more compulsion to obey. They were free to act as they pleased.

Yet unlike Reynolds, Hairston had left her memory of all the spell's words and workings intact. She repeated, "Nolens volens," and the creatures stilled. Wisps of ecstasy stirred at the base of her spine.

She had not eaten since Hairston called at her duplex. Still somehow, she doubled over and vomited green bile until she couldn't breathe. The creatures, which did not breathe, remained huddled in the growing lake of Reynolds's blood. The vice compressing her lungs wouldn't release.

Outside, a car engine puttered to a stop. The creatures relayed to her mind the sounds of soft footsteps, a key clicking in a lock, a need for new sacrifice.

"Jeffrey?" Ferguson called. "Penny?"

Perhaps the attorney and the PI had a link beyond employment, a bond extended by the unholy arts they trafficked in. Surely Ferguson had seen Sonja's car, must have driven around it. The eagerness of the creatures expanded through her body, their desire overcoming her revulsion.

Sonja wasn't alone as she descended the stairs.

Ferguson realized much more quickly than Reynolds that the creatures would ignore his command, and as he fled through the house, they gave chase. Sonja fought the temptation to follow the creatures, to indulge the pleasures worming through her and exult in the hunt and impending feast. When they were out of eyesight, she instead dashed out the front door, across the lawn, and into the woods, fumbling for her car keys as clouds hid the moon.

If she could reach the road, she would drive as far from the city as her gas tank would let her. Headlights blazing, she began the painstaking back-and-forth turns to swivel her car around. She hoped Ferguson could fend the creatures off a long time because if he died before she reached the end of the driveway, she knew she'd never get away.

She glanced in the rearview mirror and shrieked at the sight of her husband's death-paled face, anguish twisting his mouth, red-rimmed eyes bulging. But the back seat was empty, and when she checked the mirror again, he was gone.

§

World Fantasy, Shirley Jackson, and Nebula Award finalist **Mike Allen**
has written several poetry collections, including *Strange Wisdoms of
the Dead* (a *Philadephia Inquirer* editor's choice selection), *The Journey
to Kailash*, and *Hungry Constellations*; a twisted dark fantasy novel,
The Black Fire Concerto; and three collections of strange and scary
short fictions, *Unseaming*, *The Spider Tapestries: Seven Strange Stories*,
and *Aftermath of an Industrial Accident* (forthcoming 2020). Recently
he gave a talk, "Horror and the Weird," at the Library of Congress
(which you can listen to on the *Outer Dark* podcast). With his wife
Anita, he runs the Mythic Delirium Books imprint, home to the
Clockwork Phoenix anthology series and critically acclaimed works
of fiction by C.S.E. Cooney, Theodora Goss, Nicole Kornher-Stace, and
Barbara Krasnoff. By day, he works as the arts and culture columnist
for the daily newspaper in Roanoke, VA, where he and Anita live
with a cat so full of trouble she's named Pandora. You can follow
Mike's exploits as a writer at descentintolight.com, as an editor at
mythicdelirium.com, and all at once on Twitter at @mythicdelirium.

   Mike would like to thank Stephanie Berkeley De La Fuente, Martha
Simmons De La Fuente, and Carlos Hernandez for their help with the
Spanish dialogue in "Nolens Volens."

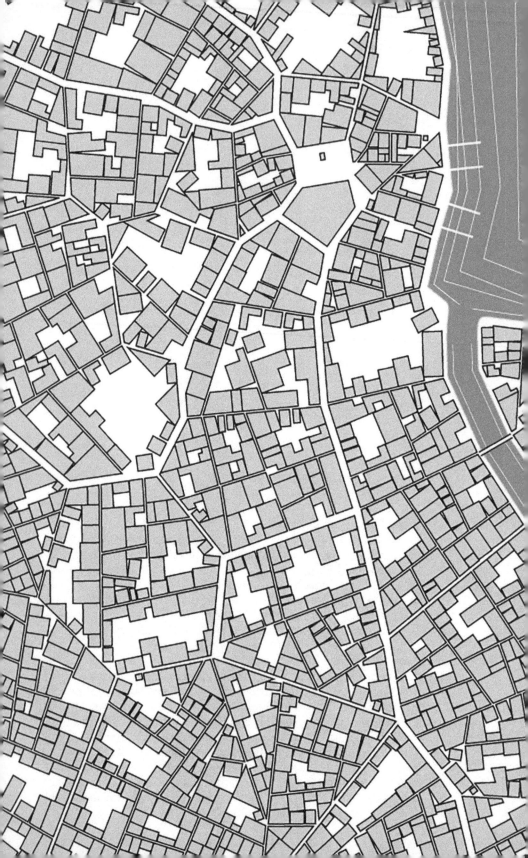

Vertices

JEFFREY THOMAS

VERY DAY, THE INVERTED PYRAMID THAT HAD APPEARED in the sky above the city grew somewhat smaller. When it had first manifested, it blotted out quite a substantial portion of the sky—bearing in mind that with all its massive towers, sometimes not much of the sky could be viewed from the streets of Punktown, depending upon one's location of course—but two months later, it was just large enough to block the sun when the two happened to align. (At such a time, a great shadow fell upon the city, pouring into the gaps between towers, the spaces between the lesser buildings at the base of the towers, and collected in a chilly pool at street level.) The pyramid, as people had taken to calling it, was actually just a triangle without depth, and so utterly black, it did not reflect light or reveal any detail within its borders.

When it had first materialized, Vera D'Cruz had read about it a bit on the net, but she still hadn't fully grasped what the pyramid was or how it had enabled the race called the Vertice to come to Punktown. (Something about creating an orthocenter through which they could pass.) Their numbers entering the city had diminished by now to a trickle, and when the pyramid would eventually shrink so much that it disappeared, it was said that would be the end of their migration. That much she knew.

Vera had more personal, day-to-day concerns, vastly smaller in scope, but for her, they eclipsed that black shape suspended in the sky. For instance, today, if Dario was late to come pick up their daughter Mia *again*, then she would be late to her 5 p.m. to 1 a.m. shift at the pub *again*, and she would get another berating from her boss, Cheng. She was gearing up to berate Dario first. Still, if there was one good thing about their divorce, it was that Dario was a good father and welcomed his daughter sleeping over at his place every weeknight. Weekends, Vera had her turn for that. Their work arrangements made it so that Mia didn't have to spend any time being watched by anyone but her parents. (Dario said she was overprotective, but Vera didn't trust anyone else to watch her child; it might have been different if either of them had family in the city, but they were all down south in the Outback Colony.) And since Mia had begun going to school a couple years ago, that had made it easier for Vera to sleep more during the day.

Vera had set out a snack for Mia who sat in front of the vidtank, encompassing one wall of the flat's living room, to tide her over until Dario could feed her dinner. She paced the room behind her child, already dressed in her waitress uniform of white blouse and black slacks with the holographic logo of the Drunken Caterpillar and other badge-like holographic "flare" floating about her chest. She desperately wanted to light a cigarette, but she didn't smoke when Mia was around. Better yet, a seaweed cigarette, but she was afraid Dario would smell it. She'd told him she had quit.

To tamp down her anger, she distracted herself by talking with Mia. It took a couple of times saying her name to crowbar the seven-year-old's eyes from the VT. "So how was school, honey? Anything fun today?"

"Alicekraa was funny today," Mia giggled, turning toward her mother. "She's always funny."

"Alice what?"

"Alicekraa. You know. I told you about her. The girl with the long—"

"The Vertex girl," Vera said.

"Vertice, Mom. She's a Vertice."

"Right, okay. Why, what did that thing do?"

"She's not a thing, Mom. She's a kid." Mia laughed again as she recalled. "That long thingy sticking out of her head is always poking everybody. Today"—she burst into wild laughter for a few seconds before she could get the words out—"when Judge dropped his stylus and bent down to get it"—a renewed burst of laughter—"Alicekraa turned around to look, and her thingy poked him in the butt!"

"Nice," Vera said.

"You should see her try to walk through a door, Mom. She's always bumping her thingy into the wall. One time, Jackie came *this* close to shutting her thingy in the girls' room door!"

"That *is* pretty crazy," Vera said. "In fact, I wonder if she should even be in the same school with the rest of you. They've only been in town for a couple months. How do they know these people are really . . . oh, never mind, honey."

"Are really what, Mom?"

"Never mind."

The apartment's door buzzer sounded, and Vera darted to the kitchen. She let in Dario who was practically panting, no doubt for effect. "Sorry!" he gasped. "Traffic was insane . . . there was an accident . . ."

"Don't make me accidentally yell at you," Vera said, slinging Mia's overnight bag from the floor and into his hand. "I have to run. I had to run fifteen minutes ago. I hope I don't run into an accident on my way."

"Said I was sorry, Ver."

As Mia crossed the room—"Daddy!"—Vera looked past Dario, out the screen door of her second-floor tenement flat, and down at the parking lot. She saw Dario's vehicle idling, hovering two feet off the ground, and a figure was silhouetted in the passenger's seat. She asked, "Who's that in your car?"

Dario looked up from hugging Mia. "Someone I'm seeing."

"Oh? *Someone* must mean you aren't seeing that Sinanese cutie anymore."

"That Sinanese cutie is named Lhi. And no, we stopped seeing each other a few weeks ago."

"Good to know."

"I don't ask you about who you date."

"Well maybe you should. Maybe you should know who I have around your daughter. Just like I'd prefer to know."

Dario opened the door, his hand resting on Mia's shoulder. "I thought you were in a big hurry."

Vera bit back an obscenity. Not in front of Mia.

"See you in the morning," Dario said. "Have a good night at work."

"Right." As she watched her ex-husband and daughter start down the stairs, she asked, "So what's this one's name?"

Dario looked back up at her and said not too loudly, "Katylaa."

"What?"

"Katylaa." Then Dario continued hustling his daughter down to the waiting hovercar and the dark figure waiting inside.

"Any of you guys interested in dessert?" Vera asked the table of young men, coworkers who'd just gotten off the job.

"Are you on the menu?" one of them asked, smiling up at her.

"Nope, sorry, but we have . . ." and she launched into a description of the offerings. She wasn't much fazed; it happened all the time.

She keyed their dessert and coffee orders into her wrist comp, saw an alert that the meals for table three were ready for pickup, and started toward the kitchen. On her way, she glanced again at one of the booths lining the Drunken Caterpillar's far wall. A business meeting apparently. Two Choom men in five-piece suits sat on one bench. The Choom were the indigenous race of this world, Oasis, though people of Earth ancestry now outnumbered them in Punktown. They looked fully human except for their mouths, which extended back to the ears. She was familiar with far stranger beings; how could she not be, living in this city? For instance, at the bar with its third bottle of Zub in front of it sulked a lone Mo-mo-mo-mo: a race with features that, not only didn't begin to compare to the physiognomy of humans, didn't resemble any terrestrial animal living or extinct and whose very asymmetry almost hurt her eyes, preventing considering their appearance overly much. So what was it about the Vertice over there—sitting opposite the two Choom businessmen in the booth—that so unnerved her?

She supposed it was that, because they were almost human, the thing that set them apart seemed all the more grotesque by contrast. Still, weren't the Choom almost human? But there was more to it. Not only the circumstances of their arrival—that portal or whatever it was, a starkly outlined hole in the sky by day that shut out a patch of stars by night—but the history of their origin. She had read of that on the net.

This Vertice appeared mostly as a human man in his early thirties, deeply tanned, and dressed in a handsome, well-fitted business suit. In conversation, he smiled and nodded at the pair of Choom. When he nodded, the long protuberance that jutted from his forehead bounced in the air. It looked like a reddish-brown stick that someone had jammed through his skull, piercing his brain. She saw this extremity, which had one joint toward the middle, fold down a little to avoid poking his tablemates opposite when the Vertice leaned forward to pluck some of the complimentary popcorn that had been brought by their waitress. Vera was grateful she was working the tables today, not the booths.

Vera had read about how, ninety-one years ago, a group of scientist-explorers had gone forth from Earth in a now outdated teleportation pod that had malfunctioned en route and gone missing, thought to have been lost to an alternate continuum at best or "unconstituted" at worst. Only with the recent arrival of the Vertice had the fate of those people come to be known. The explorers had ended up on an inhospitable world where they had encountered the last of a dying sentient race. These beings had the appearance of a tripod, their forms chiefly comprising three long reddish-brown legs, hard and jointed like those of a king crab but smooth instead of spiny. Each leg ended with an opening through which a cluster of thin, black tendrils could be extended, so the race could manipulate objects and communicate with these in a kind of sign language. Where the three legs converged, there was only an orb the size of a baseball, housing certain organs. The brain, such as it was, was distributed throughout the entire tripod.

The race in this form was extinct now, but in order to preserve something of themselves—and, as the Vertice claimed, in order to adapt the suffering humans to the hostile planet they were trapped on—the tripod beings had merged with the explorers.

The Vertice were the descendants of those explorers in whom the last tripod beings had taken refuge, but they were not considered as that race merely inhabiting human vehicles. They were not being thought of as two races in one body but had been accepted for what they claimed to be: a third race, independent and unique. They had developed their own culture and their own technology as their arrival attested. Because of the origin of their ancestors and because Punktown was a melting pot by its very nature, they had been allowed to come through. Only a few months since their appearance, they were settling in Punktown's neighborhoods. Joining its workforce. Entering its schools.

When she was bringing the meals to table three, one plate in each hand, she stole another look at the booth with the Vertice and two Choom. Their waitress, Dhi, had brought their meals too. Dhi was Sinanese, herself human in appearance but for her pale blue skin. Sinanese women were touted for their beauty, and Vera was surprised that Dario and his girlfriend had split up. Well, maybe he felt it was a blessing; Vera had heard the woman had been a handful— hot-tempered and a gambling addict. But what was it with her ex-husband and non-Earth women? Before the Sinanese, he'd gone with a Choom. (At least Vera had liked her well enough.) Was it the exotic factor? Was he jaded with women of his own kind or just trying to see how many non-Earth races he could sleep his way through?

As his dish was being laid before him, the Vertice bent his forehead protuberance down a bit again, and from the hole at its end, a batch of thread-like black tendrils emerged to wriggle in the air—as if to take in the smells wafting off his food—just very briefly like the flicking tongue of a snake, and Vera shuddered.

"Go do your homework, honey," Vera said, toweling from her shower.

"I will, Mom, in a second," said Mia, filling a glass at the bathroom sink before heading back to her room.

"Your father better not be late today," Vera said after her.

"I told him to stop being late, Mom!" Mia called.

"*Thank* you."

Vera went to her bedroom, donned her outfit for the Drunken Caterpillar. She had asked Cheng, once, the meaning of the pub's name. He'd told her it referred to an elixir sold in Asia, long ago, as an aphrodisiac and cure for cancer—its chief component being the larva of the ghost moth turned by a fungus into a fruiting body. He then said, "But we all know booze is the best elixir because it makes you *forget* about limp dick and diseases."

Vera came out into the living room, saw Mia sitting on the sofa staring at overlapping holographic screens floating in front of her. Good. It was her second-grade homework. She went on to the kitchen, lifted her coffee mug from the counter, and slurped at its tepid contents. Her eyes fell on a drinking glass resting on the windowsill over the sink. It was filled with water, and in the water leaned a tubular brownish chunk of something, trailing long black roots from one broken end.

"Mia," she yelled behind her. "What is this?"

"What, Mom?"

"Get in here."

Mia bounced across the threshold, and Vera pointed. "What's this thing here? Some school project?"

"Alicekraa gave it to me, Mom," Mia explained. "She told me to put it in water for a few days, and it will grow."

Vera's mouth opened a bit, and she stared at the drinking glass. "I have to get rid of this, Mia."

"What? Why, Mom? Alicekraa gave it to me as a gift!"

Vera wheeled around. "Why? What did she say it would do?"

"She said it was a surprise, Mom!"

Vera whirled back, picked up the glass, stepped to the trash zapper, and dropped it in. Water and brown thing and all. She punched the activate key.

"Mom!" Mia cried. "That was mine! Alicekraa gave it to me!"

Vera turned to see tears in her daughter's eyes. "I'm sorry, honey, but Alicekraa shouldn't have given it to you."

"*Why*?" Mia wailed.

"It isn't . . ." Vera didn't know what to say. She didn't know what she'd destroyed. "Come on . . . here." She snatched up her pocketbook, dug out her wallet, extracted a twenty-munit bill from it, and held this out to her child. "Here, Mia. You can have this instead. I bought that thing from you, okay? You can spend this with Daddy the next time he takes you to the Canberra Mall."

"Okay, Mom," Mia sniffled, accepting the bill.

"That bitch," Vera said to herself, looking at the trash zapper. It had finished "unconstituting" its contents. "That little bitch."

"What is it, Mom? Who's a bitch?"

"Don't say that," Vera told her. She was shaking outside and in. "Never mind."

It was raining today. Vera had come to like such days. The inverted triangle, as seen through the breaks between skyscrapers, was subdued by the approach of evening and veiled behind the bunched gray clouds—not so starkly, vividly black. Sometimes, gazing up at it on brighter days, she suffered something like vertigo and had the impression the so-called pyramid was not just delivering the Vertice here but sucking something *into* itself at the same time. Feeding on something in Punktown. Its energy. Maybe its sanity. In some small way, she felt, it preyed on hers.

Just before her shift began, taking advantage of a break in the rain, Vera went out to the Drunken Caterpillar's parking lot with its puddles and wet vehicles reflecting neon and holographs, had a cigarette. On her wrist comp, she called the home number Mia's teacher, Ms. Qualoon, had given parents a few months ago at the start of the school year. She left a message, but only a minute later, the teacher returned her call. Looking back from the wrist comp's screen was an attractive Choom woman with a bowl cut dyed metallic orange. Vera idly wondered if Dario would want to go to bed with her if he could.

Vera described to Ms. Qualoon the gift that Mia's classmate, Alicekraa, had sent home with her and what she had done with it. "Now I wish I hadn't destroyed it, though, until I could show it to you. I'm concerned it might have been something dangerous."

"How so?"

"Well, you know . . . like the larva of a parasite or something."

"Ms. D'Cruz, the Vertice are not parasitized. They started as two races who willingly combined to better their chances at survival."

"So the Vertice tell us. Their ancestors aren't alive to back that up."

"They reproduce as humans do. They're born just the way you see them now with the proboscis and nonhuman internal features in place. They've shown that. The Colonial Network wouldn't allow them here if they considered them a threat."

To Vera, it sounded like Ms. Qualoon was regurgitating indoctrination.

"With all respect, Ms. D'Cruz, Punktown as we know it today was built by colonists—by your people colonizing my world—and it remains a city that welcomes all sentient lifeforms. All these identities are the identity of Punktown."

"Look, I'm not a racist!" Vera said. "It's just . . . look at the insane level of crime in this city. Not everyone who comes here is a saint exactly."

"The descendants of the *Earth* colonists here are just as responsible for those crimes as non-Earth races," the teacher pointed out, the long line of her Choom mouth bowed down sternly.

"So what was that thing Alicekraa gave my daughter?"

"From the sound of it, a plant, maybe a flower. But if it will make you feel better, Ms. D'Cruz, I'll speak to Alicekraa and tell her not to give Mia any more gifts of that nature."

"Of *any* nature," Vera said in a tight voice, itching for another cigarette.

"I just want to mention that Alicekraa is a very sweet and considerate little girl."

"Right. Thanks." Vera broke the call.

Looking up at the spongy clouds in the slate sky to gauge whether the rain might resume, Vera saw a glittering speck emerge from the misted triangle and begin its descent toward the city. Another shuttle. More Vertice come to settle.

With her work week finished, looking forward to a weekend with Mia all to herself, Vera took the subway to the Canberra Mall to pick her up from Dario. Having gotten home from work around 2 a.m., she had slept in until ten and was to meet Dario at noon. There he would turn Mia over to her, and he'd told Vera—to rub it in, knowing she wasn't currently seeing anyone?—that he and his new girlfriend would go on to eat at one of the mall's numerous restaurants. Vera planned on taking her daughter to the mall level that was one great arcade and indoor carnival, after which they'd get lunch themselves elsewhere in the mall at someplace Mia liked.

Despite these pleasant plans, however, she arrived at the sprawling Canberra Mall shaken and angry. She had had to switch lines at Johnson Station, and while waiting for her train—listening to a guitar-playing busker sing a decent version of a Del Kahn song—a man had shuffled up to her. She'd pretended he didn't exist, a skill one developed in Punktown, up until she peripherally noticed the long, reddish-brown appendage bobbing from the center of his forehead.

"Can you spare a munit or two, miss?" said a gravelly voice.

Vera had turned on the man with her eyes already bulging. He had the prerequisite unkempt beard and layers of dirty clothes of the countless homeless men in Punktown, but he was a Vertice.

"*Really*?" said Vera. "You're really begging for money? How long have you been here—two months? One month? Is this what you people have to offer us?"

"A munit or two, pretty lady?" repeated the homeless Vertice. His skin was bronzed by the harsh sun of his homeworld, its wrinkles like cracks in a dried-out mud bed. Just the tips of his black tendrils had poked out shyly from the opening of his protuberance.

"Blast you!" snapped Vera, backing away from him. "Don't come here if you can't take care of yourselves!"

"You don't understand, miss," the old man had said in a voice tottering from drink or drugs. "It's a hell back there. I couldn't get my feet under me. I can do that here with just a little help."

"I pay my taxes. That's all the blood I'm giving you. Go lie down on the tracks if you want an easy solution."

With his glassy, drunk-or-drugged eyes—human eyes or merely portholes for something inhuman hiding within?—still on her, the Vertice had straightened his proboscis. A horrible screech had come from the little hole at its end— looking very much to Vera like the meatus of a penis—like a chunk of iron dragged agonizingly across a sheet of tin. Vera had clapped her hands over her ears, turned, and run farther down the platform, and luckily just then, her train had come whooshing along through the tunnel.

But here she was now on the mall's ground floor just inside its main entrance, waiting for her daughter, and that was a good thing. The best thing. While she waited for Dario, she strolled along the inner curve of the circular vestibule, looking into the shop displays spaced there. Pocketbooks, shoes, and clothing hung on automatonic mannequins going through endless loops of graceful movement.

She stopped in front of one curved window with her mouth falling open. The mannequins displayed behind it were not automatonic, did not move. They had featureless gold faces: no hair, no eyes, only a suggestion of a nose and mouth. But they did sport a long gold appendage, jointed once toward its middle, sprouting from the forehead of each.

"Are you kidding me?" Vera said aloud. The mannequins modeled autumn fashions, and two of them wore turtleneck tops. How did they even get those tops on the mannequins with those long proboscises without taking the things' heads off?

Vera wondered why the governing body of Punktown, indeed the Colonial Network, was shoving the Vertice down their throats. What did they have to offer? Because there had to be some benefit for them to spread their arms so invitingly. Was it the technology the Vertice had developed that had enabled them to jump here from so far away? Well, if so, the network would have to improve on that, wouldn't they? Because that window was closing tighter by the day.

Inside the shop behind the mannequins, she saw a Fekah moving amongst the hung clothing, its gender not apparent to her. It looked like a bipedal albino toad, its head and its feathery pink gills enclosed inside a red-tinted bubble helmet. Looking away from the window, she saw a gray-skinned Kalian woman with a blue turban-like headwrap and ritualistic facial scars, crossing the vestibule, and in the opposite direction, with shopping bags clutched in each hand, went a Torgessi, its towering nude body sheathed in turquoise and black scales, its massive head like a cattle skull missing its horns.

Truth be told, Vera was always nervous around the Fekah because without their protective helmets the very sound of their respiration could deafen a human in close proximity. She was suspicious of the Kalians because she'd heard they worshipped a demon called Ugghiutu, which in fact might be an actual extradimensional entity, and she disapproved of the way women were repressed in their culture. And the Torgessi . . . well, they were fearsome if angered, and she found their very height and bulk imposing. But when she was out and amongst these and other races that disturbed her, she tried not to acknowledge them too much . . . in the same way she had tried unseeing that homeless person until he'd accosted her. She was even able to do this at work, even while waiting on such races. She didn't look at them too closely. She would look at her wrist comp, look elsewhere around her, smiling like a mannequin herself while taking their orders. It wasn't all non-Earth races . . . oh no. It really wasn't. She thought the Choom were okay—they were pretty inoffensive on the whole. Well, except for gang kids, criminal types . . . and she hadn't been happy with the way Mia's teacher Ms. Qualoon had said—without emphasizing the words, but she might as well have done so—"Punktown as we know it today was built by colonists, by *your* people, colonizing *my* world."

"Mom!" she heard a familiar voice cry, and she saw Mia skipping toward her. Falling behind a little was Dario, and Dario was holding hands with a woman in a snug rust-colored turtleneck and black leggings, an ensemble that showed off her slender figure. The woman had gold-brown skin and long black hair and a jointed appendage curving out from the middle of her forehead like an insect's antenna, serving as a third eye.

"Oh . . . come on, Dario," Vera said, staring, but Mia was crashing into her lower body, and they put their arms around each other.

"Mom, I can't wait to go to the arcade!" Mia chirped.

Dario and the Vertice woman had caught up now, and Dario smiled and said, "Hey. This is Katylaa. Katylaa, this is Mia's mom, Vera."

"Hi, Vera," said Katylaa, smiling too, showing off perfect teeth that glowed against her sun-gilded skin. She held out her right hand. Vera pretended it didn't exist. She looked only at Dario now.

"Can we talk for a minute? Over there?" She jerked her head.

"Uh, okay." Dario wasn't smiling anymore. Vera could tell he didn't like that she hadn't accepted the Vertice's hand . . . hadn't returned her greeting. "Mia, you stay here with Katylaa for a minute."

"No," said Vera. "She can come over there with us."

"She'll be fine right *here* with Katylaa for a *minute*," Dario snapped, and he started walking in the direction Vera had indicated. She went after him, and close to one of the shop windows, they faced each other.

"You're something else," Vera said to him through gritted teeth. "Why don't you fuck a Mo-mo-mo-mo next?"

"What is the problem, Vera?"

"How can you stomach being with that creature, Dario? How can you overlook that *thing* sticking out of her head?"

"She's a person, not a *creature!*" he hissed. "And why should I overlook that thing sticking out of her head any more than I'd overlook her arm or her leg? It's part of who she is."

"Oh, so you like it, huh? What does she do with it . . . stick it up your ass?"

"Oh for . . . Vera, I can't believe you. You don't know Katylaa at all, and you're talking about her like this?"

"That's right. I don't know her. I don't know her kind, and it's too soon yet for *any* of us to know them! But here you are exposing my daughter to her. Tell me, Dario, has she moved in with you yet?"

"No! But what if she did?"

"Because if she did, I wouldn't allow my daughter to sleep under the same roof with her!" Vera cried, her voice growing louder.

"Look, we share custody. You can't tell me my daughter can't stay at my apartment."

"I can if she's endangered!"

"Endangered *how?* Endangered *how*, Vera? What is it with you? Are you smoking seaweed again or gone back to the hard stuff from your druggie teenage years? Because if that's the case, I can talk about endangering Mia too."

"Blast you, Dario. I'd never go back to hard stuff again. But you can't keep your hard stuff out of every wet, alien hole."

"I think you're just jealous, and this 'alien' thing is only an excuse."

"I'm telling you . . . I won't have my daughter living in the same apartment with a being we know so little about. And I will not allow my daughter to be alone with that person *ever.*" She motioned toward where Mia stood looking their way, Katylaa standing beside her with her hand resting on top of the child's head. From here, Vera couldn't tell if the Vertice had heard them. If so, her neutral expression didn't give away her reaction.

"Just take Mia," Dario said, "and have a good weekend with her. Okay, it's a shock . . . I should have told you beforehand . . . I'm sorry. You'll calm down. You *have* to calm down, Vera."

"I don't *have* to do anything! You're the one who'd better be watching out. Not just for my daughter's sake but your own."

Dario sighed, wagged his head, and gestured for Mia to join them. She ran to him, and he kissed the top of her head where Katylaa's hand had been. "Be good for Mommy, honey."

"Always, Daddy."

Uncertainly, Katylaa was drifting toward them, but Dario went to intercept her before she could get too close. He took her hand again and guided her toward the entrance into the mall proper.

Vera saw Katylaa glance back at her over her shoulder. Her attractive face was still neutral, but for one second, black tendrils flashed from the tip of her proboscis, whipped the air, and sucked back in again.

After the weekend, when Dario came to pick Mia up again so that Vera could return to work, they had further words. Dario took his daughter by the hand and led her from the apartment while Vera was still yelling. She went out to the landing of her stairs and continued shouting down after him. At the foot of the stairs, he glared back up at her and exclaimed, "Will you stop carrying on like this? You're going to scare her!"

"Who? Mia or *her*?" Vera stabbed a finger toward Dario's hovercar, in the shadowy interior of which a dark shape could barely be discerned.

"Come on, honey," Dario said to Mia.

Every day, Mia got on and off her school bus in front of Vera's tenement building. Vera would nap for a while when she got home from her job around 2 a.m. until Dario dropped Mia off on his way to work. Vera would see Mia onto the bus and go back to bed. She would wake in the early afternoon, get ready for work, await Mia's return on the bus and thereafter Dario's arrival. This fractured sleep pattern left her in a constant state of weariness, often bleariness. She would fall asleep watching VT while she waited for the bus, awake with a jolt, and forget whether she had to get Mia onto the bus just then or off it. Would forget if it was a weekday or the weekend.

As she had done before, she flinched awake on the sofa, glancing around wildly looking for Mia. The time told her it was afternoon . . . the bus would be here in twenty minutes. She let out a relieved if exhausted sigh, got to her feet, and straightened the blouse of her uniform.

That morning when Dario had brought Mia back from staying overnight, Vera had stripped her down and pulled her into the bathroom. "You're going to have a shower," she'd told her.

"But, Mom, I had a shower last night!"

"Don't argue."

Sitting on the toilet cover, Vera held her disrobed daughter by the arms and examined her boyish body, turned her around, leaned in close, and rubbed her thumb over the center of the girl's forehead. No odd mark there . . . blemish or wound.

"Has Katylaa tried to give you any gifts?" Vera asked her. "Anything like Alicekraa gave you?"

"No, Mom."

"If she does, you tell me, okay?" Vera shook her just a little to emphasize the point. "You tell me. And you tell me if you see anything like that in Daddy's apartment. Got it?"

"Okay, Mom, okay! Jeesh."

Now as she considered stepping outside early to smoke a cigarette while she waited—or remaining inside to smoke a seaweed cigarette to soothe herself— Vera returned her attention to the murmuring VT and saw there had been a news feature running about the Vertice. She commanded the VT to increase the volume. A Choom news reporter was saying, "—3 p.m., by which time every last one of the Vertice will have safely arrived on Oasis for a total of thirty-seven thousand, seven hundred twenty individuals who will be residing in Punktown—leaving not one Vertice behind on the world they lived on for so long."

"All of them?" Vera said. "*All* of them?"

The Choom spread his huge grin at Vera as if to mock her and said, "Punktown welcomes them all to their new home."

No time left to smoke seaweed before the bus came, though she craved it. Vera commanded the VT to shut off and went out her flat's front door and down the steep front steps of the embankment her tenement building was perched on, to street level.

There was a factory across the street, which emitted a headache-inducing smell like burning plastic, so Vera never opened her windows on that side of her building. It also emitted strange sounds: a constant hum of power, which nagged her like tinnitus, spiced with the occasional clang or rattle or rumble. It was giving off another sound at the moment, one she hadn't heard before: a shrill, continuous metallic whine. It was like a fiddle bow of infinite length dragging along her spinal cord.

From the left, down the street, she could see the yellow hoverbus approaching. However, something in the sky caused her to gaze upward, squinting against the sun, and she saw the inverted triangle. She hadn't noticed it before because it had now grown so small it looked like a stationary aircraft, one of many craft that floated above the city. It was the metallic shriek that had drawn her eye to it because she had realized then that the sound was coming from there.

The bus floated to a stop directly in front of her, but Vera didn't look away from the three-cornered black hole in the sky. She saw a bright spark emerge from it—a shuttle . . . the final shuttle—and streak downward toward Punktown.

The screech radically jumped in volume. Icicles in her ears, and Vera shot her hands up to clamp her palms over them, but she couldn't look away even as her daughter came bounding down the bus's steps. "Mom!" she cried happily.

The metallic shriek intensified, grew deafening. Didn't Mia hear it? It reminded Vera of the sound that homeless man had made from his proboscis when she'd confronted him.

As she watched, gripping her head, the black triangle closed up and was gone, and the screech was abruptly cut off, and Mia threw her arms around her waist.

The bus's door slid shut and the vehicle started into motion again. As it passed, with eyes streaming tears, Vera saw a little girl looking back at her through one of its windows, her forehead appendage pushed up against the glass, and from its tip for just a second, black tendrils flickered out like a serpent's tongue and sucked back in again.

§§

Jeffrey Thomas is an American author of weird fiction, the creator of the acclaimed setting Punktown. Books in the Punktown universe include the short story collections *Punktown*, *Voices From Punktown*, *Punktown: Shades of Grey* (with his brother, Scott Thomas), and *Ghosts of Punktown*. Novels in that setting include *Deadstock*, *Blue War*, *Monstrocity*, *Health Agent*, *Everybody Scream!*, and *Red Cells*. Dark Regions Press has recently published the shared-world anthology *Transmissions from Punktown*, and Miskatonic River Press/Chronicle City have released an RPG set in the world of Punktown. Thomas's stories have been selected for inclusion in *The Year's Best Horror Stories* (editor, Karl Edward Wagner), *The Year's Best Fantasy and Horror* (editors, Ellen Datlow and Terri Windling), and *Year's Best Weird Fiction* (editor, Laird Barron). Thomas lives in Massachusetts.

Like Fleas on a Tired Dog's Back

ERICA L. SATIFKA

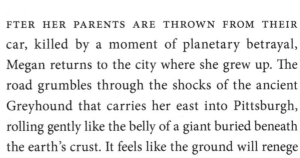

FTER HER PARENTS ARE THROWN FROM THEIR car, killed by a moment of planetary betrayal, Megan returns to the city where she grew up. The road grumbles through the shocks of the ancient Greyhound that carries her east into Pittsburgh, rolling gently like the belly of a giant buried beneath the earth's crust. It feels like the ground will renege on her any second. It feels like death.

She calls the number she'd been given, the one for the foster family that's been taking care of Kyle. The arrangements are made, and before too long, they're staring at each other across a room that is not his. It has a football motif. Kyle hates sports; she hasn't seen him in three years, but she remembers that much about him.

"I made it," she says.

"You're too late. You missed the funeral." Her little brother gets to his feet, grabs his cane, motions at his packed luggage.

Megan doesn't apologize because she knows she can never make it up to him. Instead, she changes the topic. "I got us an apartment. You'll have your own room."

"I have my own room *here*." Kyle's fingers shake as he steadies himself against the royal-blue wall. They're a mere four floors up in an old building, barely out of the realm of danger, and this room hasn't been earth-proofed. She can't wait to leave.

Megan hoists Kyle's packed duffel bag onto her shoulder. "It'll be okay. I miss them too, you know."

Kyle glares at her, and even though she's ten years older than him and could easily kick his ass, she backs away. "You don't know a damn thing about it. You weren't here."

Forty-five seconds. That's all the longer it lasted. But forty-five seconds had been enough. The earth had grown tired of life, the scientists said. The planet was activating its immune system.

The Event. The Dying. The Adjustment. You could use any of these or over a dozen other euphemisms interchangeably. Everyone knew what you were talking about.

Megan tips the cab driver, a turkey-necked old man. He tucks the bills inside his cashbox, his hands quivering almost as much as those of her brother. She picks up Kyle's duffel bag; her things are already inside the rented duplex. She nods toward the door on the right side of the long porch. "C'mon."

Kyle slowly makes his way down the sidewalk, his bad leg dragging. Just as they both reach the wide wooden porch, she feels a spasm pulse up from the earth like a muffled belch. Instinctively, she grabs Kyle's hand. He flings it away in disgust.

They weren't earthquakes. When the earth activated its immune response, it was evenly felt all over the planet from Pittsburgh to New Zealand. They could probably even sense it in Antarctica, Megan thought. No earthquake worked like that, nor did any act of terrorism. Compared to the Event, the aftershocks are only an annoyance, but one that hints at a greater destruction possibly to come.

It was safest in the cities with their new smart architecture and ready access to medical care, so people flocked to them. They left the machines in the fields. The random belly-rumbles and occasional blasts of magma that periodically break through the surface don't bother the machines.

Megan and Kyle's duplex isn't smart architecture, but their bedrooms have been retrofitted to offer at least a little bit of protection. Kyle sneers at the smooth obsidian walls. "It won't hold. Not if the Big One happens."

"That *was* the Big One," she says, not clarifying "that."

"You don't know. You don't have the dreams." Kyle looks much older than his fourteen years, and very little of that is because of the cane.

"You're right. I don't." She throws the duffel bag down on the living room floor. "So maybe I should shut my mouth."

Megan stalks into the kitchen. She wonders why she's mad at Kyle. Because she *is* mad, she realizes, her hands clutched into tight fists at her sides.

It's not his fault their road woke up when Mom and Dad were driving on it, she thinks. Not at all, but still it had changed her life. She'd had to move back here from Chicago, a land of high-rises, where she had slept through the Event just as her parents' car had skidded on the awakened asphalt, throwing Kyle from it, sailing off West End Bridge, pitching itself into the Ohio River.

Not that Chicago had been any better, at least in the days directly following the Event. Because anyone who was adjacent to the earth's surface, whether on the first story of a house or out in a field or in a vehicle, was in the impact zone.

The death toll was less than one might have expected but still reached into the tens of millions with injuries far exceeding that. Even if one hadn't been affected physically by the heaving of the planet or its brief exhale of toxic gases, many survivors have the dreams. Whether they were glimpses of the future or a symptom of post-traumatic stress is a matter of considerable scientific debate.

People who have the dreams don't like to talk about them to anyone who doesn't, and it isn't polite to ask.

Megan wheels around. She wants to ask Kyle about the dreams, ask him what he meant by the Big One happening. Even if they're not close, he's still her brother. He has to tell her.

She walks into the living room. Kyle is slumped in the corner, a pouting expression on his face. "No couch?"

"It's being delivered on Thursday."

"Not going to be a Thursday," he says. "The planet's ending tomorrow. It's blowing itself up this time instead of trying to shake us off." He makes an explosion gesture. "The dreams told me."

Fear drips like cold water down Megan's spine.

Kyle waits a few moments and speaks again right before she feels herself about to pass out. "I'm just fucking with you, sis."

The smart architecture hums at night and runs deathly hot. Megan twists and turns on her bed, stripped down to only a T-shirt and underwear. Despite the padding between them, she can hear Kyle's screams. Not everyone who has the dreams screams at night, but Kyle apparently does.

She knots a thin robe around herself and pads into the unsafe yet cooled kitchen. Cracking eggs against the side of a pan, she quickly cooks and eats a too-early breakfast.

Megan reads the paper for an hour—the former tenant hadn't cancelled their subscription—until Kyle limps from his sweltering room to join her at the table. She motions toward the remaining eggs, which have been set to warm on the stove.

She lets him finish his breakfast before she asks the question. Asks it slantwise anyway. "Seems like last night was hard."

Kyle shrugs. "It was fine. You get used to the humming."

"What's in them? The walls?"

"The Technology." He pronounces the word with a capital letter. There are a lot of capitalized phrases in the world these days.

"Is it safe? These things aren't going to give us cancer, are they?"

He doesn't respond, just awkwardly rises to his feet. Kyle has to go to school; she'd forgotten about that.

The life insurance money had put Kyle in a good school, a safe structure built of gleaming, black smart architecture, newly erected in the ruins of PNC Park. It's in the new style, ninety stories tall with its bottom levels reserved for equipment to keep the building running. Copters composed of the same insulating technology shuttle residents from place to place, so one's feet need never touch the ground. Every city in the world that could afford it was being rebuilt along these lines, identical black monoliths designed for safety, not aesthetics. Megan has the feeling that tourism is going to become a lot less popular when all the cities are done rebuilding.

But right now, the world is in transition and will be for the next several years at least. So for now, most people live on the ground instead of the near sky and take their chances with cheap retrofitting of the existing structures. In places that can't even afford retrofitting, they insulate themselves with prayer.

Megan misses her Chicago apartment, the one that had saved her out of sheer luck. She'd wanted to sign a new lease, maybe bring Kyle over to live with her. But then her rent doubled. High-rise buildings are a precious commodity now. Only peons sleep on the ground, and that includes Megan and Kyle.

She drains her third cup of coffee and catches the trolley downtown. It trembles on its tracks as if aware how precarious its situation is.

The earth moves just enough to remind her, to remind everyone in the world, that it is alive.

A few weeks later, after a summer spent either roasting in her smart room or taking her chances in the kitchen, Megan sees her first balloonman.

The balloons of the balloonmen are carnival-colored, a riot of pigment against the newborn black monoliths of downtown Pittsburgh. The balloonmen are brightly clothed as well and are often known to sport unusual facial hair. To Megan, they look like steampunk cosplayers trying just a little too hard.

"Halloooo," yells the balloonman from his wicker basket, hanging ever so delicately from the round bulb of nylon itself.

The balloon touches down on Liberty Avenue where traffic has been blocked off for it. Only the rich can afford to live this way, spending upward of 99 percent of their time in the air, completely free from the earth's violent immune response to the humans living on its surface.

Out comes the balloonman, followed by a robotic servant. A security system, constructed of the same material that makes smart architecture, snaps around the basket. Clearly, historical accuracy has its limits.

Megan slows her work, only halfheartedly stapling the progress reports together for that afternoon's executive meeting. She squints at the scene twenty-four floors down.

Only fifteen minutes later, the balloonman sprints from the shopping center he'd walked into, his arms bulging with rations and kerosene. The robot, even more laden with packages, follows behind. The security system snaps open, and before Megan can staple another report, it's gone, a speck in the sky.

Some people give the balloon the finger as it leaves the earth's rollicking surface, and Megan hears a few shouted *Fuck Yous*. But mostly, people accept the balloons. Because balloonmen mean tax money. Fully one-fifth of Pittsburgh's income relies on taxes paid by passing balloonmen.

That's what I need to get for Kyle and me, she thinks. *A balloon of our own. It's the only way to be really safe.*

But even as Megan thinks these thoughts, she knows it's a pipe dream. Balloonmen are techie types; they'd been millionaires before the Event, and they were still millionaires. Many of them had gotten into smart architecture on the ground floor. She and Kyle will never catch up.

Megan beats Kyle home that day. She ignores the news—it's just another recalibration of the death count as it's been for the past four months—and pulls up an application form.

She doesn't have the money for a balloon. She doesn't even have the money for this, but chances are meant to be taken.

Kyle isn't happy. "I'm not living in one of those places."

"We're all going to be living in those places soon. I'm just getting us in there a little faster."

He glares at her, takes his dinner into his black-walled smart room, and she spends the night alone.

Megan and Kyle are eighteen stories up on a monolith in an apartment less than half the size of their duplex, which wasn't exactly roomy. She's tried to hang Mom's photographs and Kyle's music posters up on the walls, but the slippery material won't allow decoration. Megan throws a colorful blanket over their ratty old couch and calls it a day.

The monolith provides complimentary transportation for all of its residents, which is part of the reason rent is so high. Gleaming black copters shuttle Kyle to school and Megan to work, and the ground and all of its ominous twitching becomes somewhat of a memory.

Kyle's dreams have stopped, or at least, Megan doesn't hear them anymore. In fact, the entire monolith is as soundless as the duplex was cacophonous, and Megan gets a white noise machine to compensate.

One Saturday morning, Kyle picks at his food. He hasn't eaten any of it.

"What's wrong?"

Kyle keeps pushing eggs around on his plate as if debating whether to talk. "I'm tired."

"But you're sleeping better," Megan says before reminding herself that she's not supposed to ask him about the dreams. Or reference them even.

"I'm going out." He pushes his plate forward, grabs his cane. Megan doesn't ask him where, and when his black copter spins away, she gets dressed for her own second job and takes the elevator down to ground level.

Salvage duty. On the surface of the sickened earth, unprotected. Kyle doesn't know she works down here. She doesn't intend for him to ever find out. If he does, he'll tell her to quit, say that he doesn't want to live in a monolith anyway. Which is basically the truth.

Megan crests one of the humps of broken-down detritus that surround the base of the monolith, which used to be a hospital. Other salvagers are there as well, throwing concrete chunks and gloppy medical waste into one of the several recyclers set up. They too are made of the black material. They contain Technology.

The ground rumbles only faintly today, and like everyone here, she's gotten used to it. She takes out her pointed stick and begins to collect old newspapers.

A shadow occludes the sky, and Megan looks up, expecting a balloonman. Instead, it's a copter, but one that appears to be diverting from its normal flight plan. It looks as if it's about to crash into the next monolith over, but at the last second, the copter bucks and pivots, driving itself into the earth about two blocks from where Megan and the rest of the salvage crew work.

The majority of the humans on the ground stampede for the elevator, but Megan and a few others push forward, picking their way down the broken pavement to gawk at the copter.

The machines aren't manned, or at least, they're not supposed to be. But when Megan peers into the cracked windshield of the copter, she sees a person wired into it. Young, probably female. Definitely dead.

A man near her blanches; she thinks he's about to throw up. Nobody says a thing. They return to salvaging.

It's around six o'clock on a weeknight, and Kyle still isn't back. He's been going out more and more often for long stretches at a time. His walkabouts were originally a weekend-only thing, but they've bled into the rest of the week. Megan waits for him at the shuttle landing and calls for one herself. She has a pretty good idea of where he'll be.

She stares at the wall of black in front of her, separating her from the cockpit. Is there a person in there too? Was that even a person? Megan taps on the cockpit, which resonates faintly.

"Hello? Is someone in there?"

No response.

When she gets to her parents' ruined house, it's nearly full dark. The copter won't land on the spasming earth, but it does hover for long enough to show her that Kyle isn't there after all.

Fuck, she thinks. Her eyes fill with unwanted tears as the memory of their house, the memory of her dead parents, flashes through her brain. The copter carries her back to the monolith, acting as if it can't wait to get back to the place where it belongs.

The next morning, Megan calls the school, but he's not there either. She would call the parents of Kyle's friends, but she's not even sure if he has any. If so, he's never talked about them. She goes into his black-walled room and hunts for clues, but he's left nothing behind. As if he knew he was going to do this.

"You ran away," Megan says to nobody.

She leans against the smart architecture, feels it hum. She thinks she hears something deep within, a signal in the noise. It's like a voice speaking to her through layers of thick fabric.

You know something, don't you?

Megan's head rushes with images, and an electrical sensation runs down her spine, coursing across her leg, down to her foot. She shakes it violently, falling down on Kyle's bed in the process, tangling herself in his faded Batman sheets.

He never wanted to come here. He was afraid of this place, afraid of what it would do to him. Maybe he'd known about that pilot or whatever powered the machinery in the lower floors of the monolith. Perhaps he'd dreamed about these things.

Megan wonders if Kyle is closer to her than she thought he was.

Down in the belly of the apartment building, churning machines exhale a vague, sweet-smelling vapor, and the engines of the monolith sing in her ears like tinnitus.

Nobody's tried to stop Megan from coming down here, which makes her worry. Surely these levels have to be restricted? This area is for technology only. Technology . . . and maybe something else.

"Kyle?" Megan holds up her flashlight like a club; it turned out not to have been necessary in the brightness of the monolith's control chamber. "Kyle!"

She inspects each of the humming machines, the technology that makes the heaving landscape livable. Like the buildings themselves, they are blocks of seemingly impenetrable black slabs. Megan slams her fist down upon one; the pain is blinding.

At the end of the rows of machines is a door. Could Kyle be behind there? She rams her shoulder against the door as if it would do something, as if she's able to destroy the door and even the monolith itself through sheer force of will.

Something cracks under Megan's skin, and she staggers away from the door, swearing.

"You have him in there, don't you? *Don't you?*" But even though the monolith talks, it doesn't talk to her.

I should call a medical copter, Megan thinks as she climbs the black stairs to the lobby of the monolith, which is actually the seventh floor. She very nearly makes it before collapsing.

The camera of Megan's mind judders when she awakens, doubling the image of the camp around her: its fires, its huddled residents. The arm she'd broken is bound to her chest in a sling.

"Kyle?" The earth sighs, and Megan realizes that she's on the surface, unprotected. Her teeth chatter.

"Over here," says a voice behind her.

Megan swivels and gropes her way toward a nearby fire where Kyle sits cross-legged, his cane across his lap, his hands extended. For the first time, she realizes how cold it is. Almost a season has passed with them sealed into the monolith.

Daybreak splashes color on the mountains that surround the outskirts of Pittsburgh, and the monoliths jut from the landscape, the smart architecture alien and jarring.

Kyle hands her a charred piece of spitted meat. "Eat this."

Megan squints at it, trying to determine the source and then shrugs and digs in.

A balloon sails over the closest ridge at its full height, not touching down any time soon. Megan hands the spit back to Kyle. "I just wanted to keep you safe. Keep us safe."

Her brother feeds a wood scrap into the fire. "We'll be safe," he says, "if we listen to what the ground is saying. If we don't overstep our boundaries. The planet doesn't want to kill us. It's just . . . sick."

Sick of us, Megan thinks. *We're the fleas on its back, the sand in its eye.* "We'd be safer in the monoliths."

"I'm not going back there."

"*Why?*" Even as she says it, she thinks she knows why. The technology has a price. All miracles do. Megan can almost hear the sound of the technology talking, burrowing its way into the minds of the people still inside. Her leg still aches from her one-way conversation with the wall of Kyle's room, almost more than her arm.

"Trust me, sis. I'm the one with the dreams. And you don't want to see what those buildings will do." He pauses. "Eventually, anyway."

"But how are we going to live down here? *How,* Kyle?" As she speaks, the ground shifts beneath them, the living earth rolling around its digestive juices.

He doesn't respond, just pokes at the fire, his expression full of resignation and beneath that hope.

§

Erica L. Satifka is the author of the British Fantasy Award–winning *Stay Crazy* (Apex Publications) and the forthcoming rural cyberpunk novella *Busted Synapses* (Broken Eye Books). Her short fiction has or will appear in *Interzone*, *Clarkesworld*, and *It Came from Miskatonic University*. She lives in Portland, OR, with her husband/occasional co-writer, Rob, and an assortment of strange cats. Visit her online at ericasatifka.com.

Urb Civ

KATHE KOJA

ERE, YOU—YOU, SELMA—

Mr. Bertrand, uh, her name is Salma—

What? Be quiet, you, newbie—the sudden flick of a bead of flux, molten and dripping, he jerks back his arm just in time—*Selma, Salma, show them,* the old man offering the ancient welding wand that Salma accepts with one dexterous hand, flipping the green eyeguard down with the other, demonstrating to the class clustered behind the steel worktable how to mend a spankbot's broken arm. At the table's head the old man watches, right eye in perpetual squint, right arm clumsy to dig in his jacket pocket for what, for a contraband cigarette that Salma lights for him with a soldering gun: *Merci,* to her, then *You see?* to the rest, a brief scowl aimed his way, *see how she did? Good work! Next, we gonna fix up a dragonfly.*

And Salma nods, he nods, they all nod: two women, six men, motorbike roughriders and teenage malcontents, shaved heads and black-wrapped braids and a wispy purple beard, all the students of this cold late afternoon, but *Smoke break first,* says Mr. Bertrand, carefully checking the street before heading for the stairs, his tread heavy and uneven, like a machine on the verge of breaking down—

—*want to come?* and it takes a moment, a wasted moment to realize Salma is talking to him—*Me? Sure! Sure, I'll go*—then follow her down, past four grim

floors of pinch locks and accordion gates, repurposed security flats, a squatters'
stronghold under permanent siege and *The Gunnysackers*, says Salma over her
shoulder, *used to have, like, the whole second floor here. You heard of them, right?*

Sure. They were a rebel army, holding the heavy blast door for her to exit, into
the alley with its lone bulging trash bin, out to the street's winter sun where he
shivers inside his waterproof parka; Salma in her nylon anorak seems unaffected
and *Bertrand knew them*, she says, nodding toward the old man standing now
at the corner, hunched and wary as a sentinel, Mr. Bertrand whose school has
always been the go-to place, the place to learn how to build and burn, hack a sex
toy, defy the government. *Bertrand knows everybody. Ask him sometime about
his friend the poet, the one who broke off a citizen cuff—*

Broke a cuff? That couldn't have happened.

It did happen. Lightstick fished from a kangaroo pocket, she offers him a
cigarette, he shakes his head; blowing smoke, her throat is smooth and brown
as buckwheat honey. *He broke it off and got away.*

The citizen cuffs were unbreakable—

They say dragonflies are unbreakable, too, white smile around the yellowed
cigarette but *Material flaw*, he says firmly. *The dragonfly design is flawless, only
the material can fail—*

You're sticking up for a dragonfly? one eye screwed shut, right eye, like
Bertrand's—and then she smiles again, a joking smile because it must be a joke,
who would stick up for dragonflies, and the police state that launches them,
their lasers and tasers and *Flawless design*, he says, with a smile of his own, half
a feint, half at that skin, those hazel eyes below the fireproof bandana, Salma like
a princess in welder's drag. *You have to give credit where credit's due.*

Is that how they do it uptown?

Uptown? No, no actually I'm from Montréal—

Canada? they still have that? another joke, waiting for his smile in return
then *Montréal*, she says, *that's a long way away. How'd you wind up here?* as a
cough booms, Mr. Bertrand's ugly and wet, no wonder cigarettes are illegal!
but Salma drags deep, waiting for his answer so *I came from school*, he says. *My
master's in Urb Civ—placement derangement, but it's really about how things
work together. Or fall apart—*

You mean like this, her backhand gesture to the building, the scorched and
boarded block: a storefront mosque and silent tavern, old transit shelter greyed

out by years of vandalism, sharp piss smell even in this cold. *My degree's in folklore studies . . . I bet your profs never saw anything like this in real life.*

You bet right, which is exactly why he came here, why he volunteered for active service—call it spying, call it infiltration, without boots on the ground nothing will ever change. And this place, this city is overdue for change, for rescue, black rings of decay around all the world's cities like a fable of rot and danger, the dark forest strangling the fair castle; folklore, sure. *I wanted to see if I could help, so instead of wasting time in grad school, I came here.*

Do you like it here?

What do you mean? and when she does not answer, *It's a great city in some ways,* thinking of where he stays, the quiet dormlike apartment uptown: there are other agents in the building, he knows, though none of them know each other or each other's names, even at university they never knew each other's names. In his neighborhood the sidewalks are busy and the trains are mainly clean, the tea kiosks on the corners are clean, the signs and billboards advertise products that, on this street, a person would be jumped or worse for even having. *It's better than where I came from*—not Montréal after all but New Miami, where the security still depends on drones, slow and clunky as an old man stumping downstairs: nothing like these dragonflies, fast and accurate, nearly silent, once you hear it it's already deployed . . . The first time he saw one here he nearly gasped: that something so useful and lethal could be so beautiful, too.

You ever been to Pumptown? That's where I live.

By the, the water treatment plants—People live there? You live there?

A lot of us do, nodding toward the building, *Jorge does, and his sister . . . It's kind of rough, but at least you can drink the water, right? And the river's right there, you get a nice breeze on warm nights—it's pretty.*

Pretty? with such flat disbelief that she laughs and, *The old sodium lights,* she says, *they shine orange, like a harvest moon. And when the sharks come out—*

Sharks—

The kayakers, sketching a shape in the air, strange beast, a bullet with fins. *They race bank to bank, like shadows, they go so fast—*

Isn't that prohibited? To be on the water?

Prohibited? Yeah. This, flicking ash, *is prohibited too. So is Bertrand, so are we,* and she gives him a gentle push, nudge, shoulder to shoulder, so close he can smell her, past the cigarette stink her skin is like soap and flowers and *How did you know my name?* with a different kind of smile and *I asked that one kid, with the beard,* looking at her then away, as if clumsy, abashed but *You,* she says, *could have asked me.*

He says nothing, formulating the best answer, best response—because Salma is why he came here, to befriend her, learn what he can from her, all the tactics and plans; and turn her if he can, turn her the right way, and her friends with her, the kid with the beard, Jorge, who is Jorge—and *A folklore degree,* he says at last, bantering, nudging back. *What can you do with a folklore degree?* to bring her shrug: *"All learning comes to use,"* that's what my professor used to say. And *folklore is history, right, it's based in—*

History? History's over, it's dead. This is what's real, recalling with scorn his own professors' toothless classroom philosophies, their fantasies of block-by-block reclamation, gentrification, like posh blinds on smashed windows, their dither and dismay at the steep rise in state security, the surrender of personal freedom—but what if they saw this city up close? Freedom! like illegal kayaks racing in filthy water, dirty waste canisters rolling loose at the curbs, in the subway—on his way here today, on the train, he sat reading or trying to read as a man in a hat with plastic bull's horns slumped next to him, squirming and panting, masturbating? having a seizure? but no security available, no one there to make it stop: so he got off at the next stop but the next train was nowhere, the arrival display pulsing and falsing, unreadable runes so he headed for the stairs—as sounds assailed him from the shadows, sly and sourceless, something like footsteps but not footsteps, three-legged, what walks like that? and who on the platform to ask for help? No transit police, no buzzbox to push, nothing to do but shine his phone in the direction of the sounds and *I can see you,* he called, loud, lying, voice too high, *I'm recording you!* And be answered with nothing but a mocking silence, a metallic chuckle that turned out to be another canister, waste canister rolling drunkenly toward him, to fall with a hollow thunk on the tracks, an invisible hazard to any oncoming train—and he hurrying up to the street again, to the breakage and emptiness, the roaming trashhawks with their sagging sacks and sharp sticks, the trucker-fuckers who flash themselves to any passing vehicle, down to this building where the blast door wears an ugly red glyph that means, who knows what it means? folklore, some sign from history, here be monsters? Does Salma understand what this school, this "learning", is *about*?

And what if he took her to his building, his quiet street lined by containment walls, firm blue blast-resistant concrete, and the clean new public park with its smart pickets, that waist-high white fencing that self-multiplies as needed, put down three and in an hour there are thirty, or three hundred, a thousand, some people call them dragon's teeth; folklore again. And the dragonflies, what would folklore call them? everything but what they are, eyes to see and power to patrol, control, punish if need be, every legal citizen in this city should have one, like sleepless guardian angels: because in real live actual life, bad things happen that need to be punished, cities rot and die if they are not properly policed, professors are idiots and agents are recruited and rebels are removed so that one day cities, all the cities, this city can be safe again, can be a place to live and not a place to fear, here be monsters—

—*even in folklore. No one's exempt, the heroes, the villains*—she is talking, what is she saying, something about good and evil, some romantic's fable, the anorak's hood framing her face, princess in the gutter—then *Hey,* she says, voice changing, one hand on his arm. *Are you OK?*

I'm fine. He realizes he is shivering, a quick hard shudder, another. *It's just, it's cold out here,* cold enough, now, to snow, fresh spinning flakes from the clustering clouds, and upstairs will be nearly as cold, no real heat in this building or Mr. Bertrand's rooms—

—as here comes Mr. Bertrand, crippled and slow, not long for this world yet how much harm has he already done, how many have been trained in his lawless school with its Gunnysacker pedigree, its stolen tools and siphoned power, corrupting people like Salma who set out to do good? But no one is exempt from law, yes, or force, take a hex head screwdriver, and pop! goes an eye, the other eye, how many students can a blind man teach? If it were up to him—

And *You trying to school him, too, this blockhead?* Mr. Bertrand gruff to Salma, and then to him, *The women are smarter, always, that's why there's five boys here for every girl. You keep watching, you'll learn . . . Inside, inside now*—

—as Salma holds the blast door, this time, for him, following close, companionably close, close enough to abruptly pivot then press him to the stairwell, her forearm hard against his throat and *Did you think,* she says, her voice changing again, her face changing with it, like a mask removed, *we didn't know about you? Did you think we didn't see you coming?*

What—Wait, Salma, I don't—

Canada my ass—

Salma no—as that strong arm presses, and presses, as he struggles against her, struggles for air, for freedom as Mr. Bertrand holds the blast door closed, Mr. Bertrand who knows everybody, Mr. Bertrand watching as his own eyes roll up and his knees give way, Salma's arm harder still, like iron, like a machine, her face without expression, beautiful useful le

For Carter Scholz

§

Kathe Koja is a writer, performer, director, and independent producer whose work crosses and combines genres, from historical to contemporary to YA to horror. Her novels have won awards, been multiply translated, and optioned for film and performance. With her production company, Loudermilk LLC, she creates immersive events, solo and in collaboration with an ensemble of creative artists.

You can find out more at www.kathekoja.com.

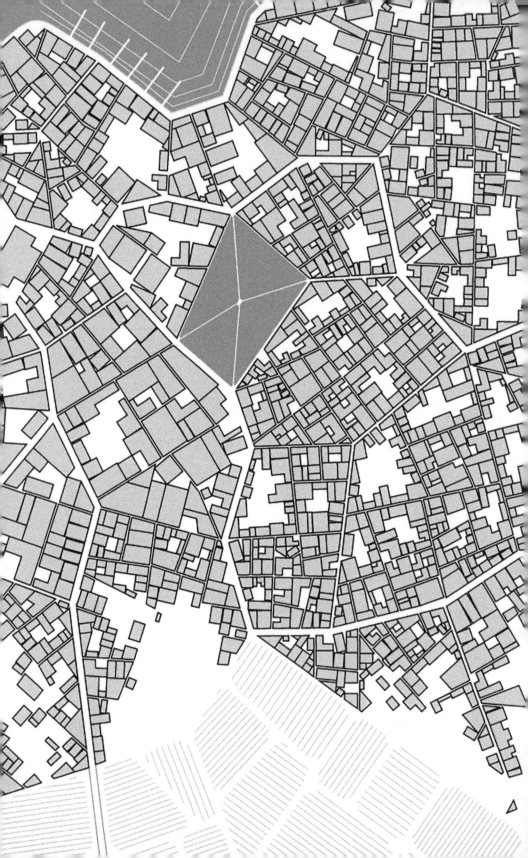

Over/Under

LEAH BOBET

SPLITTING UP WAS THE SENSIBLE THING. THERE WAS TOO much ground to cover, and Resha could be anywhere at this hour.

"She did *not* go back to him," Jeremy said, stomping down the hall. Cleo, your downstairs neighbour, banged the ceiling to tell you both to shut up, and you held your head, feeling it fill with static. You'd already been up since five, working the safe injection site, and your thoughts were going out one by one, dead pixels in the billboard of your brain.

"Jesus Christ," Jeremy said, but lower. "It's minus fifteen tonight."

"She's on transit," you said. "She took my Metropass." *And,* you didn't say, *my wallet.*

Jeremy swore again, and Cleo banged again, louder and faster 'til the floorboards shuddered. You pictured dust falling, hundred-year-old house dust, onto Cleo and her grimy basement kitchen and her fists. "That's it. I'm calling the cops."

"No cops," you snapped and ran your hands through your hair to the tips. "How in hell is this even a conversation anymore?"

Jeremy looked at you with that long-lashed, wistful stare—the one he saved for those times when he wished you were a different girl. Not a lot different, just subtle tints and filters: a desk job instead of frontline in the cold in Moss Park. A sister who did juice cleanses, not oxy and beer. A smile brighter lit, less shaded, wrought in primary colours.

"I told you," you said low and pulled your boots on. You told him the first time you brought him home to your place instead of not staying the night at his: you and Resha were a package deal. You were each other's mirror-girl, anti-twins, two-way shadows. *You learn to love my sister if you want to love me.*

He clenched his teeth around whatever he knew better than to say next.

"You take surface routes," you said and dug out a thick knit hat and scarf. "I'll go down."

"Fine," Jer said and hunched out the door.

When Resha loses the plot sometimes she just rides, not able to stay tethered in your orderly house of straightened picture frames and potted avocado plants, not able to go all the way back to Nick's sublet in the Jameson blocks. You found her twice just riding the Queen car—a full hour west to Long Branch, a full hour back to Jarvis—too paralyzed to get off at his streetcar stop or yours and decide which one is home.

Those times, you sat down beside her, held her hands, talked soft until you could coax her off the streetcar and through your lighted door. But other times she's gone for days, a smudge wiped casually off the downtown, and comes back thin and obviously using, eyes trained to the floor, hating herself. She doesn't tell you where she goes those bad times, but N.K.'s worked harm reduction a lot more years than you and said delicately, hand on your arm, that he saw her once at the shooting gallery in old Lower Bay Station. Down in the perfect mirror of Bay Station above it, one full of Bloor Street businessmen and the other scattered with needles, a girl once took his flyer for the safe injection site, and she looked just like you.

"You okay?" he asked afterward, his professional carer's eyes watching your unprofessional face for need, and because it was your habit, you said, *Yeah. Of course.*

You grab Resha's extra scarf, throw it on over your own. If she's down there— so help you God if she's down there—she'll be cold tonight.

And it's somehow colder than an hour ago, your nostrils sticking on every breath. You shove her red scarf over your nose and take off for Dundas Station, digging in your pockets for a token now that your wallet is gone.

There's nothing. The last one went to Pilar at work, and nobody you can call is coming out tonight. The station's empty except for one of the block regulars:

a hunched old woman who hobbles up and down Yonge, waving her hand perpetually in front of her face. Susie. Pilar told you her name was Susie.

You can't believe you're doing this. You have no right to ask.

"Susie? Can I trade you for a token?" you ask, and she stares at you. People downtown don't talk to the homeless, or not with anything polite to say. Toronto is a precarious détente; its two worlds touch rarely, and there are always sparks. "I've got an extra hat. It's an emergency. My sister's in trouble. I know you might not have—"

She looks at you, still shaking slightly, and you stop. You've never seen her upturned face before. It's seamed and a little fragile.

"Please," you say, and she opens her hand on a circle of gold and white.

"Oh god, thanks so much," you breathe and pass her your cable-knitted hat. She mumbles something you don't catch before the security guard from the mall materializes—"Right, let's not bother the lady"—and his body's already between you, backing her away.

"Don't kick her out!" you yell after him, and he turns around, incredulous. You hear your voice crack. "Don't. It's really cold outside."

"Right, lady," he says and turns back around. She's already gone. *Goddamn.*

You drop the token in, get on the train, and text N.K. even though he's on-shift and won't get it for hours: *Hey buddy, emergency. Going to Lower Bay to look for Resha. Send backup if I don't check in by midnight?*

You hop off at Museum, deserted except for its ghostly pillars: Toltec warriors, First Nations house posts, Forbidden City columns, and Osiris, guarding the doorway to the dead. You pick your way to the edge of the platform, looking back and forth for commuters or even a station guard. A breath of cold wind licks down the outside stairs.

When N.K. goes down, TTC workers unlock the door on the Bay Station platform, pretending they don't know what's inside. It is insane to contemplate how your clients get in: a broken gate lock and a sprint through an active subway tunnel, past the third rail, into the disused station. It's dangerous as hell. That's why N.K. has his project: some night soon, someone down there will die.

You stare alone down the mouth of the subway tunnel, yawning, festooned with potato chip bags, a tumbled sneaker, soft grey mice, soot, rats.

It made sense to split up. It was sensible. It made sense.

Jer almost slips going down the steps, and wouldn't that take the goddamned cake: breaking his ass on his own front porch two weeks before Christmas because Resha took off again.

It's cold, and he's tired—not just from ten hours at the office and two more at the gym. Annie never wants to admit that Resha is a bad bet. They'll drag her home, she'll cry, Annie will cry—all night probably—and then Resha'll do what she always does: reset to the last familiar self-destruction the next time shit gets hard.

He and Annie talked about this last time—that it would be the last time. That her sister's habits couldn't blow a hole in their lives anymore. Something's got to change.

Tonight, he is changing it.

He takes a look around: north, east, south, west. *West,* he chooses and heads across Jarvis to Yonge Street, the mall, the city lights. Annie's overthinking it with her lists of Resha's favourite transit routes and endless hypotheticals. There's only one place Resha goes that she won't admit to, and that's back to Nick, even after the broken arm last winter and this spring's cigarette burns.

He dials the non-emergency number. Holds the line. Says, "Yes, I'd like to file a missing persons report."

He's got one picture of Annie's sister on his phone: a shot from this summer at Cherry Beach when Resha promised she was getting into counseling for sure this time, and Annie dragged all three of them out to eat soft serve even though she had to know Resha would flake out two weeks later. He texts it to the officer once they hang up: that awkward, turned-away face. Annie will kill him for this, for even implying there's a problem in public, but then she will cry, and he can soothe her, and it'll be done. And she'll realize how good it is, not living under the shadow of Resha's outspread wings.

It's starting to snow: little hard pellets that prick skin like straight pins. It's worse than minus fifteen—minus fifteen and falling, with an Extreme Cold Weather Alert scrolling across every billboard screen under the same video of the mayor opening emergency shelter space. Everyone in the city is trying to get home, and the 501 is bunching like it always does. Two full streetcars roll right by him until the third one spits out a few people, and Jer just goes for it: jams himself up the stairs and into the car, well in front of the goddamned yellow line. Someone's Chinese grandma gives him a filthy look and sticks her elbows out, but he grabs the fare box and holds his ground.

The driver scowls at him, and Jer says, "Look, dude, I'm off the stairs."

He can see the driver think about throwing him off, really consider it. He looks the guy in the eye, not hard-assed but firm, like the partners do during a client meeting. And it works: the driver decides he's not worth the fight and takes off, and the Queen streetcar blows its way through the pilling snow westward, past the limits of his neighbourhood. Out to Jameson Avenue and parts unknown.

You haven't thought this through.

You take your phone out, put it back, take it out again, but there's no signal; TTC wifi is capricious, and cell signal down here even flightier. The cameras work, though, and someone is going to notice you pacing the platform around that open-jawed tunnel and send security to roust you out of here.

And then what'll happen is what always happens to people like Resha when no one looks for them: frozen stiff on the sidewalk, stepped around, stepped over. Their dismembered bodies dumped in Rosedale Ravine.

You glance up at the camera one last time, slip the safety gate open, and head into the tunnel.

You're brave for a whole minute, until the light recedes and you're choking on the smell of live electricity and dead earth. This was a terrible idea. Your footsteps are so loud, loud enough that someone has to have heard you, and everything your boot touches makes you jump. *You'll jump right into the third rail, and they'll find you down here weeks later. Your body will derail a subway train.* You edge along the platform inch by inch, praying that you're almost there.

You've hit the downslope—surely you must be getting somewhere—when you see motion. *Rat,* you think, and your whole body freezes. But then a shadow moves between the shadows, and a very human voice wisps, "Hey."

You squeak. Your breath plumes under the dim emergency lights, disappears up to the tunnel ceiling. You can make out the shape of the face: a beard, a ratted trench coat. The squatters in Lower Bay have set a guard on the tracks, here where the trains don't actually run.

"What you want?" he says in a cracked-plastic voice. He smells ripe but not too bad compared to most guys you see sleeping rough.

"I'm looking for a friend." You don't want to say *sister*. For a lot of people sleeping rough, family doesn't mean *safe* or *home*.

He sizes you up. You don't move. People size you up at work all day. "You spare change?" he asks. It's not a question.

"Don't have change," you say softly, "sorry. But are you cold?"

He looks you up and down, and you unwind the red scarf from your face, damp with breath-sweat. "It's wool," you say, and the cold air plucks at your tender mouth, your nose. You wipe it off on your coat and press it into his hand. It's Resha's. Your belly twinges. You'll buy her a new one.

"You got somewhere to sleep?" you ask, and he gives a little half-shrug, shoulders jitterbugging up-down. "They've got emergency shelters tonight."

"Shelters are shit," he says, and you've seen them, so you can't really disagree. "God bless, miss."

There's a light up ahead: dim, rounded. The murmur of voices.

"Take care," you say and pass into that perfect replica of Bay Station, underground.

No one answers the buzzer at the apartment on Jameson, the one Jer hauled Resha's things out of the last time she decided to turn her life around. That's no big shocker. Guys like Nick don't put much stock into shit like doorbells, and in buildings like this, half the buzzers are broken.

The cops said thirty minutes. Maybe an hour. Maybe two. It's busy tonight. There is a volume of calls.

It's past eleven, he hasn't eaten, and his hands are numb. Every guy who comes in and out of here is eyeing him like he's here to buy drugs, or sell them maybe. He's got his hand on his wallet through his pants pocket, and if Annie was around he might feel like shit about that, but as it stands, he can't spare the guilt. He knows what his firm mentor would say: *take initiative. Change the game.*

"Aw, shit," Jer says under his breath and loiters by the buzzer until someone with a key comes by and lets themselves in. It's an old trick: one shoe stuck out, and he's caught the door.

The hallways of Nick's building stink: onions, mold, weed smoke, wet carpet, nobody giving a shit. Loud TV in five languages blasts from behind every other door. He works his way down the hall to the apartment number he still has written down in his phone—in case the cops needed a statement—and gives three loud, hard-assed knocks.

There's no answer.

The TV down the hall flips into blaring commercials: pawnshop jewellery and Taco Bell. He knocks again, harder, listening for an echo, for the rustle somewhere, in all this noise, of Nick breathing hard on the other side of that door.

It doesn't happen. He grits his teeth, bangs again, and the door next to Nick's opens: a South Asian guy in flip-flops and a cleaner's uniform stitched with *Robert*. "What the hell?"

Jer flushes. "You see a girl come in here tonight?"

The dude's face doesn't change. He's weighing Jer, how much trouble he might be. "Nobody's in there," he says. "Nobody's out of there."

"What?"

"Your buddy *died*, man. Couple days ago."

Jer blinks.

"Now you stop banging, huh?" the guy says and slams his own door hard.

Jer looks at the red knuckles on his right hand. Nick's dead. Resha isn't here. Nick's *dead*.

He tucks himself smaller and hits the elevator button, fidgets waiting, just takes the stairs. There's piss in the corner of the stairwell, pooling. He dances around it with his boot and bursts outside into the icy air, the rime of ice building up on the sidewalks. His stomach feels oddly deflated, a strange shed skin. He was sure. He was so sure.

He texts Annie: *Not at Nick's.*

Look, I'm done with this shit tonight.

There's no answer. She never looks for him first when her sister's involved.

He taps out, erases, retypes, sends: *I called the cops. I'm done with this shit. I'm done.*

She's unmistakable. You'd know her anywhere: perched on a folding chair in the middle of that subway platform like a queen, a goddess of the air and dark. You've found her, your mirror-girl, anti-twin, two-way shadow, and she is all fucked up.

"Resha," you breathe, and she looks up at you with—you swear—a flash of hurt before her heavy eyelids lower and she turns away, like a kid. You are the little sister, and she the older, but you've always felt like it was the other way around. And maybe that's what started this between you, flitting in and out of each other's shadows. Bound like knife fighters at the wrist.

Either way, you know your job here. Be calm for her and take her home.

"This is not a good idea, Resh," you say softly.

She coughs. "Right, you and your rich boy from the suburbs know everything now."

Addicts do and don't mean what they say. What Resha says when she's coming down is a needle aimed between where she thinks your armor is, and because she's your anti-twin, she's usually right. No one knows how to hurt you like she does. You know she's projecting, and they didn't need to teach you that in nursing school. You got early training in what Resha means when she says things that are so mean: *I hurt. Don't leave me alone to hurt.*

You reach out one naked palm. "Resha, what's wrong?"

Her eyelids open, sharp, and agony bubbles into her face. "He's *dead* is what's wrong, and I wasn't there, and it's *all your fault.*"

Your mouth opens. Nick's dead. Nick, the guy who broke her arm and her face and her heart, and she's grieving. And Resha's absolute downfall has always been the weight of her grief.

"Oh, Resha," you say and put her jacket across her shoulders. She shrugs it away, haphazard, already tired. Her lips are blue. Your brain instantly enumerates the signs of hypothermia. "C'mon, let me warm you up."

She's not moving. She spits something broken and incomprehensible at you. You suck in a breath. You've got to get her somewhere heated. She's too heavy to lift.

You peel off your own coat, warm from your body heat, and wrap it around her. The cold hits hard: it's freezing down here. "Resha, if I go get help, will you be okay?"

She's not okay. Her eyelids flutter. You chafe her hands, her feet, trying to get the blood moving. Your teeth are chattering. You're down here in a sweater and jeans, your boots icing even indoors, and Resha's fading hard beside you, bundled in your coat and your scarf.

"C'mon, stay with me. Please stay with me," you beg.

"You're *shit*," your sister mumbles.

I am shit, you translate, and tears prick your eyes.

You do not start a career in harm reduction without understanding that the addict is the only one who can make the decision to quit. Resha has always been the first and last word when it comes to her scrambled life. No matter how much you wish you could get behind her eyes and make her see how she's killing herself, you both know no one else can decide for a person that it's time to get clean. But you can't leave her here tonight, slurring and shivering. You can't leave your sister to die.

It's cold.

You lean back against the pillar beside her, pressing your body heat to hers. It's past midnight. N.K.'s got to be coming if he saw your text—if he didn't just turn his phone off before heading to bed. She's cold. You've just got to keep her warm until he comes.

Your head is swimming. You lean it back, and the ceiling is a quicksilver mirror. It must be ice, leaking down, pipes freezing under the good subway station, the one with the suits, malls, and high heels. But the dark above you glistens, it moves, and from Resha's mouth, a meltwater stream of words bubbles up: *Useless selfish stupid stuck-up abandoning bitch.*

"I wish you were *dead*—" she scrapes out, and you feel it like a hook in your guts.

The quicksilver is moving on the ceiling again, a thin membrane between who you turned out to be and who she did. The mirror that reflects the words Resha can't tell you but slantwise: *I wish I was dead.*

"No," you say, definitive, but it doesn't come out. You're not cold anymore. At least that's not going wrong.

Your phone buzzes somewhere in your pocket. It's far. You hold Resha's hand, enumerating the knuckles with your fingertips, and close your eyes. Just for a minute.

Resha's in pain.

You've always had a sense of when she hurt, your anti-twin; the feeling that something wasn't right. She used tonight, and suddenly she's come down hard. You lean your cheek against the cold tile, feeling nothing, and watch someone in your coat, in your hat, bend over on the platform and cough up brown, stringy puke. She's writhing like a chestburster's kicking in her belly, and you know you should clear her airway, get her on her side, but you can't quite connect your hands with your head right now. You can't connect Resha with this vomiting doppelganger, this other version of you.

Keep her warm until N.K. comes, you repeat to yourself. *Just stay warm.*

Something clanks; metal on tile, loud voices. Then N.K.'s leaning over you, his warm face tense and sorrowful. "Annie? Annie, oh shit."

"Resha," you say and shake him off. He follows your eyes to where she's still puking, and then he's holding her upright, telling her to breathe, shaking out pills. Of course he's got a kit from the clinic.

Resha swims out of your field of view, creaking upward. "It *hurts.*"

She's alive. You did it. They made it in time.

There are blue lights. There are red lights and heavy boots and paramedics talking in clipped voices about a stretcher and steep station stairs. *They're going to take her to the hospital,* you think, and the paramedics wrap a blanket around you and say, "All right, we're ready to lift."

I'm the wrong one, you think. And then, *They're not here for her.*

They lift you onto the stretcher; the blanket tucks under your arms and legs. The ceiling is quicksilver. Your shadows dance upside down in it: you on a stretcher, immobile, broken; Resha coughing, sitting up, wrapped in your clothes. You could make that real if you wanted. You're strong. You could, you judge—clearly, considered—take that on.

You reach for the shimmer on the ceiling.

"Let's keep you nice and warm," the paramedic says, eases your arm down, and wheels you away.

It's four in the morning when they finally give you the update: withdrawal, garden-variety withdrawal sickness, exacerbated by hypothermia from the severe cold. You lean back in the emergency room chair still wrapped in an orange blanket, a rehydration IV in your arm. They're warming you slowly, in increments, so your blood pressure doesn't crash. "You were very lucky," the emergency doctor tells you, and you don't tell him what you do for a living. It would be too embarrassing and too hard to explain.

Jeremy sits in the corner of the curtained-off cubicle, turning his phone over and over in his hands. It rang once in the first half hour, and he had a low conversation in the vestibule where it's still warm. He came back quiet and pale.

"We have to talk about your sister," Jeremy says, and you shake your head. You can't do this. Not now.

"Yes," he says flatly. "You almost died tonight."

"I'm sorry," you say.

"Jesus, Annie," he snaps and puts his head in his hands. "You can't win this fight, okay? Please. Just let her go."

It was never about winning, you think and finally, perhaps, understand:

Jeremy doesn't have the tools for this kind of situation: the endurance to watch her come home all fucked up, to hold the needle, to go to work with a smile on every day not sure which client they found frozen on the street last night. To open the door to some dude who called you a fucking cunt last week because he's sick, and he's a person and deserves medical care too. Jeremy doesn't have the tools to get beaten down and wipe blood off his mouth and get back up again. He believes in endings. He believes in the kind of evil that gets defeated and lets you make the long walk home.

"She's going to get better," you tell him, because that's a story he can have faith in.

He takes your face in his warm hands and looks you in the eye. "Babe, I wouldn't bet on it."

Your nose twitches. There is beer on his breath.

"Where were you?" you ask, sharp.

He leans back. "What?"

"We don't keep beer in the house."

"Look, I was waiting—" he starts, and his hand goes to his phone.

You whip it out of his hand and read the line of text messages, one after another. *I'm done with this shit. I'm done.*

You and Resha are two-way shadows, the shadows each other casts. Down the hall in an emergency bed, she is heartbroken. And here you are.

"You said you'd go over if I went under."

"Look," he says. "I can't."

Your sister's shadow is a close, dark thing. You reach for it, wrap it around you like a blanket.

You told him: you couldn't love someone who couldn't love Resha, the hurt in her, the scrabble, the worth, the beauty, the fight. Who doesn't understand that if there's so much of you in her, beaten down, spit-toothed, standing back up, there's so much of her in you too, and that's why it's important to love people when it's hard. Because one day, you know it'll be hard to love you. One day, you were going to need him there, going overland for you or digging down.

The ceiling shimmers, dark on white. It's easier than you think to reverse gravity, and fall.

It is a long way down into her shadow, into its gates and byways, through its throat. He kicks a little on the way down. But you have been there, and you know the path.

The ceiling in Toronto General is white. White with a thousand pinpoint holes, white made of shadow, or shadow studded with white. It's hard to tell at the moment. Your head hurts. Your mouth tastes of sick, and your heart is a dead thud under your ribs. *Broken,* you think. You thought it could work somehow: that this charming, flashy Bay Street boy could see the darker depths of you and love them. That he'd walk the dark.

There's an IV line in the crook of your elbow. *Concussion,* you think, but that's not right. *I fell.*

Something has changed. Something's wrong.

You roll your head agonizingly left, and Resha is sitting by your bedside, clear-eyed after so many years: your anti-twin, your mirror-girl, your shadow, the shadow you live in, wrapped in your own coat and scarf.

"What did you *do*?" she asks softly.

You start, stop. Words bubble. You can't speak right. There's a mask over your face, and your stomach hurts. Your mouth's wanting something you can't define. What you've done is perfectly natural, what you should have done all along. You've taken the choice away.

Your stomach convulses. Everything hurts.

Resha waits until the shudders stop and lifts the mask from your face. "Annie?"

"I don't want you to die," you say, and Resha stares down at you, mouth open.

"Oh, little sister," she whispers, "I'm coming." And with fragile fingers, bruised and knobbed, she gently takes your hand.

§

Leah Bobet's latest novel, *An Inheritance of Ashes*, won the Sunburst, Copper Cylinder, and Prix Aurora Awards and was an OLA Best Bets book; her short fiction is anthologized worldwide. She lives in Toronto, where she works as an editor and book reviewer, makes jam, and builds civic engagement spaces.

A Name For Every Home

RAMSEY CAMPBELL

"Don't you know your ABC, Pad? Are they letting people go to university without it now?"

Patrick didn't look up from the map on his phone. A pad was where you lived, he thought, or what a dog did. "Just trying to do my job, Carl."

"Sort your post in alpha order. That's how you'll get round Garden Mile."

"Let Patrick learn for himself." Not quite without a pause their supervisor said "If that's how he works."

"That's not how Frank sorts the Mile, Eunice."

"Frank's off sick," she said.

She gazed at Carl until he returned to filling in a card to tell someone they couldn't have their mail before they paid a customs charge. Even if her rebuke was focused on Carl, Patrick felt less accepted than ever. She couldn't expect him to race through sorting when hardly a house in the suburb was numbered. "I expect he's right," he said and abandoned searching for house names on the map.

Carl watched him set about alphabetising envelopes on the wide desk topped by pigeonholes. "You won't get far if you aren't true to yourself, Pad."

Patrick twisted around, and a muscle throbbed as if someone had punched him in the back. "If you want the real me then for a start that's not my name."

Nearby workmates hooted with amusement. "Don't get in a paddy, Paddy," Carl said.

"That isn't either."

"There'll be time for jokes when everything's delivered," Eunice said.

Patrick tried and failed not to respond. "I didn't hear much of a joke."

"You might like to try a bit harder to get on with your colleagues."

Sensing their contempt, Patrick took a silent breath so fierce it sucked in a smell of envelopes. The huge room put him in mind of a hive—the apian buzz of strip lights, letters fluttering like wings, postal workers bumbling at their honeycombs of pigeonholes—but if this made everybody into drones, didn't that include him? His clammy hands were stained with ink by the time he finished transferring letters and packages to the delivery trolley. "Done," he said, but nobody bothered to respond.

A prematurely autumnal September wind chilled his bare knees as he wheeled the trolley into the shopping precinct, where people were queuing to collect their undelivered mail. The first time he'd worn his postman's uniform he'd felt like an overgrown schoolboy condemned to walk the streets as a punishment for failure. Beyond the precinct—charity shops, off-licences, coin arcades, betting shops—the residential streets began. In ten minutes houses trapped between one another gave way to larger buildings split into apartments, one of which was Patrick's. A carer was coaxing a large slack-faced youth into the house next door, while on the other side two families were sitting on the doorstep and conferring in a language Patrick didn't recognise. They gazed expectantly at him until he realised they saw a postman, not a neighbour. "I'm not your man," he called, "he should be along soon," but all six of them sent him a frown that suggested he was talking nonsense.

The Victorian streets led to a wide dual carriageway, across which lay Garden Mile. The suburb appeared to possess its own exclusive stretch of sky, dark with a threat of rain. As Patrick crossed the road, having waited quite some time for a green sketch of a man to scrounge light from the red, a silver Bentley saloon raced in front of him just inches from the trolley. By the time he found breath for an appropriate word the car was swerving through a gap in the central reservation to speed around a bend into Garden Mile.

A car door and a boot slammed somewhere ahead as Patrick wheeled the trolley into the broad road. Every house was resolutely individual and surrounded by a garden several times its area. Each garden boasted at least one vehicle expensive enough to star in a showroom—a Jaguar, a Mercedes, a Rolls Royce—and each gate displayed a name. Patrick was past the first bend by the time he saw a name he recalled from sorting the mail—Dogs Home.

The displaced Swiss chalet didn't look as though it boarded dogs, and no kennels were apparent, but as Patrick dropped a letter in the box attached to the bars of the gate, a Doberman bounded around the house, baring its yellowed teeth. It clawed at the top of the gate as if determined to clamber over, and he'd put the trolley between himself and the animal when a man yelled "Gutter."

Patrick might have felt directed there if the dog hadn't dropped to all fours with a frustrated snarl and trudged back to the house. So that was the dog's name, and the words on the gate could have been a warning. He wheeled the trolley around a bend to the next house he had mail for, an Italianate villa called the Watch. It lived up to its name by taking his photograph with a security camera as he approached the solid seven-foot gate. He pushed a package under the metal flap of the wide slot in the gate, and it was yanked out of his hand. Surprise made him blurt out the last thought he'd had. "I'd have said cheese if I'd known you were after my photograph."

"We don't have smilers in our gallery."

Though the woman's sharp voice invited no response, Patrick retorted "Which one is that?"

"The one we keep rogues in."

"I'm not one of those. I'm your postman."

The metal flap gave him a glimpse of a pair of eyes brimming with moisture and clanked shut at once. "You're not the usual man."

"He's ill. Won't I do?"

"We'll have him back." Her voice was receding, and Patrick heard slippers shuffling along a path. "We trust him," she said.

Patrick wasn't going to let her make him feel like an intruder, never mind a criminal looking for properties to rob or otherwise up to mischief. He trundled the trolley along the middle of the road while he peered at names on gates, and caught sight of a plaque he must be misreading. He had to laugh at his mistake, and then at the mistake the laugh was. When he pushed the trolley up the ramp leading over the pavement to the open gates he saw that the house was indeed called the Pad.

It pointed jazzy angles of white concrete in every direction, no two of them alike. Just the windows were rectangular. One displayed the front room and, beyond sliding doors, a kitchen and an outdoor barbecue. Among the cars parked on the drive he saw a silver Bentley that he recognised from letters on the registration plate—DRG. He was making to move onwards when two rather less than teenage children ran around the house. "Got something for us?" the girl scarcely asked, and the boy supplied a translation or an additional demand. "Got us something?"

They were plainly twins, and they looked oddly familiar—their small skinny angular faces expressive of a dull dogged hunger their owners mightn't even have defined. "Nothing today, I'm afraid," Patrick said.

Their tired eyes narrowed and their thin lips drooped. "It's our birthday," the boy complained, and his sister was anxious to establish "Both of ours."

"Happy birthday, both."

"Kiera," the girl said as if Patrick should have known, and jabbed a finger with a chewed nail at the trolley. "Look for me."

"And Kieron," the boy urged him.

"Trust me, I'd know if there was anything for this house."

"Why would you?" Kiera demanded, and Kieron contributed "You heard, why?"

"You mightn't believe me if I told you." In a bid to end the confrontation Patrick said "Just enjoy your day. I expect that's why you're off school."

"Who's asking that? Who wants to know?"

This came from the man who stalked around the house, a wiry fellow with muscular veinous arms and a larger version of the children's face. Despite its size, the features—meagre eyes and mouth, aggressively pointed nose and chin—looked even more compressed. He halted for a moment, staring at Patrick, and then marched faster at him. "Fucking Nora," he said. "Paddy Ransome."

"Mel Cousins. Well, good lord."

Mel stuck out a hand only to take it back. "Weren't you supposed to go to uni?"

"I did." When Mel's red-eyed stare persisted Patrick said "I've been a waiter and worked in a bar, and this is what I'm doing now."

"Fucking Nora." Mel jerked his head at the trolley. "Bring it round," he said. "Shouldn't think you're in a panic."

"No rush," Patrick said and followed him around the house.

About a dozen people sat on garden chairs near the paved patio where the barbecue stood. Children were bouncing somewhat desultorily on an inflated castle at the far end of an expansive lawn. "You've done well for yourself," Patrick felt he should remark.

"It's my old man's too."

Patrick thought the women in the audience might appreciate a further comment. "Just yours?"

"We got rid of the wives if they're what you mean. They weren't helping the firm," Mel said and showed Patrick his back. "Dad, here's Paddy Ransome we called Pad at school. He went to uni but this is all it got him."

A stocky man was turning burgers over on the barbecue as though searching under stones for some unwelcome lurker. He raised a puffy instance of the Cousins face to squint at Patrick. "Old friend, are you, Pad?"

Patrick felt it might be unwise to object to the name. "I expect you could say so," he said with equal caution.

"Fancy making yourself a bit of extra? We could use you and your wagon."

"I don't know if I could do that." When not just all the adults but the Cousins twins stared at him, Patrick gave way to saying "What would it involve?"

"Better stuff than I ever sold at school," Mel said. "Give it here, Rod."

A man in a garden chair passed him a device Patrick had assumed was a cigarette substitute. When Mel held it out Patrick said awkwardly "I never liked it much. I'd rather not go back there. My mind's in enough of a state."

"It's the cleanest you can get. It's oil." Since Patrick remained unpersuaded, Mel said "Watch."

He depressed a button on the pipe and applied a lighter, inhaling at such length that Patrick held his breath. As Mel let out a protracted plume of smoke Patrick sucked in a lungful of air, only to find it brought him the smoke. "Whoa," Mel said. "You got some after all."

His delight appeared to spread his features, slowly and relentlessly. His head nodded towards Patrick, bobbing like a balloon on the string of his neck. "I'd rather not have anything to do with it," Patrick heard himself declare too late.

"You just did," an amused spectator told him.

Patrick turned to argue, not least to persuade himself they were wrong, and felt as if he might never stop turning. As he seized the trolley for support Mel's father said "No call for that, Pad. Nobody's going to rob your mail."

"I wasn't. I didn't mean." Patrick left the rest of the sentences behind while he stumbled in search of an empty chair. A herbal odour had lodged in his nostrils and was extending tendrils to net his brain. How could that be? Perhaps if he found words to define the sensation, it would go away—perhaps its effects would. He sank onto a skeletal canvas chair, but he couldn't hide in it when everyone's attention had settled on him like a web. In the hope of subduing his sensations he said "Could I have a drink?"

Mel was refilling the pipe. "Fetch Pad a can, Kieron."

The boy slouched into the kitchen, which was tiled white as a morgue, and hauled open a freezer Patrick could imagine lying in to chill his unhappily clammy self. Of course nobody would shut him in there, but he kept a nervous eye on it until Kieron slammed the lid. When the boy brought him the prize Patrick grabbed the can of lager and rolled it across his forehead, which had grown so tight it was squeezing out trickles of sweat. "Show some fucking manners," Mel's father warned him. "Never mind snatching off the kid."

"Sorry," Patrick blurted, though he wasn't sure to whom. He peeled off the metal tag, remembering barely in time not to lob the grenade, however much he might feel he was acting in a film. He poured a metallic mouthful into himself, belatedly recalling how to swallow. "Needed that," he spluttered before admitting "Thought I did."

Was it quelling the effects of the pipe? When Mel had passed around a sample joint at school there had been nothing to counteract them, and now Patrick couldn't tell how the combination of substances was affecting him. The pipe was advancing towards him along the line of chairs, marking its progress with clouds of smoke he could smell. Mustn't this mean he was breathing them in? He covered his nose and mouth with a moist bloated hand, but his neighbour offered him the pipe. "No, please no," Patrick babbled from behind his hand and made a grab for dignity. "I said not for me, thanks."

Kiera nudged her brother, giggling. "Scared to do a pipe, him."

Patrick lowered his ponderous unwieldy hand so as to deal them a stern look. "I hope you both are. Stay that way."

As the stereoscopic image—one face for each of his eyes—opened its mouths, Mel's father said "Watch out who you think's your friend, son."

"I'd like to think I can tell," Patrick said.

"Not you, you twat. When's he going, Mel?"

The balloon that bobbed at Patrick had regained its dissatisfied look. "Give us what you've got and you can take your can with you," Mel said.

Patrick peered along the line of chairs in search of sympathetic witnesses, but those who weren't indifferent were no better than amused. "Your father said you wouldn't rob me," he pleaded.

Mel's face swelled towards him, and Patrick was afraid it wouldn't stop short of merging with his own head. "What are you calling us, Pad?"

"Nothing if I shouldn't. I didn't think you were that kind of, not that kind of anything, any kind at all."

As Patrick managed to catch up with his own words and restrain them, Mel's father said "Kind of what?"

"No kind. That's what I said, only what do you want to take? I don't mean drugs," Patrick said, outrun by his speech again. "That's nothing to do with me."

"Better believe it. Better remember."

"He's saying we're villains. That right, Pad?"

Patrick would have said anything that might fend off the face, which seemed as huge and hostile as the world. "I was saying you wouldn't steal from me."

"Who'd we rob instead?" The face lurched closer before receding so swiftly that Patrick saw it deflate. "Give us what you've got for us and you can piss off with the rest," the newly shrunken Mel said.

"I told your two, I've got nothing. Perhaps whoever's on the next round will have some."

"What the fuck are you doing here, then?"

"I thought you invited me."

"Guess what I'm telling you now."

For a paralysed moment Patrick assumed he was required to read Mel's thoughts and voice them. As he wobbled to his feet he kept hold of the can of lager, which emitted a screechy creak. "Can I still take this?"

"Take your brew and your walker and best of the lot yourself," Mel's father said. "And get them to send us someone else next time."

He couldn't want that more than Patrick did. Patrick managed to relax his grip on the can as he planted it on one of the lids of the trolley, and felt he ought to say "Thank you for the drink."

"Just keep your garbage to yourself," Mel told him.

"Why do you have to say that? Your father wanted manners. I was trying to be polite."

Mel let his mouth hang open in an idiot's grimace and jerked a thumb at the trolley. "Your garbage there, you stupe."

"I don't think you can call it that just because there wasn't anything for here."

"He's a giggle," Mel's father said without providing any evidence and stared at Patrick. "Mel's saying keep your can out of our road."

"Is it all right if I drop it in somebody else's?"

Presumably Patrick didn't say this, even though he heard himself, since nobody reacted. He was taking care not to dislodge the can while he swivelled the trolley when a woman said "You want to get yourself a car."

"How do you know what I want?" To head off this retort Patrick made haste to ask "Why?"

"Then you wouldn't have to potter about with that contraption. You look like some old feller with a walker."

"At least I won't be killing anyone with it."

This prompted an ominous silence broken only by his irregular rubbery heartbeat—no, the thumps of unshod feet inside the giant blancmange—the castle, rather. "What are you calling us now?" Mel said.

"I was just wondering who nearly ran me over on their way to your house."

"That was you in the road, was it? If we'd wanted you dead you'd be dead."

Patrick saw Kiera and Kieron exchange an eager look, which he was less than anxious to understand. As he turned away he saw the castle set the house prancing. The concrete building calmed down as he hurried past it, and the nearby houses gradually ceased their dance. Perhaps the dark sky was some use if it had restrained them by weighing on them.

Was it safe to walk in the road? Might a car try to run him down? Surely Mel had said not, and Patrick emptied the can of lager down his throat to quell his nervousness. If that made him wander across the roadway, imitating its curves but in reverse, the deliveries ought to keep him on track. He had to veer towards each house to read its name, not the easiest of tasks while the letters jittered like faulty digital displays, if indeed that wasn't what they were. His footsteps and the stormy rumble of the trolley were the only sounds, because everyone in Garden Mile was staying quiet so as to listen to him. They would have heard him announce a name he had mail for—the Spikes, where the package barely fitted through the slot in the gate. Despite the barbs that topped the wall he thought the name might denote needles too, but couldn't be sure if he'd said so aloud. He had a bunch of bills for High Walls, and mustn't think high balls or bills for balls, let alone utter the words, or he might never stop laughing. Wasn't that preferable to feeling afraid? He couldn't afford either while he had a job to finish, and soon he came to Justus with a sheaf of envelopes. "Not justice," he told himself, only to find the comment menacing. The riverine meandering of the road had brought him behind the Pad, and as the antics of the castle threatened to infect the houses he anticipated seeing the Cousins family and all their guests bounce in unison above the wall. He gripped his mouth to trap hilarity, and was glad to find he'd reached another house with mail, the Palms. It greeted him by raising its green hands on their scaly arms above a hedge, and he was about to slip the envelopes through its expressionless mouth on the gate when he recalled sorting just one item for this house. He peered at the second envelope and saw it was addressed to the Pad.

The envelopes must have been stuck together when he'd sorted them. He would surely have noticed if his workmates hadn't distracted him. Best to deliver everything else first, and he drove the trolley through the gathering gloom. Harmoney House, the Manshun, Ray 'n' Beau's End . . . These and others kept him murmuring observations, and he was sure he'd walked considerably more than a mile by the time he completed the round. As he dropped the empty can in a compartment of the trolley he was overtaken by a notion that he'd misdelivered some item. Surely the recipient could take it to their neighbour.

The engine of his vehicle rattled all the way back to the Pad. If he ever owned a car he suspected that was how it might sound. He should have had it fixed, because the relentless clatter brought Mel around the house as Patrick ventured through the gate. "What are you snooping round here now for?" Mel demanded.

His children were behind him. "It's the old man with his walker," Kieron wanted somebody to know.

"It's a baby with a buggy," Kiera was determined to suggest.

"Shut it, you. What are you after, Pad? Seeing what else we do?"

"I'm just doing my job."

"Not making a bit on the side. Not spying on us for the law." As Patrick made to laugh this off Mel said "Don't waste your time. Some of those are out the back."

Patrick would have been entirely happy not to learn so much. He couldn't judge how closely his answering noise resembled a laugh, and it felt unhelpfully belated. "I'm nothing but a postman," he insisted. "I had mail for you after all."

"You told these you'd got none."

"I'd mixed it up with someone else's."

Mel remained suspicious when Patrick retrieved the envelope, which was large and pink. Was he wondering how Patrick could have overlooked such an item? The children ran to seize it, and Patrick was afraid they might rip the contents apart. "Who's going to open it?" he said, holding it above his head. "Better be just one."

"What are you making them jump for? They're not fucking dogs."

"I just thought you mightn't want it destroyed, Mel."

"Never mind thinking what I want. I'll have you destroyed, pal." With no lessening of menace Mel said "Give it here."

Too late Patrick realised he could have ascertained who the mail was for. He'd assumed the birthday card would be addressed to both the children, unless the envelope contained a pair of cards, though was it bulky enough? As he made to examine it, Mel snatched it, and Patrick had to refrain from saying that the elder Cousins would have found that impolite. He was heading for the gate when Mel said "Tell us you're having a laugh."

As Patrick turned, the untimely gloom hindered him like water if not mud. Mel was brandishing the open envelope at him—the empty envelope. "Where's the card?" Patrick protested, he scarcely knew to whom.

"No card in here, Pad. No fucking thing else either."

Patrick stared at the yawning beak, the pink entrance to a woman, the way back into a womb, and fought to concentrate. "Someone must have taken it."

"Who are you calling a thief now?"

"I can't say, can I?" Patrick struggled not to let his gaze stray across Mel and the children in case it looked accusing. Surely it made sense to ask "Who was it for?"

Mel glared at the envelope and then at him. "Looks like you, Pad."

Since he didn't move, Patrick had to venture back to him. As Mel turned the envelope towards him he spat on it—no, a large raindrop fell on a line of handwriting. The line was all Patrick had previously seen, and now he saw it was the whole of the address. *To the Pad*, it said. "You're right," Patrick told Mel. "It must be a joke."

"Who's having one of them?"

Patrick watched the letters settle down from writhing and assume a final shape. The scrawl looked childish, which made him think Kiera or Kieron was responsible. Might they have slipped the envelope into the trolley while Mel's father had diverted him away from it? He could equally suspect any of a number of his workmates. "I can't say that either," he said.

"Bet you can't. More like it's an excuse for you to come sneaking back."

"Why would I want to do that?" Patrick saw the answer in Mel's eyes, considerably worse than a warning. If he'd been closer to escaping through the gate he mightn't have lingered to be rational. "Don't be paranoid, Mel," he said.

"What's going to make me that, Pad?"

"What you had before. You won't say you aren't stoned."

"So are we," Kieron said.

"It's our birthday," Kiera said as if this hadn't been made plain.

"I've got to say I am a bit myself." In case it helped, Patrick added "In honour of the occasion."

"Don't try making out you're like us." Some element of the exchange had infuriated Mel. "Pity I didn't run you over," he said, "while I had the chance."

"You can't really mean that. There are children listening."

"And don't you fucking tell them what I mean. Here's your message." He thrust the envelope at Patrick and turned to the children. "Watch out for him," he said. "You wouldn't like to be him if he came back."

Patrick dropped the envelope in the compartment that wasn't occupied by the empty can and made with a defiant series of clanks for the gate. From the pavement he saw the children watching him like guards. On his way back to the barbecue Mel shouted "You're not kidding us you didn't write it, Pad."

How could Patrick have been responsible? Where would he have found the envelope or the opportunity to write on it, or a reason? Mel's suggestion had left him feeling that his memory was wrong—that his whole mind was. He needed to show Eunice the item in the hope that somebody owned up. As he headed for the main road he grew anxious to locate a bin where he could bring the clatter of the trolley to an end. The dark sky looked too burdened to keep hold of its rain, but so far not a drop had touched him. Lightning flashed as he passed the Watch—no, the security camera caught him once more. He turned the bend that brought Dogs Home in sight, and Gutter started barking. Patrick wasn't about to be driven off the pavement, and he was marching past the gate when a man called "Hi there, postman. Just wait, will you."

His voice was as clipped as his grey hair and moustache. He was waving an envelope—the first item Patrick had delivered. "This isn't ours," he complained. "It's not remotely like."

The Doberman sprang up as Patrick took the envelope, and the dog's jaws clicked shut only inches from his hand. "Down, you brute," the man said. "It doesn't care for strangers."

Patrick had to squint hard at the restless letters to grasp that the house where he should have left it was called Boosome. Even if the name made no sense, how could he have misread it? Mel hadn't affected his mind then, but Patrick felt as if their encounter had undermined time. Though the savage antics of the dog gave him little chance to think, he seemed to recall having seen the name somewhere on his round, surely not just on the envelope. "Sorry to have troubled you," he said.

As the dog bounded at the gate again its owner strode back to the house. For long enough to let the gloom droop lower overhead Patrick tried to think which way to move. He felt as if he was attempting to look down on Garden Mile, still at his desk and searching the map. How distant was the address he had to find? The Doberman was leaping higher, snarling through its teeth, and he had a sense that the entire suburb was growling at him. It wouldn't stop him performing his job. He wasn't going to give anyone an excuse to criticise him, and he tramped back along the road. At the bend he turned to bid some kind of farewell to the dog, which seemed to need no breath to bark. He'd hardly met its eyes when it vaulted over the gate and raced after him.

He wasted seconds in fancying this was his latest hallucination, and then he fled. The Watch greeted his clangourous approach with another flash of lightning, and the pavement around him broke out in a nervous rash. More of the rain streamed down his face, unless that was the juice of his panic. It blurred his vision while he dashed towards the Pad, where he saw faces at an upstairs window. As the dog appeared at the bend in the road Patrick rushed the trolley to the open gates. He hadn't reached them when Kiera and Kieron came out of the house.

They had been at the window, and he thought they'd been watching for him. Kiera was jigging to a repetitive ditty on her phone, and her brother had a gun. Patrick floundered through the gates after the trolley, and the boy pointed the toy at him. "Is that a birthday present?" Patrick said. "It looks real."

"It's our grandad's and you have to piss off."

Kiera continued to jerk like a puppet as if neither she nor the phone felt the rain. "You come in," she warned, "and you'll get what dad said."

Patrick heard claws clacking on the tarmac and a snarl that grew lower but closer. He flung back one of the lids of the trolley to see just his envelope and the Boosome item. "Not them," he pleaded and found the empty can to shy at the dog. It bounced off the animal's head, and the dog gave a yelp before redoubling its snarl and padding towards him. "Let me stay," Patrick begged the children.

"I'll make it right with your father."

Through the house he saw Mel and others busy erecting a shelter beyond the crowded kitchen. He took another step, and Kieron raised the pistol. "Not me," Patrick blurted. "The dog."

He stooped to yank the bolt of the left-hand gate out of its socket, and was shutting the gate when he heard his vehicle backfire. It couldn't, since it had no engine, but he'd been distracted by a dull punch on his back. He clung to the gate while he stumbled to face the children. Kiera was continuing to prance, and her brother had him covered. "He's not gone yet," Kiera said.

Patrick tried joining in the dance as he lunged at the other gate. His capering impressed neither of the children, and might even have provoked the blow his chest took. Somebody behind the house—Mel or his father—wondered loudly what had just happened, but nobody came to look. "All right," Patrick said with more dignity than he'd realised he possessed, "I'll take my chances with the dog," and staggered past the gates. Perhaps he hadn't made himself heard, unless it didn't matter, because he received a parting thump on the back of his skull.

It carried him into the road, where he sprawled face down on the tarmac. The sky collapsed on him—the downpour did, at any rate. Perhaps that was why he could barely see the dog until its muzzle met his cheek. He couldn't move enough to flinch, but in any case the dog was only licking rain off him. Was it merely rain that was inundating the road around him? Dance music grew louder as the children came to view him, and he thought lightning had accompanied them until he heard the whir of a shutter on a phone. In the distance a man gave a cry of disgust or frustration about him if not the weather. As Patrick felt himself begin to spread through Garden Mile, he could only wonder if this would help him deliver the last of the mail.

§

The Oxford Companion to English Literature describes **Ramsey Campbell** as "Britain's most respected living horror writer." He has been given more awards than any other writer in the field, including the Grand Master Award of the World Horror Convention, the Lifetime Achievement Award of the Horror Writers Association, the Living Legend Award of the International Horror Guild and the World Fantasy Lifetime Achievement Award. In 2015 he was made an Honorary Fellow of Liverpool John Moores University for outstanding services to literature.

Tends to Zero

WOLE TALABI

$$e^{i\pi} + 1 = 0$$

WHEN THE SUN RISES, SO DO I. THROUGH THE curtains, filtered dawnlight kisses my eyes. I wake.

It's 7:05 a.m., and I should still be fast asleep. After a long night of drinking, first at Freedom Park and later at Quilox Club, ending in a deeply unsatisfying threesome with Chiamaka and Ronke—runs girls I'd picked up from Swe Bar—I'd finally drifted off into dreamless slumber at about five. Now I am awake. Laying in this soft bed, in the softly lit executive suite of the InterContinental Hotel, nestled between two soft, naked bodies, I find myself thinking of last night, of the early minutes before the start of Afropolitan Vibes at Freedom Park, the only part of the evening that I genuinely remember.

We'd arrived early—Asiru, Lekan, Chris, and I. In the cloudy sky, the sun had taken on an orange halo as it sank against a field of dizzying purples, red, blues, and yellows. We found a nice table near the stage where the air was scheduled to vibrate with loud, live music in a few hours and settled down with two bowls of pepper soup, a plateful of suya, and a calabash of allegedly fresh palm wine.

A young man who looked like a vagrant with a goje was sitting on the sand at the edge of the stage, playing softly. I'd watched the sun slowly drown in the horizon while my old friends from university, whom I hadn't seen in months, tried to distract me from memories of my dead brother. They meant well, but I couldn't bring myself to care about their words. When they realized I wasn't really paying attention, they slowly pivoted their discussion to arguments about football and politics.

Sitting there silently in the strange light of sundown, I momentarily regressed into a sort of dream state and, in so doing, found myself free of sadness for the first time since my mother had called screaming into the phone that Tunji was dead. But as the sun finally fell, I became aware of the thick white wall surrounding the park, and the memory of its history, which I had learned about in the process of failing my first year at university, poisoned my mood.

Freedom Park was built on the old, colonial-era Broad Street Prison, the first prison set up after the British seized Lagos in 1861. Originally built with mud and thatch, it was repeatedly arsoned by anti-colonial freedom fighters, so the British rebuilt it with brick. Thousands were imprisoned and executed by enforcers of the British colonial will, including many of Nigeria's founding fathers, but after independence, Nigeria took control of her own destiny and became responsible for her own cruelties. Many people were kept incarcerated there in the years following, including highway robbers and separatists that had been on the losing side of the civil war. The prison was finally pulled down in 1976, and Freedom Park developed over it. Imprisonment was replaced by artistic expression. A history of pain was overwritten with the promise of regularly scheduled pleasures.

Perhaps I was sitting in the exact spot where someone had been kept in chains like an animal for resisting foreign invaders, perhaps I was eating from a table that stood where someone had been killed, offered as a sacrifice on the altar of law and order in the new republic. Freedom Park was a palimpsest, and whatever fragment of happiness I'd glimpsed in the drowning sun could no longer be perceived clearly through its history. I wished then that I hadn't known anything about the park and its history of pain and violence, perhaps I'd have been able to hold on to that feeling longer. History is a burden, knowledge is misery, and I know too much about this city where I was born and where I, like my brother, will probably die. I'd spent the rest of the night in a blur, and more money than I reasonably should have, blunting my mind and memories with marijuana, lust, and alcohol in an effort to recapture the feeling. I failed.

I rise, lift Ronke's perfectly manicured hand off my chest, push Chiamaka gently until she rolls over, and slide out from between them, underneath the covers at the end of the bed. I put on the fluffy white robe, with a stitched gold emblem, and comfortable straw slippers provided by the hotel. The lights are off, but immature daylight illuminates the clothes, condoms, receipts, underwear, bundles of cash, and bottles on the floor. The slick, modern decor of the room that I had admired when I booked it seems tainted by what we did here yesterday, three people caring nothing for each other, licking, rubbing, and slapping flesh against flesh desperately. The place now seems sleazy.

I catch my dim reflection in the large rectangular mirror set in an old mahogany frame, carved with leaf and flower designs, and notice that my entire body somehow seems substantially smaller, somewhat shrunken and skinny, like I have lost a sixth or so of my weight in the last few days. I choose not to think about it too much. It's probably just an optical illusion, light and shadow playing games at dawn. Or the result of a residual high. I grab a half-empty bottle of Jack Daniels from the floor and walk over to the window. The sun glints over the lagoon, making it shimmer like liquid silver, and for a moment, I forget just how filthy the water is beneath the soft waveforms of the surface.

I take a large swig of the whiskey, throw the bottle on the bed between the girls, and sink to my knees. Tears roll down my face. I kneel there, weeping softly, watching the sun rise over the water until the sudden trill of my phone drags me back to the present.

I rise from the floor, wipe away the tears, and walk to the dresser where my phone sits insistent. The caller ID reads "Mum," and I instinctively reach for it before pausing. I gaze at the screen, my hand frozen. On the other end of the call, she is probably sitting on her bed, morning prayers just completed, bible in her thin hand, and her hair bound up in a silk scarf. I would love to talk to her now, to share memories of playing with Tunji in the sand at Bar Beach, to tell her how desperately I wish I could bring him back, but I know she will only cry and wail and tell me how terrible my life is and that I should come with her to church before God takes me too. Often, I find myself wishing he'd done just that.

I can't talk to her now. Not when I'm like this. My body thaws, I pick up the phone, swipe to dismiss the call without answering, and put it on silent. My skin feels too tight, my legs unsteady. Ashamed, I walk to the bed and fall back into the valley between the two naked women, narrowly avoiding the bottle. I feel like Adam, hiding among the trees of the Garden of Eden.

I am alone. I mean, I have always felt alone, living more in my head and in the bottle than in the world, keeping most of my thoughts and emotions to myself, but Tunji's death has triggered something. I have been feeling a new kind of aloneness, a deeper and more complete kind of aloneness that has suffused every thought and emotion I have. It hurts. I don't want it.

I wrap my arm around Ronke's waist and pull her to me. Her voice, sultry with drowsiness, drifts to me, "Ah ahn, you're awake already?"

She moans, pulling a pillow to her chest as I rub myself against her. She sighs.

"Let me put you back to bed. Try for a little pleasure before the end."

I ignore the strange conclusion to her sentence, not understanding what she means by it, and we have joyless sex for a quarter of an hour while Chiamaka pretends to sleep. When we are done, I fall asleep again, exhausted and empty.

By noon, we are all awake. I give them ₦125,000 to get back to their campus and take care of themselves when they get there, slipping an extra ₦25,000 into Ronke's hand while Chiamaka is putting on her makeup in the bathroom. She rewards me with a wink but doesn't take the money, pressing the cash and my hand back against my chest. Her long hair swishes as she shakes her head and adjusts her dress like a second skin.

"It's okay. I really don't need this," she says before she kisses me on the cheek and looks at me with something like pity in her impossibly grey eyes. Ashamed, I look away and say goodbye without returning her gaze.

I take a shower, slip into my T-shirt, jeans, and sunglasses, which all seem a bit too big, and then check out of the hotel and drive back down to Swe Bar in Onikan where music with incomprehensible lyrics set to bass as thick as the heartbeat of a decadent god and the cloying smell of whiskey welcome me like a womb.

$$1 + \frac{1}{\varphi} = \varphi$$

With dawn comes sharp flares of pain, red needles of light beneath my eyelids.

I turn away from the rapidly rising sun, my hands instinctively covering my face as the hangover begins to blossom in my head. My hands are the familiar wet of vomit and dew. My back is sore from sleeping on the unforgiving concrete sidewalk leading out of Tafawa Balewa Square, less than a mile from the bar. A woolen echo fills my head, silencing the world. My bones press against my skin, making my body feel small and not quite fully developed. I feel like an accident.

Peeking out from between my fingers, the upside-down city smiles back at me in the fading twilight, its badly maintained buildings and hastily constructed steel towers like uneven teeth in a yellow-grey mouth of sky.

There is a bus stop near me. I can tell by the tangle of traffic—mostly beat-up danfos and molues, secondhand motorcycles and scratched cars. Old men sit by the roadside on low stools under brightly colored umbrellas, their hands moving rapidly as they ready their stalls and kiosks for the day into which I have clumsily emerged. There is a carnival of bright plastic buckets and metal trays carried by women, children and young men hawking wares. The colors are too bright, the silence in my head too unnatural.

In a sudden surge, sound returns to the world, and the hysteria of feet slapping against the concrete and tires crunching pot-holed road, car horns blaring, and engines growling all explode into my consciousness. Four roads dance into a roundabout a little distance away, and there are no traffic lights. It's pure Lagos chaos, and it makes my hangover feel like an irresolute death.

I groan and sit up, hanging my heavy head between my legs and leaning my back against a cracked, upright concrete slab that should have been covering a gutter for support as people walk past me, staring, shaking their heads and hissing. Tears and saliva fall from my face to the ground as I wonder wretchedly why I hadn't been the one to die instead of my brother.

Tunji had always been the ambitious one. The smart one with the scholarship to UNILAG, the handsome one who got married to a beautiful wife at 24, the fun one who had friends everywhere and who had gone from being an accountant to a five-star restaurant owner, and the one who'd planned to retire a millionaire at 50 just like our father. I was the mediocre one, the plain one who got below average grades in class, who barely managed to graduate from Osun State University after stumbling through four years of English literature, who worked as a DJ and producer for street musicians and dodgy radio stations.

Despite this achievement gulf between us and the constant remarks of our parents who fetishized their public image and the way our lives reflected on them, Tunji and I always remained friends. Perhaps even more than we were family, we were inexplicably friends. When we were children, we always insisted on playing together no matter what our vastly disparate cliques thought of the other. Whenever Tunji got picked as football team captain and the captains took turns selecting team members, he would always pick me to join his team first, even though my feet were as clumsy with a ball then as they usually are after a dozen or so glasses of shepe now. Whenever my friends and I went to smoke igbo on the rooftop of our hostel, I always insisted that they allow Tunji to join us despite his reputation as a "scholarship boy" because I knew he liked the mental freedom that came with the herbal high, even if he didn't like the dank, cloying smell of weed. He was the first person that I told when I failed my first year at university, and he drove all the way to Ikire to drink with me and be beside me when our father arrived to tell me what a shame I was to the entire family. I was the best man at his wedding, and I ran around Lagos like a wild animal for eight weeks helping to make arrangements with caterers and florists and musicians and the million other vendors, so the couple wouldn't have to. And even though once the ceremony was over I got drunk and passed out in the carpark a few minutes to midnight, Tunji came to find me, put ice packs on my face, pour water down my throat until I woke up, and drag me back to the after-party, laughing all the while. Our moments of connection were always like that, characterized by us just being there for each other, not necessitated by anything beyond who we were to one another.

But they were also characterized by this: my constant failing, my constant falling, and Tunji's unwillingness to let me hit rock bottom and break. The truth is, I gave up on myself early. I became an alcoholic wastrel when I was about nineteen. Since then, I have had little ambition in life beyond drinking myself into some semblance of ignorant bliss and making myself as small as possible, trying not to disappoint my parents much more than I already had once I realized I'd never be able to live up to my father and brother.

My father was a legendary hotelier with properties dotting the city, and Tunji, he was going places. At least he was until an articulated truck skidded off the Ojuelegba Bridge and fell to the road below, smashing him into a pulpy mess in the front seat of his Range Rover SUV.

My mother has been crying and praying for three weeks, inconsolable. I've been drinking. Whiskey. I've been drinking whiskey. I've been drinking because I don't know what else to do. Palm wine is best for celebration, but whiskey is good for pain.

"You're lucky armed robbers or policemen didn't kill you while you were sleeping," says a rusty old voice in confident Yoruba. It sounds like it's coming from both inside my head and above me at the same time. I raise my head to see two thin eyes set into a wide, wrinkled face, smiling at me.

"But then again, you don't have much time left."

"Who are you?" I groan. The man speaking to me is a small, shriveled old man with a big grey afro and small grey eyes; he has a wise, seen-the-world look to him like a living sunset. He is wearing a green and brown Ankara shirt and trouser combination with plain brown sandals and a gold watch that looks more expensive than he should be able to afford.

"Doesn't matter," he says and tosses a ₦500 note onto the ground in front of me. "That should be enough to get you home. I think you'll find that your wallet is no longer with you."

"I don't need your help, old man," I shout, louder than I intend to, as I reach for the note to hand it back to him. My fingers settle on sandy concrete, my vision swims, and I fall over, banging my head hard.

The man looks down at me pitifully as he pushes his money into the front pocket of my shirt.

"Foolish boy," he says. "Go home and wait. There's no need for all this drama. You'll be gone soon enough."

The calmness with which he makes this strange statement and the familiarity of it jolts me out of my drunken haze just long enough to ask, "What the hell does that mean?"

"If I tell you . . ." begins the old man before a brief pause and tilt of the head. And then, "Forget it. I've already done what I can to make this easier for you. Just take the money, and go home."

I drag myself up from the floor and grab hold of his trousers. "Why did you say I will be gone soon? Are you cursing we with juju?"

"I don't curse people," he says as he shakes his leg free of my grasp. "I'm not a babalawo. I'm . . . no one."

He walks along the sidewalk, whispering something to himself, and I start to think that he will leave without saying more, but he stops and turns to face me and says, "Look, this isn't easy for me either. It has only ever happened twice before."

"What the hell are you talking about?"

He sighs and shakes his head before finally speaking. "What would you say if I told you that this city, like you, is alive? It was born, it grows, it eats, it loves, it will die. Since it was a child, it has learned to eat what it needs from the lives of the ever-growing flood of people that come into it, become part of it. Its riverbanks have become cradles, its slums have developed into fists; its grey roads have grown teeth; its traffic and owambes and construction and beaches have developed a rhythm like a pounding heartbeat. And the city, like all living things, will always do what it needs to survive, fight to stay alive, defend itself from threats to its life. And what would you say if I told you that you, young man, have somehow found a way to make yourself a threat to the city?"

I hear the words he says, but they don't make sense to me. I know from experience that words can sometimes shake free of meaning and become abstract noises when heard in hangover or post-high, but this is different. He is talking of Lagos like it's a person, a real human. Not in metaphor but in substance. Puzzled and hungry for understanding, I can only mutter, "The city is alive?"

"Yes," he says. "Look, go home. You won't understand now. Take the money I gave you, and go home. Drink some more and forget all this. In the evening, you'll really notice the change, and maybe you'll start to understand."

"What will I understand? What will I see? What is happening to me?"

"Bloody hell. I should have just stayed away. Give me your hand," he says impatiently as he kneels on the ground beside me. The pedestrians on the increasingly busy street stare at us even more than they did before, but I don't care. I do as I'm told.

He puts his hand into mine, and it feels like an old earthenware plate, but what is even stranger, it feels like this small old man's hand is larger than mine. Much larger.

"This is what I mean. First in your depression and now in your grief, you have been thinking strangely of this city, viewing it all wrong through the lens of your pain. You have linked parts of the city with negative memories, with painful histories, with almost everything wrong in your life, with everything wrong in so many lives. Usually most people link parts of the city with both good and bad memory and emotion. There is a balance, and the city works it out. But you, with your sadness and grief, have threaded a pure and persistent pain to the very essence of the things with which cities are made flesh, and it has obstructed the city's breathing, pressed against its organs. You have become a sickness, a cancer, so the city is pressing back against you. You must understand, none of this is malicious. Now you will shrink as the city destroys you. You will become smaller and smaller and smaller, and eventually you will disappear into nothing because Lagos can no longer survive with you in it."

The air around me smells of reused cooking oil, sweat, and exhaust. A danfo heading to Yaba passes by, the conductor calling out the destination. There is a white sticker on its back window where in faded red font it declares, "God's Time is Best."

Dazed, I ask the strange old man, "How long do I have?"

"In one or two days, it will be as though you never existed. You will be forgotten. Your mother will not remember that she had more than one son. Your friends will not miss you. You will be subject to a great and instant forgetting. You will have been nothing but a wick, nameless, snuffed out. A discarded bundle of memories and experiences without a name. The city will absorb you and your experiences and purge them. It must to survive. And when it is done, it will adjust itself and its people so that it may continue to live."

I throw my head back and close my eyes to shut out the sun, and I start to laugh and laugh a long laugh that becomes a cough, and before long, I am choking.

I feel the eyes on the old man on the back of my head and his hand on my shoulder, so I ask, "This is ridiculous. Why should I even believe any of the rubbish you just said to me?"

He rises to his feet and straightens his back.

"Because I *am* the city. And I *will* not let your twisted pain kill me."

And with that, he scatters into a billion tiny pieces that are seamlessly absorbed by the air and concrete and mud and madness, leaving me hungover and confused on the cracked Lagos pavement, wondering if he was ever really there at all.

$$\lim_{t \to \infty} \sum u(t) = 0$$

A sharp knife of sunlight cuts through the space between the curtains of my bedroom and across my body, separating my consciousness and leaving me half-awake for the third time this morning. A part of me wants to rise early, but the bed is warm and soft, and exhaustion keeps dragging me back into sleep like an anchor until memories of the old man penetrate the fog, and I remember. I remember. I am disappearing.

I sit up, my torso crossing the line of light, and am surprised at the alien nature of my own movements, the arcs my limbs trace are unfamiliar and strange, so strange. I am afraid of my changing self. The fear paralyzes me, but what do men who are shrinking into themselves do? There is a half-empty bottle of whiskey on the bedside table, its glass edges and amber liquid beautiful in the light of the young sun. I stare at it for what could be seconds or hours—I am not sure—yearning for the familiar comfort and knowing that it will not, cannot, help me anymore. I turn back to the window and watch as dawn unravels, skeins of light spreading across the wide sky, and think of the artists selling cheap paintings of sunrise on canvas in Jakande Market alongside wooden art, beads, bracelets, necklaces, talking drums. If Lagos truly is alive, then its many markets must be its beating heart. I almost smile.

When the sun is high and bright, I briefly consider visiting my mother, taking her up on her open offer to take me to church. Perhaps her pastor can pray for me when he is finished counting his profits from last Sunday's collection.

No. But I should at least talk to her. I want to talk to her. I need to. She is the only family I have left even if the old man, who says he is the city, says she will not remember me when I am gone.

I rise on unsteady legs like a newborn calf and go into the living room, stumbling. Falling into the middle of the sofa, fighting to breathe evenly and cleanly, I pull my phone out of my pocket, press "Mum" on the smooth screen, and hold it up to my ear with a skeletal hand. My grip is so weak; the phone slips from my hand when she answers, and it takes me a few seconds to retrieve it.

"Goodbye?" she repeats when I finally say the word. "What do you mean goodbye? Where are you going?"

"Yes," I confirm. "I know things have been difficult between us lately, but I just wanted to say goodbye, and I love you."

"Where are you going?" she asks again.

"I don't know," I tell her because even though I want to confess to her that her son is being consumed by a city, it would be too confusing and too cruel.

"What does that mean, ehn?" she asks before retreating into the safety of her religion. "You've started with your wahala again, but this is not the time for it, so I need you to listen to me. Don't go anywhere yet. There is midweek service today, and pastor Chris has been asking of you since the funeral. Come with me, and let us—"

She is still speaking, but her words are too familiar to mean anything to me. She keeps talking. I drop the phone to my rake-thin thighs and stare at it, mesmerized, like it is a gemstone or a small, talking animal. The tears begin to flow, and I find myself once again confronted by the widening gap between myself and the woman who birthed me. We used to be very close when I was younger and my mind more malleable, but my entire adulthood has been a series of estrangements. I want to talk to her now, to tell her how sad, angry, confused, and scared I am at everything and nothing, how desperately I need to feel like something about my presence in this world mattered before I am gone from it, but all she can do, all she has ever done, is tell me to come to church. She has no other counsel to offer but the comfort of her god. I wish that once, just this once, she would try to talk to me without the wall of her faith between us, even if she has no assurances to offer me. I just want to know that in this moment we are equally human. I put the phone back to my ear and repeat myself, ignoring her own stream of words, "Goodbye, Mum. I love you."

She will forget me soon, and perhaps that's for the best. Sometimes even family means nothing in the end. I wish Tunji were still here. Lagos is a cruel city to take him like that, to erase me in retaliation for poisoning it with my grief. I throw my phone at the wall, and it shatters into a hundred useless pieces. And then all the fear and anger and pain and grief and disappointment and depression and confusion congeal into something liquid in my chest that drips down my ribs, tickling me as I laugh and laugh with all the bitterness in me until tears run down my face like a poisoned river, and I close my eyes to keep them in.

I drift into something like sleep, and there I feel the flowering within me of a potential for something like happiness, something much deeper and something more unique than the chemically induced highs and obliviousness of alcohol. Something beyond my strange circumstances and my changing body. Something so much . . . more. When I open my eyes, it hits me.

I imagine myself as I used to be a few days ago, heavily and intentionally, until I feel like my imagination has taken form, has physical weight. I imagine a hand shaped like a city with expressway fingers, open air market palms, and beach surf fingernails squeezing me. Just like the old man said, I see the city compress me, and I lift my left hand up and stare at it.

My forearms thin almost immediately. I see my skin tighten and the flesh padding my bone diminish like it is evaporating. My stomach twists with fear and excitement. But I don't stop. I press on, my mind swelling with imagination as I picture more of the city in the hand that squeezes me. In that hand, I see the filth and congestion of Obalende, its winding, yellow molue queues and ugly, dirty shanties where so many in Lagos pass through on their way to the day's labors like callouses on the palms. I see the lovely colonial townhouses, mansions, clubs, and hotels of Ikoyi where the rich and powerful nest themselves like the lines in the little finger of the city. I picture the filthy canals, waterways, and shacks on stilts of Makoko, running along the lagoon where the Egun fishermen who migrated from Badagary eke out a living, and in my mind, it is the back of the hand of the city that squeezes me. I see the new rows of apartment buildings and townhouses that are being built in Ajah, the place for the once-growing middle class that seems separate from but flows into the city like its cephalic vein. I see the roiling, dirty waves of Bar Beach like Ronke's fingernails, long and extended and pressed against my chest. I inhale air and exhale myself. I feel my ribs contracting, my chest emptying me out into the city, as I imagine what it is doing to me, and I will it to press against me even harder, to accelerate the process. It is exhilarating. Spittle collects in the corners of my mouth as I collapse back on the couch and continue my fading away.

It gets easier and easier as I do it, my imagination yielding more of the city and less of myself. My legs become thin stalks, and my torso reduces to thin board after a few cycles of squeezing and letting go, squeezing and letting go. I am developing a muscle for erasing myself, strengthening it with high-intensity exercise.

I have reduced myself to little more than a skeleton before I feel the urge to be out in the city as I do this. To insert the unreality of my situation into the absolute reality of Lagos, to be in the open city as I picture it pressing onto me.

I push up from the couch and struggle outside to my car. The difficulty of walking outside is expected, but pulling open the door takes far more effort than I thought it would. It has been so hot and humid that the air outside is thick, hazy, saturated with water vapor, smoke, prayers, and dreams. The sun feels heavy on my head. I nestle myself in the driver's seat and look at my face in the mirror.

I am gaunt. Adrenaline erupts and surges through my veins as I rev the engine and press the horn until Ladi the gateman comes out to open the gate, holding up his sagging trousers with one hand. When I pass, I floor the accelerator and swing the car out onto the road, rear tires smoking and showering everything with dust, sand, and gravel. By the time Ladi is a speck in the mirror, too small to distinguish from the hundreds of other pedestrians, I am sweating profusely.

The wind blows wildly through the windows as I barrel down Okobaba Street, ignoring the traffic lights and dipping in and out of potholes recklessly.

And then, suddenly, there is a large, lovely woman in the car with me. I know it is Lagos because it can be no one and nothing else. She is wearing a spectacular gold and blue traditional iro and buba made with expensive aso-oke. The iro is tight against her wide hips, and the buba has a low-cut neck that would be revealing if it wasn't for the half dozen matching stringed-bead necklaces around her neck. Her stiff, blue gele is a large and elaborate affair like the train of a wild peacock wrapped around her head and pressing against the roof of my car. She speaks as I round the highway exit and climb up the causeway that leads to the third mainland bridge.

"What are you doing?" Lagos asks as she adjusts her gele and turns to face me with piercing grey eyes. "You can't stop this once it has begun."

"I am not trying to stop it. I am embracing it," I reply, bizarrely buoyant. I no longer fear anything, not my mediocre and pointless life, not this overwhelming and cruel city and its history, not even my coming demise. Even my grief for Tunji has morphed into something new. There is freedom in acceptance. With practiced ease, I take the image of the woman sitting beside me into my mind, and in my imagination, I picture this manifestation of Lagos, broad and beautiful, sitting on my chest, compressing me. I am delighted when I see my fingers, tight against the wheel, shrink. To imagine the city is to lose myself.

"You should have done this sooner," says Lagos. "Accepted things. You should have accepted the life you had. Perhaps I wouldn't have had to purge you."

"Perhaps," I say because I cannot think of anything else to say.

"Do you want me to stay with you?" the city asks. "Until the end?"

"No need," I say. "I want to do this alone."

"I understand. And I am sorry," says the city. "I am only trying to survive."

I mouth the words, "I understand."

"Is there anything you want before you're gone? Any final requests?"

"I want to see Tunji, even if only for a moment, right before the end. Can you do that?"

"I'll see what I can do," she says.

When I glance to my right, there is nothing but a gourd of palm wine in the chair where the woman that is the city had been. I wonder what we are celebrating as I reach for it and take a swig. It tastes like freedom.

An okada whizzes by, barely an inch from me, and I almost hit it. My arms and fingers are so small; it is difficult to control the car now. My vision is blurring at the edges. Shapes and colors are bleeding into each other like reality around me has been stabbed. Or perhaps my eyes are becoming too small to see clearly. I look up through the windscreen. Above, the sun is retreating behind a curtain of silver and black clouds. The skyscrapers of the marina in the distance, the shanties on the edge of the water, all of it now seems less real than the dream-images I have of them in my head pressing against me. The horizon of my existence grows nearer and nearer. I am carrying my version of the city in my mind, a private and complete burden that I will soon be free of just as the city will soon be free of me.

The sky begins to weep rain.

I press my foot down harder against the accelerator, and the vehicle vibrates intensely like a lover in orgasm.

When I can no longer keep control of the careening car, I swerve right, hard.

Tires scream, the world spirals, and I crash through the barrier. Everything slows as jagged metal and hot rubber slam into my windscreen, cracking it and bringing in the smell of smoke and the raw bite of pain. I fall. I fall for what seems like a long time.

When the car breaks the surface of the lagoon, water rushes in. I close my eyes and imagine that all of Lagos, from Badagry to Ikeja is liquid around me. It gets harder to breathe, but I am not sure if it is because my lungs are shrinking rapidly or because I am drowning. I feel myself become small, so small and slight. I turn my body over to this water that is the city and so much larger than myself.

In the instant before there is no more of me, I see Tunji's eyes blossom open like flowers in the darkness. I hear his voice in my head, and his voice is my voice, the voice of the city, which is the only voice that exists, the only voice that has ever existed, and it says, *Everything dies, and everything will be forgotten. Ideas. Feelings. Lives. Cities. Monuments. Gods. Memories. Everything. Everything tends to zero.*

Wole Talabi is a full-time engineer, part-time writer, and some-time editor from Nigeria. His stories have appeared in *The Magazine of Fantasy and Science Fiction (F&SF)*, *Lightspeed*, *Terraform*, *AfroSF (v3)*, and several other places. He has edited two anthologies and co-written a play. His fiction has been nominated for several awards, including the Caine Prize and the Nommo Award, which he won in 2018. His work has also been translated into Spanish, Norwegian, Chinese, and French. His debut collection of stories, *Incomplete Solutions* (2019), is published by Luna Press, Scotland. He likes scuba diving, elegant equations, and oddly shaped things. He currently lives and works in Malaysia. Find him online at wtalabi.wordpress.com and @wtalabi on Twitter.

My Lying-Down Smiley Face

STEPHEN GRAHAM JONES

T HE WAY AUDREY FIGURED IT, IT WASN'T REALLY STEALING.

First, outside of practice biopsies for medical students, a tumor from a seventy-three-year old deceased woman doesn't really have any intrinsic value. A dime a dozen, right? Audrey couldn't sell it on the street by the ounce, she couldn't build a sideshow around it, and she couldn't put it on the good side of an organ donor list. Nobody was going to miss it.

Second, had her mother had a fluttery heart during pre-op—getting the vapors, as she would have tried to call it—and been unable to continue with the surgery, she'd have had that exact tumor inside her still, and it would have been hers, not the hospital's.

Just because she'd died on the operating table didn't mean ownership changed. Sure, there was no "owner" anymore, exactly. But there was an heir. A daughter.

When they gave Audrey a couple of minutes alone with her mother to say goodbye—*to be sure*, Audrey corrected in her head—she'd noticed the tumor in a plastic specimen bottle on a cart on the other side of the operating room. Hours and hours ago, the nurse at Admitting had printed out a sheet of labels with Audrey's mother's last name and first initial on them, and one of those labels had been applied to the side of that bottle.

Inside, the tumor wasn't suspended in foggy Victorian liquid like they always were on television. The tumor was slumped against the side of the bottle as if spent from the operation. From how hard it had tried to resist the blade.

It was grey and smooth with veins or tubules or something still attached. Fibers, tendrils, tentacles? Ducts of some biological sort? Was that how a tumor did its thing, by sending feelers out into the body, little mouths opening at the end of those long tubes?

If Audrey hadn't known what her mother's surgery was for, she would have assumed the tumor to be a liver, a kidney, a gall bladder. The tumor looked as if it had purpose, like it had evolved for some obscure internal task, one it would have completed if not for the disruption of this surgery. The cart it was on had had its four upright posts wrapped with red BIO-WASTE tape, like a barber pole. *Waste,* as in headed for the trash bin. *Waste,* as in nobody would miss it.

The bottle fit in Audrey's shoulder bag perfectly, right alongside the plastic container she'd had her lunch in, and because there was no embalming or preserving fluid, it didn't slosh when she walked back out into the hall.

The cause of death as it had been explained to her had been—to put it in terms for grieving daughters who obviously don't know anything, who don't work at labs themselves—simply the strain of a fragile chest cracking open for the first time in its seventy-three years. There had always been a distinct level of risk associated with surgery like this, the surgeon was sure to reiterate, and Audrey's mother's doctors never would have recommended her for a dangerous operation like this had the tumor not become life threatening, and then on and on with apologies and regrets and condolences and assurances, all of which Audrey nodded politely to and feigned appreciation for.

Really?

It was better this way.

Now, no more calls at four in the morning, accusing Audrey of abandoning her mother to a system that didn't have her best interests at heart. No more judgments for the way Audrey was living her life—the sinful way she was *choosing* to live her life. This marked the end of the all-caps texts complaining about the medium of texting itself, and why couldn't Audrey just pick up her phone and *talk* through it? Wasn't that why it's called a phone? Was Audrey's mother missing something here?

Those texts reminded Audrey too much of growing up.

In the privacy of her teenage diary—that her mother had made *un*-private one loud afternoon—Audrey had spent page after page wondering what had lodged in her mother in her teens or twenties to make her like she was now. The way Audrey pictured it in words her mother ended up reading out loud to her, her mother had been walking down the sidewalk one otherwise normal day, just taking in the city in all its hustle and bustle, when, as bad luck would have it, a speck of resentment had been lolling about on the breeze, waiting to get breathed in by some hapless passerby. Audrey's mother was that passerby. She had inhaled that fleck of corruption, and the way Audrey imagined it, she'd then put the palm of her right hand to her upper chest while blinking twice fast.

Which her mother in the living room that afternoon, diary in her other hand, had been sure to mime.

It was her go-to gesture, after all.

But in Audrey's version, no one had noticed that this random girl had breathed this random irritant in. There was no need to grin this away, no need to play it off.

So Audrey's mother kept right on walking down that sidewalk. Only, it was inside her now, this resentment blooming into bitterness and bile, which she would spew over her only daughter for her only daughter's first eighteen years.

But who was Audrey trying to fool?

Her mother had been on her case for more like four and a half decades. And while Audrey'd been conditioned and conditioned well to no longer write things down—"casting aspersions in your smutty little book" had been the precise wording—her imagination had never gone into any kind of remission. That speck had lodged deep in her mother's chest, yes, and in her mind, Audrey knew her mother had been playing the oyster ever since: locking the door to her bedroom and curling around this irritant, layering saliva around this intrusion into what had been going to be her perfect life, licking her recriminations and regret onto it, polishing that grain into something exquisite and harsh.

When she'd started spitting up blood six months ago? That just proved that this wasn't just all in Audrey's head. It made sense that her mother's own hatred had started eating her from the inside. It made sense that medical imaging showed a crude, hungry mass in her chest, trying to gnaw its way through as much life as it could.

Audrey had known it was there all along. It was the only explanation.

When, as a last resort, her mother would text her in all caps? Audrey, on the advice of her therapist, would text back a simple bland emoticon, which she then, on her next visit, would have to explain to her mother all over again: an emoticon is a textual representation of a face—yes, Mom, sideways because you have to use colons and parentheses and all that, and those are all straight up and down. It's a way of sneaking an expression in amongst the words, since there's no italics or bold or any of that to get it across.

Audrey's mother considered it a nuisance, having to angle the tiny screen of her flip phone over to make sense of whether Audrey was smiling or frowning or winking.

It was a small victory, the effort her mother was having to expend to get the intended tone or miss the sharp irony of Audrey's texts, but in a lifetime of large defeats, a small victory felt pretty all right.

Had Audrey's therapist had a tip jar on her desk, Audrey would have left it rattling for that good advice about the emoticon. Come to think of it, she would have tipped her mother's surgeon as well after he was done explaining the day's tragic events to her.

Audrey stood there and nodded, her lips prim, her eyes fixed on a spot well behind the surgeon, the hustle and bustle of the busy hospital swirling around the little island of stillness they were standing on.

Her voice wavered the appropriate amount when she thanked him for his effort. She touched his forearm with the fingertips of her right hand in farewell, and then she waltzed right out of that hospital into the brightest Wednesday she'd seen in a while, her mother's tumor tucked neatly under her arm.

Aside from a sudden certainty that people could see through the leather of her purse, Audrey's walk to the subway was nothing.

But then she didn't go down those stairs.

She could smell the port. Not with her own nose but with her mother's.

What no one but her only child ever knew about Audrey's mother, it was that her sense of smell was so sensitive it was practically a disability. Whenever she had to mill among the rabble, as she called the other members of her species, she would always come away with a headache from continually holding her breath. She could tell the moment mayonnaise turned. She knew a bad egg through the shell. She couldn't be in the same room with corn nuts or flavored chips. And she wasn't shy narrating to Audrey about who around them used the all-natural deodorant, who sprung for the synthetic stuff.

Audrey hated that, because of her mother's sense of propriety—which is to say, the snobbishness she came to through her sense of smell—she in response, unlike her wife, quietly used a roll-on that was probably, she imagined, responsible for ninety percent of global warming.

She also hated that, catching the whiff of the wharf, she crinkled her nose exactly as her mother would have.

But there was a remedy. Oh yes, there was a remedy.

Audrey might have to make all the proper obeisances with her mother's public remains—embalming, the casket she'd already picked out, the plot that was already paid for—but there was zero compulsion to do anything proper with her mother's medical waste.

Audrey stepped around the subway's stairway and walked into the wind, grandly inhaling that salty, rotting flavor.

If this tumor was her mother's vilest essence distilled, her core, her yolk, her soul, then dumping it into the brackish waters her mother considered the most putrid, the least palatable, that would have to be a lot like sending her to her own personal hell, wouldn't it?

"At least symbolically."

Audrey was already practicing how she was going to couch this for her therapist. She was already preparing for her therapist's approval—not enough to make her an accessory after the fact, just enough to let her know that, first, this was permanently between them and, second, it was supremely healthy. All the therapist's clients should be so bold, so decisive.

Audrey quickened her step. Her lips were pursed, neat. Not quite a smile since she didn't want to announce her intentions—who would ever guess though?—but "prim satisfaction" wasn't an admission of guilt either.

Bonnie, her wife, was going to find this hilarious. They were going to have to break out a second bottle tonight, more than likely.

And why not? No more bills from the home now. No more reminders of all the bad times. No more complainy calls before acceptable hours. No more of those sour texts in all caps. No more carefully measured emoticons in response.

From here on out, Audrey was just going to emoticon naturally like she should have been able to do all along.

It was a whole new world.

Had the surgeon been able to tell she was about to collapse into laughter or had he thought those were tears she was holding back?

It didn't matter. Not anymore.

Audrey shifted her purse to the other shoulder just to confirm the extra weight in there. The bulge of medical waste.

Once to the stubby little pier, though, Audrey hesitated. Not because of the flotsam scumming the surface of the water, and not because of the trash clinging to the pylons.

Because of the depth.

Were Audrey to pour her mother over the railing *here*, her mother would find the shore in a matter of minutes. And that would be far too easy—a kindness, practically.

No, Audrey's mother, she deserved the deep water.

It was time to take a ferry ride.

While waiting for the ferry to chug back over to her side of the water, Audrey called Bonnie. She wasn't sure exactly why. She couldn't have articulated it anyway.

Maybe it came down to not wanting to be all the way alone for a ritual so momentous? She didn't say that into Bonnie's voicemail though. The voicemail that meant she was in with a client.

"Um," Audrey said, "just wanted to . . . the surgery was a success. They got the tumor out."

It wasn't a lie. Technically.

Why didn't she want to say it though? *Mom's dead.*

She was afraid her voice might crack. It was stupid—it was stupid times ten, times fifty, but there it was.

Audrey wasn't sure if thinking this way, letting her sentimentality rise up, heat her eyes, was specific to her mother dying or just generally what society had trained her to feel upon the death of a parent.

If so, then Audrey supposed what she might really be feeling was guilty.

She had the specimen bottle out now. She was sitting on one of the wooden benches, passing the bottle back and forth from her left hand to her right.

It was the color of a tick, she'd decided a few minutes ago. The tumor had a color that suggested that, if you drained it, let it shrink back to the size it had been years ago, it would be that coppery dull brown a tick is when it's not latched onto a host.

As-was, though, the tumor was distended, its skin stretched out thin and grey.

Audrey shoved the plastic bottle back in her purse and signed off on the voicemail the way she always did: "Lying down happy face!"

It's how you do an emoticon out loud—it's what a colon followed by a closing parenthesis *made*: the stupidly grinning face of someone lying on her side.

It was how Audrey was telling Bonnie she was all right.

And she was, wasn't she?

The ferry bellowed its horn when it pulled in, startling Audrey from her trance—what her therapist called her "Audrey is *thinking*" face.

Audrey bought a round-trip, of course, as the plan was to stay on, circle back. An hour and a half all-told, but it was going to be worth it. Mother's last ferry ride. And for all Audrey knew, her first in twenty years too. Maybe longer.

Stepping off the platform onto the deck of the ferry, ready to accommodate the rocking that turned out not to be there in the slightest, Audrey was ninety percent sure the tumor sloughed over onto the floor of the bottle, its own adhesive qualities finally giving up on clinging to the side anymore. As if Audrey's mother was reacting to being here of all places. As if she were showing her displeasure with a choreographed, overdramatic swoon. The indignity. The *smell*.

Everybody moving from shore to ship, if this even counted as a ship—as grimy as the ferry was, wasn't it just a floating portion of the city, calved off into the murky river?—everybody had to have felt the tumor shift its weight, Audrey assumed. She was practically screaming in her head, loud enough that her legs went mechanical, forgot how to walk naturally.

She pressed the underside of the four fingers of her right hand to the hollow of her throat as if surprised and embarrassed to have just burped.

No one noticed. No one was watching her.

Looking down, she also confirmed that her purse had yet to become transparent. And the tumor had yet to raise its shrill voice, play its tubules like the bagpipe it most definitely wasn't. And there was no mass of people in aquamarine scrubs and surgical masks building up behind her, skipping their breaks and lunches to retrieve these few ounces of medical waste.

"You're being stupid, old girl," Audrey said to herself and cast about for the loneliest, most private stretch of rail.

While Audrey would have allowed that there might be kids on the ferry, had she even thought that far ahead, she was a bit taken aback by the lanky speckled happy-happy dog running from person to person, nuzzling their fingertips for the treat it knew was here somewhere if this ferry was anything like its own home.

When it was Audrey's turn for this inspection, she pulled her hand up to her purse strap and clamped tighter onto the rail with her other hand. She was sure a dog could give the alarm about what her fingertips had been touching.

"Allergic," she explained for anyone watching and listening.

No one was. That's the thing about the city.

She shifted her shoulder under the purse strap, and the tumor shifted with her, lolling to what felt like the other side of the specimen bottle.

Since no one was listening or watching, Audrey said to the tumor, "Just a moment now. Won't be long."

The ferry shuddered and started pulling for the other shore. At first, nothing changed but the pitch of the diesel engine, but then, like the world was on delay, the boat moved in its sluggish way. Audrey's phone buzzed in her purse—she could feel it buzz even a room away lately—but she let it go to voicemail. It would either be Bonnie, returning Audrey's call, or it would be the hospital, tactfully asking about a certain irregularity they were experiencing. A problem with, um, inventory.

Now that Audrey's mother was gone, Audrey guessed it was someone else's turn to start in with the veiled accusations. And if it was Bonnie calling, not the hospital, Audrey felt certain that now that she was actually *doing* it, now that she was actually engaging in this dark ritual, she might lie about where she was this precise instant, even though the ferry sounds and gulls would be giving her away. And she didn't want to have to lie. That would be a bad first step into this new part of her life.

Another bad first step: stalling.

This section of the railing was hers, wasn't it? It was her own private little part of the ferry. Her own little ritual space. And surely she couldn't be the first mourner—ha—to dump a loved one's remains into the water like this. Should she get caught, then she could just say that what she'd just dumped overboard had been the lunch she'd forgotten in the break-room refrigerator last week. It had been a large dumpling, say, from that new place two streets over. She would even dig for the receipt, frowning at the ridiculousness of this inquiry. The only way to prove she was lying would be to go into the water after her mother. Which is to say, she would be fine even when the receipt wasn't there.

There was no reason not to do this, she told herself. The world was *asking* her to do it, pretty much. Insisting, even.

So.

Audrey cased her immediate area again in what she knew had to be a suspicious way, and she pulled her purse around and extracted the specimen bottle, holding it by the white lid.

To anyone watching, maybe it could be a thermos. Maybe this was going to be a drink of coffee. Or maybe Audrey could be a secret alcoholic, cupping herself around this shame.

Still holding onto the lid, Audrey grasped onto the side of the bottle to hold it in place so that her other hand could twist. She'd just started to apply pressure when the tumor squelched across the inside of the bottle, sucked up against what would have been Audrey's palm, only a sixteenth of an inch of clear plastic between her skin and that deflated mass.

Audrey dropped the bottle, stepping back from it like you do when you've just let half a quart of milk slip in the kitchen: you don't want to get splashed.

This was plastic though.

The bottle rebounded into her shin, causing Audrey to take another step back, and then—Audrey still shaking her hand as if trying to unremember the heat of that almost-touch and how the tumor had felt *alive*—the lid popped off, rolled on its edge like a coin.

"Oh," Audrey said, and she covered her mouth.

The mouth of the bottle was of course smaller than the body, but not by much. It had been just small enough to keep the tumor from spurting out onto the deck though.

Except. Except the tumor was coming out anyway, wasn't it?

One tendril had either fallen just past the bottle's mouth, or it had slapped out into that open air to adhere to the decking. It tightened, straining, maybe pulling, maybe *being* pulled by the bottle trying to roll away, and the tumor's shiny greyness—a bulging tick, ready to burst—filled the mouth. It slumped out.

Audrey noted, and wasn't the least bit surprised by this, that the direction the tumor had either spilled or pulled itself was *away* from the railing. *Away* from the stinky, brackish water.

This confirmed to her that a sea burial was the proper method of disposal for her mother's innermost self.

"Not so fast, deary," she said, lowering herself to scoop her mother back into the make-do coffin, and at the exact moment she'd picked the bottle up, that damnable dog was there in a flurry of Christmas excitement and Valentine's Day slobber—another saying of her mother's.

The dog barked once, more of a yip—*I found it, guys, I found it!*—and it bit down at the tumor the way Audrey had once seen a dog snap at a crab on the beach. Like testing.

When nothing pinched the big dog's nose or snipped at its whiskers, when nothing hot spurted into its eyes, it struck down deeper, the wolf in it coming alive for a moment. Its great white teeth dug into the fibrous grey meat, and it pulled the tumor up from the deck, angled its head back, and slurped the thing down all at once, its eyes seeming to bulge from the effort.

Audrey stood, felt behind her for the railing, her eyes never leaving this thing that was happening.

"Bad dog, bad dog!" a young blond woman was saying now, just suddenly there, her left hand hooked in the dog's red collar, her right hand managing a toddler on her hip.

"It's . . . it's," Audrey said, "it was just some old food. A dumpling from that place on the—"

"Not chocolate, right?" the woman said, somehow containing the dog and the child and her concern all at once.

"Dumpling," Audrey spurted out again.

"Here," the woman said, flapping her purse open with her child-hand somehow, making to pay, but Audrey waved the effort away.

"I didn't even want it," she said.

"Are you sure?" the woman asked back, the dog slipping her grip at last, blasting off to the front of the ferry in a rollicking animation of paws and ears and jowls and satisfaction.

"It's nothing," Audrey said.

"Thank you," the woman said, "and I'm so sorry."

At which point Audrey noticed she was being offered the specimen bottle lid. That was why the woman had let the dog slip: she'd been going after the lid.

The moments were clumping together for Audrey and then slipping ahead all at once before she could process them all.

Audrey took the lid, screwed it back onto the bottle, only twisting the lid, not the bottle itself, so as to keep the hospital label hidden.

"How long until—?" Audrey said, tilting her head at the far shore, which she wasn't even going to set foot on.

"Twenty-five minutes?" the woman said back, finally setting the child down. It could barely walk—*he, he* could barely walk at the age he was.

Audrey wasn't going to fall into the stereotype so many of her gay friends did—well, the male ones—of turning her lip up at children.

The boy tottered off after the dog.

The woman looked up to Audrey with a comical exhaustion and gave chase, herding and worrying. Audrey turned back to the railing and, when she was sure no one was looking, let the specimen bottle slip over.

Instead of bobbing in the wave like she expected, it was sucked under the boat nearly immediately. A draft to the propeller, Audrey surmised, and imagined a world where she knew fluid dynamics or whatever science it was that would explain the bottle's immediate disappearance.

But?

It was done, wasn't it?

Maybe not how she'd planned, but in what she had to admit was a pretty repulsive way. The smelly water would have been fitting, but the inside of a dog was no heaven either.

"Goodbye, Mother," she said.

And to herself: *twenty-five minutes.*

Probably more like twenty-two now.

The screaming didn't sound like screaming at first.

Audrey was having a private session in her head with her therapist and had on her "Audrey is *thinking*" face, she knew.

They were discussing what the memorial service had been like and whether it had shut the door on that part of Audrey's life. Right then, right when the screaming started in for real and honest, Audrey was listening to her therapist explain to her how the metaphor of "shutting a door" on an event or time or memory was actually just asking it to all avalanche out into the hallway of a life at some later, less convenient time. Audrey was taking this lecture not as intended, precisely, but as an admonishment to better watch her figurative language. Except now someone was screaming. Not in the many hallways of her mind but at the front of the boat.

Audrey pursed her lips and fell into the stream of ferry riders tending that way, to whatever the emergency was. Her phone buzzed in her pocket, and before she could remember not to answer, she had it pressed to her ear.

The call was just empty sound, hollowness. It prompted Audrey to look behind the ferry at the diminishing skyline of the city. It was broken and jagged and smoggy all at once. And then she was rushing along with everyone else toward the sound at the front of the ferry. Before shoving her phone back into her purse, she chanced a peek at the screen. It had been a text, not a call. But it was gibberish—a whole little speech bubble of capital letters.

Her phone asked if Audrey wanted a translation, but Audrey didn't.

She knew who it was. She knew who only used capital letters like that.

The tone and volume were getting across, even if transmission from death to life was garbling the words. It's not easy to text from the churning insides of a dog bouncing with happiness.

In the diary Audrey still kept in her head, she scribbled down that she was sorry, that she didn't mean to steal it: she didn't think it would matter, it was just medical waste, it wasn't really *her*, this was supposed to have been just an exercise, part of her healing, a symbolic gesture, a guilty secret, a final get-back.

But then she was to the source of the commotion, along with everyone else.

It was the woman, the one with the dog and the child.

She was propped in a corner behind the bolted-down fiberglass benches. Her throat had been gnawed out. The chunks that gnawing had left behind trailed down her chest, had pooled in her lap. Her eyes were still open. The screaming wasn't from her but from a young woman in a tight skirt and sneakers. Everyone else was just looking. Just watching.

Nobody understood but Audrey.

"Oh," she said, steepling her hands over her mouth, shaking her head no, please no.

But yes.

Random voices were clamoring about authorities, and cell phones were all drawn. Some were snapping pictures, some were calling emergency services, and some were narrating this to who knew who, like they were reporters on assignment.

Audrey was all alone in the crowd.

She stumbled back, out of it, casting her eyes every direction at once for her mother's distinct profile, but what she saw instead was the dog.

It was standing on a supply chest, white fiberglass like the benches. It was wagging its tail and doing the canine version of a smile, its eyes casting around for the next wonderful thing the world had to offer.

"You," Audrey said to it.

"There it is!" a male voice boomed, and the dog snapped its face over to the crowd, its tail stopping mid-wag.

There was nothing to pull up from the deck to throw at the dog, so what came flying at it were shoes mostly. Two hairbrushes. A hot dog from the concession booth inside.

The dog sniffed the hot dog, rejected it, and the smell sickening it evidently, it dry heaved, its back humping over from it, its tail tucking down between its legs.

Again, again, these whole-body coughs from deep enough down inside it that Audrey felt her throat swelling like something was rising in her as well.

"What's it doing?" a man asked out loud.

"My dog *loves* hot dogs," a woman answered, her calmness out of place.

But she was right: dogs love hot dogs.

Just, not this dog. Not anymore.

It turned around and in a final undulation upchucked the corruption from its stomach.

The bulging grey tumor was still intact. Just shinier now. It filled the dog's mouth for a breathless moment, its eyes straining, its torso convulsing with this birth, and it passed through, slipped into the foot or two of dark space behind the supply chest.

The dog looked to the crowd. To everyone gathered around it.

It shrunk back, its tail fully curled under, and a full bottle of water slung out at it, caught it on the shoulder.

The dog yelped, cowered, and that was the crowd's cue to advance.

The dog edged back, dropped a foot into the dark space it had just thrown up in and, sensing that there was no retreat in this corner, darted forward, slipping through legs. Those with shoes could still kick though. The dog caught a wingtip to the ribs, went sliding, scrabbling for purchase, and then a mid-heel came down hard on its foreleg, and the dog cried out, all its Christmas excitement gone, all its Valentine's Day slobber dried up, and it rose yelping its confusion, limped back to the railing. When the bodies and legs closed over it, that was Audrey's chance.

She backed up to the supply chest and extracted the plastic container she carried her lunch in, peeled the top off.

She had to collect Mother. She had to stop this before anyone else got hurt. Only, when she stepped neatly around to reach back, leading with the square container, the dead mother's child was there. The boy. The toddler.

The woman must have thrown him there when the dog came for her. A last maternal impulse. All she could do. It's how mothers are supposed to be, Audrey knows.

Her eyes heated up.

The toddler was unharmed. Except for the mealy blackness on his hands. Except for the black stains around his mouth. Audrey cast all around him for the tumor, but of course, it was exactly where she thought it had to be.

Tumors don't like being in the open air. They prefer the insides of bodies.

The toddler looked up to Audrey and blabbered its words that weren't words, and a grey bubble stretched out at the corner of its mouth.

This toddler had eaten Audrey's mother.

No—Audrey's mother had *invaded* this toddler.

The dog hadn't been an acceptable host. Not even close. With a sense of smell that developed, the world would be a constant assault on someone with her mother's delicate sensibilities.

No, this, this speck of evil floating on the wind, this bulging parasite, this pearl of resentment, it needed a *human* life to pervert. And it had found this one even younger than it had found Audrey's mother. It would grow up into . . . Audrey shuddered. Into something worse than her mother had been. First, it would be a man, so it would have strength and social position, and it would probably use being orphaned like a moral high ground. Second, it would definitely have the judginess of Audrey's mother. That ability to sharpen a simple declarative statement—about a skirt, perhaps, or a pair of earrings—into not just an instrument of surgical precision but one with an infected blade, so the wound festers for years.

Audrey could tell this was all true simply by the eyes this toddler was settling on her, and the outfit she'd chosen to attend her mother's surgery in. *It doesn't matter how you look in a waiting room,* she hissed in her head. It matters that you're comfortable sitting there for hours. It matters that your feet don't hurt.

"Comfortable now?" the toddler was saying to Audrey with its eyes. With its unbreaking stare. "Happy with your petty little theft?"

Its chubby hand opened and closed slowly. In invitation? As if the tumor was testing the limits of its new body? As if Mother was showing Audrey how cute and vulnerable this body was, which of course translated to untouchable.

Audrey pressed her lips together and knew that she should have just left after the surgeon delivered his self-assessment in the hall. She should have just turned, walked out, never looked back. The tumor would have wound up in a medical waste bin with all the other tumors and abortions, with all the other amputations and liposuction leftovers.

Yes, perhaps there it could have Frankensteined something together, lumbered up out of that dumpster.

But maybe *not* too. Maybe it would have all just ended there.

A mother dies and stays dead, end of story.

If not for *me*, Audrey told herself.

She let the lunch container fall down, clatter away with its empty plastic sound, and a teenage boy hovering at the periphery of the dog-killing crowd—it was exciting, Audrey guessed, but all scary—he seemed to feel the impact in the deck. He turned, looked from the container up to Audrey, and like second nature, he bopped over, picked it up, handed it to her.

The toddler, now in the presence of a witness, of a savior, reached up with both arms, palms up, fingers spread wide.

Now the teenager was looking from Audrey to the toddler like, *Did you drop that too, miss?*

Audrey looked back to the crowd, enacting its justice on the screaming dog, and then she did it: she claimed this. "You'll get dirty," she said to the toddler and leaned down, hiked the toddler up by its chubby arms, settled it on her hip—settled *him* on her hip. The boy. The boy the boy the boy. He fit perfectly. She turned her beaming smile onto the teenager and accepted his offer of an empty plastic container.

"Crazy, huh?" the teenager said about this day on the ferry.

"The city," Audrey said back, and the teenager—a preview of the toddler Audrey was holding?—wheeled around with a grin, his duty done.

So now Audrey was holding it. This. *Him.*

"Um, well," she was saying in her head to Bonnie, "you know how we were never going to have children?"

But no.

Audrey was *not* going to raise her own mother. She was not going to cultivate that evil, push it out into the world to continue destroying lives just for its own amusement. She wasn't going to let Bonnie get pulled into its path, made victim of all the resentment and recriminations and bile Audrey had had to live with for so long. Most of all, Audrey had *escaped*. It was over. Over over over.

Almost.

Except this toddler, this boy, he had his hand snaked behind her head now, wasn't so much tugging on the hair at the base of her skull with his tiny fist as clamping onto it. Holding on. It was probably something his mother had grown used to, this little thing he did. It was something she was going to miss in a few years, those little monkey hands. Or something she had been *going* to miss, had there been more years for her.

He wasn't crying either. He had at first, surely when he'd fallen behind the supply chest—when he'd been *thrown*, Audrey made herself face up to. There was no way it could have been gentle. His mother, the woman with too many hands, she'd seen the family dog rising for her throat, and she'd pushed her child as far away from what was happening as possible. Audrey didn't doubt that that woman, in her last moments, with her last few pumps of blood, had even tried to direct the dog away from her child's hiding place.

And now Audrey was crying, dammit.

The boy started sniffling as well.

"It's okay, it's okay," Audrey said to him—*him*, him, yes—"I'm just being . . . you're probably hungry, aren't you, dear?"

Audrey hiked him over to her other hip, rolled her shoulder on the side he'd been on.

She could get used to this.

It was terrifying.

"Bobo," the boy said, pointing with a chubby index finger, and Audrey looked up just in time to see the dog, broken and bleeding, arcing out over the railing, its paws pedaling in the air, its bloody mouth open, tongue lolling. Her mind took a snapshot of that, a snapshot she immediately realized she didn't want. But not wanting an image like that only sends it down to the photomart on the corner, brings it back enlarged. In a frame.

Audrey turned around fast to try to keep this from imprinting in the boy's head and realized she had her own set of instincts that could completely override what she knew to be true.

"Bobo," she heard herself saying.

"Ma-ma," the boy said as if correcting her, as if actually conversing, and Audrey had to see what she'd turned him around to face: the woman thrown into that white corner as if discarded, a bib of red over her shirt, her eyes open.

Had no one thought to cover her yet? What was this, some voyage of the damned?

"It's okay, it's okay," Audrey said, hugging the boy's head to her chest and shuttling the two of them inside, away from all of this.

The concession stand spread wide before them. The source of the hot dog that had become a sort of weapon just a minute or two ago.

Everything was happening so fast.

Audrey's phone buzzed its reminder buzz, telling her to look at the text she'd only seen on the lockscreen, hadn't actually tapped open.

Ignore, ignore.

She fumbled for her change purse, the one Bonnie had given her almost ceremonially when Audrey had turned forty, informing Audrey that "it was time."

Audrey supposed it was.

"Now what do you like?" she asked the boy, and instead of actually buying one of everything within the boy's small orbit, they took one of everything and left a loose pile of quarters and dimes and nickels on the counter.

Out on deck it was a madhouse, a jumble, a mob.

In here, it was ghost-town city. Not even a clerk. Just one old woman in the corner with a walker and an oxygen tank. She was looking out the window at the water, maybe didn't even know something was going on.

When they pulled into the other shore, Audrey knew there were going to be emergency responders and layers and layers of police and probably a barricade and reporters as well. This was news, wasn't it? A murder, some crowd justice, and then—though this knowledge would be well delayed she was sure—an abduction.

To say nothing of illegal disposal of medical waste.

"I'm so sorry," Audrey said like that could cleanse her of this afternoon.

And then, just to be sure it couldn't be so, she set the boy on the counter and turned him around on his rump, so they could see each other face to face. His fingers were sticky with candy, his mouth ringed red with it. Because Auntie Audrey lets little boys have treats.

Audrey grinned about this, that it was already happening.

Bonnie would understand, wouldn't she?

Just, first, Audrey had to get rational, had to disabuse herself of the flight of fancy her head kept trying to take her on.

All that had happened was that, yes, a random dog had eaten her mother's tumor. As any dog would have, given the chance. But it was just meat to the dog. What else could it really be? Eating a symbol isn't going to determine a dog's behavior, is it? It's not going to make it a killer. And then—completely unrelated, not even circumstantial—that dog, that had already proved itself a nuisance all over the ferry, it had attacked and killed its owner when that owner tried to get it to behave.

Easy as that. Rational as anything.

Granted, Audrey was still going to have to relay it to her therapist, but her therapist would just nod in her deliberative way about it all, ask Audrey what had her read been on the whole scene—what had her read been in the *moment*, and how did that differ from her interpretation *now*?

Now was already starting, Audrey told herself. No more irrational certainties. No more paranoia. No more believing in things that could never be.

To prove it, she looked directly into the boy's face—"the boy who wasn't yet missing," she corrected in her head—and held his eyes, waiting to see if he was going to dismiss her as worthless, as a disappointment, as a walking talking failure of a woman.

If he did, then she would know, and have no choice but to act accordingly.

But he wouldn't judge her like that, Audrey knew. This was all in her head. You think wrong things on the day your mother dies. That's a biological rule.

The boy held her gaze for three seconds, for five seconds, and then the cherry-flavored candy in his hand won out, and he was back to that.

"Well then," Audrey said and scooped him back up, looked around the cabin for witnesses. So this was it, then: her punishment for any part she'd played in the death of the boy's mother, Audrey would now pay for it for eighteen years. And Bonnie would as well. And it would all be fine. This is life, this is how life happens. There're bumps, but you keep on driving to the next place and the next place.

When there weren't any witnesses—when the oxygen woman was still trancing out the window—Audrey nodded to herself, walked out a different door than she'd walked in.

It deposited her at the section of the ferry she'd started on. That lonely stretch of railing where she'd meant to perform a memorial service or—*Be honest,* her therapist admonished, *at least with yourself*—to exact some long-overdue revenge. Some years-in-the-making justice.

Full circle, Audrey told herself and crossed to the chipped blue railing and leaned against it, careful to keep the boy on her other hip. He could still see the vastness of the ocean, but he couldn't reach for it and overbalance, go over.

"Mo, mo," he said then.

"Your mommy's . . . she's sick," Audrey said, not sure how to phrase it or whether it really mattered precisely what words she used.

"Mo, mo," the boy said again anyway, opening and closing his sticky red hands, and Audrey got it: *more, more.*

"My, you are a hungry one," she said and repositioned his weight so as to unsnap her purse—*the goody bag,* she was already calling it in her head.

God, Bonnie was going to hit the ceiling, wasn't she?

But then she was going to melt into the floor.

Anybody would.

And, Audrey decided, she wasn't even going to tell her about the tumor. In the story already spinning in her head, she'd taken a ferry ride to commemorate her mother's passing, to be alone in the middle of all that water. It could still be symbolic, but now what the ride would be standing for would be a daughter, suddenly alone in the world.

Which would give Bonnie a chance to nuzzle in, say how Audrey wasn't alone. Did she think she was?

It's a big thing when your mother dies though. You're allowed some latitude.

As for why she'd rescued this child, this toddler, this boy . . . Audrey didn't know yet. It was probably going to have something to do with the difficulty of adopting. That, coupled with her and Bonnie's maternal instincts, meant that this boy had fallen into their lives for a *reason.* He was a gift, wasn't he? It was meant to be.

This was the end of the candy free-for-all though. Else those chubby hands might just stay chubby, right? But then, Audrey reminded herself, the boy had lost a mother as well, hadn't he?

Maybe just one more candy, to get him to trust her.

She let him reach in, careless of her sunglasses, her keys, and what he came out with, it proved that Audrey's mother's tumor wasn't alive in him, sending its black tendrils all through his tiny body.

Corn nuts. The stinkiest of the bad. The snack that would send her mother retching.

"Think I'll have one too," Audrey said and tore at the indicated tearing place, tilted the tube of a bag back into her mouth and held it across for the boy.

He reached in like it was Christmas, came out with a grand total of three dusty nuts, but then he stopped.

Not because of what he was holding.

Because of what Audrey was chewing. What Audrey was breathing.

The boy drew his head back, a cry building on his face, and while he didn't quite throw up like the dog had done—as Audrey had actually seen her mother do once around a discrete corner—he did spit up his red candy.

It spread into a chunky bib on his shirt front.

"No," Audrey said and held him away from her—held *it* away from her—and because she had no other choice now, she completed the action she'd started what felt like hours earlier: she held her mother's tumor along with its current host out over the railing of the ferry, and she opened her hands.

The child plopped straight down just as the specimen bottle had, and, just like the specimen bottle, it sucked immediately under the ferry.

Behind them, Audrey knew there would be a brief scum of unsymbolic candy red on the surface of the dirty water. At last. But he had hardly even weighed forty pounds. She doubted even the gulls would find him. Or the corruption he'd been harboring inside.

It was done. It was over at last.

"Bye, Mom," Audrey said, the skin of her face cold now, cold enough she could feel the warm breeze sighing in. The warm, spectacularly rank breeze. She sighed back, her breath dusted with the corruption of the dread corn nut. That was the only thing she'd missed: she should have stuffed the rest of the bag into his mouth before dropping him. It would have been the final insult, the best insult.

But this, this, now, it wasn't bad either.

Audrey had both hands to the rail, her reminder buzz going off in her purse, the sky wide and empty all around her—she literally *was* a daughter alone in the big world now—and she closed her eyes to soak it in, realized after a breath or two that the silence around her was too thick. Was all wrong.

She turned around to the crowd, most of them without a left shoe, all of them with unbrushed hair. And thirsty. Desperately thirsty.

For justice.

"You don't, you don't—" Audrey said, shying away from the half-eaten bean burrito sailing into the side of her face. "You don't understand. He was, he was my—"

A right shoe caught her sharply on the shin and went on past over the railing.

"*I had to!*" Audrey said, hiking her left foot up onto the railing to follow her mother in, to get away from this, swim to some distant shore where what she'd done could make the right kind of sense.

The crowd hauled her back down. The crowd hauled her down hard.

Audrey landed on the deck on her chest and knees, her cheek pressed to the wood where thousands of grimy, dirty shoes had ground out cigarettes, and the last clear thought she had before the heels came down into her back and head and face, it was that her phone, it was buzzing with a text, an all-caps one. From Mom.

"*It's not funny!*" a woman shrieked above Audrey, raising her whole leg to show Audrey just how funny this wasn't. But it was. It so was.

Following her therapist's advice, Audrey had been replying to her mother's screamy texts with simple emoticons for months now. And she still was: *This is my lying-down smiley face,* she said in her head, smiling a beatific smile, the smile of one finally at peace, and then the shrieking woman, possibly a mother herself, brought her heel down, hitting Audrey's Send button for her.

§

Stephen Graham Jones is the author of sixteen novels, six story collections, and so far one comic book. Stephen's been an NEA recipient, has won the Texas Institute of Letters Award for Fiction, the Independent Publishers Award for Multicultural Fiction, a Bram Stoker Award, four This is Horror Awards, and he's been a finalist for the Shirley Jackson Award and the World Fantasy Award. He's also made Bloody Disgusting's Top Ten Horror Novels and is that guy who wrote *Mongrels*. Stephen lives in Boulder, Colorado.

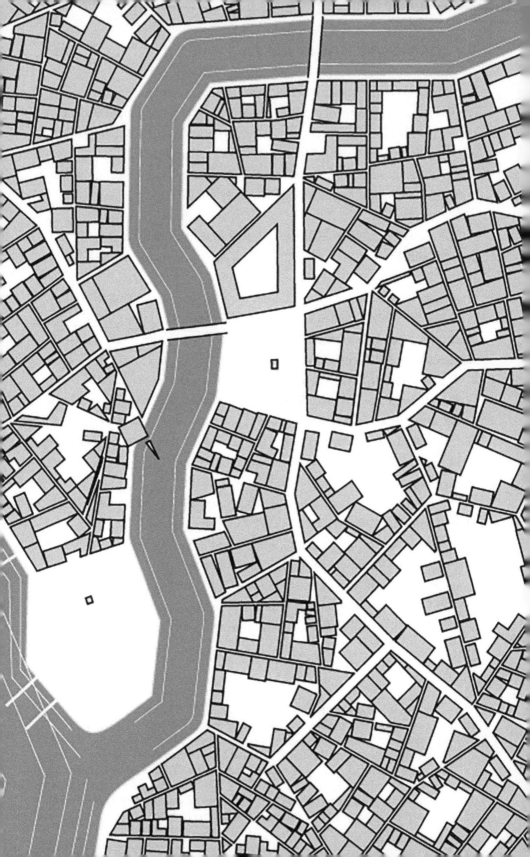

Luriberg-That-Was

R.B. LEMBERG

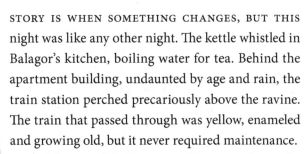

STORY IS WHEN SOMETHING CHANGES, BUT THIS night was like any other night. The kettle whistled in Balagor's kitchen, boiling water for tea. Behind the apartment building, undaunted by age and rain, the train station perched precariously above the ravine. The train that passed through was yellow, enameled and growing old, but it never required maintenance.

It had been a long time since Balagor spoke to anyone. All he noticed were the absences: those empty, narrow streets of Luriberg once paved in cobblestones before the big Soviet machines came to extract all the stones and pour down concrete. The darkened absence of the mezuzah on his door—a slanted, narrow strip of dark, unpainted wood. When he touched the spot, something stirred inside as if the motion used to mean something.

Sometimes, even his name felt strange. It wasn't Balagor, it was Berl—Berl the fiddler. There had always been fiddlers in Luriberg since the dawn of time when Prince Zbigniew established the city. In all the old stories, the Polish prince rode up the hill, and behind him, the tsaddik reb Lurje rode, fiddling the tune that turned G-d's benevolent face toward Zbigniew and all his endeavors. Out of the fertile earth, reb Lurje's music called out stones, big stones for the fortification of the walls and small cobblestones.

Balagor-Berl woke up in darkness. The shadow of the heavy brass eagle on the top of the closet shook its wings in impatient jerks. He could not see the train, but he could sense it in his bones, speeding toward the ravine. It was the same train, hurrying somewhere, its windows shadowed by curtains.

Stories are when something changes. He no longer remembered who told him that. It's not a story if everything stays the same. But he did not remember when something last changed.

He put on his cap and walked over to the train station in the morning. Mornings were dim in Luriberg those days, gray like pigeon wings and rain. But the yellow train whistled past him, climbing up on the tracks and over them, out of sight in the ravine. It was as if it had fallen down.

Balagor-Berl climbed up the steep hill. The very top of it was shorn as if sliced off with a knife; the train tracks sank, blue and glistening, into the wet brown earth. He looked around for the train, for the noise and echo of it, but heard nothing. Did it really topple into the ravine? If it had indeed fallen, he heard no sound.

Balagor-Berl clambered over the dangerous tracks toward the very edge where clumps of grass and a few spent dandelions clung to the pebbles and rocks. He was Berl just then, Berl the fiddler, the fiddle alive and beating inside his chest. Over the rim of the hill, Berl saw the steep sides of the ravine, jagged and barren, all the way down to the ground below.

No train. It was as if it had never existed. Far below him, the earth was covered in bones: not the white bones of stories but dirty, splintered, moss-covered bones, grayish and heaving as if something moved among them.

"Who's there," Balagor cried, and a thousand voices echoed: *Over and over and over and over again.*

He knew that he'd fallen down the ravine before, his cheek on the wet earth and his arms cradling bodies—clinging to the bloodied coats of people he had once known. Above him, others clutched at his coat just as desperately, but none of them moved, spoke, or breathed.

Balagor-Berl jerked backward, away from the ravine.

Between the edge of the hill and the tracks, there perched the train station. He'd missed it earlier as if it had toppled into the abyss with the train. But now it was back. It was a small building, more of a coop than a building—and flimsy, hastily constructed of corrugated metal. The sole wide window was open. It was a ticket counter, and behind it, he saw the shadow of the ticket-master.

Up close, the ticket-master was a stout woman with a sad and serious face, her graying curls barely constrained by a faded yellow kerchief. Her dress too was yellow.

"Tickets needed?" she said in that gruff, no-nonsense voice of Soviet ticket-sellers. "Or are you intending to fare as a hare?"

"Yes. No." Balagor mumbled. A hare was what they called a ticketless passenger who snuck on the train for a free ride.

"Not a hare. I want tickets. Ticket." He wanted to ask a thousand questions, but shyness tied his tongue. He asked instead, "Where does the train go?"

"The yellow train? No, no, you cannot board that today. Today I have blue. Wrong line, see?" The train whirred past just then with its clanging and yellow enamel and curtains. Behind them, he thought he saw shadows.

"I thought it fell over the ravine," Balagor said. "I thought it had gone."

"For sure, for sure. Your ticket," she said, thrusting a slip of hard paper into his hands. "Don't forget: the ticket is for midnight."

"There is another train here at midnight?"

"No. You were told already. This is the yellow. Your ticket is for the blue."

Balagor pocketed the ticket. With each step away from the station, he became Berl again as if the old fiddle unclenched in his chest.

He wasn't asleep, Berl; he was just lying on the couch in his only room, as still as a corpse, the ticket clutched in his hand. Precisely at midnight, his kitchen filled up. He heard voices.

"Stories are when something changes." A deep voice he'd heard so many times before, perhaps when he was ticketless. Asleep. He remembered going out at night, stumbling over invisible roots and bones toward the train station perched on the hill. At night, the train was all mass and sound, whirling past him until it plummeted into the ravine.

"Stories are for when something changes," the deep voice intoned. "But if nothing changes, we are erased as if we have never existed at all."

Balagor swung his stiff legs over the edge of the couch and tiptoed as silently as he could toward the kitchen. Light oozed from under the door, spilling its warmth over his toes, and he heard the sounds of slurping.

"Add sugar rafinad," a very young voice said, immediately followed by a sound of a small weight splashing into liquid. A sugar cube, falling into tea.

"Come in, come in." That was addressed to him, Balagor—or perhaps also Berl then—shuffling from leg to leg before the closed door of the kitchen. Slowly the door creaked open, and he stepped over the threshold as if he was a guest in his own apartment.

The small kitchen was full but not because of the number of people: only two others. At the head of the table, there sat a girl of about eight; she had pigtails with bows, one in blue and the other in yellow. A much larger someone was squeezed in between the stove and the table, paws on the cheap kleyonka tablecloth. This second guest was an enormous green crocodile, its skin shining like a pair of patent leather shoes. The crocodile's mischievous eyes sparkled behind a pair of tiny, lopsided spectacles. In front of the crocodile was a glass of tea in a silvery podstakannik, a glass of tea like he'd never possessed, a glass of tea like they served on trains: the liquid inside steamy, dark brown with the potent and brooding smell of the road, drunk in tiny gulps while the heavy wagon shook with the percussion of rails.

"Good evening," said Balagor. "Who are you?"

"I'm Shprintse," said the girl. It was too old a name for her. Berl had never heard it attached to anyone younger than sixty. "But if you must, Nadya. It is the same as Shprintse. Some call me Shura though. On the blue line."

The crocodile seized a cube of sugar rafinad in its paw and tossed it into the tea. Without waiting for it to melt, it grabbed the silvery handle of the podstakannik and upended the whole glass into its suddenly open jaws festooned with rows of sharp teeth—some of them golden. The tilting glass emptied into the open maw and then inevitably fell out of its podstakannik. Berl twitched, waiting for the crunch of broken glass, but the crocodile's paw dove after the empty glass, deftly extracting it and returning it to the podstakannik and to the table.

"Uncle," said Nadya-Shura-Shprintse. "Uncle, you need to introduce yourself."

The crocodile clanged its teeth. "Do I really need to? Do I?"

"Yes, Uncle."

The crocodile sighed in weary resignation. "Oh, all right, very well."

From somewhere under the seat, it extracted a checkered cap and donned it. Its long, patent-leather nose began to shrink, and the vivid green began to mellow until a person sat in the crocodile's place. Well, almost entirely a person because the paws were still very much in evidence, wrapped around the silver podstakannik with its empty glass. The rest of the crocodile now looked like an overly thin human man—thirtyish, slightly wrinkled, bespectacled, dark-eyed, his curly hair venturing forth from under the cap—in short, a regular shtetl yidele, if perhaps too tall and still green about the paws.

The yidele shook his paws into hands. "Allow me to introduce myself. I am your train-respected well-conductor."

After a lengthy pause, Berl realized that a name was not forthcoming.

"Your ticket," said the train-respected personage, and Berl obediently gave it to him.

"This says . . . Balagor-Berl," the ex-crocodile intoned. "But there's only one ticket, so only one of you will venture forth."

"There's only one of me," said Balagor-Berl. "This is the whole of me." But he wasn't sure that it was true. Here, in his kitchen filled tightly by an ex-crocodile and a girl, squeezed between the peeling wooden table with its kleyonka tablecloth and the inner door to the room, between the warmth and the tea and the cubes of sugar rafinad, Berl felt like Balagor receded. This was heimish like a long time ago that he no longer recalled, but it felt like an easing. No need to think about the peeling train station or sleeping alone on his couch; instead, his chest once again contained a fiddle.

"Where are we going?" Berl asked.

"The blue line goes underneath the city," said the girl.

"Underneath," the ex-crocodile echoed. "Where everyone went who did not go into the ravine." And he winked.

Balagor hated that wink.

"People are in there." He was not quite sure what he meant. In the ravine. Fallen. Forgotten. "Our people are in there. I thought that venturing under the city would be a more somber occasion."

"Do you think Jewish history must always be lachrymose? No, we'll keep joking even beyond the grave. At least, as long as we can."

Shprintse-Nadya elbowed him. "You're not dead yet, Uncle."

"Only because nothing changes. When the story progresses, I'll be dead all right, but somebody might remember the extraordinary capacity of my jaws." He fell silent for a moment as if falling asleep but jerked awake and said, "Where were we? Even more importantly, when were we?" The ex-crocodile thrust his hand into his enormous jacket, hanging loose from his human frame and checkered black and brown. From the jacket, he extracted a large clock. Its small hand was stuck at the number two. The large hand was at five past the hour. "Ah. Yes. Hope. Please help me out, Shprintse-Nadezhda."

"One moment." The girl reached toward the clock and pushed the small hand all the way to twelve. The large hand she also rotated, much gentler, until the whole showed two minutes before midnight. "Hope keeps the train going, but it keeps circling back."

Her voice blended with the voice of the clock that came alive in that moment. Tick. Tock. Tick. Tock.

"Hurry," said the train-respected conductor. "Tell me who you are and get on the train."

"I'm . . . I'm . . ." Balagor-Berl stammered. He was Berl for sure, the one with the fiddle for a heart, the one whose bones ached the closer he got to the ravine. In front of his eyes, darkness spun, striated in red. He opened his lips, but the sounds of his name would not form.

The train-respected conductor sighed, and his whole body twisted with it. "Please. Your name."

"Balagor," said the girl.

"He gets to choose," said the ex-crocodile. "That's the deal."

"I told you," said Shprintse-Nadya. "I told you, he needs to be better protected."

"Balagor," said Balagor. He was just repeating what the girl had said. It felt heavy, inevitable almost. The large hand of the clock moved forward, and the girl prodded him.

"It leaves from the restroom."

"You're not coming?" Balagor said.

"To the restroom, even the tzar goes alone," the ex-crocodile intoned. But he sounded sad.

As if in a dream, Balagor shuffled over to the narrow, peeling-pink corridor and opened the door to the small bathroom. Above the cast-iron tub, the old water heater hummed with a bluish row of gas flames, heating up the water.

Balagor blinked. The thin whistling of gas intensified and built up until it was no longer humming—not the gas heater but the train, the train, the train, approaching from somewhere beyond the wall, behind the heating unit, no, the heating unit itself was the lights of the train, whistling past him on top of the bathtub. Wagon after wagon passed by as the train slowed, its locomotive somewhere out of sight beyond the walls of his apartment. A blue wagon filled the bathroom—not like the one above the ravine—it was tidy and sparkling and clean. A red star was painted by the doors.

The doors opened, and Balagor clambered in.

Inside, the train car was dark; only a single small window looked back into his bathroom. He remembered when the bathroom was first put in: the Soviets divided the building into twenty apartments, each with its own kitchen and bath. His apartment, like the others, was shared with another family; he had family too. A daughter, perhaps a grandmother. He did not remember. For years now, he lived in the building alone.

He was also alone here in the train coupe designed for two with two long seats flanking a table. He had nothing to put on it: no snacks, no stuffed cabbage, no fried chicken in its three-liter jar. When the train moved, the view of his bathroom flashed by and was gone and with it the light. Balagor sat alone in the darkness.

What was his daughter's name? *Nadya* came unbidden to his mind, but that could not be right. The little girl's uncle was a crocodile. And Balagor always lived alone. There was never anyone else anywhere.

I want him better protected.

He was better protected now, and that's why he could not remember.

The train whistled and rattled out of the brick tunnel into a real railway that wasn't the rim of the bath. They were somewhere.

Balagor peeked out of the window. This felt city-like, but there were no buildings here, just earth and the bright silver rails of the train. But above him— above, the buildings hung upside down, suspended from an earthy sky.

Balagor blinked, but the vision remained. It was Luriberg all right. He recognized his own street with its maple and horse chestnut trees that sprouted downward, their broad arms shading the earth-sky. Small trees hung down from the tops of the hanging-down buildings. The street—in his sky, which was the upended earth—the street was full of people, small people he could not quite make out because of the distance, walking and running and just milling everywhere, people moving slowly, people talking, people with canes, people in hats that did not fall down, people with strollers.

The train whistled, speeding, but Balagor had to see more. He pushed against the window—the one that had once been a door to his bathroom—and pried it open. The air of the underground Luriberg bloomed in his nostrils, all wet like the earth and a little bit stale. The train was slowing down again.

It came to a halt in front of a train station. The train station was small like the building above a ravine but in better repair; instead of corrugated metal, it had imposing tall walls of dove-gray with stone-arch windows and delicate lace curtains. In the middle of the building was a wide, open counter. Instead of tickets, the dark polished wood of the counter was piled high with pirozhki, glazed brown pockets of dough with many different fillings. Balagor's nose distinguished potato and cabbage and egg and something sweet, probably cherry. Behind the counter stood a stout woman with a kindly, soft face, graying curls peeking from under a blue kerchief the color of Nadya-Shprintse's blue ribbon. Her dress too was blue.

"I've seen you before," said Balagor.

"Maybe," she said. "Maybe not. You always come through here in one way or the other."

"What do you mean?" said Balagor, but something stirred inside him where his fiddle heart used to be. But no, he was Balagor now. Protected.

The pirozhki-seller shrugged. "Reb Lurje had passed here. Over and over he passed, riding this train you came in on. He stopped at this stop, and he fiddled here, right here where you're standing, in exchange for my pirozhki. But he ate nothing. He was trying to bring Luriberg back."

"I thought this was Luriberg . . ." said Balagor, his tongue heavy and thick in his mouth.

"This? This is just decorations. Illustrations. Evocations. Commemorations. All painted like these—" and she tapped on the gray imposing stone wall of the station behind her. It echoed hollowly like no stone wall had any right to do. Balagor took a step sideways and peeked into the alley. The building had no side—the building had no back—there was no building, only a thin layer of unpainted cardboard sticking from the ground. The pirozhki-seller was cardboard too with a flat, unpainted back reinforced with a stick. He felt bile rise in his throat as he jerked himself back to the station and the pirozhki-seller in her blue dress and kerchief, three-dimensional from this side and alive.

"It takes more than protection of a name not your own to bring back Luriberg-That-Was. But you don't want to pay the price. That's what I told reb Lurje. Still, the truth cannot be constrained behind these veneers of paint. Open your hand, and you will see."

Obediently, Balagor turned his hand palm up, and a drop of rain fell onto it. And another. They were reddish-brown and fell on his face, drop after drop until he could taste the salt.

It was blood. Blood falling from the upside-down earth, raining down from the people and the buildings as if the sky itself was emptying out.

"See?" said the pirozhki-seller. "See? You can bring it all back for the price of your heart." She dove under the counter and lifted up a violin. It was painted on cardboard like everything else in this place—flat from the side and making no sound. "But not this one. Your real one." Her voice was so loud now. "Only the real fiddle heart will bring it back—Luriberg-That-Was, Luriberg-That-Was. It is coming and going, it's coming and going."

At Balagor's side, the train was moving again and leaving him behind, leaving him alone with that fear of becoming cardboard like the pirozhki-seller, slowly dissolving under the bloody rain.

He turned his back upon the station and ran after the departing train, jumping and landing on the steps of a wagon. He pushed open a door and fell inside into a different wagon than before—a passenger wagon third class. There were berths here, three per wall, one above the other, and people sat or lay on them—people like the ones he knew before the war, elderly women in kerchiefs and children, chattering or frightened; young people huddled together. Opposite him stood an older Jewish man with a long, salt-and-pepper beard and burning dark eyes. His dress was slightly old-fashioned, a longer black coat over knee-length pants. It felt like Balagor knew him, had known him forever and always. The man held onto a rail with one hand; another clutched at his ravaged and gaping chest.

"You cannot give your fiddle heart. The price of your heart is too high."

"Where are we going?" said Balagor.

"Where we're always going," said the heartless old man. "Over and over, we're going because it is always the same without sacrificing the heart. But that price is too high, so the story never changes."

"I want . . ." said Balagor, but he was interrupted by a large, burly man in official clothes.

"Present your ticket, citizen," said the officer.

"But . . . I gave it. I gave it to the train-respected well-conductor?" Balagor mumbled.

"Got it. You're riding hare-style, and that won't work," said the burly man.

"Out you go." The wagon door opened, and Balagor was flung from the train and into his bathtub.

Balagor lay on his sofa, bruised and shaking, curled upon himself. He'd been protected. *Protected,* the girl had said. But now, the other side of all things looked like cardboard. The walls, the sofa. The wardrobe, its doors creaking in the darkness of the room. The brass eagle on top of the wardrobe. Nothing felt real. He was afraid to touch his back for the fear of finding it flat and painted while the rest of him lived and breathed. His kitchen was empty when he emerged from the bathtub. He creeped past it, past the empty chairs that once held an enormous, sparkling-green crocodile and a girl with two thin braids with yellow and blue ribbons tied into festive bows. The kitchen was clean. There was no train-style tea glass in its podstakannik. No cubes of sugar rafinad.

After he returned, he did not dare venture out of his apartment. He did not eat and did not miss it. He did not drink and did not go to the bathroom with its humming gas and no departing train. He hid here under the blanket, which felt like cardboard, protected by the name Balagor, which came out of nowhere and meant nothing—it wasn't even Soviet.

Protected. Then why did the blood drip from the upside-down city? What did it mean to be protected? From what? *The truth cannot be constrained under these veneers of paint.* The truth was in him under these veneers of paint. His name was inside this other name's letters.

His kitchen had been empty just one cardboard moment ago, but just then, he heard it. A deep, familiar voice, a voice he'd heard many times before.

"Stories are when something changes."

He forced himself off the sofa, out from under the blanket.

"Stories are when something changes," the deep voice intoned. "But if nothing changes, the story cannot move on. It runs around and around like the train on the blue line, going nowhere, arriving nowhere. As if we had never existed at all."

"But we continue," said the girl. Balagor-Berl tiptoed over to the threshold and pushed open the door. "We continue," she said, "even if we do not exist anywhere else. As long as we're here, there is still hope."

"There's no hope if nothing changes," said the crocodile, the checkered cap mashed between his green paws.

Balagor-Berl stepped over the threshold.

"And if everything changes and he loses his heart, then what? Into the ravine we all go," said the girl. "The price is too high. It's too high."

"Excuse me." He coughed into his hand.

Both of them looked at him. The crocodile adjusted the spectacles on its nose. The girl tugged at the yellow ribbon on her left pigtail. "Balagor?"

"Berl," he said. "Berl, my name is Berl." Inside his chest, his fiddle heart stirred with the sweetness of reborn pain.

The crocodile sighed. "Can I see your ticket?"

"You took it from me before," Berl mumbled.

"No, silly, that was for the blue line. You need another. There's no riding hare-style on that one."

"Don't do it," said Nadya-Shprintse. "Don't do it, Balagor. It is too dangerous—"

"I'll get another ticket."

He squeezed out of the narrow, full kitchen. Into the corridor. Past the dark bathroom humming with gas. Into the cold gray streets, cobblestoned and empty and wavering slightly with the fog.

He had been walking and walking when behind him he heard a rhythmic noise. As if of something huge also walking.

Berl should have broken into a run, but he slowed, his fiddle heart keening with the resonance of its thinnest, most brittle string. He gulped a breath and turned.

Behind him, people marched in a crowd.

They were of all ages—children and grandparents and families, young and old, their faces somber with hunger and cold and at once eager, looking beyond him up the hill. Toward the train station. They wore gray and brown coats, some tattered and others unblemished, all with the same large yellow star sewn to the chest. They did not hold hands, even the small ones, each walking alone. Nadya-Shprintse was there, walking calmly with Berl's mother. They did not look at him. None of the people did. Their feet drummed the pavement rhythmically, in unison, like a train that drummed on the rails. Their eyes sparkled like the headlights of the train. They were the train, the large yellow train, enameled and tattered around the edges, rushing toward him. Berl tried to snap out from his frozenness, to get out of its way, but the train-crowd engulfed him.

It was like swimming upstream in a body of ghosts, semi-solid and rushing around him and through him until he was gasping for air, trying to move against tight, taut bodies, drowning in yellow rushing and the sound of the horn closer, closer, closer—and suddenly he was inside the train.

It was stiff there, stiff with bodies. Bodies old, bodies young, bodies unmoving. His mother was here somewhere, and Nadya. Maybe alive, maybe dead, definitely dead, each rigid and spilling over with blood. Berl could not move. Inside him, the fiddle was voiceless from screaming.

"You again," said the crocodile-conductor, squeezing around the bodies. He was different now, official-looking and angry, not unlike the officer from the blue train. "Your ticket."

I was trying to get it for you, Berl wanted to say, but nothing came out; no air remained in his lungs.

"You miserable shlimazl of a hare," the crocodile hissed, grabbing him by the hand. And into his ear, "Lucky bastard." A door that had not been there before opened up, and Berl was thrown out onto the cobblestoned earth.

He tried to sit up. Look up. The yellow train, doorless and windowless, swished past him, laboring higher toward the ravine.

Behind the train marched the executioners. Always before when he'd seen them, they appeared faceless, but now he saw their faces—youngish and older, serious, stern, gleeful, smug, expressionless. Slowly they walked up the hill after the speeding train, but they did not fall behind.

When they reached the top of the hill, they took their guns off their shoulders and stood in position. As one, they fired their weapons after the train.

Behind the executioners now came the people in blue. They were the same as the executioners in number and shape, and only the color of their uniforms and their red shining stars distinguished them in the gloom. They watched the train topple over the brink of the ravine. Only then did the soldiers in blue lift their guns with the same exact motion and fire after the executioners, spreading them into dust.

Berl's whole body was a long groan of pain, but he made himself get up and climb. The executioners were gone. Not a shadow. Not a sigh. As if someone had erased them from history and story.

He looked down. The train had disappeared as always, but he saw his people.

Gaping wounds in their chests, shoulders, heads. Gaping wounds where their chests and their heads should have been. They were all falling down the steep ravine all the way to its jagged and barren ground. Thud, thud. Thud. Thud.

The soldiers in blue were behind him, their guns now pointing at his chest.

"My people are falling!" He screamed. "Do something—"

As one, they shrugged. "Say thank you that you're still here. Now take your passport and shut up."

When he blinked, each of the soldiers became a letter, shimmering in front of his eyes. They spelled one word: *Balagor.*

Balagor recoiled from them, turned back to look at the ravine. There was no evidence of the train and its people. The bottom of the ravine was now covered in bones, not the white gleaming bones that the stories were made of but dirty and splintered old bones, grayish and heaving as if something moved among them. Then even that movement ceased.

The soldiers were gone. Balagor took a step back and then another, and then he was standing in front of the small, lopsided train station. It hadn't been there before, but it reappeared. The ticket counter was open. The ticket-master nodded at him with no mirth—the same stout woman in her kerchief the color of Nadya's yellow ribbon.

Balagor stepped back and peered behind the train station. It was three-dimensional, real, and he breathed in relief. No cardboard.

"Tickets needed?" said the ticket-master gruffly.

One for the yellow train, he wanted to say, but he couldn't. He had been inside it, he saw where that train went, and now his name changed again. "I don't know."

"You cannot change anything if you ride as a hare. You need to pay the price," she said.

Didn't you tell me it's dangerous? Is this you? Are you Shprintse-Nadya? I saw her marching with the others. I saw her topple, shattered, into the ravine, the back of her head smashed—is that the wound your kerchief conceals? Is she family? Is she you?

"What do you need?" Balagor asked instead.

"The price of the ticket is your fiddle heart. You never play it anyway. Not anymore. What do you need it for, reb Lurje, that you keep coming here?"

Lurje and Balagor and Berl were all the same, he thought, trying to move on from here. But he couldn't. "Stories are when something changes."

"Then cut up your chest and give it to me, that old fiddle you carry that played for Zbigniew when the city was built. Give that fiddle to me so that it will call up the cobblestones and the streets and the buildings of Luriberg-That-Was, Luriberg-That-Was." She was not cardboard, but now she took her whole face off as if it was a mask. Not Nadya-Shprintse grown up; there was nothing behind it, just cardboard with an empty mouth cutout. It spoke on. "Give your fiddle to me so that the city will be as it should be while you leave on the yellow train."

Berl backed away slowly. He was Balagor, the fiddle inside him swathed in layers of names and debris, tucked away in Soviet communal apartments. He was grateful that he was still here—wasn't he?—neither going away nor moving forward, neither living nor dying. The fiddle was somewhere inside.

"You changed," he called out to Nadya, but it wasn't her. It was just the ticket-master with the cardboard face, the gaping cutout mouth and eyes that led nowhere. She could not run after him. But she said, "Nothing changes. Because you will not accept the truth. Or do you think that the story is about you? That the city wanted the Jews here ever? No, it wanted to be built, it wanted to be called up from stone—and then to get rid of you. Except you are still here, hovering around. Nothing changes until you go. So call the true, brilliant city up again and board the train as a passenger for one last time and not a hare."

Shaking, he stepped away from her. Down the hill. The little train station disappeared from view and the ticket-master with it. Cobblestones under his feet.

He was in his city alone. It wasn't the truth. He was not sure what the truth was or who he was, but he was not leaving. *If we agree to just go, then surely we are erased*, he thought, *as if we had never existed at all.*

He walked down the hill toward his apartment as the air thickened with darkness. Perhaps there would be other people in his kitchen, perhaps there would not.

It did not matter. Stories are when something changes, but this night was like any other night.

R.B. Lemberg is a queer, bigender immigrant from Ukraine, Russia, and Israel to the US. Their stories and poems have appeared in *Lightspeed's Queers Destroy Science Fiction, Beneath Ceaseless Skies, Uncanny Magazine, Sisters of the Revolution: A Feminist Speculative Fiction Anthology, People of the Book: A Decade of Jewish Science Fiction and Fantasy,* and more. R.B.'s work has been a finalist for the Nebula, Crawford, and other awards. Many of R.B.'s stories are situated in Birdverse, an LGBTQIA+-focused secondary world. Their Birdverse novella *The Four Profound Weaves* is forthcoming from Tachyon Press in 2020. "Luriberg-That-Was" is a story situated in R.B.'s Luriberg continuity, a magic realist/surrealist place inspired by Jewish history, Jewish-Russian literature, R.B.'s childhood, and their family history.

In their academic life, R.B. is a sociolinguist working on immigrant discourse, identity, and gender. R.B. lives in Lawrence, KS, with their spouse Bogi Takács, child Mati, and a large and vibrant community of books. You can find R.B. online on Twitter at @rb_lemberg, on Patreon at http://patreon.com/rblemberg, and at rblemberg.net.

The Sister City

CODY GOODFELLOW

HEN LOREN LEFT, HE SAID IT WASN'T ME BUT the city. "This place hates me, Julian," he said of LA. "I have to live in a city that loves me like this shithole loves that douchebag from the Red Hot Chili Peppers." Typically, he buried the casual cruelty under a bad joke, but it was the first crack in a reservoir of obsession he'd kept completely secret. When he abruptly left for Portland, he didn't ask me to come with him, and I wouldn't shame myself by following him.

Fast-forward three months: Loren's parents come to me to find out what happened to him, and I take their money and buy a ticket to fly up there. Even dignity has an expiration date.

Call it morbid curiosity. Call it a need for closure. Call it revenge. Call it anything but what it really was.

I met his mother for brunch in Malibu. Old Hollywood technocrat class—dad a sitcom editor, mom a costume designer for the Disney mill—they wholeheartedly approved of Loren's sexuality, but they never hid their disdain for his trashy taste in men. When he wanted to be a painter, they sent him to CalArts, and when he refused to produce anything commercial or salable, they let him move back into their compound in Pacific Palisades.

They didn't even cut him off when he went up north, but within a few weeks of renting a frowsy bungalow in the dingiest corner of Southeast Portland, he stopped drawing on his allowance, picking up his medications from the pharmacy, and answering his phone. Mom kept calling, and once, a month ago, a strange, catatonically high person of indeterminate gender answered and told her Loren gave them his phone at a "potlatch."

She told me what it was before I could look it up on my phone. "The Pacific Northwest Indians celebrated their material wealth by giving it all away," she sniffed.

"Crazy," I said. "Not wanting to be rich, I mean."

She pursed her lips in an expression her plastic surgeon probably warned her against. Anyway, this person who barely knew Loren told her that he gave away everything at this party. Trashed the place. Invited kids off the street to squat there. "Even you wouldn't believe the state of it," she told me. Before they hung up and ripped the phone to a new number, the kid told her that as far as they knew, Loren went to live on the street or, as they put it, to "the Real City."

I knew she was huffing class resentment to stave off her own self-loathing, so I didn't poke, no matter how badly I wanted to. They marinated Loren in privilege and were flabbergasted that he'd use it to punish them for the unforgivable sin of bringing him into the world without preparing him for it, that his acting out was the closest thing their son had come so far to expressing love at all.

Local police and FBI failed to do anything about it. The more homeless kids disappeared, they seemed to think, the better. Two private detectives combed Portland's tent villages and labyrinthine underground for weeks without finding anything she couldn't learn from home, didn't bring her anything but excuses to spend more of her money.

So now . . . she was asking me to find him. I'd seen where it was headed when she didn't just pump me for information. She would pay for my expenses, naturally, but by the flinty gleam, I knew she was banking I'd be cheaper than the detectives and more diligent than the law because I loved her son and because I must know quite a bit about the underside of rocks.

I only said yes, so help me, because I was broke and the gallery was shuttered until the owner got out of a bottomless tax pit—not because I gave a damn what happened to her son or because that gleam in her eye reminded me of him.

One thing that hooked me, but should have made me stay away, was the video.

The second detective promised he'd be able to locate Loren in a matter of days by combing through TriMet and some commercial security video using face-recognition software. It was hideously expensive and produced a slew of false positives but eventually yielded one hit, which she was told was itself strange, but it was all too possible, given the genius of Portland's homeless for slipping into every crack in the city to get out of the rain.

The video was a month old, and it showed a twitching stick figure on a light rail platform, fighting up the stream of rush-hour foot traffic. Face contorted, the low resolution and frame rate made him jitter across the frame like a whirligig, but it was unmistakably Loren. For one frame, the rolling eyes seem to pin the camera defiantly, to silently condemn and cry for help. You could dig up an unmarked grave and show me a dirt-clotted skull, and I'd recognize that smile.

His mother paused the video on his face and bolted down half her mimosa before she continued. It had to be some kind of prank, she said. The detective couldn't explain it as glibly as he had Loren's popping up out of nowhere, but she knew it couldn't be true. I had to ask her what she meant three times before she fumbled her way to the Play button.

Loren's manic rictus shrivels as he breaks the camera's gaze and throws his arms around a short, skinny person with a shaved head, hard enough to make me twitch with jealousy. He windmills his arms so furiously that the sleepwalking commuters fall over each other to give him a wide berth. His arms go down to his sides, he tucks his head with the steely focus of a gymnast sizing up a pommel horse, and he runs and leaps off the platform into the path of the train, screaming into the station.

There were no suicides or accidental deaths on the TriMet red line train or on any other MAX line that day, that week, or that year. Unlike the lethal meatplows beneath New York and Los Angeles, the MAX trains were like cuddly plush toys that made it almost impossible to get seriously injured. The city said the video was a hoax when she showed it to them, and though it wasn't doctored, they quietly threatened to sue her if she didn't keep it to herself.

So she fired the detective, and after fighting several times with her husband, she called me.

Loren always insisted the absence of seasons was why everyone in California acted like they did. A little seasonal depression was essential for healthy human development.

Portland was one big seasonal depression support group. Since nearly every day was cold, wet, and miserable, there was a muted patience and sweetness, a sly acceptance of whatever it took to get through the colder, wetter nights and a winking shared knowledge of some unnamable factor that made it all worth it.

It was supposed to be spring in Portland, but even when the sun came out, it was pale and weak as a stepfather's love, with deep-blue vampire shadows you could still freeze to death in.

Perhaps a lifetime of learning geography from wall-mounted maps had ingrained in me a sense of the Pacific coast as a vertical surface, a continuous climb from the slough of Southern California to the foggy heights of Oregon and Washington. Even after weeks in Portland, I never lost that queasy vertigo sense that one false step would send me tumbling south, all the way back to where I belonged.

It should have been easy to find him. Compared to LA, Portland was a baby city, a bunch of parks and absent-minded grid-sprawl you could see from one end to the other even as the plane circled the airport. If Loren was missing, it was because he wanted to be.

But then you set foot on the street, and you fight to keep from turning a reflexive, protective blind eye to the city within the city. Blink and it's gone, lost in that flicker between blackness and sight.

Hollywood has its infamous locust hordes who come to be discovered but end up turning tricks in hour-rate motels, shinnying up stripper poles, and sleeping in campers or under bridges, but the climate is forgiving, even if the city is not. The dream is real and alive even if it might as well be on another planet. You could at least understand why so many come and stay to be eaten alive.

But why did they come *here*? The weather wept, and the streets buckled and broke under their own weight. Bloating woodwork, swelling moss and mushrooms, and eroding bricks. Hillsides strewn with tents and trash, begging bowls and incoherent cardboard epitaphs, shivering with the soul-sapping chill under every bus shelter—these uninvited pilgrims come to witness a miracle they could not begin to describe, numbered in the tens of thousands on top of the old, infirm, alcoholic, mentally ill, unwanted, superfluous citizens trapped there by birth, all here to feed themselves to a fiery dream of a new utopia that burned all the brighter for the certainty that it existed nowhere on this earth, that the dreams of those manicured yuppie houses in the nice neighborhoods were some kind of lure like the glowing bit on a deep-sea predator's snout.

I couldn't begin to understand how Loren could want to lose himself among them, but to an artist addicted to hopelessness and doom, they must have attracted and inspired him as powerfully as whatever it was that kept them here.

Loren's last known address off Burnside was being remodeled, and the new occupants wouldn't let me see it, so I wandered the neighborhood, showing Loren's picture to anyone on the street, offering them money. I gave a lot of it away but got nowhere.

I ate breakfast at a place that only served biscuits and thirty flavors of gravy, bought vetiver and rhubarb essence at a Goth aromatherapy boutique called Euphobia, and ate sundew salad at a vegan café that only served carnivorous plants. Everything I saw, I imagined him mocking it as I searched every passing face pushing a shopping cart.

In a coffee shop twelve blocks away, I stopped to order a mocha when I chanced to look at the art on the walls. Like every café in the area, they were crowded with borderline amateur paintings and photography by local artists with hilarious price tags, but looking at the series beside the register, I got a weird rush of familiarity.

The pics were of a demolished house, poorly lighted attempts to make abstract textures out of the damage, with craters kicked in drywall and slogans scrawled in spray paint and blown out until they were satellite imagery of an utterly digested landscape. The words *metamorphosis*, *dream* and *reality*, *before* and *after* . . . appeared over and over . . . and always surrounded by a pink corona like a halo of worms—"The Really Real" . . . and "The Sister City." And everywhere, a black squiggle like a question mark clutching a staring, lidless eye.

"Yeah, Topher took those," the cashier said in response to my staring. "Squat house down the block. Street kids threw a rager there. My housemate got a sweet egg chair out of it . . ."

I went to the men's room. It had a poster from *The Cars That Ate Paris*, a diorama of half-melted vintage action figures, and an empty crimson square on the peeling purple wall with a grubby paper caption taped nearby that read, *Unknown, Metrocorpus IX (Julian), oil on canvas, $75.*

My hands shook so bad I pissed on my shoes. I washed up and pulled my sweater up over my shoulders, turned around to look at the tattoo I'd gotten right before Loren left LA.

It was lifted directly from my favorite of his paintings, from the one that had until recently hung on this wall. I rolled my shoulders to make the spiny, leech-like creature curled around a staring hazel eye seem to undulate under my skin. I'd hoped Loren would feel inspired by it, but he dismissed me as one more canvas he couldn't bear to look at and asked me to keep my shirt on in the future.

Thankful as always that I wasn't in North Carolina, I nerved myself up to go look in the women's room. The decor was similar, and between posters for *Picnic at Hanging Rock* and *The Exterminating Angel*, a small, unframed canvas hung on the wall. The caption said, *Unknown, Metrocorpus IX (Julian), oil on canvas, $75*. The abstract bramble of nested translucent forms was mostly the rosy pink of blood-flushed tissue, tessellated organic shapes that could be sexual organs or the topography of a mammoth organic landscape. Branching hairs suggested veins and arteries or bridges, causeways, and castles. The small canvas had a catalog sticker on the back from Morphos Gallery with a phone number.

I ran outside into a downpour, like waves crashing down on your head, and nearly crashed into a naked guy.

Without looking at him, I apologized and walked down the street holding the painting to my chest to keep the rain off it when I realized he was following me.

The guy stood a good head and a half taller than me. He staggered, growling and red with road rash like he'd just been thrown from a moving car. He was completely naked, except for a white gym sock on his left foot. A passing car splashed him, and he nearly veered off the curb to chase it but turned to challenge me. When I foolishly made eye contact, he charged, holding something out in front of him in both hands.

I turned to run and hit a traffic signpost hard enough to make it sing. I staggered backward into the path of the naked man.

He stopped me from falling in the street and gently draped something over my shoulders. I jerked away involuntarily, my fight or flight instincts flying right out of my head. It was a thick overcoat, raindrops streaming off its waterproof shell, the lining warm and dry, but in my terror, I thrashed out of it. He turned like a matador and threw it over the next person walking down the street, a slight, short woman with purple hair staring into her phone and smoking furiously. She accepted the overcoat as her due and kept walking.

I was thoroughly dumbstruck, and it dawned on me that I recognized the beatific vacancy in his smile. Before I could stop him, before I could frame the words, he threw his arms out and leapt into traffic.

I thought because of this that I was hot on the trail, that this was the city pushing back, but perhaps, if I was not trying to be a real detective, I would have recognized that this was just Loren, saying goodbye.

The last time I saw Loren was on a rare rainy Sunday in LA after his last show at the gallery. We collected the uneaten sandwiches and hors d'oeuvres and took them down to an impromptu campground near the Echoplex. The city wouldn't tolerate anything that looked like a dwelling in plain sight, but the gaggle of shamefaced people huddled under tarps stretched between shopping carts and wheelchairs had lived there for months.

Loren offered them the food. "Nobody else even sees them," he said.

"That's a survival reflex. You couldn't help more than a few of them without going hungry yourself. And what if they don't deserve it?"

I don't know why I was taking up his parents' bullshit arguments against him. Maybe because fighting with him was the only way to get a response at all.

"I've seen the people at the top," he said. "Seen what it takes to get there and stay there. Trust me, they don't deserve what they have . . ."

He finished distributing the sandwiches and finally let me drag him away. I needled, "Do you feel any less guilty?"

"Do you?" he asked.

He asked to see my wallet. I took it out without thinking, and he walked over to an odd patch of dry pavement beside the curb. He took out some cash and held it out to the knife-bright wind. It disappeared, but the wind didn't take it.

He came back over and handed me my wallet, several dollars lighter. I started to yell at him, but for just a moment, staring at that spot where he'd given away my money, I could see something stopping the rain, something that almost had a face.

In the car, I told him to quit clowning and give me my money, I didn't have parents to replace it for me. He sighed like I'd missed the whole point. "You don't see them," he said. "Not the ones who really need help."

He must have been right because I didn't see him again after that day either.

It took Loren's mother another month before she withdrew her support. An angry message told me she hadn't hired me as a surrogate trust-fund brat, and if I didn't intend to produce results, I could shift for myself. By that time, I had already stopped spending her money after splurging on a new laptop and an ancient Volvo station wagon. If I was going to find Loren, I wouldn't need it; I would never even perceive him if I didn't reject it. I wasn't trying to find her for him anyway.

He had vanished like a raindrop in a puddle, but he left ripples. I tried everything I could to trace them, working at coffee shops and pizza parlors and volunteering at halfway houses, but no matter how many free slices and mochas I dished out, no matter how patient I was listening to anything a street person cared to share with me—and they love to talk once they know someone's really listening, and for much of their day, they have nothing to do but talk, if only to themselves—but there are things nobody who has never slept rough can ever truly know. Even if we ask.

There was no weird conspiratorial vibe when they shrugged off your questions, but the eyes always went glassy when you asked about a particular person or about how they lived, that was deeper than shame, or if you asked about the striking surge in the numbers of the mentally ill, even if you heard them tell each other constantly that there were more and more checked-out basket-cases among them, and most weren't like that before they came here.

There may not have been any suicides on the TriMet lines, but there had been an obvious spike in overdoses, bridge dives, and hit-and-run accidents where the victims were homeless and couldn't account for their actions. You heard kids share stories about friends committed and diagnosed with exotic brain dysfunctions only to be turned out on the street by an overloaded social care system, about friends vanishing for days on end and returning with no memory of their whereabouts but with weird new second-hand habits and patchwork personalities, about weird incidents like when a vegan hippie who overdosed on Fentanyl came to and sucked her boyfriend's eye out of his face before running into freeway traffic. They were superstitiously afraid of talking about this shit with outsiders unless you provoked them—by speculating, for instance, that it must be a dangerous new drug.

"It's not a drug that's got 'em so fucked up," a toothless young lady told me on Hawthorne as she ran off with my last few cigarettes. "It's the dream."

I had made a lot of friends and started to feel like a welcome guest, if not a part of the city, so long as I kept my mouth shut about being from California. But after talking to hundreds of people—kids younger than me, refugees from culture wars, burnouts who'd licked sin's ashtray and never quite recovered, hippies for whom homelessness was just an endless folk festival, and so, so many decent, normal people that society had no use for, just hanging on and hoping it wouldn't get worse when it had never gotten better—I never got any closer to Loren.

The solution, when it came, might have been sent by the same agency that delivered the image of him jumping in front of the train. It was so obvious, I should have seen it the first day.

I lost my job and couldn't find another one. The following week, I got kicked out of my apartment and overnight found myself sleeping in the Volvo. By then, I knew all the seldom-patrolled dead-end streets, all the parks and backwater neighborhoods where the residents didn't call the cops at first sight of someone sleeping in their car.

It all happened so fast; it was like being swallowed and eaten alive. I had been living in my car for a couple days before the shock wore off. But even when my car was towed and I took to the streets with a dome tent and sleeping bag bought with the last of Loren's family's guilt funds, it took weeks before anyone believed me enough to tell me about the Dream of the Sister City.

If it wasn't what brought them here in the tens of thousands, it was still spoken of in enough halfway houses and bus shelters to feed a myth that plagued seekers after stranger visions than those the mainstream faithful sought at Sedona or Kathmandu, stranger miracles than could be had at Lourdes or Graceland, and it was what made so many of them stay long after the city had decisively spit them out.

They talked about it in haunted stage whispers. For each, it was different in its particulars but so uniform in its qualities, in the ineffable nature of the *true* experience, in its superior clarity that made waking reality seem like a faded filmstrip projected in a well-lighted room, that you knew it was not a dream they were talking about but *the* Dream.

Arguments raged about every aspect of it, from how and where to sleep to make it come to what it meant and which was the true Dream. Some people dreamt it their first night on the street and never again. Others who'd lived on the streets for years didn't believe in it until it came for them once in drug-deep sleep and left them chasing it forever after. Some claimed it only found them when they were dead drunk or stoned while straight-edge fanatics swore that any drugs at all prevented a true visitation.

I soaked up every tidbit I could ferret out or eavesdrop on. I ditched alcohol, meat, my phone, all contacts or memories from my old city, my name. I stopped bathing and started smoking pot, panhandling, foraging from dumpsters, letting whoever I was with name me, so I was a reflection of the City to my peers and invisible to everyone else.

What was known and accepted was that it only came to those whom surface reality had abandoned or cast out, a secret frequency only perceptible to those who'd tuned out the city's fake dream of a perfect world you could buy, marry, fuck, or kill your way into, only to those who slept in the streets and parks in the cold, naked embrace of the really real, who lived or died by its mercy.

In the Dream, you walk the streets of the Sister City. Sunlight poured like wine through gorgeous blown-glass towers and tree-temples, grown rather than hewn, in an eternal Maxfield Parrish afternoon. Tiny shops gave away miracles, libraries creaked with doors to deeper dreams, museums cluttered with everything not yet invented or imagined, galleries of blank canvases exploded with the contents of your imagination the moment you walked in.

Everyone had a memory palace for a home—a museum of self, limited only by the imagination that furnished it. Or they lived on the infinitely hospitable street, drifting from one generous gourmet cart to the next, idling in beer gardens and vineyards, arcades and cafés, botanical gardens and patches of untamed wilderness teeming with gentle wild animals; chasing parades and carnival processions and fanciful phantoms in need of rescue or ravishing; riding gondolas across glassy azure canals fringed with the minarets of pleasure palaces, meditation temples, hanging gardens, and mercurial follies that melted or mutated into ever-stranger forms when you stared at them; or flying like kites high above it all, and somehow you knew that if you wanted to join them, all you had to do was climb to the top of one of the iridescent spires and jump into the wind.

Always the arguments over details and geography, but always left unsaid the certainty that it wasn't something from their subconscious, that it persisted when they woke up with eyes gummed shut and cheeks encrusted with happy tears, that it was more than merely real, that it was somehow the real face of their city, the true essence, open only to those who had nothing else.

Even when you could get someone talking about the Dream, they would clam up if you tried to connect it to the incidents, the disappearances. *Those* people were fucked up on some new drug. *Those* people were doing it wrong. Those people weren't what the Sister City wanted, so they fried out. They slurred the ones who never came back from wherever their dreams took them as "cotards," without knowing what it meant or where it came from.

And even when you'd pulled a dumpster run with someone to steal rubbery pot stickers and rancid rice for a late-night snack, they would just walk away if you pressed them about Ovid and Circe Crawley.

Portland's answer to Peggy Guggenheim, Circe Brewer used the last of her family's timber fortune to bankroll a series of storefront art galleries and ill-advised forays into radical street art that led her to Ovid Crawley.

A notorious local poet and performance artist, Ovid Crawley captivated Circe and offered a way to burn her upper-class peers and cement her legend, through him and her abiding obsession with the young homeless community of Portland.

While they lavishly supported soup kitchens, fund-raiser concerts, libraries, art and education programs, and even mobile showers and a free barbershop for the homeless community, they moved into a three-story loft downtown that soon became a clearing house for parties, drug abuse, and orgies involving intoxicated minors. Police were called by neighbors to clean up after fights, overdoses, and confrontational art installations like enormous quantities of spoiled meat assembled into a church.

While they reveled for years in their scandalous lifestyle, the local scene eventually saw the sexually omnivorous Crawleys as perverted poseurs and users who exploited homeless youth without trying to get them off the streets at all. Indeed, Ovid preached that the homeless were Brahmins, the soul of the sister city, and must be protected from the system rather than absorbed back into it.

One by one, their venues and parties shut down. The last, Morphos Gallery, was replaced with a sensory-deprivation tank salon only a week before I arrived in town. The faded flyers for the last show still littered the cobweb-strewn atrium of the new salon—*Dream of the Sister City*, slated to premiere a few days after their closure, presumably would have featured the work I'd stolen from the coffee shop.

Street rumor had it that the Crawleys had gone underground, themselves now homeless and squatting on their own foreclosed properties, but anyone who still hung with them was forbidden to associate with outsiders, which gave it the mystique of a cult. And the seekers most consumed with the pursuit of the Dream tended to be those who ran with the Crawleys.

I slept in parks and under overpasses. I cadged spare change outside Powell's. I ate unfinished breakfasts out of trash cans. I hooked up with younger men, older men, and even a couple women when it was really cold, and the loneliness was more than I could take. I disappeared from the sight of normal people, slowly became invisible. While I never remembered my dreams, I began to wake up to my leaky tent sagging under a torrent with a formless feeling of having just been somewhere wonderful.

I asked only the ones I felt I could trust about the Crawleys and still lost more friends than I made. I never found anyone who supported them, but the rest were too afraid even to admit there was anything to be afraid of. But finally, I found a kid who told me that there was a park in St. Johns where some said you could catch the Dream any night of the year that the moon was visible. He was no more specific than that, but I had nothing but time and the rains had finally tapered off, so I camped in every park in the north end of town until I found it.

Every tree in the park and the surrounding street was in feverish full bloom, petals like carpets of cotton candy and sherbet in the gutters, musky sick-sweet perfume of tree-semen so thick it congealed in a paste on your palate.

A caravan of battered, moss-infested campers lined the back of the park and dirtbag nomads squatted over a latrine trench they'd dug in the bushes. A little girl threw a tantrum outside a camper over a kite tangled in a nearby tree. Someone inside hollered back, "You climb up and get it. You still got toes . . ."

A guy stood on a picnic table, shouting at a slouching crowd of losers sharing a bottle of Boone's Farm. He wore a spotless white shirt and white pants in a place where such clothing, without stains or soil from work, was a miracle. His shirt shouted, IF YOU DON'T LIKE THE PROGRAM, CHANGE THE DAMN CHANNEL.

He shouted, "The Sister City remains invisible because it requires new eyes, but who will make it see itself?!" A few disaffected high school kids heckled him, but a fringe of random people in telltale grimy clothes several layers too thick for the rare sunny weather nodded vigorously as he shouted.

An old man in a thrift store's worth of raincoats sat at the picnic table across from the playground, hunched over in miserable contemplation of the trash between his mismatched sandals. Cars and trucks cruised up and parked on the potholed dirt road backing the park, waiting for childlike women to come out of the bushes to take them around the world. I wondered if any of them were visible to the snarl of rush-hour traffic creeping past on Fessenden, if I was visible even to them.

No one protested as I pitched my tent and unrolled my sleeping bag, ate leftovers scrounged from behind the taqueria down the street, studiously avoided looking at the other squatters setting up their own miserable camps beside mine, and waited for the moon to come up.

I drifted off to sleep listening to the traffic and the cackling of middle school kids sharing some truly deadly sativa on the playground.

And I went there.

The tent had become a gigantic lotus flower on a lily pad adrift on a burgundy lake. Musical swarms of chirping tropical fish burst from trees like towers of coral as the first rays of wine-thick moonglow peered through the jeweled domes and crystal spires that fractured them into a shower of kaleidoscopic light. On the great lawn where the playground had been, a pavilion spread out under firefly lanterns, teeming with acrobats, jugglers, and floral displays dripping with gemstone fruits and sultry perfume. Translucent crowds of robed and crowned sightseers gathered round an exhibit, their bubbling awe and appreciation competing with the flying fish.

The lily pad meandered to the shore, and I stepped off it to float among them, conscious of piercing stares prickling my skin, of waves of whispers at my back as I pressed through the crowd to face the object of their adoration.

A painting glistened, the pigments still wet, the canvas a pale skin stretched on a frame of bone. The subject was me.

I lay paralyzed in my clammy sleeping bag, swimming in sweat. Fingers of milk-pale daylight combed the grass. A camper peeled out of the parking lot, leaving a child wailing like an air raid siren at the curb. A small mushroom village of tents had sprung up around me while I was asleep. A woman in a parka held together with duct tape screamed, "You don't know the difference between real and lies anymore," at a shell-shocked man pushing a shopping cart overflowing with books in tattered trash bags. "We can't live in a lie!"

The hunchback in the raincoats backed out of the sagging Coleman pup tent next to mine, dragging a sleeping man out by his ankles. As I watched, he rolled the man onto a low gurney and wheeled him across the lawn and the unimproved road to a ruin of a house almost swallowed by trees at the back of the park.

I struggled with my own limbs, heavy and foreign, and after maybe an hour I crawled out of the tent. No one else was awake, no one else saw what happened.

The towering five-story oaks bordering the park loomed over it like a green tidal wave poised to crush it or forcefully trying to hide it from the sky. The deep, shaggy thicket of the yard was a riot of flowers, completely obscuring the flagstone path across the long-gone lawn. A dead tree overrun with vines studded with coral-pink buds that dangled down to brush the ground formed a semi-private bower where two naked people of indeterminate age and gender listlessly coupled on a bed of crushed comfrey.

It was the kind of house somebody probably ordered from a Sears & Roebuck catalog a hundred years ago, but the warranty had long since expired. Something shaped like a man sat and smoked and watched me from the green nest of the porch, curtained off by spills of vine thick as garden hoses.

Blackberry and wisteria and more aggressive and exotic weed species scaled the walls and slowly pried off the Masonite siding, ripped down the fern-clotted rain gutter, and made inroads to conquering the sunken, mossy meadow of the steeply pitched roof as if the undergrowth had been tasked with razing the house to its foundations for some unspeakable offense against the fundamental laws of nature.

As I approached, the man on the porch retreated inside and slammed the door, but leaves and moldy newspapers kept it open. I hesitated before climbing onto the porch, noticed the light from the recessed windows set into the foundation. I climbed the stairs and forced the door wide enough to squeeze into a ruined room.

Black mold spewed across the ceiling wherever rats did not brazenly watch from gaping holes admitting on the attic. The floor buckled underfoot, curled tiles skidding away like stingrays from my creeping feet. Circling round a sunken spot in the demolished kitchen, I pushed open another trash-clogged door and went down the basement stairs.

The basement was lit only by a dim green light that spilled over a labyrinth of bodies. Pale, naked skin on rows of cots and inflatable mattresses, some with IV tubes snaking into arms and necks.

"They die if someone don't care for them," a voice like steel wool on silk said in my ear. I turned with my hands up in surrender, knowing it would be the man in the raincoats and knowing he was Ovid Crawley.

"They're lost in the Dream," I said, and he shook his head.

"If it's just a dream, go show me proof that all this"—he waved contemptuously at the world—"isn't just a nightmare."

I said, "I've been there. I was there last night."

"You've never been anywhere but your own head, boy." He grimaced and gurned gray, toothless gums. Bloodshot eyes, like dirty pearls, and long, matted yellow-white hair like the roots of some poison plant. "If you'd been to the Sister City, if you saw it as it *really* is, you'd never come back."

He took my arm, tugging me back upstairs. I offered to clean, to help take care of them, anything, if he could tell me what became of Loren Estes. He shook his head like a man for whom all names meant nothing, but he told me about the dreamers in the basement, and he let me help for a while.

The first, worst cases were committed to state homes and diagnosed with Cotard's Syndrome, a brain dysfunction that left them unaware of, or unable to operate, their own bodies, but this was missing the point. A few who managed to get PET scans before they were discharged for inability to pay showed enlarged pineal glands and severe parietal lesions, leading to identity and memory disorders but also to strange new perceptions. Some of them could see into the Dream while awake. Bad things happened to sleepwalkers. Some stayed away so long that the Dream took over their uninhabited bodies.

"Nobody can face the Sister City in its true form. Even the seekers only perceive it through a stack of illusions because to see what it really is you have to face what *you* really are."

I told him I was ready, and he spat in the air, caught it on his own face, smiling like it was the kiss of the sea. "You're not ready, but she's hungry, so I'll give you to her, and she'll let me alone."

I asked if he meant to give me to the Sister City.

"No," he laughed until blood vessels burst in his nose and cheeks. "I'm giving you to my wife."

TOXIC HUMAN DUMP, said the graffiti sprayed on the faded official warning signs on the cyclone fence around the old Portland Gas & Coke Plant. The hulking Gothic Revival ruin was impregnated with asbestos, and the soil was inundated with petroleum by-products, and the water of the nearby Willamette was rife with PCBs and DDT, the whole coastline branded as one of the biggest and worst Superfund sites in North America, so it was the perfect place for a rogue artists' collective. The sun wilted behind the shaggy green hills, and oily shadows seeped up out of the sour ground.

Ovid Crawley dropped me off at a rip in the fence in an ancient ice cream truck, offered me a surgical mask.

They were waiting on the other side to take me in. They ignored my words, pinned me down, and took my shoes, my clothes. When I shivered naked in front of them, someone traced the lines of my tattoo on my back, and I was allowed to stay.

I was kept in a closet, fed moldy bread and river water for I don't know how long. I didn't care, I didn't keep track, because in between freezing, vomiting interludes of unwelcome wakefulness, I walked the streets of the Sister City.

Until one time when I woke to find them standing over me. I recognized the intense bald woman from the TriMet security video. With eager eyes, she searched me as a gang of hairless girl-boys presented and cavity-searched me.

"If you came to take him away," she said, "we'll feed you to the river."

I told her I didn't want to take him away. I only wanted to see him, to be with him. They half-dragged, half-carried me up four flights of stairs, out of the basement and through cavernous rooms with bolts and amputated struts where all the coal-burning apparatus once stood, dragged me up stairs like a ladder into the cupola on the roof, like a bell tower, a studio with a breathtaking panopticon view of all of North Portland across the river, the forbidding mountains of Forest Park, the green soapstone sentinel of the St. Johns Bridge, and in the distance, the ghostly snowcapped fang of Mount Hood suspended on the eastern horizon.

I had eyes for none of it just then. For I had found him.

He stood shaking, naked, painting. The canvas was half-again his height, and he stood on a ladder. The subject might have been a pornographic landscape or a panoramic vista of some monstrous god's half-flaccid genitalia. The brush strokes were crude, impasto scabs of layered oils littering the image like a malignant aura, but through it, I saw something I recognized . . . a lake, a lily pad, a pavilion, a staring hazel eye enthroned on an altar and suckling an eyeless army of starving larvae . . .

He turned and blinked those maddening hazel eyes at me, and something like a smile pinched his face. He did not recognize me, and in those eyes, I saw no sign of Loren Estes.

Of course it wasn't him, Circe Crawley told me. Loren was the deepest Dreamer she'd ever seen. He would stay under for days on end and emerge with the most remarkable work, but under her wing, he went to sleep for weeks. He sleepwalked, even threw himself in front of a train once, but when someone thought to confine him up here and give him supplies, he began to paint.

The paintings in and all over the walls of the cupola studio turned Loren's old work inside out, depicting with a crude literalism what he had painfully forced out in expressionistic fits when he could withstand going off his meds. It was as if someone else was painting Loren's nightmares, someone who had not only seen them but could claim citizenship inside them.

Loren's sleepwalking series was highly sought after by private, subterranean collectors who would pay anything for them because it was as close as anyone who hoped to cling to some shred of sanity could come to seeing the true Sister City.

She said some people think it's the collective memory palace of the city, if not all mankind. The people who wander its streets were the homeless, and the people who lived and worked and sold their souls to the city were its bricks, its buildings and trees and books. Some thought it was a Platonic trip into the sphere of ideals, the archetypal city. Some were even dumb enough to believe it was heaven. But they were wrong.

The Sister City is a sleeping god, aloof of all attempts to awaken it. An unknowable other, dreaming its own dreams, and those who shared the Dream of it little more than bacteria at play in the fields of its flesh.

She had commissioned Loren to paint its portrait, but now she liked the one who'd take his place better.

But where is he, I demanded to know. I begged her to wake him up just long enough for him to see me.

Go and find him yourself, she said. Someone pressed a rag reeking of ether over my mouth, and someone else pinned my arms for a third someone to tie them down as Loren's body came shuffling over, brush and cock equally engorged and shiny with crimson paint.

I understand now why they couldn't operate their own bodies properly after waking up. After taking a body in the Sister City—the true Sister City with all its illusions stripped away—it's not that the human form is so difficult to operate so much as returning to it is like being buried in a cage of bone, an avalanche of unwelcome sensation, a nightmare of nerves. All that unnecessary complexity, all that evolution to create so much misery . . .

The Sister City could be all we know of God, that other we feel in the back of our minds, in dreams and visions when we are all but unmoored from the illusions of this world. It could be the sum of us, the integrated, unruly hivemind of humankind, but what to make of us, we uninvited parasites who crawl and feed upon it?

In the form of a flatworm infested with a rash of exquisitely sensitive eyes, on a foot that was also a tongue, I crawled across a sea of shit and a world of hurt to find him.

Across monstrous plains of inflamed epidermis, gasping, cavernous pores clogged with flukeworm winos, runaway teenaged amoebae, and schizophrenic fungi. I had no doubt that the parasitic fauna of the Sister City had something like intelligence, even some vestigial self-awareness, for I had seen one painting with my lover's hand. But we were making them into ourselves with those infections of eyes and other sensory apparatus, though not one in a hundred saw the world they inhabited as it really is.

In recesses where the landscape was utterly engulfed by torpid swarms of parasites, I crawled among them, vaguely sensing the humanity in the ones I ate and the ones that tried to eat me. As I bored through the hermetic membrane of a Canadian woman named Libby MacEachern, I swallowed her spicy cytoplasm along with commingled memories of Providence Hospital emergency room and exploring a museum of dolls while riding the back of a giant cat in the Sister City.

I gorged myself on the mitochondrial ghost of a young man named Dylan Martin, a Californian beloved by friends for his sense of humor but never to be trusted with animals, laid low by Rohypnol in his drink at a bar only to wander an infinite library in pursuit of the most beautiful song he'd ever heard and convinced he'd nearly found it when I sheared him open and consumed his nucleus.

The crushing guilt I felt over devouring them was nothing to the agony of hunger, the ache of loneliness that made even the fleeting contact of predation seem like the promise of true love.

Crawled over wishbone bridges of crystal and cartilage, over dunes of shed cells and seas of sebaceous cysts, and at the end, I found him.

I knew it was him, as surely as I knew the mind occupying his body was not his, when I finally found it. Even as a segmented worm, he was magnificent. Cilia trees with compound eyes for fruit erupted all over his embattled membrane. A cloud of gray tumorous antibodies leeched his moribund body, but they couldn't pry him away from his obsession any more than I could.

With hundreds of acid-dripping vacuole mouths, he clung to and burrowed into a nest of burnt-out nerves, trying to ignite the dead skyscraper neurons, trying to wake it and make it see itself.

I came back, and I freely admit that I killed his body to stop them using it, and as long as they force me to take my meds, I can't go back, but I know he's there in the Sister City, doing what he was born to do. The metropolis of neurons is firing like dying neutron stars, and soon everyone will see.

Soon all of us will wake up from this Dream.

{§

Cody Goodfellow has written seven novels, and his collections, *Silent Weapons for Quiet Wars* and *All-Monster Action*, both received the Wonderland Book Award. His recent short fiction has been featured in *Black Static*, *Flight or Fright*, *Monsters of Any Kind*, and *Best of the Best Horror of the Year*. As an actor, he has appeared in numerous short films, TV shows, music videos, and commercials. He is also a cofounder of Perilous Press, an occasional micropublisher of modern cosmic horror.

BROKEN EYE BOOKS

The Hole Behind Midnight, by Clinton J. Boomer
Crooked, by Richard Pett
Scourge of the Realm, by Erik Scott de Bie
Izanami's Choice, by Adam Heine
Never Now Always, by Desirina Boskovich
Pretty Marys All in a Row, by Gwendolyn Kiste
Queen of No Tomorrows, by Matt Maxwell
The Great Faerie Strike, by Spencer Ellsworth
Catfish Lullaby, by A.C. Wise

COLLECTIONS
Royden Poole's Field Guide to the 25th Hour, by Clinton J. Boomer

ANTHOLOGIES
(edited by Scott Gable & C. Dombrowski)
By Faerie Light: Tales of the Fair Folk
Ghost in the Cogs: Steam-Powered Ghost Stories
Tomorrow's Cthulhu: Stories at the Dawn of Posthumanity
Ride the Star Wind: Cthulhu, Space Opera, and the Cosmic Weird
Welcome to Miskatonic University: Fantastically Weird Tales of Campus Life
It Came from Miskatonic University: Weirdly Fantastical Tales of Campus Life
Nowhereville: Weird Is Other People

Stay weird.
Read books.
Repeat.

brokeneyebooks.com
twitter.com/brokeneyebooks
facebook.com/brokeneyebooks
instagram.com/brokeneyebooks
patreon.com/brokeneyebooks

now here

CPSIA information can be obtained
at www.ICGtesting.com
Printed in the USA
LVHW041811270220
648406LV00004B/806